Niya:

Rainbow Dreams

Niya:

Rainbow Dreams

Fabiola Joseph

URBAN
Renaissance

www.urbanbooks.net

Urban Books, LLC
300 Farmingdale Road, NY-Route 109
Farmingdale, NY 11735

ISBN 13: 978-1-62286-785-1
ISBN 10: 1-62286-785-8

First Trade Paperback Printing January 2017
Printed in the United States of America

10 9 8 7 6 5 4 3 2 1

This is a work of fiction. Any references or similarities to actual events, real people, living or dead, or to real locales are intended to give the novel a sense of reality. Any similarity in other names, characters, places, and incidents is entirely coincidental.

Distributed by Kensington Publishing Corp.
Submit Orders to:
Customer Service
400 Hahn Road
Westminster, MD 21157-4627
Phone: 1-800-733-3000
Fax: 1-800-659-2436

This book is for anyone who is dying to be free.

For the souls who roam and can't find a home.

If I could help it, you would never feel alone.

For the ones who are bold enough to say, "Fuck the world. I can only be me."

For the people who just want to love freely.

This book is for everyone who believes in true love.

Gay, bi, and even straight, it doesn't really matter much.

We all bleed red, so loving each other is a must.

ACT I

Rainbow Dreams

Niya, you saw it all.

As I walk through life, it is as if I am invisible.

A ghost who is still living but is ignored nonetheless.

I watch other people just to make sure it's not just me, but as I look at them, they look right through me.

I know that I am different. I know that I stand out. So why is it that they are all blinded to the beauty I house?

Just when I thought that life wasn't worth living, you came along and actually looked at me.

You took the time to see things that I hadn't even seen in myself.

You know not what you do, because it just comes so naturally.

You love me, and that will always be enough.

So with you I stand through the good and the bad.

I will forever love you for taking me from a ghost no one saw to a women standing proud and tall.

Niya, my love, you saw me. You saw it all.

Jamilla

Chapter 1

Niya

"Why are you fucking with me?"

The block was packed, and all eyes turned to me. Brooklyn in the summertime brought everyone outside. The kids and their parents littered the streets, hoping to escape the sweltering heat. The corner boys served their poison to paying customers, and as for me, I was having another argument with Rodney.

"What the fuck is your problem?" I asked, hoping that my lowered tone would convince him to do the same.

"You know what the fuck I'm talking about. You say that you're my friend, but you are lying to me. You're gay, Niya. Just admit that shit."

I was shocked. I couldn't believe that my best friend had just outed me like that. Well, maybe that was the problem. I looked at him as if he was still and only my best friend, and not as if he was the lover he wanted to be.

"Fuck you, Rodney." I started to walk away, but he just caught up with me and turned me around.

"No one out here is surprised. Look at you. You dress like a nigga. You act like a nigga. You even wear men's cologne. I thought that maybe, just maybe, you were a tomboy, and that maybe what they said wasn't true, but we all have to face the truth."

"What the fuck would it matter if it were true? You ain't my nigga."

My heart felt as if it would beat out of my chest. All my life, I had kept one secret. I had never let anyone in on this one thing about myself. I had battled this thing all my life, and I thought I had hid it well. There were plenty of straight girls who dressed like me and wore their hair in cornrows like me. So what made me so damn different? I asked myself while staring into Rodney's face. I was still me. I was the friend he had always known. Why would admitting out loud the fact that I liked girls change any of that for him? It wasn't like he didn't already know. How could he do this to me? He was my one and only true friend. I even trusted this nigga with my life. I just couldn't understand what had pushed him to embarrass me in front of everyone who was outside. I would never have done that to anyone I care about.

"I love you, Niya, but I can't have a friendship that's not real. You don't like dudes, and that's okay, but at least be real with yourself."

I could feel my eyes watering up, but I couldn't let the whole damn block see me cry. "I'm not gay." As soon as the words left my mouth, I wanted to take them back. The truth was, I just couldn't bring myself to say it out loud.

"Are you fucking kidding me? I just gave you an out. Are you that fucking weak?"

"Fuck you! I ain't weak. I—I just . . ." The words were fighting to get out. They were jumbled only because my brain was getting in the way.

"Say it. Say that you like girls. Can you do that?"

With my heart dying to tell the truth, I let my lies turn me around and allow me to walk away. I could feel everyone's eyes burning a hole into my back as I walked away from the block where everyone already knew the reality of my sexuality.

***

When I got to my building after a short ten-minute walk, she was sitting there, at the bottom of the stairs, as always, writing in her damn notebook. I took the stairs two at a time, but as I turned to go into the building, I changed my mind. She was still sitting at the bottom of the stairs that led to my building, so I stayed at the top. I pulled out a Black & Mild and just sat down above her. I needed to cool off before I went into the house. I needed to clear my head. I just couldn't understand why Rodney would do that to me. We had always been close, close enough for me to allow him to be my best friend.

I had thought that being around him would mask who I really was, but how could that last? I allowed him to bring girls to my house when my grandmother was out. We would freak off, but that was between us. He would bring in a third party so I could watch her, touch her, fuck her, and make it look like a threesome, but I wasn't fooling anyone but myself. Of course, he would be mad. I had used him to mask who I really was.

"The least you can do is say hello."

She had never spoken to me before. I would always see her, look at her, write something about her, and keep it moving. I had almost forgotten about her being at the bottom of the stairs. It was a good thing she spoke.

"My bad. I was caught up in my own thoughts. Hello," I said. She didn't turn around when I spoke, so I was talking to the back of her head.

"Upset about what your friend said?" she asked.

I damn near choked on the smoke I had just pulled in. "That dude's buggin'."

"Is he?"

I remained quiet. I thought that I had momentarily lost my hearing, because Brooklyn had never been so silent.

When I didn't answer, she turned around, which only added pressure to the situation. "Are you going to answer me, or are you just going to sit there all bug-eyed?"

"Um, nah. He has things all messed up. I just, you know, I—"

"Okay. I understand," she said, cutting me off. Her answer sounded sarcastic, and that didn't sit well with me.

"Bitch, who the fuck are you? You don't even know me!"

"I said, 'Okay. I understand.' No need to call me a bitch 'cause you can't admit to who you really are."

I was down those stairs before her last word left her mouth.

"You don't understand shit, 'cause there's nothing to fucking understand. All you do is sit on these fucking stairs, writing in your fucking notebook. What the fuck would you understand about what I'm going through?" I yelled. I snatched her notebook out of her hand and kept it from her as she reached for it.

"Give me back my fucking notebook," she demanded.

"Fuck you, bitch! Mind your fucking business next time."

She looked at me as if she was hurt, but I was way too lost in my sea of bullshit to empathize with her. "Fine. Keep it," she said, looking down at my hand before continuing. "Taking that from me, it won't change anything that has happened tonight. It won't change who you really are. You can yell 'Fuck you' all you want. It's your lie, not everyone else's."

I was so taken aback by her words that I was speechless. I watched her walk into the building, and I instantly wished that things had gone differently.

10/05/2020

Marshville Branch 704-283-8184

Chambers,
Alice Huntley

Arrived Request Slip

****

Telephone

Title :
Niya : rainbow dreams /
Fabiola Joseph.
Item Id :
871091005993007

Chapter 2

Jamilla

I had felt her behind me, and that had shit irked me. I hadn't been sure if she could see what I was writing, so that had made me stop. I had seen what went down between her and her friend as I walked out of the corner store. The whole block had seemed to be watching. In a way, I was kind of shocked that she didn't light Rodney's ass up. Niya seemed so tough. Although we had never uttered a word to each other, she just came off that way.

She hung with the rough crowd, the dope boys, the good-for-nothings. I didn't even know why I always noticed her, though I guessed it was because she just seemed so different. I thought that it was a known fact that she was gay. She looked like a stud, wore guy clothes, and never had on any makeup, so I was lost. I knew that I should have kept my mouth shut, but being a writer had got the best of me. I had to know what she was feeling and why. I hadn't thought that things would turn out the way they had, and the worst thing was that she had taken my notebook.

As I stood face-to-face with her for the first time, I noticed how beautiful she was, but in an "I'm not a girl" way. Sure, she had nice lips, nice hair, which most people would say was being wasted on a butch girl who would never curl it. Her skin showed the mix of her Dominican and Haitian roots. It was smooth, light, but looked tanned at the same time. Her eyes were on fire, yet they held so much in them. They were dark, beneath long natural lashes. Most women would kill for her eyes, which seemed also to be naturally lined with dark pencil. I watched her peach-colored lips as she spit her lies at me. I wanted to ask her to calm down just so I could talk to her, but that wasn't going to happen. She was all of five feet eight, maybe five feet nine, but her anger made it seem as if she towered over my five-feet-seven-inch frame.

"You can yell 'Fuck you' all you want. It's your lie, not everyone else's," I yelled at her. I had had enough. I just wanted to talk to her.

I had thought that maybe she had had enough of staring at me. For months, that had been all she did. I didn't mind it, unlike some of the other girls had during our high school years, but now we were headed to college after the summer was over. I would have thought that she would feel free enough to be herself. But fuck it. She wasn't in the right frame of mind tonight. As I walked into my building, I prayed that she didn't open that notebook and read what was inside of it. But a small part of me wondered what would happen if she did.

Chapter 3

Niya

As I walked into my grandmother's apartment, my cell phone rang. I looked at the name on the screen, and it was White Boy, an albino nigga who would buy some shit off me from time to time. I wasn't in the mood to deal with his ass, so I sent him to voice mail. It just hadn't been my night. Two arguments with two people in a matter of minutes, and it had left me drained. If I'd known any better, I would have just gone to bed.

"Niya, *mi amor*, what all that yelling I hear outside? You know I keep window open. Why you yell 'Fuck you' like that?"

I looked at my grandmother as she made her way over to the fridge to take out my plate and warm it up. I headed to my room, threw Jamilla's notebook down on my nightstand, and headed back to my granny to finish our conversation and eat.

"You can't do that, Niya. You can't curse people in the streets like that, my love. Don't act like your mama. She used to—"

Her comparing me to my mother only added fuel to my dying fire. I had vowed to be nothing like her, a crackhead who roamed the streets, turning tricks for a hit. Not that my father was any better: he was locked away in jail for robbing a bank. Neither of them cared enough about me to get shit right.

"My mother? Are you for real?" I said, interrupting her.

"Sí. Igual que ella."

"Just like her! Are you crazy?" I couldn't believe my ears.

"Ay, watch your mouth. You are the crazy, speaking to me like that in my house," my grandma said with her heavy Dominican accent. She walked over to the table, pulled out a chair, and told me to sit. She walked back into the kitchen and brought my plate out. "Now, tell me why you yell 'Fuck you' to the nice girl."

I looked at her as I picked up my fork, and for a second, I thought about lying to her. "'Cause she overheard Rodney calling me gay."

I watched her scrunch up her face before she asked, "He called you what?"

I put down my fork and looked right at her. "A gay. Lesbian, Grandma. A lesbian."

Her mouth dropped open. She got up and went into the kitchen. I followed her, but she wouldn't face me.

"Mi amor, why he call you that? And why you yell at her for him calling you that?"

"Because she wasn't minding her business."

She was quiet for a while, and I would have given anything to know what she was thinking. She never turned around, though. "Why you tell me this Rodney and her think you're lesbian?" she finally asked.

My heart rate quickened. Was she about to flip out? She started to wash dishes, as she just couldn't stand still. She even washed what was already clean.

"Why, Niya? Why you tell me this, huh? That's crazy. Rodney tell you that, she tell you that, and now you tell me?"

I started to cry. What would make her ask me why? I thought that I would be safe with her, thought that she would shield me from others, and even from myself.

Was this a mistake? I hadn't even got a chance to tell her yet, and she was already acting funny. Either way, I told myself, I was just going to tell her the truth. I had lied to two different people on the same day, and those lies would end with the only woman I knew who truly loved me. I was afraid, I was worried, but I couldn't face knowing that I was a liar just one more time that night.

"Grandma, look at me." I touched her back, but still, she didn't turn around. "Look at me! Do I look straight to you? Why do you always ask me who I am going out with? It's 'cause you already know. You always ask *his* name. You know there is no he, Grandma."

"So why you tell me this, huh?"

"Because I'm a lesbian."

Her hands no longer moved. The water was running, but she didn't say a word. Nor did she wash another dish. I backed out of the kitchen. With anger and hurt filling my airways, I needed some air. I grabbed my cell and opened the door. I heard her call my name, but I just couldn't go back in there. I had said it. For the first time, I had said it out loud, and at that moment, the truth was suffocating me. Once I was outside, I called White Boy and told him that we could meet up. When I hung up with him, I called Roxie and told her I would see her within an hour or two, after I made a deal.

Eye to eye with the barrel of the gun, and all I could think about was how much of a shitty night I was having. First Rodney, then Jamilla, though that shit with my grandma was just the worst.

"You got one minute, bitch. If you don't come up off them bricks, I'm gonna put a hole in your chest."

See, now, why did he have to call me a bitch? 'Cause I got tits? I shook my head before getting out of the car.

"Don't you know that this is a man's game? Ain't no room for no pussy in this shit. Fucking dyke running around here like you a nigga. I should put this dick in your ass and remind you that you're a bitch. You got a pussy just like the rest of them hoes around here."

I looked back and looked him up and down. This little nigga was poppin' big shit, but I couldn't worry about that right now. I had other things to think about. Like how this dude knew that I was holding. The only people who knew about this deal were White Boy, who was buying the shit from me, and Roxie, the bitch I was fucking with. Could it be that this nigga had just got lucky, or had White Boy sent his ass?

As soon as I'd pulled up to pick up my packages, he was right on my ass. Either way, I was going to find out. Whoever he was, he had to know something about me. He was taking my sexual orientation a little too personal for him not to. I walked him to the shed behind the abandoned house and popped the lock.

"Hurry up, bitch. I ain't got all damn day."

We walked into the shed. I moved some things around and pulled out the two bricks. Even through his ski mask, I could tell that he was smiling.

"If I wasn't in a hurry, I would dick your dyke ass down. Maybe it would remind you that you should like dick, not walk around like you have one. I should—"

"Nigga, maybe if you weren't so caught up on the pussy that I'm getting, you would actual get some real-life pussy, instead of just talking about what you should do. Small dick motherfuckers always got a problem 'cause I'm fucking bitches better than they ever could!"

As the words left my mouth, I couldn't help but question if they would be my last. But he didn't shoot me. He punched me in the lip instead.

"Bitch, I'm giving you ten seconds to get the fuck out of here."

I spit out the blood that was dripping into my mouth from my busted lip. "All right. My bad. I'm leaving."

I left the shed, made a left, and prayed that I was moving fast enough. I walked over to the plant, lifted it up, and stood there for a minute. I had never had to use the gun. I'd just cracked a few niggas in the head. I'd never really pulled the trigger. That night, it was as if everything was moving in slow motion. I cocked the gun, made my way back to the shed, and prayed to God. I was about to take a man's life, and I wanted him to forgive me. A few things ran through my mind, but the thought of him dying didn't have the importance it should have. I thought about who I was and who I was going to be after that day. I thought about the people in my life, and how they'd reacted to the person I had always been but had hidden, and it pissed me off. I turned the corner and crept into the doorway of the shed. There he was, walking out, as if what he held belonged to him.

"Ay, you still wanna fuck this dyke bitch straight?" I asked as I aimed the gun at him.

He tried to reach for his gun, but I moved faster. I let out three rounds, hitting him only once. He fell back, but he was still breathing. I walked up on him, took the duffel bag from his fingertips, and did the world a favor. I shot him again, hopefully ending the life of a homophobic thief who would otherwise rob again. I got the rest of my things, moved them to a new place, and went straight home.

I didn't get much sleep that night. The dead man ran through my mind as I tried to get some rest. It wasn't as easy as I thought it would be, taking a life, but I tried to act as normal as possible when I awoke the next morning to the smell of bacon and eggs on the stove. I stumbled down to the kitchen.

"Hey, Grandma. Anything good to eat?" I asked as I tried to rub the sleepiness from my eyes. I wasn't going to bring up the night before if she didn't.

"Niya, mi amor, you have to get some rest. You too handsome to go around looking like zombie."

I looked over at my grandmother and had to smile. She always knew how to brighten up my day. Just hearing the word *handsome* made my heart skip a beat. I took a seat at the table, and as she brought over a plate of eggs and bacon, I asked myself if she got it. Did she understand what I had told her last night? If so, was she okay with it?

As I ate, she watched me. I knew she had a mouthful to say, so I waited.

"You know, your uncle George was a gay in Santo Domingo. My father kick him out because he gay. He struggle so much. He didn't have no money, no food, no clothes. So . . ." She had to stop for a minute. I waited for her to wipe her tears so she could continue.

"So he live on the streets, did anything for money. Soon he start to take the drugs to be able to stay up, work more, sell his body. Well, we beg my father. Me, my mother, and my sisters, we beg him. We say, 'Please, Papa, let him come back. He still your son.' He say, 'No. He dead to me.' For two years, we beg him, and he say no. Well, one day, we in the house, making dinner, and we hear yelling from outside. We run out. It's my papa covered in blood. He hold George in his hands. He skinny like broom, almost dead. Someone beat him, rape him. We bring him in house, call doctor, clean him, give him medicine. Three days later George die."

I got up, got the box of tissues, took one, handed her the box, and watched her wipe her tears as I wiped my own.

"See, my father, he cry the hardest. He cry the loudest. He know this no happen if he let George stay. My mother hate him after that. They never the same. They fight.

They hit every day after that. Life never the same again. My father die with this on his heart. So, Niya, when I ask why you tell me this, it's 'cause I know already. I know for years. I love you, Niya. That don't matter. Forever, I love you. No matter what. Understand me?"

I couldn't take it anymore. I got out of my chair and kneeled down in front of her. I threw my head onto her lap and just cried. I cried for her dead brother; I cried for my broken family. I cried because I loved her and she loved me. I cried because she loved me, no matter what. Most of all, I cried because I was free. As long as my grandmother knew and accepted me, I could start to come to terms with who I was. I could say "Fuck the world" and just be me.

"Mi amor, as long as I love you, that's all that matters. 'Fuck you' to anybody who no love you. You are great, Niya, the best, no matter who you love or sex with. I love you."

Chapter 4

Jamilla

I hadn't seen Niya for a week. My heart raced as I thought of my notebook. I didn't want her to take anything she might have read the wrong way. Or worse, I didn't want her to think that I was some obsessed person who wrote about her. I hoped that she just thought that I was writing about some random person.

"Jamilla, we need to talk. *Ki kote ou ye*?"

"I'm here, in my room," I said to my mother.

She came into my bedroom and sat down at the foot of my bed. She waited for me to put my laptop down before she started to speak. "How are you and Marie?"

I rolled my eyes. I had got a new stepdad, and a stepsister, Marie, had come with him. "Everything is fine," I answered coldly. My mother shifted on the bed, and I waited for the bullshit.

"You are still wetting the bed?"

I didn't answer.

"Marie said you wet the bed four times this week. She said—"

"Mom, I don't want to talk about this. The doctor said that it's a side effect."

My mother stood up and looked at me. "Side effect? *Kisa sa ye*?"

I couldn't believe that my mother had just asked me what a side effect was.

"From what happened, Mom. The doctor said—"

"*Ban'm tèt mwen*. I don't care what he say. You need to stop this, and since you can't, you have to move out of the room." She had told me to "give her her head." Meaning she didn't want to hear anymore.

"What? Why do I have to move? This is my room."

"You keep wetting the bed. Marie can't take it, and I can't expect her to live like that."

I thought I was losing my damn mind. My mother was kicking me out of my own room for Marie? I couldn't understand what was happening. I wasn't wetting the bed on purpose. I prayed every night, before I went to bed, that the sheets would be dry when I woke up. It was embarrassing. I couldn't sleep over at anyone's house because of this, and it just ate at my self-esteem.

"You are taking her side on this? You are going to make me leave my own room for her? Where will I sleep? In the living room?"

"You wet the bed and won't stop. What do you want me to do? Jackson is not happy that his daughter is mad. You cannot sleep in the living room. You will ruin Jackson's couch. You will have to sleep in the kitchen. The floor can be mopped if you pee on it."

I didn't know what to say. My heart felt as if it was being ripped out of my chest.

"What do you mean, in the kitchen? I can't sleep in there. *This* is my room."

"Listen, I have to do what is going to make everyone happy. You keep peeing in the bed, and that's not right." My mother's Haitian accent seemed to get stronger, the angrier she got.

"But, Mom, it's not my fault. I have tried to stop."

She was actually mad at me, and she yelled, "No, you are not trying hard enough."

I started to cry. I felt like I was in the twilight zone. I knew that my mother liked to brush whatever happened under the rug, but the bed-wetting was a result of her refusing to deal with things.

"I am not leaving my own goddamned room for that bitch. Let *her* go sleep in the kitchen."

"Hey! *Veye bouch ou nan kay mwen.* It is over. You do what I ask, okay?"

I got off the bed and stood face-to-face with my mother. "You are asking me to watch my mouth? Fuck her! She is not your daughter. I am."

"Yes, you are my daughter, but why can't you be good, like Marie? All day you sit outside. I say study, and you go outside. I say clean, and you go outside. I say stop peeing in the bed, and you still pee."

"Are you kidding me? I get straight As, maybe one B, if that. I do everything, while Marie sits on her ass. It's not my fault she would rather stay in the house, watching TV all day."

"Listen, I don't care what you say. You do what I tell you."

I looked at my mother and lost all respect for her in that very moment. "Fuck all of you. This is my room, and I'm not leaving."

Chapter 5

Niya

I sat back as Roxie danced for me. There was something about her body that just drove me crazy. Her dark skin, her jet-black hair, her eyes, her lips—they all told the story of a Negro Puerto Rican. Well, that was what she told me her family called her. I guessed she had always been some sort of outcast, because the rest of them were light. But she was the most beautiful. I met her when she came over to my house with Rodney. I had thought that we would freak off, but she hadn't wanted Rodney to touch her at all. We'd just ended up drinking and smoking. But before she left, she gave me her number.

She was very open about who she was, but I met up with her only in private or after dark. She loved to fuck with me. She knew that I didn't like her hugging or kissing on me in public, so she would do it all the time.

"You bring something for me today?" she asked as she made her ass jump to the music. She was thick, had ass and breasts for days. Her body was that of a grown woman, but she had just turned eighteen.

"Maybe, maybe not. Aren't you just happy to see me?"

She walked over to me, straddled me, and let her hair down. It swept past her shoulders and made her even sexier. "Come on, *Papi*. Don't play with me. You know it makes me wet to see something sparkle."

I knew what type of chick she was, but I just couldn't help it. Looking at her in her bra and thong, so pretty, so deceivingly pleasing to the eye, I just had to feel her, be around her, feast on her.

"You feel that, Papi?" she asked as she took my hand and slipped it into her undies. "You feel how wet that pussy is? Make it wetter, baby. Show me what you bought for me."

Like her fucking lapdog, I reached into my pocket and pulled out a bracelet.

"Oh, baby. I love it. Look at that! How many carats?"

"Two," I answered. I was a sucker for a bad bitch with good pussy. She had me right where she wanted me.

She stood up, put on her gift, and took the rest of what she had on . . . off. She got on top of me and let me taste her lips. They were just as sweet as I remembered. The cash I had dropped on her jewels was money well spent. With Roxie, sex was always exciting. Just the sound of her moaning turned me on. She was a straight freak. Her pussy was always wet, and no lie, once I slipped my fingers between her legs again now, I'd be damned if she hadn't managed to get even wetter than she was before. I flipped her on the bed, and as always, she played her little games. She pushed me away, sat up, and waited for me to pull her close again.

"I changed my mind. I'm not horny anymore," she said with a smile. "Fuck that bullshit. You give me that pussy when I want it."

I laid her back down and pushed her legs open. She had the prettiest kitty. Well groomed, fat lips, and just juicy.

"I wanna watch you," I said.

She didn't move, so I took her hand and slid it down her belly. I placed her fingers against her clit and waited. Still nothing.

"Why you always have to do shit the hard way?" I asked as I wrapped my hand around her neck. At first, I put only minimal pressure on her neck, but the longer she made me wait, the more I squeezed. I watched as a vein in her forehead bulged, and slowly, she started to move her fingers. I eased up. The rougher I got with her, the more turned on she would become.

As I watched her, I pushed her legs as far back as they could go. I pushed her hand out of the way and plunged into her wet spot. She tasted sweet, and I couldn't get enough of her. I licked every inch of her cave. I sucked her engorged clit, and I tongue fucked her until she came in my mouth. She was a wildcat. Pulling at my hair, screaming my name, telling me how much she loved her papi. I fantasized about having a dick, just so I could feel her with something besides my fingers and tongue. She was so fucking sexy, and I wished that I could just give her the real thing. So, as she reached for the strap-on, I shook my head no. I just wasn't ready.

"Where were you that night you were supposed to come and see me?"

I looked at her as if I didn't know what she was talking about.

"You better not have been with no bitch."

I rolled my eyes at her. She was always talking about me being with other girls, though she knew damn well that she and Smiley were the only ones.

"Don't start that shit. We just had a good time," I said as I passed her the blunt. I picked up my drink glass, which was damn near empty, and drank down the rest of my cranberry and vodka.

"So, where were you?"

I didn't answer her, but when she asked me again, I pushed her off me and told her that I was going into the shower. Once I was out, I got dressed, counted off a few bills, and tried to hand them to her.

"You think that I am just your pussy piece? You come here, fuck me, and pay me. I'm not your fucking slut!"

I knew what time it was, and I wasn't going to play her game. I left the money on the bed and started for her door.

"Niya, I will fucking kill you, do you hear me? You better not be fucking around." She was following me, tugging at my shirt. Turning my V-neck into a U-neck.

"What the fuck is wrong with you? Why do you always have to end this shit on a sour note?"

She wasn't letting up, and I didn't expect her to. "What's wrong with me? No. What's wrong with *you*? You can't even kiss me in front of people. You treat me like a ho, and I am far from it."

"A *ho*? Would I buy a ho this?" I asked pointing at her neck. "Or how about this?" I pointed at her wrist. Every piece of jewelry she had on, I had bought, yet I always had to deal with her crazy bullshit.

"Man . . . I'm out. Call me when you get some fucking sense," she declared.

She was still holding on to me, so I asked her to let me go.

"I'm not letting you go. Tell me where you were, who you were with," she answered.

I yanked her toward me and grabbed her wrist. I twisted it, making sure not to cause too much pain, but enough to make her let go of me. Once loose from her vise grip, I pushed her away from me.

"You're a crazy bitch. Hit me when you are back to normal," I told her.

***

I stopped on my way home and picked up another bottle. Once I was around my hood, I just strolled the streets as a perfect ending to my night. I sipped slowly as I walked and thought about Roxie. She always had to start shit right after we had sex. But I couldn't lie; I could dig her crazy ways at times. It added spice. She was wild, fought damn near every girl in the hood, and always had some crazy shit poppin' off. She was fun that way. She was the type to eat a meal and skip out on the tab, just to have a story for that day. As I let the liquor warm my chest, my phone rang. The same number had been calling me for the past week or so. I was in just the right mood to deal with the call, so I picked up.

"Yeah, it's me, nigga. You calling to see if I'm still breathing?"

"Where the hell have you been? I went to meet up with you, but you never showed up."

The urgency in White Boy's voice made me stop walking.

"You tried to set me up, nigga. Sent a goon to take my shit and shoot me!"

"Now, why the fuck would I do that? You the only one out here I can trust. I wouldn't do no shit like that. Can we hook up?"

I laughed into the phone. "After what you did, hell no. I could have—"

"Listen to me. I didn't do that shit. How long have I been doing this with you? Why would I rob you now?" As White Boy spoke, I saw Jamilla turning the corner.

"Yeah, well, miss me with all that shit you talkin'. I hit that nigga a few times, and I hope he's not still breathing. I'll hit you up if I change my mind."

I hung up the phone as Jamilla walked by me. At first, I thought she was ignoring me, but by the look of things, she was closed off to the world. I walked behind her for a good block before I decided to call out her name. She didn't hear me until the third time.

"Jamilla."

She stopped walking and turned around. When she saw me, she rolled her eyes and picked up her pace. I walked a little faster until I caught up to her.

"Where are you going in such a hurry? I wanted to—" I stopped talking once I noticed that she had been crying.

"What's wrong?" I asked as she walked away. Again, I caught up to her. I took her arm and tugged on it to make her stop.

"Nothing is wrong. You got my notebook?"

I diverted my eyes from hers. I hadn't even thought of her notebook until she brought it up now. I guessed I had too much going on even to remember it. "I don't have it on me, but I will get it back to you. Tell me what's wrong, though."

She looked at me, and I hadn't seen that much pain in someone's eyes since the last time I looked in the mirror. "Life. That's what's always wrong."

"I hear that. Look, I don't know if you drink, but I just got a bottle. Wanna go to the courts? Maybe talk, hang out a bit?"

She looked at me as if she was trying to read me. I smiled as I thought of what could possibly be going through her head. I had been a total dick the first time we spoke. She was probably trying to understand my kindness and why I was showing any to her.

"I don't want to talk about what's wrong. Just get me drunk."

I knew how she felt. Sometimes drowning your reality in liquor felt like the only way out . . . for the moment.

Chapter 6

Jamilla

The air felt nice. It smelled like rain would soon come and rip us apart. The breeze cooled us New Yorkers and blessed us with a much-needed hiatus from the blazing night's heat that came with summer. Thirty minutes into Niya's bottle, and I was already half past drunk.

"Why did you take my notebook from me? Did it make you feel any better to read what I wrote?" I asked her, praying that she had never cracked it open.

"I didn't read it. I did it out of anger. I will give it back to you the next time I see you."

I took a swig off her bottle and handed it to her. "Have you seen Rodney?" I asked. I was doing it again, but I had to know.

"No. He called, but there's nothing left to say."

"Are you sure?" I asked, hoping that she didn't go off on me again.

"Yeah, I'm sure. I'm too hurt to go back to that. Whatever that was, 'cause it wasn't a friendship."

I frowned and continued with our conversation. "I forgive you, and we are talking right now. Is it fair to hold a grudge when you have been forgiven?" I watched her. Even though she was drunk, it didn't impair her thought process.

"What he did to me . . . that's unforgivable. He was supposed to be my friend. He betrayed me, and I will never forgive him."

A long silence fell between us. I didn't know what to say. As for her, she just looked lost in her own thoughts.

"What he said . . . is it true?" I finally asked.

She tried to hand me the bottle, but I shook my head no, and she downed the rest of the harsh liquor. "Maybe, maybe not," she said. As she answered my question, big raindrops started to fall, causing us to jump up and head for our building.

We walked in silence. When the rain began to fall harder, we ran. Once inside the building, neither of us had much to say. Our building had two sets of stairs. Each led to one side of the building. I live on the A side; she lived on the B side. We looked at each other and said good night. It was hard just to walk away. I just wanted to grab her and kiss her. The longing stare that settled in her eyes before we turned our backs on each other and parted ways told me that maybe, just maybe, if I did kissed her, she wouldn't pull away. But I just wasn't sure yet.

I felt better while inebriated. My home situation became a distant memory as thoughts of Niya and our conversation invaded my brain. I got into the house, and it was clear that everyone was asleep. I locked up, stayed quiet, and longed to pass out in my bed. I walked down the hallway, hoping that my stepdad wouldn't come out. I made it to my bedroom door and went to turn the knob. It didn't budge. At first, I thought that because I was drunk, I wasn't turning the knob the right way. I stood there for ten minutes, trying to get that door open, before it dawned on me. My knob was different. They had put a lock on the bedroom door. This angered me, so I started to bang on that door like a madwoman.

"Open up this fucking door. This is my room," I screamed and yelled, but Marie wouldn't open the door. Instead, she spoke to me through it.

"Your mom said that this was my room now."

"I don't give a shit. Open the door."

This went on for another ten minutes or so.

"At least let me get my things." I said, trying to sound defeated.

"Your mother took them out already. Look in the hall closet."

My mother did what? I asked myself. I staggered to the hallway, flipped on the lights, and opened the closet door. A gasp escaped my lips. There were all my things. My clothes, everything I owned, was stuffed in this one little coat closet. I wanted to cry. I really did. But I couldn't. I was too irritated, too upset, too angry. How could she do this to me? I knew what I would do. I was going to sleep on the couch, which she had told me I couldn't sleep on. I was going to show her. With all the will in me to do no good, I couldn't. They had flipped over the couches in the living room.

I tried my best to flip one of them back over, but with the alcohol in my bloodstream, I didn't have the balance or the strength. I sat on the living-room floor for a very long time, just thinking. I had a conversation with God that night, asking Him, "Why me?" I wanted to know why my life was the way it was. Why was I birthed from the woman I called Mom. I wanted to know why He had let things happen to me that would later put me right there on that living-room floor. There were so many bad people in the world who didn't have it half as bad as me. But there I was, a young girl doing her best, and I was living a life that I felt shouldn't belong to me. "What did I do, God? Tell me, what did I do?" I asked this so many times, I lost count.

When no answer came, I went into the kitchen to see where I could make a bed for myself, but my mother had already made it. I guessed that was the least she could have done. I lay there and figured it all out. *Ours is not to question why. Our purpose in life is to do or die*, I thought. I couldn't wait to get the fuck out of that house and just do, 'cause in the house . . . I was dying.

Chapter 7

Niya

I staggered into the apartment and stopped in the kitchen. I put the plate of food that my grandma always left for me in the fridge. I checked her box of "tea" to make sure that she had enough weed in there. My grandmother never drank, hardly cursed, but her weed she had to have. I filled up her box and headed straight for my bedroom. I turned on my underground mixtape and undressed. I had had a long day, and at that point nothing felt better than my bed. As I hummed to the rap song that came out of my speakers, I picked up my rhyme pad and jotted down some lines that came to mind.

What do you hide? As if I am not holding back mine. But deep in your eyes, I see things that coincide, with pain from life and unbinding love. Milla, for real'ah, this fever you give me is a killa. She usin' me for everything but my mind. Clothes, jewels, and money send chills up her spine. Her body be calling, and I'm always there to answer. 'Cause shorty looks good and giving her time to shine eats away at the anger. Baby thinks I don't know, but with me hiding who I am, I will have to deal'ah with everything that ain't realer . . . than you. Shit won't last long. There's only so much dancing you can do in a thong. When it's over, I just hope that you are there and know that this ain't just a song but some real shit I been feeling and was just too afraid to tell you, so I put it in this song.

Secrets, everybody has them . . . and I wish you were mine. Untold truths bury true feelings from within, but deep in your eyes, I see the need to align with a real nigga that always stays trill'ah. You the one I want beside me when I'm sittin' on a mill. Them other bitches, I'm ready to kill. Ain't shit real about them. They're just looking for someone to pay their bills.

I read over what I'd written and laughed. Wasn't my best, but it was real. Writing down my feelings for the day always kept me sane. I always had thoughts running around in my head, and writing them down had always been better than telling them. I put down my pen and turned over to put the pad on my nightstand, and there it was. I sat up and just looked at it. I had told her that I didn't read it, but sitting there, I wanted to. I wanted to know more about her, and this was the way to do it without asking her a bunch of questions. I needed to use the bathroom, so I got up. As I emptied my bladder, I used that time to think. I asked myself how mad I would be if someone read my notepad. I also told myself that no one would know. I washed my hands, returned to my bedroom, went into my backpack, took out some weed, and rolled up a blunt. I sat there smoking, contemplating what to do. I tried to think of other things, but soon enough, she would find her way back into my thoughts, and after her came thoughts of her notebook.

"Fuck it," I said out loud. I picked up the notebook and flipped it open to the first page. There was no writing on that page, just little things that she'd drawn. Lots of hearts, butterflies, and flowers, and I didn't know why, but it made me smile. She was a great artist. Even her doodles were very detailed, very well drawn. As I flipped to the second page, I took in a deep breath of smoke. I saw writing and got a little nervous as I began to read her written thoughts.

On the way home I look around and wonder how many of the kids out here wish that they weren't going home at all, or maybe that they were going to a different home, at least.

Why do you just stare? What are you trying to see? Do you see my secrets, or do you stare so you don't have to think of your own? Do you see in me what you see in her? I hope not. I want you to see better things in me than you do in her. Tell me. I need to know. I am dying to know. I lose sleep asking, why do you stare?

I put out my blunt. That shit was making me bug out. I knew I was high and way past tipsy, but could she be talking about me? I knew that I stared at her a lot, but I didn't think that she'd noticed. I read on.

When I was with him, I didn't feel loved. Was it him, or was it me? I looked at him, my first boyfriend, and felt empty. When he was on top of me, I wished he wasn't. Damn. Please, God, don't say that this is what love is supposed to be!

I have heard people say that if they could, they would want to be invisible. I have lived my life this way, and I wish I could tell them the truth about it all. Not being seen hurts more than anything in this world. Living like a ghost just eats away at your soul.

So you write about me. Don't ask how I know. I just do. Who else sits with a blue notepad and just stares at somebody? So why don't you just come over and talk to me? Is it because I am not her? Yes, I know all about her. She first came with Rodney, and now . . . off the late night, she just comes with you. Guess I'll never know.

My fucking heart was racing a mile a minute. She was talking about me. . . . *Oh shit.* I picked up the blunt I had just put out and lit it back up. I sat there for a few, just smoking, with the notebook facedown in my lap. I finished off the weed before I picked the notebook back up again.

I love that you see me. You look *at me and* see *me. I don't know why I think of you so much. I even question my sexuality, although you do not turn me on . . . sexually. I just wish I knew you. I wish that we could be friends. I need someone. I need someone to save me from all this emptiness. But I thank you. You see me, and that counts.*

Why does life have to be this way? Why must I be alone in a world of billions? My mother doesn't get me, my stepfamily hates me, and everyone else just doesn't see me.

Finally, during our last year in high school, you left your notepad behind. I was hoping that we wouldn't part ways without me ever knowing what you wrote about. I sat there wondering if I should. I knew that everything that you had tried to hide littered those pages. I knew that the words that were neatly printed on the page had emerged from the deepest part of your soul. Therefore, I had to look. I wanted to know what was behind those wondering eyes. I needed to know what you saw from the inside, looking out. You intrigue me; therefore, I had to know. When you came back into the class, looking for it, I handed it to you with somewhat of a better understanding of who you are.

Page after page, she revealed herself to me without even knowing it. She made me laugh, she made me sad, and thinking about her sadness also made me angry. I picked up my pen and wrote a few thoughts of my own in her notebook.

This city holds every sound known to man, or so it seems. But when I look at you, the whole world seems to go silent. You sit as if you're in your own realm, where love is free and tears don't fall. I wish I knew what it is about you, but I am too afraid to speak. Hidden in darkness, too scared to let my light shine freely, I don't know you, but I feel as if I need you. Will my apology ever mean anything to you? It's funny how we have barely uttered a word to each other, but when you look at me, I feel like you knew me long before I knew myself.

I wonder if you are the only one who noticed her. She is one of only two, but lost in her beauty, body, moans, and groans, I just can't seem to find my way out.

I see you. Always have. When you're near, my tunnel vision kicks in. I see no one but you. But you know what I want you to know. I can see the pain that dwells far beneath your smile. I know that pain. Have felt it a time or two myself.

No, you are not gay (lol). I just have that effect on people.

I don't know what it is about you, either. You just seem like the person who I want to love. . . . Damn. I just wrote that . . . and you're reading it. Damn. I just couldn't help it.

I wrote the following as soon as I got home. I loved spending time with you. You were on my mind. It's not my best, as I didn't even get a chance to clean it up, but these are raw emotions. Enjoy! P.S. Don't be mad that I read your notebook. Just look at it as it making us even!

I added what I had written only an hour before, along with my cell number, and hoped that she wouldn't be too pissed. I read a bit more before sleep tiptoed into my room and soon invaded my body. I fell asleep with thoughts of bringing Jamilla her notebook in the morning, and with visions of her face dancing around in my mind.

Chapter 8

Jamilla

"Jamilla, wake up. You have someone here." I heard my mother, but I was tired. I had got in late and needed to sleep off the liquor. "Jamilla."

"What?" I asked as I sat up out of annoyance. I rubbed my eyes and waited for my mother to speak up.

"You have—"

"What are you doing here?" I said.

Niya was standing in my house. Then it dawned on me that I was sleeping on the kitchen floor. Oh my God. She was standing in my kitchen. I pulled the covers over my chest and slipped my hand under them and felt around. *Fuck*. It was wet. *Fuck, fuck, fuck*.

"Get up, Jamilla. Don't just lie there," Marie said with an evil grin. I prayed that no one ever felt the embarrassment that I felt that morning. There I sat, soaked by my own urine, wishing that just once I could become what I dreaded—invisible.

Everyone seemed to be staring at me, waiting for me to make a move, but I couldn't. I couldn't even look at Niya. I diverted my eyes, looked at the floor, and spoke. My voice was low, but she heard me. "What are you doing here, Niya? What are you doing here?"

She took a step forward, and before she could take another, I stopped her.

"Stay right there," I yelled without meaning to. I just didn't want her to get close enough to see a wet spot or, even worse, smell it.

"I just came by to bring you your notebook. You left it outside," she lied, having noticed how interested my mother and my stepsister were in our conversation.

"Just leave it on the counter, please." I never looked at her. I couldn't.

"Okay. Well, I guess I'll see you around?"

I gripped the covers and prayed her away. "Sure," I answered. I raised my eyes just so I could watch her leave.

"Who was that?" my mother asked after she heard the front door close. Her face was all scrunched up. I knew that Niya's appearance would bring questions.

"That's the gay girl you bumped into at the graduation," Marie answered with a smile. She knew that saying this would get my mother worked up.

"How would you know? You sleep with her or something?" My questions wiped that smile clear off her face.

"Jamilla, stop it. That's a crazy question you asked her. How do you know her, this gay girl?"

"Mom," I said as I got up and put my sheets in the washer, "I don't really know her. I just used to see her around at school. I left my notebook outside, and she brought it in for me, that's all."

"You better not be friends with no gay. You hear me? I don't like no gay for your friend."

I didn't even answer her. Why would she care about who my friends were when she didn't give a shit about me sleeping on the damn kitchen floor? I went into the bathroom, got undressed, and stood in the shower and just cried. How could I ever face Niya again? Her face had told me all that I needed to know. She had looked shocked to see me on the floor. I didn't know what I was going to tell her if she asked me why I was there. I thanked God that it was summertime. I stayed in the house, avoiding her at all cost. I couldn't even bring myself to write for the first six days. All I did was think of her.

It was a Sunday evening, and my body was hurting from so many nights of sleeping on the floor. My mother was cooking, and I was just in a bad mood. I probably was going crazy from so many days in the house with the people I hated the most. I was sitting in the living room, with my face buried in a book, unknowingly tapping my foot against the table.

"Do you have to do that?" my stepfather asked.

I didn't even look up from the book. I rolled my eyes and purposely banged my foot against the table.

"What the fuck is your problem?"

I could hear my mother's stillness as she heard him yell.

"You, you are my fucking problem," I snapped.

I jumped up, went into the hall closet, and took out my notebook. I made my way to the front door. As I left the apartment, I could hear my stepdad yelling to my mother about how disrespectful I was and how he wanted me out of his house. I guessed that looking at me reminded him of what he had done to me.

I sat on the stoop, breathing in the fresh air. The breeze was cool, unusual for a July summer night. It felt good to be outside. As much as I enjoyed the nighttime air, I asked God to please keep Niya away from the outside of the building. I just wanted to sit, think, and write. As I flipped through the back of the notebook, I read over a few of my entries. When I got to the last few pages, I noticed handwriting that wasn't mine. I was confused, but I read what was written.

When I was done, I didn't know what to think. She had read my most private thoughts, and to be fair, I had done the same thing to her. I was smiling, but I wanted to know what all of this meant. She wrote that I seemed like someone she could love. It scared me, and it also made me feel wanted. I pulled out my MP3 player, put on my headphones, and let the music drown out the world. I listened to Bridget Kelly's rendition of "Thinking About Forever" and just read her words over and over and over again.

Chapter 9

Niya

I was on my way home from the Bronx. I had spent the day with a girl named Smiley. She was a cute chick who made me laugh. She was a homey, a lover, a friend. We never went all the way. I just liked to look at her, touch her. She was short and plump, a girl with curves that most men would be scared to handle, but I loved the feel of her. She was soft all over and sexy as hell. Sex dripped from her every word, and she knew how to play on that shit. She was one of those creatures who you were drawn to, and you just didn't know why.

Unlike Roxie, she never asked me for shit, so I always gave. I liked that about her. A few times I had left her some money on her dresser, only to find it in my pocket as I was on my way home. She was cool as shit and was always asking me to go to the clubs with her. After I let her read some of the things I had written, she tried all the time to get me to do open mic nights, but I wasn't ready. I told her that one day soon I would take baby steps with a gay club and then would work my way up to performing.

I had a lot of time to think as I drove. Jamilla had been on my mind since that morning I went to her apartment. What the fuck was she doing on the floor? As soon as I stepped in there, I felt sorry for her. I knew that she wouldn't want me to see her like that. I even told her mom not to wake her up, but she didn't listen. Every time I went out or came in, I hoped that I would see her outside on the stoop, but she was never there.

As I got out of the car and headed to my building, I heard my name being called. I turned around and waited for my nigga Shawn to catch up with me. We said our hellos, and we spoke as he walked with me.

"I just saw that nigga Rodney. He was asking about you," Shawn informed me.

I sucked my teeth and went on with our conversation, as if I didn't hear him. Once we were closer to my building, we saw the usual faces, and I stopped and chilled with a few of the neighborhood guys. No one brought up what Rodney had said, but they all seemed to be a bit different toward me. Now they spoke as if they knew that I was into girls.

"Ay, you know who was asking about you?" one of them asked me as we passed around a few blunts.

I remained quiet.

"That Jamaican girl with the red hair. She been asking Marco about you. You better check on that," one guy said.

I didn't answer. I just laughed it off and told them that I was good.

"White Boy been telling us to tell you to get up with him, but we told him you ain't really been hittin' the block much. You need to get back to work, nigga," another one said.

"That's why I work for myself. There's no clocking in," I answered.

The longer we stood there, the more I noticed I was getting checked out. I didn't know if it always happened and I was too afraid to acknowledge that, but it was crazy. Some even openly flirted. The more I smoked and sipped, the more I didn't care who noticed.

"Ay, there she go," Marco said, speaking of the girl with the red hair.

She was bad as shit. Damn near naked. Her outfit didn't leave much to the imagination. Her hair was short and the color of a fire hydrant, while her skin was the color of coffee with cream. We all watched her as she came our way. My heart was racing, and as bad as I wanted to talk to her, I prayed that she didn't say shit to me. She looked aggressive, and it scared me. My prayers weren't answered, because she came straight to me. The blunt that I was smoking hung from my mouth. I had forgotten about it as she approached.

"I have been looking for you," she said as she took the blunt from my mouth and put it to hers.

"I heard," was the only thing I could get out.

She was cool. She spoke about my clothes a lot. Talked about my jewels and the shoes she had seen me wear. Another Roxie, and I didn't need it. One was enough. She was hot, no doubt, but she had nothing special, no substance. As she leaned on me, spoke about me as if I wasn't there and she planned to be with me, as if I didn't have a choice, my grandmother came out of my building and called my name. As I looked Granny's way, I saw *her*.

I pushed Red off of me and almost killed myself as I tried to cross that street at a run. It felt like it had been so long since I had seen her. The car that almost ran me over stopped just in time, but I didn't care. I could tell that she had seen me and was now trying to hurry up and go back in the building. I ran faster and caught up to both her and my grandmother.

"What's up, Gran? What's up, Jamilla?" I spoke to both of them, but I was looking only at one of them.

"Your father is on the phone," Granny announced.

That shit slapped me in the face so hard, I could have sworn that my high was gone. I finally looked at my grandmother, and I could tell that she really wanted me to talk to him.

"Give me a second. I'll be right there," I told her.

Granny went into the building, and with just the two of us standing there, I didn't know what to say.

"Where you been?" I finally asked as I tried to make eye contact with Jamilla.

She didn't answer right away, which gave me a chance to really see her. When I looked down at her hands, I saw she was holding on to the notebook so tight that her nails were digging into it.

"I was in the house. Not feeling well," she lied, and we both knew it.

"I need to speak to you. Can you—"

"Niya, come in here," my grandmother yelled out the window.

I didn't want to move, afraid that it would be another week before I saw her again. I grabbed her hand, and without asking, I walked her up to my apartment.

Chapter 10

Jamilla

I sat in Niya's living room, with her right beside me. Her leg was against mine as she spoke on the phone. Not that she was doing too much talking. A yes here and a no there. I could tell that she really didn't want to be on the phone at all. After a few minutes, she called her grandmother back into the room and waited for her to take the phone back into the kitchen. Then she sat there for a minute, just breathing. I watched her nostrils flare before she took a deep breath, looked at me dead in the eyes, and asked, "Want something to drink?"

I shook my head yes and was thankful when she got up. It gave me breathing room. I didn't know why she made me so nervous. Maybe it was because I had read what she had written. A few minutes later she returned with two cups of soda and handed one of them to me. As she sat back down, the scent of her cologne blew my way, and instantly, I felt intoxicated. She smelled sweet, but not in a feminine way. Her scent wasn't strong, but it still lingered in the air, as if she had just sprayed on the cologne. She smelled fresh, with a hint of vanilla and light musk. I took my time looking at her. Not a damn hair was out of place; every strand had been pulled back in a neat ponytail. Her clothes were nice, expensive, and without one wrinkle. I was examining her as if she wasn't there. By the time I reached her face, she was smiling, as if she had caught me.

"Like what you see?" she asked.

Her question made me jump, and I spilled a few drops of the soda she had brought me. "I'm so sorry. I didn't mean to. Sorry."

She laughed as she got up, and then she disappeared into the kitchen and came back a minute later with a paper towel.

"I was only joking, unless . . . ," she said as she handed me the paper towel.

I was so damn uncomfortable, as I was holding my breath. I knew that she was being funny, but I just didn't know what to say.

"Let's go in my room," she said and stood up, but I remained seated. She looked at me as if she was asking me what was wrong.

"What about your grandmother?" I asked as I looked up at her.

"Oh, she's cool. She's about to roll up and go to bed. I keep telling her to leave the smoking to the grown folks, but she won't listen," Niya said as her grandmother came into the living room. They both laughed as I looked on.

"I tell you already, I smoke before you born. It my medicine," Granny said.

"Yeah, that's why you always go to bed after. It's all right, Granny. You can't hang, but I still love you."

I loved watching them. They seemed like friends, not just family.

Niya's granny looked at me. "You are?"

"Oh, sorry. I am Jamilla," I answered.

"Yes. I see you before. Nice to meet you. Niya, mi amor, I go to my room. Good night."

She went into her bedroom, and Niya waited for me to enter hers.

***

Niya's room was just as neat as she was, with a lot of music and posters and a lot of notepads. Her closet was packed with clothes, and she had so many shoes that some had to be lined up against the wall.

"So you're a shoe whore?" I asked as I sat on the desk chair. She got on her bed and lay back.

"Everyone has an addiction. You want to add something to that Coke?"

I wasn't in the mood to drink, so I told her no. She asked me if I wanted to smoke. To that, I said yes. She got up, turned on some music, and went to work. This gave me a chance to look at her freely. I was able to act as if I was watching her roll.

"Did you get a chance to write in your notebook?" she asked, forcing me to take my eyes off her body and bring them up to her eyes. She stopped rolling as she waited for my answer. Her sly smile let me know what she was really asking.

"I saw what you wrote," I said, answering her true question. Her eyes widened before going back to their natural size.

"I hope you're not mad that I read it, but I couldn't help it."

I smiled. "That's okay. I once read your private thoughts, too."

She lit the blunt, got back on the bed, and leaned back on her pillows. As she smoked, she looked at me through the smoke that escaped the burning bud of love.

Drake's "The Real Her" played in the background as I waited for her to pass the smoke. I was so nervous, and that song was making me think too much.

"You're too far. Come here," Niya said as she patted her bed.

I didn't move. "Just sit up."

She continued to smoke. "Nope. Come here. I won't bite. Well, I normally don't, unless . . ."

She made me laugh. I got up and sat at the foot of her bed.

"You're still too far. See?" She stretched her arm out to show me how far away I was.

"No I'm not. See? I can—" I stopped in mid-sentence when I went to reach for the blunt and she took my hand and pulled me to her. She pulled hard enough to bring me up close to her face.

"This is better. Now, let me blow you."

I didn't answer. I watched her take a long drag off the stuffed cigar and just waited.

Siya had both of our heads bobbing. "Tainted" played on Niya's radio and spoke to both of us. We had both been tainted and destroyed in our own ways, but in a weird way, I felt halfway healed by being there with her.

Niya sat up, her mouth full of smoke, and pressed her lips against mine. My heart danced not only to the beat of Siya, but also to the beat of nervousness. She gave me chills and made my palms sweat. I inhaled the smoke while keeping eye contact. She was so pretty, so handsome, just beautiful. I watched her lips curl into a smile as she sat back and rapped along with Siya. I took the blunt from her hand and looked away from her.

"Can you roll another one? I'm tryin'a get fucked up," I said.

She got up, filled her cup with vodka, and rolled two more blunts. I didn't speak as I got up and sat in the desk chair as she rolled. My mind was occupied with confusing questions. I thought about the things she had written in my notebook, the things she had read, and I wanted to know what she thought of me in the present moment.

"You sure are quiet. Is that how you get when you smoke? What are you thinking about?" she asked. She had finished rolling and was pulling off her T-shirt. Her diamond chain shone against her skin. Every time she moved, something sparkled. Either her earrings, her necklace, or her bracelet.

"I was thinking about you reading my notebook."

"What about it?" she asked as she looked dead at me.

"What do you think of me now that you have read all my inner thoughts . . . of you?"

She smiled again, and so did I. "Are you going to come up here and lie down with me, or do I have to pick you up and put you on the bed?"

This time I crawled on her queen-size bed and rested my back against her headboard. She downed her half of a cup of liquor and poured another. I asked her to add some liquor to my cup of Coke, and after she did so, I took a big sip. We smoked, with me right beside her, her arm against mine. Her skin was warm, soft, and burned weird thoughts into my mind. I listened to her speak.

"I was kind of nervous, knowing that you were writing about me," she said, finally answering my question. "I always noticed you, but you never noticed me, or so I thought. So to read what you wrote, to be able to read what you have been going through—it made me feel close to you. It also made me sad. Are you gay?"

I jerked and jumped at her question. "What? Where in the hell did that come from?"

She sipped her drink, and I pulled on the weed. I was already fucked up, and we were only on the second blunt.

"Just thought I would ask. Gay, bi, straight, curious?"

"Are you gay?" I returned, answering her question with a question. I watched her eyes as she looked into mine. "What? Not so easy to answer?" I asked. I handed her the blunt but refused to drop my eyes from hers.

"I—I am, yes."

"Yes what?"

I wanted her to say it, for me, and for her. She smoked, drank, smoked, and drank again, but I waited.

"Yes, I am gay. I like pussy. Does it change anything now that you have heard me say it again?"

I started to laugh. I didn't know why, but soon she joined me.

"No," I said as I lowered my body and rested my head against her pillows. "Do you feel any different?"

She thought about it for a minute, then said, "Maybe a bit relieved. Not that you didn't know it, anyway. So tell me, what are you?"

She was now on her pillow, only a few inches from my face. I watched her eyes travel from my eyes to my nose and down to my lips before moving back up again. I was all of a sudden comfortable with her. I was no longer nervous. It was as if her truth and her acknowledging her truth had somehow set me free.

"I am straight . . . I think," I said.

Again, we shared a slew of giggles, never taking our eyes off each other.

I had so much fun with her that night. Being near her just seemed so right, as if she, the person, could never do any wrong. Because of that one night with each other, we formed a bond that would link us together for life. Lying there, I knew that she would become my everything. My only hope was that she was feeling the same way.

Chapter 11

Niya

It was almost two in the morning when I felt her next to me. I didn't even remember falling asleep. I slid off the bed without waking her up, used the bathroom, and went back into the bedroom. At first, I just stood there looking at her. As I stood in that doorway, there was nothing more beautiful than her. There were so many things that I wanted to do to her, say to her, and make her feel, but with her telling me that she was straight . . . maybe, I didn't want to take too many chances.

I went over to my desk chair, lit up the half of a blunt that we hadn't finished, and just watched her breathe. I thought about my conversation with my dad, or the lack thereof. I thought about my grandmother and how much I loved her. I thought about my mother, who was sure to show up at any time, only to eat, shower, and head back out to the streets that were eating her alive. I thought about Roxie and Smiley, and how I had them and needed them differently, and finally, I thought about Jamilla. She was my tainted flower, my imperfect black rose, but I loved every petal that clung to her tattered soul. I wanted to get to know her more. I wanted her to be mine. I prayed that she would love me, and that I would take that love and be kind. Knowing that being loved was something so damn special, I knew that I would love her right down to the core.

I moved to the bed, with smoke-stained thoughts, and denied myself the luxury of listening to logic. I left all inhibitions behind as soon as I hit the mattress. There was no denying what I wanted to do. Truth ruled my thoughts and seeped into my actions. I wanted to touch her. I needed to experience what I had been thinking about for so damn long.

She was still sleeping when I got beside her. I put my arm around her waist and just let it sit there. My heart was beating so fast that I thought she would hear it over the radio I had on. Slowly, very slowly, I let my hand slide under her shirt. When I felt her flesh, I took in a deep breath. I let my hand travel past her navel, up her ribs, and I stopped once I felt her move. She shifted a little before going back into a deep slumber. She looked so damn perfect. Her skin, the color of caramel, had me wanting to taste it just so I could see if it was just as sweet. Her hair, draped across my pillow and her shoulders, made me want to pull on it. Pull her close and taste every last drop of her.

When my hand reached her breast, I slipped my fingers inside of her bra and felt her nipple. I ran my fingers across it as low moans crept out of Jamilla's lips. I moved closer to her as she stretched and seemingly enjoyed my touch. She lay there with her eye closed, moaning, breathing hard. I leaned in and tasted her neck. I moved to her ear, licking and sucking on her earlobe as I rolled her nipple between my fingers. The more she got into it, the bolder I got.

My hand left her chest so I could pull up her shirt and bra. Her breasts turned me on, and I wanted to taste them. I let out a low sound of ecstasy as soon as my mouth hit her nipple. Her hard nipple sent chills down my spine, and I let my hand head south. I wasn't sure if she was awake or halfway sleeping, but her eyes never opened. With my fingers at the ridge of her shorts, with her body moving to the flow of my tongue, and with her moans increasing, I hurried to unbutton her shorts. I was racing against my mind. I had too many thoughts flying around and too many fantasies about Jamilla that I needed to fulfill.

Her panties were a peach color. Nothing too fancy, but they were cute. My breathing was at a rapid pace as I sucked her nipple hungrily. As my fingers reached the sweetest spot, I damn near came. Her legs started to part wider as her pussy dripped with delight. I was like a wild fucking beast. Her kitty was so damn warm and wet, and her clit swelling under my fingers sent me into a lust-filled rage.

"Damn, Jamilla. Baby, you are so fucking wet."

If I had known better, I would have kept my mouth shut.

She opened her eyes, looked at me, and asked, "Where am I?"

Chapter 12

Jamilla

When I heard her voice, it scared the shit out of me. Lost somewhere between sleep and consciousness, I had known what was happening, but I had also thought that it was a dream.

After I heard her voice, I jumped up, for two reasons. One, Niya was touching me, and two, I was sleeping in her bed. Did I wet it?

"What's wrong? Come back here," she said.

"Why were you touching me?" I asked her as I put on my shoes.

"Was that wrong? I'm sorry. You seemed to like it."

"But I told you. I told you that I was straight. I didn't even realize that I was still here, didn't realize that it was you who was touching me."

She got off the bed and came closer to me. "I'm sorry, Milla. Please, don't go."

I was looking for my notebook when she came up beside me and took my hand. "No, really. I can't," I told her.

She looked frustrated, but I couldn't do anything about that.

"Come on, Jamilla. Don't leave like this. I really am sorry."

I looked at her and wished that things could be different. I wanted to jump back in that bed with her and just talk. I didn't want her to touch me. . . . Well, maybe I did, but I couldn't think about that. I was too busy thanking God that I hadn't wet her bed. I was too busy beating myself down because I couldn't change my past and make my present different.

"No. I have to go." I headed for her bedroom door, but she ran past me and stood in front of it, keeping it closed.

"I fucking told you that I was sorry. What the fuck is wrong with you?"

Did she really just ask me what was wrong with me?

"*You* are what's wrong with me. I told you that I was straight, yet I wake up to you touching me. That's what's fucking wrong."

Her face scrunched up, as if she wasn't buying my bullshit. "Get the fuck out of here. You were moaning and carrying on. You liked that shit."

"That's the problem with you gay girls. Always tryin'a pull someone to your side. Just because I tell you I'm straight doesn't mean that I was challenging you."

"You know what? I'm starting to think that you are fucking crazy."

She was looking at me as if she was looking into me. Her calling me crazy enraged me. I had to hear that shit from my mother all the fucking time. I wasn't going to let her get away with it.

"I'm crazy? Fuck you, Niya. How about you try walking in my shoes? How about—"

"That could never happen. You're too scared to let anyone in. What in the fuck is wrong with you? I am trying just to get close to you. Why do you have to leave? I keep saying I'm sorry, but you're not even hearing me."

"'Cause sorry don't mean shit." I took a deep breath. "You want to know why I can't stay?" I asked as I got in her face. I didn't wait for her to answer. "I can't stay, because the fear of pissing in your bed cripples me. I can't stay, because I am fucked up due to what my stepdad did to me."

"Piss in my bed?"

I wanted to take it back, but it was too late. I looked around the room for her bottle of vodka, found it, picked it up, and took three big gulps.

"That's right," I said after wiping my mouth with the back of my hand. "If I sleep here, I may wet your bed. Now, isn't that some embarrassing shit? But what's more embarrassing than you seeing me on the kitchen floor that day? See, you walk around like being gay is the worst thing that you could be going through. Well, how about every day having to look at the man who touched you when you were only seven years old? How about having to call him Dad and watch him marry your mother? How about being so fucked up over that shit that you are sixteen and are still pissing in the fucking bed? How . . . about . . ."

I started to cry. Looking at her, with so much pity in her eyes, I couldn't take it. She walked over to me, and I fell into her arms.

"You gotta tell your mother about this."

"I tried, Niya, but she just called me crazy. She took me to the doctor, and they tried to tell her, but she's not hearing it. They sent a caseworker to my house, but out of fear, I told them that I had made it up. I got in so much trouble for just telling the doctor in a roundabout way, so I knew I had to hide it once they came knocking on our door. I don't know what to do. I can't go on living like this forever."

"Is that why she makes you sleep in the kitchen?"

Shame consumed me. "Yes. Because I kept wetting the bed, and my stepsister got tired of it." I cried for the next fifteen minutes. I told her everything, and in her arms, I felt a little better.

"I don't want you going back home tonight."

"But I have to. My mom would flip. Plus—"

"You're not going back there to sleep on the damn floor, not tonight at least. I'll make sure you don't have any accidents. Don't worry."

I was terrified at the thought of going back to sleep in her bed. What if we woke up wet because of me? How would I ever be able to face her? With thoughts of totally embarrassing myself tap-dancing through my mind, I looked in her eyes while thinking about things. I really didn't want to leave, but . . . what if? Ten minutes flew by, and with reassurance from Niya, the what-ifs flew out the window. I got back in her bed, lay in her arms, and fell asleep to the sound of her breathing. To my surprise, I didn't wet her bed at all.

When I crept into my house after my first night at Niya's house, I thought that I would never be able to look at her again. I had told her some of my deepest, darkest secrets, and I thought that it would change everything. As I got in my makeshift bed on the kitchen floor, I thought about my night with her. I hadn't slept that well in years. Then I thought about the way she'd made me feel. Sure, I had been half asleep, but my God, from what I remembered, she had made me feel what I had never felt before.

I had been with only one guy, Lance, and he had never made me feel so good. Half of the time, I had just lain there, wishing that he would finish. He'd been nice and all, but there had been no sparks. I wasn't gay, had never thought of sleeping with a woman before, but she had just made me feel so good.

It was six o'clock in the morning when I got in, but I couldn't fall back to sleep. I just lay there, thinking of her, watching the time. I wanted to see her again already.

I wanted to be around her. I wanted to watch her smile, enjoy her sarcasm, and enjoy the flow of her stride. I loved the way she walked, as if she always had all the time in the world. And when she laughed, it showed her femininity. It was the cutest laugh I had ever heard. It was the kind of laughter that you couldn't help but join in on when you heard it.

She made me feel so comfortable. I had told her everything about my stepdad. Living in this house was one of the hardest things I had ever had to do. Every damn day, I had to face the man who had taken me away from myself, and it was killing me. I remembered that day so clearly.

My mother was in view. I could have called out to her, but he held my mouth shut. She was on the phone in the other room. I tried to make noise, but when he told me that he would snap my neck if I made another sound, I was too scared even to move. He held me on his lap, with his hands down my panties, and just moaned. My face was wet with tears, but crying was all that I could do.

When my mother came back into the living room, I was in the bathroom, washing my face, as instructed. She called me back into the living room, and when I got there, she was smiling. When I heard her say that Jackson had proposed to her, it was as if someone had clawed their way into my heart and ripped it out. The abuse went on for years. He never penetrated me, and because of that, he said that what he was doing to me didn't count as sexual abuse. He said that it was his way of showing me how much he loved me, and for a while, until I grew old enough, I believed him.

Telling Niya these things had been hard, but she had made me feel safe enough. I trusted her with my sordid past, and because of that, she would become everything to me.

By noon, I couldn't take it anymore. I hadn't heard from her, and the night before played over and over in my head. I had to see her; I couldn't take the waiting game any longer. I told my mother that I was taking out the trash, and then I headed to the other side of the building. I took the steps two at a time. I rushed to her door, and once there, I didn't think twice. I knocked on her door and waited. Nothing. I knocked again. Nothing. The last time, I knocked so hard that I thought her grandma would curse me out, but still no one opened the door.

I turned to leave, with slumped shoulders, damn near in tears. Was I crazy? Why was I acting like this? I told myself to get it together. I wasn't supposed to be feeling this way. *She is a lesbian. I am straight*, I reminded myself. As I gave myself a mental lashing for acting like a thirteen-year-old girl, I heard the locks on her door turn. I stopped at the top of the stairs and just waited. My heart raced, as if I had just run a mile, as the door crept open. She stood there, rubbing her sleepy eyes. I couldn't move, not until she looked at me. When she did, I just stood there smiling.

"Are you okay?" she asked.

I walked toward her. At first, my stride was slow, but the closer I got to her, the more urgent my need to feel her arms around me became. Once I was in front of her, I pressed my body against hers and hugged her tightly. I hugged her for a long time, and when she squeezed me back, the world seemed to stand still. Afterward, we went back to her bedroom, got in her bed, and slept. I stayed with her for a few hours.

When I got back home, my mom really let me have it, but it was all worth it. In the months that followed, I ate, breathed, and lived for her.

Chapter 13

Niya

With only six weeks left to our summer vacation, I made sure to see Jamilla every day. She had dropped some heavy shit on me that first night she slept over, and at first, I didn't know what to do with it. I never tried to touch her again. She was too fragile, too damaged, too broken for me to take anything from her, and that included sex. I wanted to kill her stepfather, and her mother and stepsister too. I just wanted to walk in there and shoot all of them dead, although that wouldn't change anything. I was seeing less and less of Roxie, since most of my time was spent with Jamilla. Roxie was blowing up my phone, leaving crazy messages, and she even showed up at my house a few times. I knew that I would have to see her soon, or she would lose her mind.

As I waited for Roxie on the stoop of her building, I thought about my time with Jamilla. I had learned so much about her in such a short time. I felt as if I had known her my entire life. The crazy part was, as much as I knew that I couldn't have her in the way I wanted her, it didn't stop my heart from falling for her. I was in love with her, and I knew that I could never tell her that. Instead, I had to play the best friend game. That shit was killing me. All I wanted to do was taste her lips, lick her all over. I just wanted to fuck her all the time. I wanted to feel her body against mine. I wanted to feel her wetness against my lips. I wanted to bend her over, fuck her, and pleasure her until she came. There were plenty of nights when I would touch myself to the thought of her. She drove me crazy, yet there was nothing that I would do about it.

"Where the fuck you been, Niya? I have been calling you. Didn't I tell you not to play with me? I heard you were hanging with some new bitch. Don't make me hurt the bitch."

Damn. Roxie had just walked up, and she was already starting with her bullshit.

"How you been, baby? I missed you," I said as I stood up to give her a kiss. She pushed me away and kept up with her bullshit.

"I'm gonna fuck you up. I'm supposed to be your girl, and I don't hear from you for weeks. What kind of shit is that?"

I pulled her close to me and kissed her lips. I grabbed a handful of her phat ass and instantly remembered why I put up with her shit.

"You know you my favorite bitch. Why you always talk shit? Aren't you happy to see me?" I asked before kissing her neck. I heard her moan and waited for her to embrace me back, which she did. As much as she pissed me off, I couldn't help but melt into her kiss.

"Uh, what's up with the affection in public? I thought you were against that."

What she didn't know was that in the past month, I had become more comfortable with who I was. Being around someone who I could let my guard down with had changed me, was still changing me, and I liked it.

"Things change, people change, but some things, they just stay the same . . . yes, Lawd," I said as I pushed her away from me and turned her to the side to get a look at her ass. She was just as plump as ever.

"So, if this is some new shit, does that mean that you will come out with me tonight?" Damn. She had me there.

She went on. "Come on, Papi. Please. It's time. I want to show you off. You fine as shit, and I want everyone to know that you my nigga."

She knew me well. Feeding my ego helped.

"How about this? You take me upstairs, show me what I have been missing, and maybe, I'll go out with you tonight."

I didn't have to ask twice. Twenty minutes later, I was in heaven. I loved the days when she would switch things up on me.

"I should do you how you do me. Make you spread your shit wide open," she remarked.

I laughed. "That's not gonna happen, but what you can do . . . is eat this pussy right."

She sat me on her couch and pulled off my jeans. I didn't let her do this too often, but I was in the mood. I enjoyed watching her. She made a production out of it every time. Sticking out her tongue just so I could watch the point of impact. She was so nasty with it. Slurping, moaning, pulling on my clit. It felt good, but I just couldn't fully let go with her. I tried that day. Hell, I tried every time she ate me out. I just couldn't do it. It felt good as hell, but I just couldn't bust a nut. So after a while, I switched places with her. I hit her off, and after she came, the question still lingered.

"Are you going out with me or not?"

I thought about it and said, "I'll go, but my friend Jamilla is coming with me."

I hadn't even asked Jamilla yet, but I was hoping she would come. I didn't think that I could make it to the club without her.

"Jamilla? Who the fuck is Jamilla?"

I broke it down to Roxie and told her that Jamilla was my straight friend. I left out the "maybe straight" part that she had thrown at me the first night she slept over at my house. I left Roxie some money to get fly with and headed home. I drove that day, so as soon as I got in the car, I called Jamilla and told her that I was on my way to pick her up.

Chapter 14

Jamilla

I waited for Niya in front of my building as I wrote in my notebook. Since getting close to her, I had been so inspired. I had begun writing a book, and I planned to finish it by her birthday. I was going to self-publish it and have a copy in hand as a gift to her. In the meantime, I wrote a few thoughts.

Just when I thought that there was nothing left in this world for me, you appeared. Unexpected, you filled shoes that I didn't even know were there. The feeling I get as your hand meets mine is unexplainable. Our souls connect on levels beyond this world. My heart now beats to the drum of true friendship. I love you, and soon I will find the strength to tell you so, although I think that you already know.

As I wrote the last words, my stepsister, Marie, came out of the building and just stood there.

"Do you need something?" I asked her as I rolled my eyes.

The funny thing with us was that I had always hated her. As soon as she came to live with us, I had detested her. She reminded me of her father, so therefore, I could never have any love for her.

"This ain't your stoop. I can stand here if I want," she answered with her own attitude.

I ignored her as I wished she would go back into the house. I knew that she was waiting to see what I was doing. In the past few weeks, I had been gone a lot, and they weren't used to it. A few times, she had asked me about Niya, and I had just ignored her. I didn't trust her, but I was really starting not to give a fuck about anyone in that house and their opinions.

Right after Niya pulled up, she jumped out of the car and came right over to me. "Hey, Milla boo. I wasn't late this time," Niya said as she took my hand. She tried to stand me up to give me a hug, but I pulled away from her and gave a quick glance at Marie.

"Hey. I'm Jamilla's sister," Marie said with a big grin on her face. She jumped down the steps and came over to us. She was all up in Niya's face. I guessed she really did want to meet her, as she had been telling me.

Niya's eyes met hers, and she offered her a stale hello before continuing her conversation with me. I couldn't help but laugh. "Let's take a ride. I got something to ask you."

Without even looking back, we left Marie standing on the stoop. We climbed in Niya's car and rode in silence for a few minutes. She was bumping Siya, and one of my favorite songs, "Off the Gas" was on. I waited for it to go off before I turned down the music and asked her what was up.

"Okay. Hear me out—"

"Oh, hell no. As soon as you start a sentence with 'Hear me out,' I know it's about to be some bullshit."

We laughed because we both knew that I was speaking the truth.

"Okay, you know how you been telling me that I really should start going out to clubs and performing? Well, someone invited me out tonight, and I want you to go with me."

I looked at her and smiled. She looked so fucking cute, sitting there, sounding all excited.

"Who invited you?" I asked.

"I'm kind of nervous and really want you to go with me." She had taken my hand and was holding it in hers. I looked down at it and remembered the words I had just written. I loved the affection she showed me.

"You didn't answer me. Who invited you out?"

She smiled and looked at me as she answered. "It's Roxie. I told her that I was going to ask you to come."

I didn't say anything. I just turned the volume on the radio back up and stared out the window. I was going to go and support Niya, no matter what, but I just really didn't like that girl Roxie.

We hit up Flatbush and Manhattan. I really didn't want to have her buy me anything, but she forced me, and as hard as she pushed me to give her a fashion show, I didn't give her one. I told her that I knew my size and that everything would fit. When my shoes alone rang up at two hundred dollars, I almost passed out. Who the fuck spent that much on shoes? When we went into the Manhattan shops, my mouth went dry, but Niya didn't care. She got me a few outfits. When I told her that I needed something just for that night, she ignored me. I guessed this was her way of telling me that she didn't like the way I dressed.

We stopped and had lunch before she dropped me off to get my hair done. I didn't know what the hell to do to it, so she spoke to the Dominican lady and told her what to do. Niya gave me the keys to her apartment, and since I had told my mother I was sleeping over at my cousin's house, I was going to spend the night at Niya's house. I was going to have to be careful that no one at my house saw me, but that was going to be easy. They never deviated from their norm. Niya had told her grandmother about my past with my stepdad, and from then on, her grandmother told me to come over whenever. Niya said that she had things to do and that I should take a cab to her place after my hair was done. She gave me money for the fare and told me I should just chill at her place until she got back.

Chapter 15

Niya

I drove out to the Bronx and saw Smiley. I told her that I was going to go out to a club. I felt that I owed her that much, since she had always tried to get me to go. Plus, I knew that I might run into her, and I didn't want any problems. She knew about Roxie, but she didn't like her much. She once told me about a run-in she had had with her. Although Smiley was a nice girl, she was known for putting grown men to sleep. I hung out, gave her the jeans and shoes I had picked up for her, and just chilled. She braided my hair, and before I knew it, it was going on ten o'clock and I had to head to Roxie's to get ready. Roxie had made me promise that I would get ready over there, so to keep her happy, I kept my word.

Roxie looked good, as always. Her crazy ass always looked fine as hell in all her name brands. That was one of the things I had tried to change about her, but you couldn't tell her anything. If it didn't have a brand name on it, she wasn't rocking it, the label whore. As for me, after showering, I kept shit simple. Plaid pants, black wife beater, fresh Converse, diamond studs, necklace, and ring. I sprayed on some Burberry and was ready to go. We got in the car, and the question I was waiting for came up.

"You sure this Jamilla girl ain't gay?"

I rolled my eyes before answering. "Yeah, I'm sure." I turned up Kendrick Lamar and tuned her out.

Once we got to my building, I told Roxie to wait for me as I ran up to my apartment. She knew a few girls around there, so she stood outside talking to them. I opened the door, and Granny was the first person I saw. I gave her a kiss and asked her where Jamilla was. She smiled and told me that she had just finished helping her get ready and that she was in my room. I headed back and knocked on the bedroom door. I heard her tell me to come in, so I did. When I stepped in that room, my damn heart stopped. I couldn't move. I couldn't talk. I couldn't do anything but just stand there.

"Do I look okay?" I heard her ask. It took me a while, but I managed to answer.

"You look great. Damn."

She had on the little white dress I had got for her. There were areas in the middle of her chest that were cut out, so she was showing much cleavage. The dress was short, and her legs looked like heaven. Her hair, with the presence of the weave I had had them add, hung down her back and was layered, with a part on the side. Her makeup brought out her natural beauty. It wasn't too much; it was just right. Her gold jewelry bounced off her skin and left me mesmerized.

"Not sure how long I can handle these heels, but we shall see," she said. "You ready to go?"

I would have forgotten about Roxie and the club if Jamilla hadn't asked me that. When we stepped out of the building, every eye was on Jamilla. Roxie came over to us with the stink face, and I knew she was jealous. Jamilla tried to introduce herself and shake Roxie's hand, but she was met with chills. It kind of turned me on when this seemed not to affect Jamilla like I thought it would.

***

When we first got to the club, I thought that I wouldn't be able to handle it. So many people, so many eyes. I felt like a piece of meat as the women eye fucked me. I picked a corner and just wanted to stay there. After a while, Roxie said she was going to dance. She had tried for a good twenty minutes to get me to go with her, but I just didn't feel like it. The wall felt safer. When she left, they swooped in. One after the other, they asked me to dance, asked for my name, even my number, and these were the femmes. When I looked over at Jamilla, who was on her way back with our sodas, she was laughing hard.

"What's so funny?" I asked once she got back over to me.

"You look so scared. It's good to know that the aggressor can become the prey too."

I had to laugh too. I was so used to being the shark that it felt weird being the guppy. When Smiley came through, she helped me loosen up a bit. She knew a lot of the people and was able to get us some drinks since she knew the bartender. Before I knew it, the alcohol had me relaxed, and I started to be myself. I danced with Roxie, and soon we all were on the dance floor. I was having a ball, until Roxie got in her feelings about me dancing with Smiley. She pushed Smiley. Smiley punched her, and all of a sudden, I was in the middle of a catfight.

"You have got to fucking relax!" I yelled at Roxie, but she was gone by then.

She was yelling, pushing, and trying her best to get to Smiley.

"You are just like the rest of them no-good niggas. You showing that fat bitch love as I stand right in front of you?" Roxie shouted back.

"Who you calling a fat bitch?" Smiley asked as she came charging toward Roxie.

"Man, I am so tired of your bullshit. We're just having fun," I told Roxie over the music.

No matter what I said, Roxie just wouldn't quit. So when the guard threw her out of the club, I didn't leave with her. I was done. That bitch was too fucking crazy for me. Instead, Jamilla, Smiley, and I stayed in the club. They got drunk as fuck, while I got tipsy, and we danced and had the time of our lives.

Chapter 16

Jamilla

I watched Niya on the dance floor and smiled. I was so happy that she was able to come to the club and be free. She was open about who she was. I watched her touch Smiley and kiss her without shame. She was open and honest with everyone else that night and, most importantly, with herself. By the time the last call was called, Smiley and I were a little past fucked up. Niya, although a little tipsy, didn't drink as much as we did. I liked Smiley. She was fun and didn't come off like a pure bitch the way Roxie did. When she'd punched Roxie in the face, inwardly, I'd cheered her on.

"She's gonna come home with us," Niya announced.

We got in the car, and I couldn't help but feel weird. I guessed I was sleeping in the living room. The car ride wasn't any better. They couldn't keep their hands off each other. I just kept telling Niya to keep her eyes on the road.

When we made it back to her place, I said a silent prayer and thanked God that we'd got home. We walked to Niya's door and waited for her to open it. Once inside the apartment, I headed to the living room. Niya took my hand and pulled me toward them.

"We're just going to chill. Come with us," she said.

I didn't put up a fight. Some part of me wanted to be included. I would have been lonely out there. In the bedroom, we smoked and listened to music. I enjoyed listening to Smiley tell her club tales. She knew damn near everyone, and she knew their stories. We laughed so hard that I thought Niya's grandmother would come out, but she never did. Niya said that the weed knocked her out every night. Soon Smiley started to touch Niya, and Niya started to touch Smiley. I didn't know what to do, so I just sat there, smoking, watching.

As things heated up, everything in me told me to get up and get out, but I couldn't. It was as if I were watching something forbidden, something rare, and I just couldn't pull myself away. Smiley had gotten on top of Niya, straddling her, and was kissing her. Niya was pulling off her lover's clothes, and piece by piece, I got more turned on. The sounds of their smacking lips lingered in the air. I crossed my legs, hoping to relieve the feeling brewing between them. I watched as Smiley's nipple slipped into Niya's mouth, and I wanted to scream. I had to leave. I looked at Niya and made eye contact. It was weird, and I had to leave. I got up and headed for the door.

"Don't leave," I heard her say.

"Yeah, don't go," Smiley added.

"I have to," I said in a faint voice.

Smiley got off the bed and came over to me. She got close to me, too close for comfort. I looked into her soft eyes as her lips touched mine. Inside, I was screaming, *What the hell*! But I didn't pull away from her. Her tongue roamed my mouth as I kissed her back. She pulled away just as I was getting into it, took my hand, and led me to the bed. I sat against the wall at the foot of the bed. Niya's bed was in a perfect little nook. Since it was surrounded by walls on three sides, there was only one way onto the bed and one way off. Niya, at the head of the bed, didn't take her eyes from mine. Her back was against her headboard, and with me at the opposite end, we were face-to-face, eye to eye, with just three to four feet between us.

"You are so fucking pretty," Smiley said to me as she sat beside me.

"Isn't she fucking gorgeous? She's so damn innocent looking," Niya interjected. "It makes me wonder, are you really innocent, or are you hiding the freak in you?"

I looked from Smiley to Niya, who was smiling from ear to ear, then back to Smiley. I didn't answer. When I felt Smiley's lips on mine again, I didn't resist. Her hands were everywhere. She managed to pull off my dress with little effort. My breasts graced the air, and I was a little uncomfortable. I put my hands up and covered them. Things were moving too fast, and my head was spinning. I just kept asking myself what in the hell I thought I was doing. *You are not gay. You are not gay. You are not gay.* I just kept saying it over and over to myself.

When I felt Smiley tugging at the new thong panties Niya had bought for me, I pushed her off of me. I hadn't looked at Niya in a while, and when I did, she was just sitting there, puffing on her blunt. She was staring at me through her slanted eyes. When Smiley tried to pull off my panties again, Niya spoke up.

"Leave her alone. She's straight . . . maybe."

Sarcasm dripped from her words, and the look on her face said it all. She wasn't buying my "straight, maybe" story.

Chapter 17

Niya

I tried my best to keep it cool, but my whole body was shaking. I tried to hold my breath, hoping that it would slow my heart rate, but that didn't work. As I watched Smiley and Jamilla go at it, a million thoughts ran through my mind. I wondered if she was really that damn drunk. I wondered how far this would go. I wanted to know if I would finally get to make love to her. I could see my chest heaving up and down, as my breathing had become fast. Once Jamilla's dress was off, I was a second away from going over to them, pulling Smiley off of her, and taking over. All I could think about was how sweet her nipples tasted, and I wanted more.

But as Smiley tried to pull off her panties, she held them up. She wasn't ready. Damn. I was going to have to wait. I called Smiley back over to me and tasted the lingering flavor of Jamilla left behind on her lips. I let Smiley pull off my clothes. Normally, I would have left my shirt on, but on this night, I wanted to remind Jamilla that I was a girl. Under all the masculinity, I was still a woman. A woman who was turning her on, a woman whom, I knew deep down inside, she loved.

My wife beater and bra were the first to go. I watched her the whole time, wanting to catch every reaction she was unable to hide. Last to go were my pants and boxers. I watched as her eyes widened and lowered. Her chest bounced up and down as she lusted over my body. I counted her breaths, which were fast and short. Smiley took off the rest of her clothes and let her tongue meet my neck. I moaned as I let her take over. She licked me all over. I couldn't help but moan. With my eyes on Jamilla, and with Smiley's hands and mouth traveling up and down my body, I was in heaven. I watched as Jamilla's legs crossed and uncrossed. Smiley looked at me, then over at Jamilla. Once again, Smiley left me and went to her.

"Your nipples are hard. You're turned on, yes?" Smiley asked her.

Jamilla didn't answer, just looked away from her, as if she was ashamed.

"You can trust us. We won't hurt you," Smiley said before she kissed Jamilla again. "We don't have to touch you, but we want you to enjoy what is happening. Do you trust us?"

I waited, almost salivating.

"Yes, I trust the both of you."

"Good. Now, relax, and just join in on the fun."

This time, as Smiley tugged at the sides of her panties, Jamilla let her pull them off. I reached over and put out my blunt. I picked up my cup of liquor and gulped it down. I watched as Smiley pulled at her legs and laid her down. Smiley kissed her lips, tongue kissed each of her nipples, and took Jamilla's hand. She slid it down Jamilla's stomach and, with her help, placed it against her dripping slit. I watched as Smiley moved Jamilla's hand up and down her pretty, bare pussy.

Soon Jamilla took over, and Smiley crawled back over to me. She licked down my chest, down my belly button, and soon her lips graced my waiting wet spot. I whimpered as Smiley skillfully used her tongue and lips. She pulled on my clit as my hand found Jamilla's thigh.

I wasn't going to go any higher; I just needed to feel a part of her body. Her groans met mine as she opened her eyes and looked at me. Her legs were open, and her hand ran up and down her pussy, helping me form all kinds of nasty thoughts about her. The faster her hand moved, the closer she got to cumming.

Knowing this pulled me closer to the edge. As I rubbed her thigh, I watched her slit become even wetter. Her fingers dripped with her juices as she massaged her clit, with her eyes on mine. With me moaning and her hips swirling with each stroke of her hand, we came. I grabbed the back of Smiley's head and pulled it to me. I fucked her face as I envisioned Jamilla taking her place. As my body jerked around on the bed, both of Jamilla's legs were in the air. It was the most beautiful thing I had ever seen. Her pussy was so plump, and with her hips twerking, she came long and hard. Damn. It seemed like that was the best nut either of us had ever had.

Out of breath, with hardly any energy, I got up, flipped Smiley over, and returned the favor. When I looked up, Jamilla was just lying beside her, watching me do what I did best. Smiley took her fingers and, one by one, sucked Jamilla's delicious juices off of them. That shit turned on not only me, but also Jamilla. By the look on Jamilla's face, she was only seconds away from reaching back down and handling her business again. Smiley came as I tongue fucked her, and afterward, we watched Jamilla get off for the second time that night. This time she let her fingers slip in and out of herself as her other hand rolled over her pretty little clit.

It was five in the morning when my phone started to ring. At first, I ignored it, but it just wouldn't stop ringing, so I took the call.

"Who the fuck is it?" I asked with an annoyed tone.

"I need to see you . . . right now."

I looked at the phone and instantly caught an attitude. "Nigga, it's five in the morning. What the fuck you want?"

"Remember that little problem you had when we were gonna meet up? Well, I found the troublemaker."

It was as if I had never been asleep. I sat up and paid more attention to what White Boy was saying.

"So what are you gonna do with that?" I asked as I got off the bed and sat on my desk chair.

"I need to see you. Are you home?"

"Nah," I lied before continuing. "I'm out. I can meet up with you. Where?"

He gave me the address, I wrote it down on a piece of paper, and within a few minutes, I was dressed. I looked down at Smiley and Jamilla, who were still sound asleep, and decided to leave a note just saying that I would be back.

I left the house and headed to my new stash house. I didn't quite trust White Boy, so I needed my gun. Once I got it, I headed to the address that I had written down on the paper. Once I got there, the abandoned building gave me chills. I sat in the car for a few, asking myself if I was ready to face whatever went down that morning. But with lingering questions about who had set me up, I knew I had to face it, no matter what, so I climbed out of the car.

"Happy you could make it," White Boy said as he walked over to me and shook my hand.

I looked around for the culprit but didn't see anyone but White Boy and the two guys who were always with him. "So where is he?" I asked, wanting to get everything over with.

"I tried to tell you that I had nothing to do with it. After you find out, maybe you will learn to trust me more."

I sucked my teeth. "I don't have time for 'I told you so.' Let's get this shit over with."

They led me inside the building and he signaled for his men to bring out the motherfucker who had robbed me. I watched the door that the men disappeared behind, and I waited impatiently for them to come back out.

"I know that you're young, but you really got to work on your circle. You're too trusting. In this line of work, you can't trust anyone," White Boy noted.

I looked away from the door and looked at White Boy. I searched his face, hoping that I would see the true meaning behind his words, but I saw nothing. Finally, the door swung open, and his two men came out with a bloody guy who looked like he had been through the worst beating of his life. They brought him over to me and pushed him down on the ground.

"This is the sorry piece of shit who held that gun up to you," White Boy said.

I looked at the man and then at White Boy. "How do you know?"

He pulled on his cigarette before answering. "I got some connects in a few hospitals, so when you told me you shot that nigga, I just called around to see if anyone came in that night with bullet wounds. In Brooklyn there were only three people that night, and one was a female. He wasn't that hard to track down. Plus, once we cracked his head a few times, he admitted to it."

All I could say was, "Wow." There I stood, face-to-face with the man I had hoped was dead. He had threatened to kill me, to rape me, and now he sat at my feet, begging for his life.

"Please . . . I'm so sorry. I shouldn't have done that shit. Don't kill me. Please don't kill me," he pleaded.

I could hear him, but his words were a distant sound. All I could think of was that night, and how cruel he had been.

"If you are thinking that you should let him live, there is still a piece to this puzzle that you are missing," White Boy said.

I looked at him and asked, "What now?"

White Boy was enjoying this. He took his time as he adjusted his shirt and lit another cigarette. Finally, he said, "Don't you want to know how he knew where your stash house was or who told him?"

I looked at White Boy and told him the truth. "I was going to ask him that before I killed him."

"Why ask when we can show you?" White Boy said.

White Boy told one of his men to go and get our other guest. I held my breath as I waited to see who it was. As the man came out of the back room, my eyes zeroed in on his hand. In it was a mass of black hair. I was so filled with anger that I got an instant headache.

"Put the little bitch right next to her man," White Boy ordered.

Words could not describe what I was feeling. It was betrayal in its truest form.

"Please, Papi, don't believe them. You have to trust me. I would—"

I took a few steps toward Roxie and backhanded her. Her hands were tied behind her back, so she fell flat on her back. I stood on top of her with each foot on the side of one of her shoulders.

"How could you do this to me? I gave you more than you ever had. I gave you more than you have ever wanted. I loved you, although you were fucking crazy, and I have damn near killed for you. What the fuck were you thinking?" My body was shaking. Rage was about to consume me, and I wasn't going to stop it.

"It wasn't me. Please, Papi, you have to believe me."

I looked down at her and wanted to believe her, but I knew that I couldn't. She was a snake, always had been. I had just been too blinded by pussy to see it. I walked over to the man White Boy had called her man, and made him a promise.

"If you tell me the truth, you will leave here today."

After that, he sang like a bird. He told me that they had been planning it for months. He told me that Roxie had spoken with Rodney on that day, had told him that I was gay and that I had never given a shit about him, not even as a friend. Had told him that I was only using him for pussy, and that once I could get girls on my own, I would no longer speak to him. She had done this so that he wouldn't be with me that night I got robbed. Everyone knew that Rodney and I moved together. No matter the job, we were always together. He told me that Roxie had called him and had given him the address the same night I was going to meet White Boy, and he revealed how they had planned to share the money they would make off the bricks. I had only one question, one that would seal her fate.

"Were you supposed to kill me?" I asked him.

He looked me dead in the eyes and answered, "She said to do whatever it took. Dead or alive, I was supposed to take what you got."

I walked back over to Roxie and just started kicking her. I didn't stop until I knocked out her front teeth. The more I thought about things, the more things became clear. That day she bugged out on me about where I had been because she'd been worried about the nigga. She hadn't given a shit about who I was with; she'd wanted to know if her man was all right. I was fuming.

"Let's get this show on the road," White Boy said as he walked over to me.

He tried to hand me his gun, but I told him I had my own. I stepped to the man who had been sent to kill me and held the gun to his head.

"I thought you said that I was going to leave here?" He was crying, which had no effect on me.

"You will be leaving . . . feetfirst." I pumped two bullets into his head without a second thought. I watched his body fall and just stared at it.

"You still have one left," White Boy said as he pointed at a hysterical Roxie.

I walked over to her and just wanted to know one thing. "Why, Roxie? Why?"

Through her tears, she told the truth. "I . . . I just wanted more. I just wanted more."

I shook my head at her. Greed was always the root of all evil. As I stood there looking down at her, for the first time, I saw her for who she really was. I saw her for what she always had been . . . pure evil.

"We are gonna have to wrap this up," White Boy said as he noticed my inner struggle.

I knew what had to be done, but I just couldn't do it. I tried to raise the gun to her head, but every time I did, my hand would come right back down.

"That's all right. We'll take care of it. You have blood on your hands, so I know that what went down tonight won't leave this building."

"Please, please, Niya. Don't let them do this. Please, baby, I love you."

"Bitch, you wouldn't know what love was if it stared you in the face," I said out loud.

I took the butt of my gun and hit her on the forehead. She was knocked out. I started for the door as White Boy stood on top of her and let off a few rounds. All I could think of was, at least she was passed out when her life was taken.

Chapter 18

Jamilla

I was having a dream that I was using the bathroom when I jumped up. Thank God, I was just starting to go when I woke up. A few drops had landed on her bed, but most of it was on her bathroom floor. That was a better place than Niya's mattress. I cleaned her floor and thanked God that I was naked. I jumped in the shower and put on a pair of Niya's shorts and a tee. That was when I noticed that Niya wasn't in the bed and that she had left a note. I rolled my eyes as I wondered if she'd gone to see Roxie. I had twenty dollars on me, but I needed quarters. I wanted to wash Niya's sheets as soon as Smiley got up. I knew that there wasn't much urine on them, but I wanted to clean them, anyway.

I took the twenty dollars and headed to the closest corner store that would give me a few quarters. It was about a ten-minute walk, and since the sun would be up soon, I felt safe enough. I got to the store, bought some gum, and got the change that I needed. The walk gave me time to think about my night. After what had happened, I didn't know how to classify myself. Was I gay, straight, bi? I knew that I could never go down on another woman; that just wasn't me. I also knew that I'd been the most turned on that I had ever been in my life. Could it be that I' just been horny? Could it be that I'd been drunk? No, there was no way that I was gay. I loved men; men loved me. No, I wasn't gay. I'd just been drunk. I promised myself never to let what had happened that night happen again. I was only going to confuse myself if I let lust cloud my better judgment.

Instead of going straight home, I went the long way so that I could pick up three coffees. We'd had a long night, and I knew that we would need it. I cut through a few alleys and was only a block away from my favorite coffee place when I saw Niya, a gun, and my stepfather.

Chapter 19

Niya

I had driven home with murder on my mind. The murder I had just committed bothered me, but not as much as the murder I just couldn't pull off. I should have been the one to put Roxie out of her misery. She had betrayed me, yet I just hadn't been able to do it. I was starting to wonder if what her boyfriend had said to me was true. Maybe the street game was a man's game. Maybe as a woman, I just didn't have the heart, or maybe I had too much heart.

As I parked my car, I wasn't ready to go back in the house. I needed to clear my head, so I walked. I thought about my life, everything good and bad about it. I thought about who I was, who I was becoming, and who I was hoping to be from that day on. I also thought about my night, before the call. I thought about Jamilla and how much I loved her. With every day that passed, I was falling deeper in love with her, yet she said she was straight. I thought about who she'd appeared to be the night before, and I wondered if she was just confused about her sexuality. I wondered if I would ever have her, and not just sexually. I wondered if I would have her love me the way I loved her. I asked myself if I could ever fix her and make her happy.

As I headed back to my building, I saw a car that I recognized. I saw him park his car, and instantly, I knew what I wanted to do. I raced toward him, and once I was standing in front of him, I pulled out my gun. There was no fight in him once he saw it. I asked him to walk with me and led him down a dark alleyway. I might have not been able to kill Roxie, but Jamilla's stepfather was one dead nigga.

Chapter 20

Jamilla

"What are you doing?" I asked as I watched Niya cock her gun. My stepfather was on his knees, crying, but Niya's hand was steady.

"I'm making sure that you don't have to look at this motherfucker for one more day."

"Please, Niya, don't do this. I'm begging you."

"Fuck that. This nigga has got to die. After all he did to you, he's gonna make you sleep on the floor? After all he did to you?"

I was crying, but she was strong, sturdy in her stance. I walked over to her, stood beside her, and put my hand on her shoulder. "Please, Niya, don't waste your life by taking his. Please."

She just stood there, as if she was in a trance. She showed no emotion, no pity for the monster I faced every day. I couldn't blame her. I had dreamed about killing him myself, but those were only dreams.

"Please, Jamilla. Tell her not to do this."

Just the sound of his voice made me cringe, but I also felt a rush of power. He was begging *me* now. All those nights my begging had fallen on deaf ears. His hands would roam my body, and no matter how much I pleaded, he would never stop. I couldn't help but enjoy this moment now, but still, I knew I couldn't let Niya kill him.

"Niya, baby, let him go."

"Fuck that," she answered.

For ten minutes, I pleaded with her. Finally, it worked.

"Okay, motherfucker," Niya said as she took my hand and walked me in front of him.

With him still on his knees, she continued to talk. "First, if you ever put your filthy hands on Jamilla again, I will kill you. There won't be any talking. I am just going to put my gun up to your head and pull the trigger. Second, I want Marie out of Jamilla's room, and I want Jamilla back in there."

"Okay, okay. They will share the room," my stepdad answered between tears.

"No they won't. I want your little bitch out of the room. I don't give a shit where she sleeps. I just want her out. Understand?"

Niya waited for him to tell her that he understood her, and he did.

"Third, I want you to treat her with respect. If I hear that you even raised your voice at her, I'm coming for that ass. Understand?"

Again, he said yes.

"Last," Niya said as she looked at me. "Last, I want you to promise me that as soon as we finish our first year of college, we are leaving New York together. I'm not sure what school you planned on going to, but we can register at the same one to make sure that we stay together."

I stood there and thought about it. Her birthday was September 26, and I was born on October 1. By the time we would be ready to go, we would be turning twenty, and no one, not even my crazy-ass mother or my sick-ass stepfather, could stop us. I was going to attend Kingsborough Community College, so it wouldn't be hard for Niya to get in as well.

Chapter 21

Niya

I waited for her to answer. I was damn near holding my breath. If she said no, I was going to kill that nigga out of anger and heartache.

"Yes, I'll leave with you."

I looked into her eyes and saw the truth, which was enough for me. I let her stepfather live, and for the next year, all I could think about was finishing the first year of college.

I wrote her this letter:

Jamilla,

Of course I saw you, and I still see you today. There is no one like you on this earth. The funny thing is, you saw me way before I saw myself, and that is not to be ignored. If I could just ask you one thing, it would have to be . . . why do you think that you're invisible? I can see your beauty from a mile away. Your spirit transcends the walls you have built. It is stronger than the pain that you harbor. Your outer beauty, although on a different level, comes in only second to the beauty you house within. I see you, like I always have. You are hard to ignore, hard to pass up. I have never seen anything like you, so of course, I would look. You are so pure; you are so real. You are everything I dream about at night, even when I get no sleep. I love you. Always have and always will.

Now I just have to find the guts to tell you all that I feel is real. But I am afraid that what I feel, you'll think is just a thrill. A fly by night that won't last too long. I must tell you that this is real. I have never loved and will never love like this again. So here you are, wondering if I saw you, when in fact you were the only one to see the true me and what I really feel. You don't have to say too much, just a few simple words. Just tell me that you love me, and that will forever be enough.

Niya

Act II

Dreamer's Paradise

So many love her, but only one can have her, and the shitty part is that I'm just not that one who will ever have her.
Oh, what I would give to have her be mine.
Oh, what I would say just to hear her say that shit back.
But this thing here, it's all just in my mind.
All love on my part while I wait for her to love me back.
And she does, just not the way I want her to, so let's backtrack
Back to a time when I thought that maybe I would have her
That maybe I could buy her.
But some shit just can't be bought,
Like the feelings that drive me crazy, and that shit is a fact.
See, the moment that I laid eyes on her, I stopped in my tracks.
There was something about her, and right then and there, I was caught,
Caught up in everything she had to offer, not realizing that everyone loved her.
I was one of many who sought her.
I would also be one of the few who would get close to her,

Giving me false hope that I would be the only one really to have her.

See, so many love her, but only one can have her.

The shitty part is, I'm the one who will never have her.

And the one who does, that shit shouldn't even matter, but it does . . . to her.

And in the end, that's all that matters, 'cause I'll never be that one, although I found her.

Niya

Chapter 22

Niya

Silence carved through the air like a newly sharpened knife as we walked back to our building. Jamilla had just made a promise to me that I prayed she would keep. There was nothing binding us to the city we called home. Her family was shit, and as for me, the only person I had to worry about was my granny. The morning's events played over in my head as if they were part of a film. Jamilla's stepfather was the second person I didn't kill this morning, and I wasn't sure if that was a good thing. Both he and Roxie deserved to eat dirt, to waste away, and to be considered casualties of the mean streets of Brooklyn. Although Roxie had met her Maker, it wasn't by my hands, as it should have been.

"Niya . . . *Niya*?"

I wasn't sure how long Jamilla had been calling my name, but I really didn't hear her until she yelled.

"What's up, boo?" I asked. We were at the entrance to our building when I took her hand. Something in her eyes was different, though. She seemed guarded and fearful of me. I felt it the minute our hands touched.

"We need to talk. I would say let's go back to your place, but Smiley is sleeping. I just . . . I just . . . we need—"

"Niya, mi amor, where have you been? Mommy's been waiting for you."

I froze when I heard her voice. It was as if the warm air had turned into a winter chill. I was afraid to turn around. With her, you never knew what you would get. Sure, she never looked right, but sometimes, it was worse than others.

"Is that your mom?"

The shock was written all over Jamilla's face. I knew that it was going to be bad. Slowly, I turned around to face the person who used to be my mother. The lady before me was dirty, she was too thin, had stringy hair, and she looked sick. The last time I saw her, she hadn't been this bad, but standing there in front of me, she was just a shell of who she used to be.

"Niya, mi amor, I had an accident. I need a shower, and I'm so hungry, honey. Is Mama upstairs? Maybe she can make us some nice breakfast, just like she used to."

My fucking heart was breaking. Who was this woman? I asked myself as she got close to me. I looked into her eyes, but the glaze from the drugs wouldn't let me penetrate her state of mind. As she reached out to me, my first reaction was to pull away. She was just so dirty, and she smelled of shit, but I just couldn't pull away from her. She was my mother, the woman who had birthed me. I let her touch my cheek and watched her smile before she spoke.

"You are so cute, mi amor, just like your papi. You look just like me, but with his eyes and lips. Can we go upstairs now?"

I couldn't move; I couldn't speak. All I wanted to know was if the woman standing in front of me was really my mother. She used to be so beautiful, so proud. Now she was just an empty shell. I couldn't help but stand there and cry.

Chapter 23

Jamilla

I didn't mean to look so shocked, but I was. I had seen her mother here and there over the years, but she had never looked this bad. Most knew that she was a drug addict, but she had managed to look a little decent, until that moment. My heart ached for Niya. She looked like a little girl, just broken and so hurt. I watched as she crumbled from within, and I knew that I had to step in.

"Hi. I am Jamilla, Niya's friend." I extended my hand to her and waited for her to shake it. She took it and smiled.

"How about we all go upstairs?" she said.

I nodded, stepped aside, and pulled Niya with me. Her mother was in front of us as we followed. As we went up the stairs, that was when I realized where the smell was coming from. She had defecated in her pants.

At one point, Niya just stopped climbing the stairs. I looked at her, and each one of her emotions was on her face.

"Come on, Niya. We are going to get through this," I assured her. I took her hand, got behind her, and nudged her up the stairs.

When we got to her grandmother's apartment, Niya's mother, Gloria, spoke up. "Can you go in and see if Mama is up? If so, make her go in her room until I am clean. I don't want her to see me like this."

Niya did what her mother asked of her.

Chapter 24

Niya

If it weren't for Jamilla, I would have just stood there in tears. When she said, "*We* are going to get through this," it gave me the strength to carry on. I was just so embarrassed. My mother was too good for that shit, yet there she was, knee-deep in it.

When I stepped into the apartment, it was quiet. I looked in on my grandma, and although she wasn't sleeping, she had not left her room yet. Smiley was still asleep, so this was perfect timing. I went back to the door, let Jamilla and my mother in the apartment, and led my mother straight to the bathroom. I stepped in to help her, but she asked for some privacy. I kind of gave her the side eye, but in her current situation, I could understand. I backed out of the bathroom and pulled the door closed behind me. In the hallway, I just stood there at the bathroom door. The last twenty-four hours were starting to catch up to me, and I just wanted to jump in my bed and sleep.

"I can help you clean her up. When my grandma came from Haiti, I used to help my mother take care of her. I'm used to this," Jamilla said as she stood by my side.

I turned to her, and as badly as I wanted to remain strong, I just couldn't. I had never liked to cry in front of people, but in that moment, right in that hallway, I felt safe enough to let her witness my tears. I broke down in her arms, silently, though. I didn't want my granny or Smiley to hear. She didn't say a word, but the silence spoke to me. In her arms, I found the comfort I wished I got from my mother. In her arms, I got the love I was always chasing, the same love that I would chase for the rest of my life.

As I got myself together, my bedroom door opened and Smiley emerged. I instantly wished she hadn't slept over.

"What's that smell? It smells like shit and smoke. Y'all don't smell that?" she muttered.

I had been so caught up in dealing with my own emotions that I hadn't noticed the scent that I had come to know very well. The minute Smiley finished her sentence, I sprang into action. I rushed through that bathroom door, and *boom*, there it was. The potent smell of shit and crack filled my nostrils, and I started to gag. My mother had removed her clothes and was as naked as the day she was born. Shit ran down her legs and sat in the pants she still had around her ankles. Her eyes were wide as she pulled the smoke from her pipe.

"Ma, what in the fuck are you doing?" I asked between gags.

I knocked the pipe out of her hand and tried to get it before she could get to it, and that was when she started to scream.

"You stupid little bitch! I am going to kill you!"

"Come on, Ma. You got to stop this shit."

There we were, eye to eye, heart to heart, so I waited as I looked deep into her eyes, just hoping that my voice would bring her back to reality.

"You are going to buy my shit back for me, bitch. You think it's free. Well, it's not. You think I'm selling my pussy just to have you knock my shit out my mouth?"

"What is going on?" came a voice.

My grandmother had come out of her room, and when she made it to where we all were standing, she grabbed her chest. "*Ay, Dios mio*, why you here? Why you so dirty?"

"This little bitch just took my shit, and I want it back," my mother screeched.

Between my mother and my grandmother, I couldn't take much more. I knew that this was killing my granny slowly, and it pissed me off.

"Why you come like this? You so dirty. Why you come like this?"

"Fuck you, old lady," my mother yelled. "I'm tired of always hearing your bullshit. All my life—"

I walked up to my mother and slapped her. I just couldn't help it. I couldn't take her disrespecting the woman who had stepped up and taken on her responsibilities.

I was not too sure what happened next. A tussle between my mother and me started. Right there, on the bathroom floor, mother and daughter fought as if we were enemies. She kept calling me a bitch and asking about replacing her drugs. My grandmother's cries hung in the air like thick smoke. As for me, I shouted from the heart. With each strike I landed, I begged my mother to stop this madness. I begged her to free herself and love her family, but all was in vain. When it hit me that she wouldn't give in, I lost it. She was no longer my mother, and I beat her as if she were just a dopehead on the street.

I heard Jamilla asking for help that would never come. "Help me, Smiley. Help me pull them apart!"

"I'm not touching them. They are rolling around in shit. Ugh. I have to get out of here. I can't. I can't," Smiley answered.

Once my grandmother stepped in, her voice brought me back to reality. "Niya, mi amor. Please, Niya, stop."

Slowly, with my mother still hanging on to me, I stood up, picked her frail frame up, and slammed her into the tub. I exited the hall bathroom, covered in her shit, and headed for the bathroom in my grandmother's bedroom. I stripped, jumped in the shower, and stayed there for an hour.

Chapter 25

Jamilla

Everything happened so fast. Before I knew it, it was a full-out brawl. At first, I didn't know what to do, but as I watched Niya's fist slam into her mother's face over and over again, I knew that I had to step in. I just couldn't do it on my own. When I asked Smiley for help, I really thought that she would step in. I was already trying to pull the women apart, so all she would have to do was hold one while I held the other. When she declined because they were covered in shit, I stopped for a quick second and just looked at her. It took everything in me not to walk over to her and slap the shit out of her. Who cared what they were covered in? This was her friend, her lover. How could she just stand there and watch? What was even more shocking was that she just got her clothes and left. Worse was the look on her face, as if she was totally disgusted. Sure it wasn't a beautiful situation, but damn, how could she just leave?

While Niya was in the shower, her grandmother and I had managed to calm Gloria down. I knew that it was wrong, but telling her that Niya had left to get her drugs did help. Gloria asked her mother for a few of the pills that she had lying around the house. Her mother always favored her weed instead of the pills.

"Okay, but afterward, you let us help you clean up, okay?"

After Gloria nodded her head, Niya's granny left the bathroom and returned with a few pills. Her daughter swallowed them down without water and, as promised, stepped into the tub and sat down in it as if nothing had ever happened. After we got Gloria clean, her mother walked her to Niya's bedroom and gave her a pair of Niya's pants and a T-shirt. I peeped in and watched as her mother dressed her as if she were a five-year-old kid.

"Is she okay?" I asked as I watched Gloria start to nod off.

"Si. I give her sleep pills. She need sleep."

I waited and just watched. It was sad; it was beautiful; it was a sight to see. You could see the love she had for her daughter, and you could see the pain that dwelled in her heart. It leaked from her soul and found its nesting place in her eyes. She hummed as she brushed her daughter's hair before laying her down on Niya's bed.

"Okay. I clean now," she said.

"No," I told her. "Stay with her. I will clean up. Just tell me where everything is."

At first, she just stood there and gave me a strange look. But soon after, she walked toward me and pulled me to her. I fell into her arms and cried for her.

"Thank you, mi amor. You no have to do this. Now you call me Granny, like my Niya. No cry, okay?"

With tears in my eyes, I shook my head up and down. She told me where to find the cleaning supplies, and as I left the bedroom, Granny got in the bed with her little girl and just held her in her arms.

Chapter 26

Niya

I would have killed her, and that wasn't cool. I thanked God for my grandmother's voice. I thanked God for Jamilla, as she had tried, but that Smiley shit kind of hurt. I really didn't feel the impact of her words until I was under the hot water. I was in a battle within. Sure, I could understand her feelings. The situation hadn't been a normal one, but her words still stung. I wasn't sure how I was going to handle things with her after that. I wanted to forgive her, but where were the love and understanding when I needed them the most?

As I got dressed, I thought about facing them all. Once again, I had slipped to the dark side, the dark side that seemed to run through my blood. My mother, my father, they both lived within the realm of that darkness, the same darkness that would find its way to me from time to time. The only thing that seemed to soothe the pain from so much gloom was my weed and liquor. So as I prepared myself to leave the safe haven that was my grandmother's bedroom, I rolled up a blunt from my granny's stash.

When I open the bedroom door, I could no longer smell the foul stench of shit. Instead, the scent of bleach and Pine-Sol clogged my airways. I thought about my granny and pictured her on her hands and knees, cleaning up after the daughter she loved so much. I was almost too ashamed to leave her room. What I had done was beyond disrespectful. I knew that she wouldn't be happy with me striking my mother, but I had to face the music. I walked down the hallway and was ready to face my granny. When I turned into the bathroom, it wasn't her on the floor. It was Jamilla.

"You don't have to do that. Let me." I felt so bad. This was not her problem, and she didn't have to clean up our mess, literally and figuratively. I stepped into the bathroom and tried to pull her up, but she wouldn't let me.

"Get out of here. I'm almost done. You already showered. I got this."

The look in her eyes told me that this was a fight that I wasn't going to win. I told her that I would be in my room, but she told me that my mother was in there.

"What? She didn't leave?"

That was a damn shock. I thought that she would be out of the door, looking for her next hit, by then.

"She's sleeping. Your grandma is in there with her."

I turned around and opened the door to my bedroom. When I walked in, my mother lay peacefully in my granny's arms. Instantly, I wanted to cry. My grandmother loved my mother so much, and so did I. I wondered what my granny was thinking about as she held my mother. Did she think about the good old days, before the drugs? Did she replay the days of laughter and the love that had filled this apartment before it all went to shit? Did she think about the seven months my mother was clean two years prior? These were the thoughts that flashed across my mind as I watched my mother sleep in her arms.

"Granny?"

My grandmother turned her head and looked at me with a smile.

"Granny, I am so sorry. It's just that . . . well, she made me so mad, the way she was acting, the things she was saying. She—"

"Niya, mi amor, no need for you to be sorry. I know. She make me mad too."

I walked over to my grandmother and kissed her forehead.

"I know you sorry. Never do that again. She your mother, mi amor. You love her no matter what, like I love you, okay?"

I told her yes, that I understood, although I didn't quite agree. I grabbed my bottle of vodka and my notepad and left her to her thoughts.

My mother had called me names; my mother had even stolen from me, from both of us. She had made false promises. She had abandoned me and had forced my grandmother to raise me. How could I just love her, no matter what? It wasn't fair. I didn't ask for a family like this, one with an absent jailbird father and a drug-addicted mother. They, both of them, should have loved me enough to get it together. They should have loved themselves enough to go straight and leave the drugs and the crime behind.

At times, I hated them, truth be told. It hadn't been easy to watch my friends with their parents. Or to grow up and have other kids ask me why I lived with my grandmother and not with my parents. I hated them and loved them and wanted them at the same damn time. My granny used to always say that she wished she had a daughter like me. No matter what my mother did, no matter how long she had been gone, I still loved her and needed her. When I was younger, no matter how many times she broke my heart, I had still waited for the day I would see her face, for the moment she would kiss me and comb my hair. For the days she would come home for a few hours and almost seem normal. I had known that it wouldn't last long, but having her, really having her for that brief moment, was all the happiness in the world.

Things with my father were a bit different. He had kicked his drug habit a year or two after I was born. He just hadn't been able to kick his crime habit. He would always say, "I have a thing for fast women, fast cars and, most of all, fast money." He had always said that fast money was the best money, and he'd lived by that code. He would rob a bank just because he didn't have bus money. I had always thought it was more about the thrill, the unknown. Not knowing if he would get away with it. He was a thrill seeker, and in some ways, I was the same way. I must say that he had been around way more than my mother. He just hadn't been around enough. There was one thing I had always been thankful for: he had passed on his love of music to me. So when times were bad, I would put on the radio, sing to the tunes, and forget the pain that grew within.

I went into the living room, turned on the radio that was on the side table, and lit up. I took a few swigs from my bottle and put pen to paper.

I wish I had you the way I have chosen to remember you, the pretty you, the sweet you, the good you, the clean you.

I wish you would love me the way that I love you, the way that we love you. I wish you would love yourself too.

I wish that you had never met him, the man whom I call my father. See, he was stronger than you, and he started you on that shit and left you on that shit all by yourself, and it destroyed you. He switched lanes, got off that road to hell, while you went full throttle, diving deep into the underworld.

Maybe that would mean that I wouldn't be here, but to me, that would be better than this. I wish, man . . . I really wish that I just wasn't this hurt. I am damaged now, filled with loneliness, enduring a void that will never be filled, even with the world around me. It will never be filled by the blunt in my hand or by the bottom of my beloved liquor bottle.

I'm damaged because I am afraid that I will never fully love, only because the love that was never taught to me is something that can't be bought. See, a mother's love is like no other love. Now, ain't that too bad for me? Because a mother's love . . . is something I never had, so I'll just have to go on as if it was never meant to be.

I wish that you were just as thankful for her as I am for her. Without her, I wouldn't be, because without her there would be no saving me. She raised your child as you let the streets raise you. Well, now we are both grown, you as a full-blown addict and me as a full-grown motherless child. A child forever youthful in the land of wishes that will never be.

See, Ma, I wish, I wish, I wish, even as you continue to be a nightmare that I can't escape from, because you hold the key to my loveless destiny. Unlock me, Ma. That's my only hope of saving myself!

Chapter 27

Jamilla

I was still in the shower when I called out for Niya. When she came in the bathroom, I asked her to bring me a towel and some clean clothes. The shower felt good, as if I was washing the day's events off of me. I wasn't sure how I was going to comfort Niya, but I knew that she was counting on me. I rinsed off my body after soaping up three different times and pulled the shower curtain back.

"Oh shit. I didn't know you were still in here," I said.

Niya stood leaning against the bathroom door, smoking. She seemed lost in thought as she stood and stared.

"May I have the towel please?"

It took her a few seconds to answer, and when she did, her reply was low and demanding. "Come and get it."

My heart started to race. I knew she wasn't in the right frame of mind. "Niya, come on. Stop playing."

I waited for her to hand me the towel, but she didn't budge. The smirk on her face told me that if I wanted the towel, I would have to step out of the tub and get it. I tried to hold on to the shower curtain, but it was not long enough. Soon I was standing in front of her naked. As I reached for the towel, she reached for me.

Her grip was tight. Her hands moved fast. They were all over me as her lips graced my neck. She lightly bit into me before making me weak with her tongue. My neck was my spot, and she toyed with it as if she knew this.

"Niya, what are you . . . doing?"

There were a few moments that left me speechless, and for those very brief moments, I didn't fight her. That wouldn't last too long, though. I would come back to my senses and try to fight off her roaming hands.

"Niya . . . come on . . . please."

As I pleaded with her, she covered my mouth with hers. She pushed me against the sink, and after wrapping her arms and hands around the back of each of my thighs, she lifted me up and sat me on her sink. I couldn't lie. What she was doing felt good, an escape from the morning's terror, but I just couldn't let it happen. I pushed her away, and that made her stop kissing me.

"We can't do this."

"Why not?" she asked as she got close to me again. This time, her wet lips met my nipple, and that caused me to moan out loud, giving her false hope. I tried to fight both my body and her.

"Niya, I am not gay. I told you this before."

She looked up at me and smiled. My breasts bounced with each short breath that I took.

"Oh yeah? Let's see."

I wasn't sure what that meant, but when she ran her hands up my thighs and found her way between my legs, the lightbulb was lit. I sat there, in a battle with my mind and body. It was as if everything had slowed down. I watched her fingers slide off of my thigh and land on my sweet spot. Her thumb met my clit as her middle finger slipped inside of me. I was not sure how long I watched and moaned, but when I managed to look away from her hand and up to her eyes, I had to stop. With my body screaming for more of what she was doing, I pushed her away.

"I don't want this," was all that I offered her. I could barely look at her. The thought of what she had just done to me made me feel shameful. Not because of the act, but because of how much I had liked it.

"Why can't we just fuck?"

Her question shocked me. I knew that Niya wanted to make love to me, but a fuck? We were both worth way more than just a fuck. I hopped off the counter and snatched the towel off the hook on which she had placed it.

"When are we going to fuck? Never!" I was so damn mad at that point that I could have slapped her.

"Oh, so you're okay with a finger pop, but when it comes down to really fucking, you just can't get with that gay shit, huh?"

I turned from her, hoping that the absence of her face would calm me down. "Niya, I am going to ignore you, because I know why you are acting like this. I know that what went down this morning is really fucking with you right now, so you get a pass. Just know this," I said as I started to wipe myself with my back to her. "You and I will never *just fuck*. Plus, I like men. You need to face that fact."

I waited for her smart-ass remark, and when none came, I turned around to face her again. This time, she looked like the Niya I knew. Not so aggressive, not so lost in thought.

"You're right. My bad. I need to stop coming at you like this, but I think you really need to think over that straight shit."

She turned to leave before I could even answer.

After I got dressed, I went into the living room to tell Niya that I was leaving. It was only noon, yet I was so ready for that day to be over. When I got to the living room, she wasn't there, so I checked her room and then her grandmother's room, and all were empty. As I turned to leave, thinking that she must have stepped out, I heard it. Soft whimpers coming from her grandma's bathroom.

At first, I didn't know if I should go in, but she sounded like she was in such pain that I just had to make sure that she was okay. I knocked on the door, but she didn't answer. So slowly, I turned the knob and let myself in. Niya sat on the toilet with bloodshot eyes. Her face was a light cherry red, and veins popped out of her skull. Tears ran down her face at what seemed to be a million miles a minute. I didn't say anything. I just walked over to her and stood in front of her. I pulled her hair out of her face and let her pull me to her. As I stood and she sat, she rested her head against my stomach and wrapped her arms around my waist. She hugged me tight, and I just let her cry for the next half an hour.

Gradually, her tears slowed down, and she was able to get herself together.

"I know that you have to go home, but would you mind smoking a jay with me? I feel that after the night and morning we've had, we have to talk."

She was right. I had a few things I wanted to ask her. We decided to go down to her car so we could have as much privacy as we needed.

As Niya and I walked down to her car, I thought about the many questions that needed answers. Who was that person who had stood in that alleyway? Who was that person who had almost taken off her mother's head? Her eyes were vacant; her soul no longer roamed in that beautiful body I had come to love. I felt like too much was going on at once. The halfway threesome had already fucked my head up, and after having to deal with Niya holding a gun up to my stepfather's head, that shit with her mother, and then the bathroom scenario . . . I couldn't think straight. For the first time in our friendship, I was kind of scared of Niya. Sure, a part of me felt loved and thankful that she would take a life for me, but all the stuff that had gone down made me a little afraid. . . . Who was that person?

When we got to her car, we climbed in and just sat and smoked at first. Seconds passed, and soon those seconds turned into minutes. I didn't know how to start the conversation. I didn't want to come off like an ungrateful little girl, but I needed answers.

"Niya?"

"Yes, Jamilla?"

She was looking right at me. With her eyes piercing my soul deeply, it was as if she was ready for whatever I was about to throw at her. She waited, hardly blinking, as I tried to find the right words.

"What in the fuck was all of that? Where do I even start?" That was all I could come up with. I had asked a straight question, with no curveballs, hoping for a straight answer.

"You could start wherever you would like."

I thought about it. The threesome was the least of my worries. "My stepdad . . . Were you really going to kill him if I didn't show up?"

"He was a dead man walking in my book. I was ready to kill him when you weren't there, and I was still going to kill him even after you had walked up. He hurt you, and for that reason, he was a dead man."

Boom! There it was. No filter. And she offered no chaser. I sat there as she peered into my eyes, and I was at a loss for words.

Chapter 28

Niya

I answered her the only way I knew how. Truth ruled my soul, and that was all I always wanted to give her . . . the truth. I didn't ever want Jamilla to see that side of me, but it was inevitable. That darker side, that side of me who would kill for her, it would always be there. In that moment, I would have died for her. I would have breathed my last breath for her. So as we sat in the car, smoking, I decided to let her in just a little more. I wouldn't tell her about the murders, but just about my drug dealings, White Boy, and my temper. By the time I was done, I was sure that not telling her about my murderous ways was the right thing. She was shocked enough.

"I kind of knew that you were dealing drugs. I was just hoping that it wasn't true," she sighed.

I didn't mean to laugh, but it kind of slipped out. "How did you think that I was living the way I'm living? My granny can't lace my shit like this. She didn't buy me this car. People kill me with that 'I was hoping it wasn't true' shit. You knew it was true. No need to hope."

"I was hoping that you weren't fucking dumb enough to think that you out of all people would beat this game. That you won't end up dead or in jail, like the rest of them fools out on these streets. What does your grandma think about all of this?"

I took a long drag before answering. "It breaks her heart. Her biggest fear is that I will end up like my mom or dad, but she knows that I am going to do what I want to do. She says that I get that from her. Stubborn as hell."

We shared a laugh, a mini vacation from the tension in the car. I sat there looking at her, and she looked right back at me. So many thoughts ran through my mind, but she spoke first.

"I want you to stop. I want—"

"I just can't quit, Jamilla. There are rules to this shit. I got people who count on me."

I watched as Jamilla scrunched up her face, as if she was disgusted by my words. "I don't give a shit. They are counting on you for the wrong things. Don't you have dreams? Your words are beautiful. Don't you want to live to see your dreams come true?"

"Jamilla, you know that I want to rap, but it's just a hard game to crack into."

"Please don't give me that shit. You're out here on the mean streets of Brooklyn, slanging that shit, so there's nothing you can't do. If you can make it out here, the rap game will be simple. You just have to get out of that shell and go after it. I believe in you. Now you just have to believe in yourself. Plus, look at what drugs have done to your own mother."

She had made me smile, but that mother shit threw me off. "The sad part is that you're right. My mother—"

"That's why you have to stop. Think about what went down this morning. The same drugs you're dealing are the same drugs that are turning people into the same monster your own mother has become. I am not disrespecting you or your mother, but that's the truth, Niya."

I took her hand, and as soon as I felt her fingers against mine, it was like she spoke to me without uttering a word.

It was as if I could feel her truth through her skin. She would be right by my side and would catch me if I fell. She was going to be right there to help me realize my dreams, because she truly believed in me.

"I will make you a deal. The minute I see the path to stardom, I will leave that street shit alone."

Jamilla sat there and thought about things.

"Six months," she finally said. "I am giving you only half of a year, and you really have to try. If I don't see any effort, I am going to fuck you up." We giggled as she threw up her pinkie finger. "Promise me, Niya. Promise me that you will chase your dreams, no matter what. Promise me that only death will stop you."

Jamilla brought tears to my eyes, but I held them back. I just threw up my pinkie finger and wrapped it around hers.

"I promise you, Milla boo."

Chapter 29

Jamilla

I didn't mean to bring up her mother, but she needed to face things head-on. I loved her with all my heart, and at times, you had to say and do things that were not easy just so you could save the ones you loved. I wasn't playing with her. Niya knew that I would be on her case like the damn Feds. She was too special to get caught up in the street life bullshit. I would do anything to make sure that the world got to experience the Niya I had come to know and love.

"About the shit that went down in the bathroom—"

When I came down to the car, I thought that I would have a mouthful to say about her prying hands, but once we were in the car, it didn't seem that important.

"Don't worry about it, Niya. Things happen. I just want you to face the fact that I am into men."

Her face changed a bit when I uttered those words.

"I just needed to do something to take my mind off of what was going on," she said. "I'm sorry. I should have never come at you like that."

I reached over and rubbed the back of her neck. "I knew that's why you did it. That's why I gave you a pass."

After our conversation, I walked away with a better understanding of who this beautiful creature was. She was complex, she had layers, and I was sure of one thing. I probably had so much more to learn about her.

We left her car and walked into our building hand in hand. As we stood in the hallway that would separate us for the time being, we smiled. She pulled me close and embraced me long and strong. After she let go and we retreated to our respective sides of the building, she called my name. I looked back at her, and she had that same genuine smile.

She said, "Jamilla, I will learn to respect the fact that you like men, but that means you also have to learn to respect the fact that you're also into girls. That pussy was wet as shit."

She winked and left me standing on my side of the building. I could hear her taking the steps two at a time. I thought about what she had said and brushed it off as wishful thinking on her part.

Chapter 30

Niya

I couldn't help but smile. Jamilla's face was priceless. I wasn't buying the bullshit she was selling about being straight. She was bi at best. Her body rocked to the beat of a very gay musical. I was going to try my hardest to respect her wishes, but damn, I wanted that girl so fucking bad.

As I entered the apartment, all was peaceful. I looked in my room and saw that my mother was still asleep, but without my grandmother. I went to her room and found her on her bed, puffing on a joint while reading her Bible. I crawled into her bed and laid my head in her lap. I fell asleep with her hand on my head and to the sound of her scriptures in her native tongue.

When I woke up, the first thing I did was look in my room. A small part of me hoped that she would still be there, still sleeping, still at peace. I loved to see her that way, but as I entered my room, the only person I saw was my grandmother. She had a bunch of my clothes at her feet and was taking her time to hang them up. Right away, I knew what had gone down.

"She tried to take them to sell?" I asked, already knowing the answer to my question.

"Just pray for her, mi amor. She take some shirts, but I save most."

I shook my head and answered my ringing phone. Work was just what I needed to get my mind off of shit. I set up a time to meet White Boy and, for the next week, threw myself into "work." I moved a lot of weight that week, which was good. I was stacking cash with Jamilla's voice echoing in the back of my brain. I had to have enough to make sure that when I quit, I was done for good. As for my mother, she would cross my mind here and there, but I tried just to let the thought of her go. She was gone again, not only from our lives, but also from the land of the living. She was the walking dead.

Chapter 31

Jamilla

The weeks were flying by, and I found myself writing more and more. What had started out as my thoughts on a budding new friendship was shaping up to be a full-fledged book. It was on my mind at all times, and when I would get home at night, I would go right to it and the words would just flow. It was as if my mind knew that I was in a rush. I had to get it done by Niya's birthday. I just had to.

The good thing was, after that night in the alley, things at home were going well. My stepdad stayed in his lane, I was back in my room, while Marie had to sleep on the couch, and we were moving into a three-bedroom soon. It was in the same building, but it was an apartment with an extra room for Marie. At first, my mother couldn't understand the changes in my stepdad, but soon she seemed just to be happy that there was peace in the house. That was the thing with her: as long as he seemed happy, she was happy. I guessed she just didn't give much thought to how I felt. My happiness didn't matter to her. It was all about him

In the weeks that passed, Niya, Smiley, and I were inseparable. Although I still had a bone to pick with Smiley about the stunt she had pulled when Niya and her mother were fighting, I kept my mouth shut. I just kept telling myself to forget her actions, but deep inside,

I held them against Smiley. Niya was teaching me how to drive. Plus, she had started going to more clubs with Smiley and had even started to write more herself. She was still dealing drugs, but I saw the effort, and that made me happy. I knew that her transformation from street thug to starving artist wouldn't be easy, but she was working on it.

School was going to start soon, and Niya insisted that I go into my first year of college as the "fly bitch" that I already was. She seemed too happy to take us shopping, so after a few days of trying to stop her, I gave in. As I waited for Niya and Smiley to pick me up so we could go shopping, a few words came to mind. I pulled out my notebook and jotted them down.

It was all fate, the way we met,

On a hot Brooklyn night.

Her eyes blazing, with both our souls for the taking.

I sat, as if I was waiting . . . for her.

Hurt filled the air, and while hers was splattered for all to see, mine was hidden within the pages she would later read.

The anger, the hurtful words, that hot Brooklyn night were all meant to be.

Niya, my love, fate was at play, and thank God we didn't stop to learn the rules to the game of true love.

You are, I am, we are what the Gods have aligned and this . . . you and me . . . was all meant to be!

As they pulled up, I put my yellow notebook away, stood up, and walked to the curb. Niya got out of the car and gave me my daily hug, and I melted right into it. There was just something about the way she would squeeze me tight, as if she had missed me. It was funny how I would miss her in just the few hours she would be gone. It was getting to the point where I couldn't bear to be without her; it was as if something was missing when she was not near. I lingered in her arms and breathed in her scent. As she let me go, I snapped out of it. I stepped into the car and said hello to Smiley. She didn't seem to be in the best of moods, so I bobbed my head to the music and went back to my thoughts.

Chapter 32

Niya

The summer was fleeting, and our vacation was coming to an end. I had spent every moment I could with Jamilla. It was as if I couldn't breathe without her being near. When I wasn't with her, no matter what I was doing, thoughts of her seeped into my brain. I wondered what she was doing, if she had eaten, whether she was smiling, if she was having a good day. With my love for her growing with each passing moment, I wasn't sure how long I was going to be able to be around her without breaking. Her smile was the most beautiful thing I had ever seen. Each time I saw her was like the very first time I ever laid eyes on her. My mouth would go dry; my heart would race. I would secretly steal deep breaths, hoping that this would calm my nerves. I was trying so hard to embed that "She's straight" shit in my head, but it just wouldn't stick.

As I watched her and Smiley shop, it was as if she was the only one in the store. After that night with her and Smiley and our escapade in the bathroom, all I wanted to do was fuck her . . . really fuck her, but Smiley was around more now too. At times, things would feel a little weird. I could tell that Smiley's feelings for me were growing, and truth was, my feelings for her were growing too, but Jamilla was still the one. I still needed to talk to Smiley about the incident with my mother, but I kept putting it off. It was embarrassing enough. Plus, how did you tell someone that she or he should have jumped in shit to help you out? What Jamilla did for my family that day hadn't gone unnoticed. She now held this special space in my heart that no one could touch.

A month had passed since that night, yet my mind was consumed with thoughts of Jamilla—on my bed, on her back, in the bathroom, and on the sink. Watching her touch herself and me touching her . . . My thoughts were all about her. I tried to shake that shit, but just like the imprint Jamilla had left behind on my heart, thoughts of that night were stuck in my brain.

"You like this, boo?"

Smiley was modeling a new dress for me. I took a quick glance at her and told her that I liked it. She had interrupted my thoughts of that night, and I was a bit annoyed. I didn't mean for it to happen, but my infatuation with Jamilla was starting to become unhealthy. I was annoyed more with myself than with Smiley. I knew that her feelings were hurt, so I got up and entered her dressing room.

"Baby, you looked sexy as fuck in that dress. Don't mind me. I was dumb not to notice them thick-ass legs and that nice ass. My bad, boo," I told her.

I walked up on her and wrapped my arms around her and gave her ass a squeeze. I kissed her neck and waited for the tension to leave her body, but it didn't. She pushed me off her and rolled her eyes.

"What's wrong, boo? I said I was sorry."

She sucked her teeth and turned away from me and began to get dressed. As I turned to leave her dressing room, I heard her speak.

"You act like you don't know what the fuck is wrong. I bet if I was—"

"What is taking so long?" Jamilla said as she peeked into the dressing room, cutting Smiley off in mid-sentence.

I was not sure if Jamilla felt it, but the tension in there was as thick as hell. I stood there, not knowing what to say, but knowing that there was much that needed to be said. I just stood there while Smiley got dressed. I didn't know what the hell I was going to do with these two. I knew that Smiley really liked Jamilla, but she was also able to tell that things were different when she was around. I tried to give them equal attention when they both were with me, but it didn't always work out that way.

The drive home wasn't any better. Smiley clearly had an attitude. No matter how hard Jamilla tried to make conversation, she was met with a cold shoulder from Smiley. Once we got back to my building, I gave Smiley the key to my apartment and told her to wait there for me. Once Smiley was out of the car, Jamilla couldn't wait to ask me what was wrong.

"I really don't know, but I am going to try to find out," I half lied.

As I sat there with Jamilla, thoughts of touching her started to creep into my head. She had on these little shorts that I had got her just so I could see her in them. Her toffee-colored thighs had my mouth watering. As I looked down at her legs, I also tried my hardest to see that pussy print. Damn. I wanted this girl. Licking and touching her were no longer enough. I wanted to taste what was between her thighs. I wanted to feel her hand behind my head as I licked her until she screamed. I had to do something. I felt as if insanity wasn't too far away. My eyes traveled up and down her body as she rambled on about not understanding why Smiley was upset. I had tuned her out, only to hear the last of her words.

"Look, I can't tell you what happened between this morning and now," I said. "I think that you should just chill out for the rest of the night and give me some time just to talk to her."

My tone came out a bit harsher than I would have liked, but I couldn't help it. I had found myself drowning in thoughts of her, while it was apparent that her mind was on other things and not on me, and this bothered me.

She gave me a weird look before she went to open the car door. "It's cool. I have some packing to do."

I tried to stop her by reaching for her hand, but she just shook it off.

"Leave my stuff in the trunk. I'll get it later," she said before getting out of the car and walking away.

Chapter 33

Jamilla

I sat in my room, wondering what had just happened. We had all been fine this morning. Sure, Smiley had been a bit quiet in the car, but we all got that way sometimes. The funny thing was, no matter how badly I'd wanted to try to act as if I didn't know what was going on, I'd known. I had caught it a few times, a look, a smirk, a quick show of annoyance. Smiley and Niya seemed to have gone from friends to—I didn't know—girlfriends perhaps. Hell, I didn't know what to call them. They said that what they had didn't have a label, but I wished they would make things clear. I'd tried to give them space, but Niya was always insisting that I was there. At times, I wondered if she secretly wanted a round two of that night. *Oh boy.* That night, the night that still lingered in the air.

I tried my hardest not to think about that night, but some part of me, a part that was foreign to me, wanted to reenact that night, but just with Niya. I would never let her know that, nor would I ever try it again, but . . . damn. I also thought about her touching me in her bathroom. That one really got to me, because it was just me and her. The one thing that I wished she would have done was to kiss me. See, that was where the confusing part came in. I knew that I wasn't gay—there was no way that I would ever go down on another girl—but with Niya . . . She made me want her. She made me want simple little things from her, like just a little kiss.

"Jamilla, where are you?"

I rolled my eyes when I heard my mother's voice. I didn't answer. Instead, I just waited for her to find me.

"Why you no say nothing? You did not hear me call you?" she said when she reached my bedroom door.

"Sorry. I was packing," I answered. Not that packing would stop me from hearing her.

"So, you go out all the time now, eh? All day you out now with that gay girl. I don't like no gay friend for you, Jamilla. You hear me? That gay stuff so nasty. People will look at you like you gay too."

There was so much I wanted to say to the woman I called Mom, but instead I just asked, "Mom, was there something that you needed?"

My mother sat down on my bed and just stared and sucked her teeth. I wasn't going to force her to speak, so I just went on with my packing. When she was tired of being ignored, she spoke up.

"Mwen pa renmen chanjman sa kap pase nan kay mwen an. You changing, and it's no good. I want to know why he make Marie go to the couch and you sleep here now."

She didn't like the changes that were being made in her house? I just prayed to God that I kept my cool. I just continued to fold and pack my clothes.

"Jamilla, you hear me? Why he so nice with you now? You do something to him?"

Keeping cool went out the window.

"Are you fucking kidding me? For years, he has been the one doing stuff to me, and now, because he's finally acting right, you think that *I* did something?"

"Oh, so you do something to him? Ay, I know you not sex my husband in my house. You go after your own mother's boyfriend?"

I had to stop myself from reaching out and slapping her clear across the face. "You crazy, selfish bitch, you—"

I got in her face to make sure that she would hear me well. "Your husband has had his hands in my pussy since the day he asked you to marry him. For years I have tried to tell you, but no. You—"

"Oh, shut up. You have sex with boys, and now you blame my husband. He would never do something like that."

"Yes the fuck he did. From the day you told me that you were going to marry him, he has been touching me. He—" She turned to leave, but I grabbed her arms and turned her back around. "Don't you dare walk out on me. I am your daughter. What that man did to me, it killed me. Can't you see that?"

I waited and prayed that my words were seeping into her head, and not only her head, but also her heart. Something had to give between us. I loved my mother, and I needed her, but the things she had said and hadn't done made me hate her at times.

"You go out with your boyfriends and let them touch you. Afterward, you say it's my husband? You want to whore your body with them boys, that's fine, but don't put it on my man."

"Mom, how could you say that? You know that I don't whore myself out. I have had only one boyfriend."

My body was shaking from hurt and anger. I needed this woman to understand me, to believe me, but she just wasn't listening with her heart.

"So what you tell me? You virgin? No, let me see." My mother charged me and pushed down me on the bed. She got on top of me and yanked at my shorts.

"Come on. You such a good girl, show me you virgin."

"Get off of me!"

We rolled around on the bed as she tried to get my shorts off. I couldn't understand what was going on. I had only heard stories, my mother's stories, of having to get "tested" by her mother while she was growing up. Her mother would make her and her sister lie down on their back once a month so she could make sure that they were still virgins. I wasn't quite sure how she tested them, but my mother did tell us that her mother would stick fingers inside of her. Well, that shit wasn't going down with me. I fought and screamed until Marie came into the room.

"What's going on in here?" Marie muttered.

"Help me, Marie. Hold her legs. Hurry. Hold them," my mother urged.

I tried to fight even harder. I spit vile words at both of them. I called them all kinds of molesting bitches. I kicked, I clawed, and I fought for as long as I could.

"No! Get off of me! Please, no, you fucking bitch!" I yelled as I felt my shorts coming off.

I could feel Marie's hands around my ankles, and I tried my best to kick her in her face. When my mother could no longer control my hands, I watched her climb on top of me, and after that, I felt her weight on my chest. I could hardly breathe as I cried for help.

"Louvri janm li."

Marie pushed my legs open and held them in place. As I tried to push my mother off of me, the smile on Marie's face could not be missed. She was enjoying my agony. It pleased her to see me cry and scream, to watch my mother violate me.

As my mother's fingers slid inside of me, she told me how she really felt about me.

"Uh-huh, just like I thought. You are a dirty whore who is sleeping with the no-good American hoodlums out there. You are a dirty girl, just a nasty whore."

I lay there numb, void of any emotions. I didn't even feel her fingers anymore. I could no longer feel anything, not even the life that still roamed inside of me.

"You see that, Marie? That is what a whore's vagina looks like. Push it open. You see that. For years she tried to tell me lies. Now look at this. She is no virgin. She let boys have her body. Look at it. Make sure you no have no whore vagina."

"What in the hell is going on here?" said a male voice.

My mother got off my chest but told Marie to hold my legs open. "She is a whore. I check her, and her vagina open. She no virgin."

"You can't do this. Marie, let her go. This is not Haiti. You cannot do stuff like this," he said.

Lying there, I just began to laugh. The irony of the situation was killing me. There he stood, the man who had been molesting me from a tender young age, yet that day, he was the voice of reason.

I looked at all three of them, and as tears from the pain that I knew would never leave my soul wet my pillow, I laughed. I laughed at the smirk on Marie's face; I laughed at my mother's pain. The pain from what her mother had done to her. I knew it. I had seen it when she told me about her mother testing her each month, and now she had passed that pain on to me. Why? Because I had told her the truth about her husband. And finally, I laughed at my stepdad. He knew that what my mother had done was wrong, yet for years he had done the same thing. *Fuck one. Fuck all.* I hated each and every one of them.

One by one they left my room, my mother being the last. As laughter merged with my tears, she spoke.

"If you try to take my husband, I will kill you. You are a whore. Continue to sex your boyfriends. Stay away from my husband. I see he is nice to you now. If I catch you with him, I will kill you."

Once she left my room and closed the door, my first thought was to call Niya, but what good would that do?

She would want to kill my mother *and* Marie, for that matter. Plus, how could I tell her that my own mother had had her fingers inside of me? And like a ton of bricks, it all hit me. The pain from her roaming fingers, the scar from my own mother calling me a whore, the damage from my very own existence—they all crashed down on me, and without the refuge of laughter, I cried. I howled. I screamed. And at the end of it all, another little piece of me was dead and gone.

Chapter 34

Niya

I sat across from Smiley and just stared at her. I had a lot that I wanted to say, but I didn't want it to come out the wrong way.

"So, what's your problem?" I asked as I sipped on a cup of vodka. I was annoyed and was trying to watch my temper.

"Oh, you know what's wrong."

I rolled my eyes and sucked my teeth. I was growing tired of her games. My mind was on Jamilla. I reached for my phone and texted her and waited.

"So, that's what you're gonna do? You're just gonna sit there and play with your phone?"

I took a long swig of the vodka and just sat there looking at her. I was trying to see the things in her that I had always liked, like how laid back she used to be, but I couldn't really see them. I picked my phone back up and took a look to see if Jamilla had hit me back. Still . . . nothing.

"You know what? I am so tired of this shit. I don't even know why we are trying."

"Oh, you're trying?" My tone was very sarcastic, and at that moment, I didn't give a shit.

"Fuck you, Niya."

When she said that, I was reaching for the book bag I always kept with me. I stopped midway and just looked at her. After that, I sat back in my chair and picked up my bottle of Cîroc. I drank from the bottle as I thought about her words.

"You know what, Smiley? Let that be the last time you ever say 'Fuck you' to me. Understand?" I spoke to her without even looking at her. I could feel the heat in my cheeks, which let me know that I was turning red. My anger always showed on my face, and if she was wise, she would take it as a warning.

"Niya, look at me." She waited for me to do as she asked before continuing. "Niya . . . fuck you! You think that I don't know what's going on between you and Jamilla? You are in love with that girl as you string me along, and as for her, she never gives a shit about you until I show you some attention. She—"

I had had enough. I jumped out of my chair, and before I knew it, I had her against my bedroom door, with my hand around her neck. "Didn't I tell you not to say those words to me?"

"Oh, so you gonna act like that's what you're mad at? Nah, you're mad because I pulled your card about that bitch."

I was so close to her face that I could feel her breath. I wanted to slap her, but I knew that it would be out of line. "What? You think that you're in a better position? You aren't all that you're cracked up to be. I caught that shit with my mother. I saw your face, I heard what you said, and that shit ain't cool with me."

I watched as Smiley's face twisted with confusion. I let her go, turned my back on her, and went back to my seat.

"Are you fucking kidding me? Your mom was covered in shit. What did you want me to do?"

I sat and listened to her for the next five minutes, as she went on and on about why she left that morning my mother came over. But nothing she said would change the facts.

"Look, at the end of the day, you're just not a bitch that I can count on. Plus, what the fuck are we doing? You thought Jamilla was cool before we fucked. When in the hell did this turn into a relationship? I'm not looking for a girlfriend, Smiley. We fuck around, and that's cool, but you ain't my girl, feel me?"

I knew right away that she was hurt, but hell, so was I. I was hurt and had been hiding it. The fact that she left that morning had never sat right with me.

"Who the fuck are you, Niya? You jump in my face, you choke me, and you tell me that this is not a relationship? I mean, come on. This is not the Niya I know."

I started to laugh. Not because she was funny, but to be mean. "Since when did you ever fucking know me? We fuck, and all of the sudden, you think you know me? If you knew me, you would have never left that morning. Jamilla didn't."

Jamilla's name had hardly left my mouth before I found myself ducking to avoid getting hit in the head with one of my own shoes.

"I am so fucking sick of hearing her name. That's what this is all about. You are fucking right, Niya. We could never be together. You're so far up that bitch's ass, and the funny thing is, you will never have her the way you want her. She will never be yours."

"It's a good thing you don't have to worry about it, huh? You know, being that we are not in a fucking *relationship*."

This time, it was her turn to laugh.

"I am not even going to leave here upset, and do you know why? It's because this right here, the way you love her, that will be your punishment. I am going to sleep well knowing that while you're eating yourself up over that bitch, she will never love your ass the same way. Fuck you very much, Niya, and, uh, remember that I was nice enough to warn you."

I was back on my feet. I grabbed a handful of her hair and used it to walk her to my front door.

"Get the fuck out, you fat bitch. You should have been thankful that I was with your ass," I snarled.

Again, I hated my choice of words, but I was pissed. For a brief second, we locked eyes, and I saw it. I saw all that we used to be, all that she used to be, and all that we had lost because of our poor choice of words. I knew that I would miss her as I watched her tears drop, but my drunken pride wouldn't let me say . . . "I'm sorry."

I went back to my bedroom and picked up my phone. *Fuck*. Nothing back from Jamilla. Smiley's words coasted around in my head as thoughts of Jamilla fought to take their place. I needed to get out of the house. I picked up my bottle and phone and headed out. The streets of Brooklyn always seemed to give me refuge from my dark moods and thoughts. While I walked without a destination, the last person I thought I would run into was Rodney.

There we were, on the very same street that he had outed me on, and for the first time, I didn't turn the other way when I saw him.

"I really need to talk to you, Niya."

"What the fuck do you want?"

The things Smiley said had really started to mess with my head. I knew that Jamilla loved me as a friend and even more. She was just afraid to face the truth. No straight girl would ever act the way she did; no straight girl would let me touch her the way she did. I had continued to walk, and Rodney was right beside me.

"Please, Niya, I need to talk to you."

At first, I just wanted to tell him to fuck off, but that night, I needed someone, even if it was someone who I felt couldn't be trusted. I told him to walk with me. We ended up at the basketball court. I passed him my bottle as I rolled up and waited for him to speak.

"Niya, um, I don't know where to start. Um, what I did was so fucked up. See, Roxie—"

"Yeah, I know all about Roxie. I know what she told you."

He looked a little shocked but continued. "Not that it's a good excuse, but . . ."

I waited, without saying a word. I didn't care how long it was going to take. I wanted to hear what he had to say.

"I had a thing for you. Like, I was really in love with you."

He stopped, waited for me to say something, but I offered him nothing. I was uncomfortable with the conversation and didn't have much to say.

"Look, fuck everything else. The most important thing is that I am sorry. What I did was fucked up, and I miss you, Niya. I miss my friend."

I looked at Rodney, and as much as I wanted to hate him, the truth was, I missed him too. We had always been together, and his company was missed.

For a while, we just sat together and smoked and drank. No words were needed. I was trying to decide if I could ever trust Rodney again. I wanted him back in my life, but I didn't want the hurt that he had caused me that night.

I finally spoke. "Man, as I sit here, I am fighting with myself. What you did fucked me up, Rodney. Do you know what it was like for me to stand there as the only person I had even let in outed me? I trusted you with my life. We ate together, we fucked bitches together, we even did our dirt together, and *boom*, you fucking took a knife and damn near tried to kill me with it."

"Niya, I wasn't thinking. I was so mad that night, and truth be told, a nigga was hurt. I should have stopped and thought about it, but I acted off of emotions."

"Man, fuck your emotions. I went home and came out to my granny, man. I felt as if I had no choice, as if you had given me no choice. Do you know that shit could have turned out real ugly for me? Did you think that maybe someone wouldn't be too happy hearing that I'm a dyke? What if someone had tried to hurt me because you chose to pull me out of the closet?"

"Come on, Niya. It wasn't like you tried to hide it. I questioned it. I just wouldn't let myself believe the truth. I mean . . . look at you."

"Get the fuck out of here with that shit. What you did wasn't right. I don't give a fuck how gay I look. It wasn't your information to give. I should have been able to face my truth when I wanted to, not when *you* thought it was right."

My words were met with silence. Yes, I was still angry, and most of all, I was still hurt.

A few moments passed before Rodney broke the silence. "Niya. I am just asking for a second chance. I fucked up, but let me make it right."

For a while after that, we just sat, smoked, and drank. Thoughts of that night still sent painful chills through my body. I asked myself if I could really forgive him, and the answer was I really didn't know, but something in me told me to try.

"I'm telling you, Niya, we can do some things on that Mac. People are making a lot of music on computers. Plus, you really have to start using social media," Rodney boasted with total excitement in his voice.

We were once again having a conversation about me rapping. It was the night before my first day on campus, and nightfall found us on the block, nursing another bottle. It seemed as if everyone around me was pushing me to do it—well, the people who knew about it.

"What if I put that shit out and get clowned? I don't know, man. Not really sure that I'm ready yet."

Rodney sucked his teeth and tried to get me to see things his way. "If you are waiting to be 'ready,' you never will be. Just say 'Fuck it,' and jump. You may land on your knees or you may land on your feet. Imagine—"

"But what if—"

"What if nothing, Niya. Imagine landing on your feet, and you take off running. You may be the first of your kind to really make it. Picture that shit. A real bitch spittin' some real shit. Just jump, and you know me and Milla are going to jump with you. I have a rack of beats that's sitting there ready. My brother got a nice camera. We can even film the video on. Just jump."

I sat there, sipping on the dark liquor, as he spoke. All my life all I had ever wanted to do was rap, but it was just a dream. I had never really thought of pursuing it as a career. But as I listen to Rodney and remembered my conversation with Jamilla, I felt like I could really do something, like it could be more than a dream.

"Just jump, Niya. Just jump."

I looked at Rodney and decided that he and Jamilla couldn't both be wrong. I had to try.

"Meet me here around four tomorrow. Your beats better be fire," I told him.

Chapter 35

Jamilla

I never did tell Niya about what happened with my mother. I was too afraid that she would go after her like she did my stepdad. We had moved into our new apartment, and I stayed out of everyone's way. I didn't see much of Niya in the days that passed, but through texting, I found out that she was hanging out with Rodney. I thought that it was a good thing. They were good friends, and forgiveness was the best way to get over something. I missed her so much, but my own misery was keeping me from her. I just wanted to spend time alone in my room. I felt dirty, and I just didn't want her to see me.

I hardly slept the night before school started. Niya and I were going to ride together, and I was a bit nervous. I was always nervous when it came to school, and now I was going to be a freshman all over again. In high school, the kids had always seemed to make me feel inferior. They had all seemed so happy with their big clique of friends, and the truth was, I had wanted to be them. I was happy that I would be going to campus with my new friend, though. I was going to pull up on campus with one of the most popular girls in Brooklyn, and I wanted to see how my life would change because of it.

"You look beautiful," Niya said when I met her in the lobby of our building the next morning. "I've been missing you, boo. Fuck this 'not seeing you' shit. I never even got a chance to tell you about what happened with me and Smiley."

Damn. Looking at her, I realized again that I had missed her too. As I listened to what went down between her and Smiley, I couldn't help but be in shock.

"So, she really felt as if I was getting between you and her?" I asked.

How could I have been in competition with Smiley when Niya and I weren't even like that?

"Jamilla, truth is, she wasn't lying. I know that you say constantly that you're straight, but that still doesn't make me love you any less. I know that you feel it, 'cause I am doing nothing to hide it. And at times, when it's just me and you, I feel that shit, and I know you feel it too. I can see it in your eyes."

My mind tried to catch up with my emotions. What was I supposed to do with the things Niya had just said to me? If she were a guy, I would have been hers already, but she wasn't, and that put a wrench in everything.

She went on to tell me about her and Rodney, and how he had told her that he was in love with her. I couldn't help but get a little jealous.

"So the whole time you were friends with him, he liked you?" I asked her.

"Well, damn. Don't be so shocked. I am a beautiful bitch," Niya joked.

We climbed in her car, and as we rode to school, I listened in silence to her tales of her time with Rodney. I truly was happy that she had gotten her friend back, but I couldn't help but question if their friendship would leave me in the dust. I knew that what I had with Niya was rare. And I would do anything to hold on to it.

When we pulled up to Kingsborough, all eyes were on us. Niya seemed totally comfortable with the attention, but it was all new to me. Some people whispered, while others just stared, but I noticed them all. Niya told me that a lot of the people we went to high school with were also attending the same college, so she probably felt right at home. We got out of the car, and Niya walked over to my side of the car and took my hand, as she always did when we hung out.

"Come on, Milla boo," she said as she threw her arm around my neck.

I had mixed emotions. I was excited that finally, I was no longer invisible at school. People would walk up to Niya and have short conversations, and she introduced me to each and every one. I had never noticed how popular she was as a high school senior the year before. But even the older kids on campus who hadn't gone to school with us knew who she was. I was enjoying the attention until Marlo, a girl whom I had always hated, came up to us with her little crew of followers. She was a tall brown-skinned girl who looked like a model. Everything on her face was sharp, as if she was bred from Zulu warriors. Her clothes were always tight and short and hugged her curvaceous body. She was so beautiful that looking at her was almost painful—painful because as soon as you saw her, she would make the average girl insecure. I watched her sweep her long weave off of her shoulders before she spoke.

"Hey, Niya. Is this your new girlfriend?"

Instantly, I pulled away from Niya, who happened to look a bit shocked.

"Girlfriend? What would make you think that?" Niya asked.

"I'm not gay," I announced. My words had come out louder than I'd wanted them to. Honestly, I was just as shocked as Niya looked.

"Oh, wait. I thought I heard that you came out. Oh, shit. My bad," Marlo said.

I waited for Niya to speak up. I was so embarrassed. I needed her to speak up and let Marlo know that I was not gay. Niya gave me a weird look before addressing Marlo.

"Nah. I mean, yeah, I'm gay, but Jamilla and I . . ."

"Marlo, I am not gay," I said.

I wished that I had just kept my mouth shut. The look on Niya's face told me that what I had just said hurt her. I wasn't sure if it was the words themselves or the fact that I was so adamant about letting everyone know that I wasn't one of *them*, one of what she was, a lesbian.

Marlo shrugged. "It's cool. I just thought. . . Well, it doesn't matter. You're looking good, though. I am happy to see that you have stepped your game up. Those jeans are cute as hell, Jamilla. See you around, Niya."

I watched Marlo walk away, just so I wouldn't have to face Niya, but soon I had to turn to her. I felt like shit instantly. She looked so hurt.

"Niya, I am—"

"Nah, don't worry about it. I am gonna head to class. See you at lunch?"

She didn't even wait for my answer. I watched her walk away and prayed that she would forgive me.

I was in my third class of the day when I got up to go to the bathroom. Niya had been on my mind all day. My life had changed because of her. As I thought about our summer, mixed emotions consumed me. I thought about our friendship, and then I thought about the things that had taken us way beyond that. Like my night with Smiley and her, or that morning in her bathroom. As I thought of those moments, I had to cross my legs. She had made me feel so good, but that was only my body. When I let my thoughts in, the way I felt, I decided that her touching me was wrong. To me, I was just a lonely girl who was letting a void be filled momentarily by a woman. I wasn't really a lesbian, but a lesbian was all I really had. The fact that she was gay somehow made me confused about my feelings for her. I had never felt that way before about a straight girl. *Ugh*. That shit was making my head hurt.

I sat in the bathroom for a short while, hoping to get my thoughts together. When Marlo came in as I washed my hands, I tried to wish her away.

"Hey, Jamilla. Where's your girlfriend?"

I ignored her.

"Girl, you have got to relax. I'm just fuckin' with you. I really do like your outfit, though."

Her compliment made me smile. The thought of a very stylish girl like her liking what I had on . . . I could only dream of a moment like that before that day.

"Niya got it for me. She—" I stopped once I noticed the smile that had crept across Marlo's face.

"I knew it. Let me find out you go that way."

"No, really, I don't. She's just my best friend. We really got close this summer." I had already said way more than I had wanted to, but she had to know that I was not gay.

"Girl, chill the fuck out. This isn't high school anymore. Don't nobody care if you are. It's the in thing now. Haven't you heard? I mean, I ain't never been with a girl, but Niya is cute as shit. If I were ever to try it, she would be the one."

I took a minute to look Marlo over. From what I could tell, she was being honest. "What do you mean *if* you were ever to try it? Have you ever thought about it?" I just had to know.

Marlo turned from me with a smile. She reached into her pocket, took out her lipstick, and spoke as she reapplied it. "Girl, I mean, I can't say that I have spent too much time thinking about it, but . . . a bitch like Niya . . . she could get it."

"You like her?" I asked out of curiosity, and then I waited impatiently, as if on the edge of a cliff, for her reply.

"*Like* her? I mean, she's cute and all, but what really had me taking a second look is the fact that I heard she knows how to take care of a bitch. I didn't know how true it all was, but if you're just her friend and she got you laced like this"—Marlo reached over and touched my shirt—"I know she can definitely take care of a fly bitch like me."

In that moment, I remembered why I had never liked her. She was a Roxie, a girl whose ambitions rode on her sleeve. She was easy to read, a user, a girl who was out for herself.

"I don't know, Jamilla. I may just give Niya a try. But, girl, here's a word of advice. Never do again what you did this morning. It's cool to let people know that you're straight, but damn, girl. I think you hurt Niya's feelings."

Damn. I hated that girl. I watched her walk out of the bathroom, and after she was gone, I realized that when she'd touched my shirt, she left her shade of lipstick behind on it. For the rest of that day, every time I looked down, I was reminded of her.

Chapter 36

Niya

I saw Jamilla while I was grabbing something to eat between classes, but I stayed pretty quiet. My feelings were crushed. Maybe it was because for that brief moment in time, I had almost felt like she was mine. When we were standing there and people were coming up to us and I was introducing her to them, it had felt good to have her so close, right under my arm, as everyone looked on. It had made me feel like they all saw it, saw everything that I had always seen in her. I could tell that she was nervous, but my touch had seemed to calm her down. I would steal glimpses of her. She'd been smiling, and she'd looked happy finally to be noticed. I had thought that what I was doing for her was a good thing. The whole truth, though, was that what I'd done was also for me. That shit—pretending that she was mine just for that moment— had felt good.

After our first day of classes, we drove home together, and I played the music loud. I didn't want to talk. I just wanted to get her home and out of my car. I was still upset and hurt, and I didn't want to go off on her. Once we were in front of my building, I sat in the car and just waited for her to get out. I didn't look at her or say a word. With me refusing to look at her, she turned down my music.

"Niya—"

"Jamilla, don't."

She sat there, and still, I wouldn't look at her.

"I just wanted to say that I'm sorry."

"What in the fuck are you sorry for? You're straight, and you let it be known. No need for apologies." I just wanted her out of my fucking car. I felt as if I couldn't breathe with her next to me.

"I know, but I . . . I just—"

"Jamilla, let that shit go. I heard you loud and clear today. Hell, the whole damn campus heard you. The funny thing is, Smiley warned me about this shit. She could see my feelings for you, and she could also see the lack of feelings that you have for me."

"That's not true, Niya. You know that I love you."

I started to laugh, and finally, I looked at her. "Oh yeah? You love me?" I needed a fucking drink. The sight of her was killing me.

"You know that I do, Niya."

"Nah, I really don't. Just go on home, Jamilla. I got shit to do." I was hurt, and now so was she. I knew that she cared for me, but I needed her to love me the way that I loved her.

Without another word, Jamilla climbed out of my car. She stood on the curb, waiting for me to get out and say something, I guessed, but I was all talked out. I didn't want just to drive off, but I had to. Everything that she was right there on that sidewalk, everything that she represented, all of it hurt like hell. The truth was, I just couldn't take too much more of the pain I felt when I looked at her.

I had been in Rodney's basement for an hour. I had a bottle of feel good, and the weed smoke lingered in the air. I listened to beat after beat until finally, I heard "the one." It was slow, it was moody, and the drums were just as emotional as I felt. I pulled out my notebook and had him play it over and over again. Twenty-five minutes later I had something I wanted to record.

I got a gay girl problem.
Lost in the land of easy pussy.
I'm hoping stray pussy will solve it.
She said she likes only men,
But when I'm with her,
All that bullshit transcends
The lies she tells as my hands move up her thighs and cause her body to bend.
I can hear her cries, but that shit is all lies.
Don't she know that I'm a fucking godsend?
The shit I do with just the tip of my tongue . . .
I had her before, and I'll have her again.
She got straight girl problems,
As her need for pussy is starting to blossom.
A nigga like me is the only one who could solve them.

The song went on for a whole four minutes, and I had Rodney record it. I unleashed my emotions as I sang the lyrics, and by the time I was done, I looked at Rodney for approval.

"Don't lie to me. Just give it to me straight," I told him.

"Hold up. Hold up."

Rodney left the room and came back with his brother June. When he started to replay the the song, I thought that I would die. But as I watched his brother, I saw his head start to bob.

"So, what do you think?" Rodney asked his brother when the song was over.

"I think it's hot. She went hard on that shit."

I took in a deep breath and just listened.

"The only thing is . . . I wouldn't drop that as her first single," June advised.

"Why not?" I said, jumping in.

"'Cause it's a slower beat. It's sexy as hell, but you know what these kids out here want. You got to kill 'em with a club joint first."

I was kind of disappointed, but from a business standpoint, June was right.

"Look, think about it, and if you come up with something hot, let me know. If I like it, I will call a few of the homies over and some bitches, and we gonna shoot a video," June said.

My eyes got big. I didn't think that I was ready to have anyone hear my music yet, let alone to shoot a video.

June looked hard at me. "Why are you all bug-eyed? Your shit is hot. If you can come up with a club joint, you are gonna blow them away."

I looked at Rodney, and he only confirmed what his brother had just said.

"Niya, just think about it. We could have a song and a video out this week. That shit is gonna be crazy," Rodney said with a big smile on his face.

So I said, "Fuck it." Rodney played more beats, and I found one that would be sure to have the girls rolling their hips and popping their ass, and I gave it my best. I knew it had to be cocky, I knew that I had to come off strong, and I knew that by the end of the song, I needed to have not only the gay girls on my shit, but the straight ones too.

Team take yo' bitch.
Thought she was straight.
Till I took yo' bitch.
Lesbuns give the best head, hon.
And this shit right here isn't just for fun.
Thought that dick would keep her,
Thought that dick would please her,
But I'ma pussy eater.
I'ma pussy killer.

Legs high, got her head high,
Spread-eagle, no longer eye to eye.
I'ma lick it up. I'ma beat it up.
Her nigga's name
Now a distant thought.
Team take yo' bitch.

We wrapped up the song in under an hour. By the time June came back downstairs, we had doubled over the song and had added the ad-libs of me talking shit, and this time, I knew we had a hit.

"Yo, this shit is fuckin' hot. I'm about to make some calls, and we gonna film this shit tonight," June told us after he heard the song.

I was excited. I wasn't sure where these songs were going to take me, but I couldn't wait to see.

Chapter 37

Jamilla

I must have texted Niya over twenty times, but she never answered. My heart felt as if it was being ripped out of my chest at the thought of losing her. She was my world, my everything. How could I have been so insecure, so insensitive? All I wanted to do was apologize to her. I wanted to tell her that honestly, she was making me crazy. I was stuck in the unknown. I was afraid, petrified that maybe I had feelings for her that went beyond our friendship. I wanted to tell her that the thought of loving a woman was a foreign thing to me and that this in itself was enough to make me pull away from her. I needed her to understand that my nights were filled with thoughts of her and that my days were no different.

She had to be told that I needed no one else but her, but how could I tell her these things and have her understand that I just didn't think that I was gay? Or was I? Oh my God, I didn't even know who or what I was anymore. There were so many aspects to our friendship that had me fucked up. I loved her, I needed her, I wanted her—even sexually at times—but she was a woman.

I called Niya throughout the evening, with no response. Soon day turned into night, and I was barely breathing, or so it seemed. I hadn't eaten anything, nor had I had a drink of water, since I came home. I couldn't, not until I spoke to her or saw her. So I sat at the window of my room, chewing one piece of gum after the other, and waited for her. I didn't care how long it took. I was going to wait for her and speak to her before she went into her apartment.

Chapter 38

Niya

People were everywhere. We were in Rodney's backyard, and there had to be about a hundred people out there, if not more. I was pretty fucked up and wasn't as nervous as I should have been. I just sat in one of the chairs and totally leaned back, as the liquor in my system had me ready for whatever. June was a true director and was telling people what they should be doing in the scene that was about to take place.

"How in the hell did he get so many people here so fast and so damn late?" I asked Rodney as he handed me the blunt. It was going on eleven o'clock.

"Social media. Twitter, Facebook, and Instagram. That shit is crazy. You are gonna have to be on them way more after this. Get you a fan page going. You need to start posting pictures and—"

"Posting pictures of what? I don't really do nothing special."

Rodney laughed at how naive I was before answering me. "Once you build your fan base, you can post a picture of what you're eating, and they are going to eat that shit up. Like, now go ahead and post a picture of the people here. You do have an Instagram, right?"

"Nah. Just a Facebook."

I kind of felt out of the loop as Rodney took my phone and said that he was going to set up an Instagram account for me. Twenty minutes later, it was all set up and I already had five pictures up.

"Hey, Niya. You pick out a lead for the video yet?" said a female voice.

When I looked up to see who was speaking, I smiled at the sight of her. She wasn't in the same outfit from school. Although her clothes were always short and tight, she seemed to be dressed even more scandalously.

"Marlo, damn. I mean, nah, not yet."

The shorts she had on might as well have been left at home, as they were so small. And her cut-up tank top left nothing to the imagination. Her body was fucking perfect. Nothing too big, nothing too small, and she was tall and plump in all the right places. She pushed my hand out of my lap and sat on it. I couldn't put together what was happening. Was Marlo even into girls?

"Well, there ain't a bitch out here that looks better than me. I'll be the lead, if you ask me to be," she said.

Man, as I was sitting in that chair with her in my lap, looking into her eyes, and smelling her sweet scent, truth was, I didn't see any other girl but her. I looked at Rodney, and he just gave me a nod, as if to say, "She's the one."

"Why don't you go ahead and get yourself a drink? While you're at it, fill me up too," I told her.

"So does that mean that I got the part?"

When I told her yes, she screamed as if she had gotten the lead in a Jay Z video and gave me a tight hug. I hugged her back and wasn't shy when it came to letting my hands slip down to her ass.

"Hold up. Let me get a pic of you with your leading lady," Rodney said as he grabbed my phone out of my hand. I pulled Marlo close, and he snapped a few shots.

Shooting the video was fun. It was your typical hood video, with street dudes, beautiful girls, and hood locations. It took us three hours to film in five different close locations in the city that birthed all my creativity. The crazy part was, wherever we went, the crowd followed, which only caused more people to join us. Everyone wanted to be in a frame, but the scenes I liked the most were left for last. By then most of the crowd had gone home, and it was just me, Rodney, June, and Marlo. We were filming in June's bedroom since it was a dope-ass room. The furniture was black, and the background colors, in the form of throw pillows, wall art, and the comforter, were gold and red. It looked like something straight out of a rap video.

As we filmed, with Marlo playing the perfect lead, I told myself just to be free. I wanted it to come off as real, as if she was mine and I could do what I wanted to her. She didn't stop my hands as they traveled her body, and when we kissed, that shit felt real to me. She was fucking beautiful, and when I rapped about turning a bitch out, in my mind, I pictured her. If she had a boyfriend, it only made me think that the song was fitting for the situation. She was going to be batting for my team—*team take yo' bitch*—'cause she was going to be mine.

By the time we wrapped and I came up for air, it was almost four in the morning. I was beyond fucked up, so June said he would take me home in my car and would just stay at his girl's house since she lived only a few buildings down from me. He offered to take Marlo home, and when she said yes, I was happy that I would have a bit more time with her, even if it was just for a short ride. When we got to her place, I staggered out of the car, helped her out, and had to lean against the car for support. I lit one of June's cigarettes and just waited for her to speak.

"You fucked up, huh?"

I smiled as I noticed how nervous she was. That would have been me if I didn't have liquid courage. I pulled her closer to me by her belt loop and answered her question before asking one of my own.

"Yeah, I'm really fucked up. So what about you? Are you not fucked up enough to let me do it?"

I watched her lips curl into a smile and waited.

"Let you do—"

"What do you think?" I asked, and then I leaned into her and covered her mouth with my lips. It didn't take her long to fall in line. I was not sure how long we were out there, but by the time I heard June calling my name, I was moments away from lifting her up and fucking her right there on the hood of the car. I loved how easygoing she was about my roaming hands. No matter where I touched her, she let me.

"Niya, it's late. Hit her up tomorrow," June said through the car window.

I kissed her lips one more time and pushed her away. I asked her to put her number in my phone before I got back in the car.

"You need to watch out for that girl. I heard some of the girls talking about her. They were calling her all types of thirsty bitches," June advised as he drove away from the curb.

"I bet they were. Did you see her?" I asked June.

"Yeah, I saw her. Just be careful. You're about to blow up, Niya. Once I drop this shit on the Net, your life is going to change. There are going to be a whole lot of folks out there who will wanna jump on for the ride. I've seen it a million times, and a bitch like that, they never change the formula. She's cool and all, but I can feel the thirst jumping off her ass."

We shared a laugh, but as we made small talk, I really thought about what he had said and decided that this whole Marlo thing was just going to be for fun. That is, if it turned out to be anything at all. When we got to my building, I looked at my phone and noticed another message from Jamilla. I didn't read it. I just didn't feel like dealing with everything that came with her in that moment. I had had one hell of a day, and I wanted to end it with just the feeling of satisfaction.

Chapter 39

Jamilla

I was out the door before her car came to a stop. I ran down the stairs and met her at the entrance.

"That's not happiness to see me," I said, borrowing a line from *A Perfect Murder*, which was one of my favorite movies.

"What are you doing out here so late?" Niya asked as she tried to walk without falling over.

"I need to talk to you. I have been calling you and texting you all day. Please, stop walking," I said as I tugged at her hand.

Once she got to the set of steps that were on her side of the building, she stopped and sat on the third one.

"I didn't really feel like talking to you," she confessed.

Damn. Her words kind of stung.

"Niya. This is not us. This is not what we do." I waited to see if my words would have any impact.

"Yeah, well, this is what we're about to do, 'cause I can't be chasing after no one."

I wasn't sure if it was the liquor talking, so I was going to try to ignore her harsh words. "Look, Niya, I . . . I love you. I need you in this moment, as I have always needed you since the day on the stoop." I was about to cry, so I stopped talking, hoping that silence would stop my tears from falling.

"See, there's the problem right there, Jamilla. You love me, but you need me more, and that's fucked up. The difference between us is that my love for you comes before my own selfish needs. Do you know how fucking hard it is to be around you, to see you, to even just be in the same fucking room with you, knowing that I can't have you? Well, I could have you, but you just won't let me. You're so hung up on not being gay that you just won't let yourself love the person."

"No, Niya, that's not it at all. I—"

"Yes the fuck it is. That shit that happened on campus today . . . man, that shit embarrassed the hell out of me. There I was, all proud and shit. I was standing there with the girl I love, and what does she do? She fucking crumbles as soon as someone thinks we're together." Niya looked away after she spoke. I was guessing to stop her own tears from falling. Once I saw the pain radiating from her eyes, I said, "Fuck it," and just let mine flow.

"Niya, please, you have to understand. I do love you, even more than I need you. Maybe I worded it wrong, but I do love you."

When she looked back up at me, her cheeks were wet too. "I would love for that to be true, Jamilla. I would damn near give my life for those words to be true, but they aren't. You need everything that I do for you, and don't get me wrong. I love that I am able to be there for you, but . . . what about me? Jamilla, my whole damn life has changed because of you, and that's both good and bad. Do you know how hard loving you is for me? I can't go a fucking second without thinking of you. Man . . ." Niya had to stop talking since her emotions were getting the best of her and were interrupting her speech. I cried right along with her and tried my best to get her to understand.

"Niya, this is all new to me. I have always been with men. I never even thought of a girl until I met you. That scares me. It's making me question the person I have always thought I was."

"What? A straight person?" Niya asked, and as she waited for me to answer, fear of the truth hit me and made me stumble a bit.

"I—I don't . . . I don't know what's going on, Niya. All I know is that I have always been straight. I have always liked boys, and here you come, forcing me to wonder if that's even the full truth."

For a while, we were silent. I stood in front of her with tearstained cheeks as she tried to dry her own eyes. There was just so much tension in the air, and neither of us knew how to make it go away.

"Jamilla, I love you. I do. But this shit here . . . it's not good for me. I just want you to be mine. I need you to love me the way that I love you. The sad part about that is, although I say these words, I know that it won't happen right now. Yeah, for some reason, I have faith that one day you'll wake up, but the not knowing how long I will have to wait . . ."

I kneeled down on the bottom step and leaned into her lap. I held her hand and rested my forehead against hers. "Niya, I love you with all my heart, but I just need for you to give me time. What happened in school today will never happen again. I am so sorry, Niya. I never want to hurt you. I can't promise you that you will get all that you want, but I can tell you that my love for you is true. And to keep things real, I need you in my life. Without you, I would be lost right now. It's because I have you that I didn't go crazy when my mom—"

Oh, shit. I stopped talking just in time, or so I thought. Niya's face went from sad and understanding to confused and angry, although she didn't know what had happened.

I thought about not telling her, but I realized that not telling her would only make the space between us grow wider. So I sat down beside her and held her hand as I told her every detail of the day my mother "tested" me.

"What the fuck?" Niya asked as she stood up and fell right back down again. "How could you not tell me this? I am going to fucking kill that bitch."

"Niya, no, please. That's why I didn't tell you. After what happened with my stepdad, I didn't want to find you in that same situation with my mother too. I know she's wrong, but that's still my mother."

"Man, fuck that bitch. A real mom wouldn't do no shit like that."

"Shhh. Niya, please calm down. I've lived through everything else, and I'll . . . I'll . . . live through this too." I lost it then. I threw my head into Niya's lap and just cried as flashes of that day danced before me.

"Oh, my God, Jamilla. Baby, I'm so sorry. You should have told me, Jamilla. You should have told me."

Niya held me as she ran her fingers through my hair. For a long while, I just cried in her arms. I needed to get rid of all the sadness that had entered me ever since that day. I was so filled with despair that Niya was the only one who could save me.

"Jamilla, we have to do something. How could she do that to you?"

Her voice had taken on a chilling note. I sat up, and when I looked into her eyes, they were just as cold.

"Niya, promise me that you won't do anything to my mom."

She was quiet, so I asked her again.

"Okay, okay, but if she tries to do anything to you, you need to call me and knock that bitch out, Mom or no Mom. Can we at least get Marie's ass? I can't believe she helped your mother hold you down."

"I don't want you to kill anyone, Niya. I mean it."

"Oh, I ain't gonna kill her. I won't touch a hair on the bitch, but she's gonna pay."

I would be lying if I said that I didn't want something to happen to Marie. To me, she was just as evil as her father.

"As long as she's not hurt too bad, do what you want."

Niya smiled and pulled me close again. "Let this be the last time you keep something from me. I don't care what it is, if you can't take a shit and you're constipated, you need to tell me."

We shared a laugh.

"Seriously, Milla boo. I will do anything for you, and you need to know that above everything, I am here for you."

I looked into her eyes and saw the truth. "I know, Niya. That's why I told you tonight, I don't want to hold anything from you, and doing that only adds stress. I love you too, and you need to know that I am here for you too."

She smiled and kissed my lips. The kiss was short and fast, and a little part of me wanted it to be longer, with more passion. I thought about throwing caution to the wind and kissing her the way that I wanted, but I knew that this would only add more confusion. Instead, I walked her to her apartment, got her into bed, and went back home. As I lay in my bed, thoughts of Niya were my bedtime stories.

Chapter 40

Niya

While getting ready to head out for another day of classes, I couldn't help but think of Jamilla. I was still seeing red from the night before. I had stayed up, thinking of ways to kill that bitch mother of hers but make it look like an accident. I wanted just to go up to her and choke the life out of her as I looked into her eyes, but I had made a promise to Jamilla. I did have plans for Marie, though. It wasn't going to take much to get her back. It would take a couple of days, but she was going to get hers.

"Mi amor, you have to eat before you go."

I kissed my granny and sat down at the kitchen table with her.

My grandmother sat across from me after serving me my breakfast and stared at me as I ate. "What's the problem with you?"

"Nothing, Granny."

She sucked her teeth and took a sip of her strong coffee. "Who raise you?" she asked, then waited for an answer that never came.

"Niya, mi amor, answer me, *mierda*."

I had to laugh. "You cussin' at me, Granny?"

"Why you not tell me what's wrong?"

I didn't answer her. I took one more bite of my breakfast and got up. I kissed her forehead.

"Mi amor, I love you with all my heart."

"Granny. Nothing is wrong."

"Okay. Fine. I will wait, because I know you like this," she said as she pointed to the back of her hand.

"Okay, Granny. Have a great day. I love you."

I walked out of the kitchen to her voice saying the words that were music to my ears.

"I love you always, mi amor."

I walked out of my apartment about twenty minutes early. I knew that Jamilla wouldn't be downstairs, so I used that time to speak with the "Get it done" dude. He was that nigga you went to when you needed a dirty deed taken care of. You paid him, he got it done, and you never spoke about it again. The funny thing was, he was always outside. No matter the time of day, if you were looking for him, you would find him. He was an older man, and I could only imagine the secrets he knew and kept to himself. After speaking to him about Marie, I went over to my car, looked down at my watch, and lit up a blunt. Jamilla would be out any minute, and as I waited for her, it happened.

"Yo, Niya. *Niya*."

I turned around to see my boy Trey running across the street, with June right beside him. When they got to me, Trey had his phone in his hand and a smile on his face.

"Yo, how come you ain't call a nigga? I would have showed up for the video shoot."

I looked at June like "Damn! You have a big mouth."

"I watched that shit on YouTube and—"

"You put it up already? When did you even have the time to edit it and post it?" I asked June as I pulled out my own phone. June smiled while pulling out his wireless device.

"I'm about to send you the link. I ain't even been to sleep yet 'cause of that video. I worked on it all morning."

I was only half listening to June as he spoke. I stared down at my phone, waiting for the link to appear. When it popped up, I was almost scared to click on it.

"What's going on?" Jamilla asked as she walked up to the car. I half hugged her before turning my attention back to my phone.

"Niya is about to check out the video I posted," June told her.

"What video?"

When I heard her question, I just wanted to scream, "Fuck. I forgot to tell you."

"The shit we shot for Niya's first song. Damn. How everyone know about it except for you two?" June said.

The look on Jamilla's face said it all. I knew she was hurt and shocked all at the same damn time.

"Go ahead, Niya. Watch it," she said.

I clicked on the link and waited. For the next four and a half minutes, my eyes were glued to the screen of my phone, and Jamilla didn't look away, either. I could hear June and Trey making comments, but I could not hear them clearly. My mind was solely on the video. I didn't know if I could put into words exactly how I felt. My heart danced like it had never danced before. I was watching me; I was watching my dreams unfold right in front of me. I knew that it was just an Internet video, but to me, right in that moment, it was as if I was a star. I listened to the words of the song, I watched as I rapped them, and if this hadn't been caught on video, I would have thought that I had dreamed it all. I wanted to cry, but I couldn't let my boys see me do that.

"Niya, scroll down and check the views," June said.

And when I did, my mouth fell open.

"How in the hell does this shit have ten thousand views already? What time did you post it?" I asked.

"Man, I posted it early this morning and stayed up posting that shit all over the Net. Facebook, Twitter . . . I even posted the link on Instagram. While you're on your college shit, I am going to send it out to the underground magazines and anywhere music is found. We about to blow up, baby. Just watch."

I was speechless. When I looked at Jamilla again, her frown had turned into a smile. I could tell that she was happy for me. She took my phone and watched the video again, this time with a better view. We all stood around her just to get another look at it too. I watched her smile throughout the video, just not during the parts with Marlo. When she was done, she handed me back my phone and hugged me while whispering in my ear.

"That's really good, Niya. I'm so happy for you, but I wish I'd been there."

It was as if I felt my heart crack a little bit. I was happy for myself, but I knew that out of all the people, Jamilla should have been there.

I said good-bye to June and Trey, and they went on their way. Jamilla and I got in the car, and as I drove, I tried to find the right words to say.

"Jamilla, I'm sorry. You're right. You should have been there. I could do the video over if you want."

She looked at me with no emotion on her face.

"If I *want*? No, keep it as is. The video is hot. You did a great job."

After that, I left it alone.

Chapter 41

Jamilla

How could I let her know that I was heartbroken, shocked even? What in the fuck was going on with us? Yes, she'd been mad, but damn, she hadn't even called me and told me to come by. She hadn't even told me the night before, as I cried in her arms. That was not us. Well, it wasn't what we had been. I was starting to feel like I was losing what I had just found. It seemed as if we had found each other not too long ago, but we were already pulling away from one another. It was scaring me. I was losing control too fast; I was losing her too soon. The scariest part was that I didn't know why.

It seemed as if people were just waiting for us to pull up. As soon as Niya parked her car and got out, people were crowding around her. There was a chorus of "I saw your video," "You look so good," and "Oh my God, I didn't even know you could rap." Before I knew it, I was fighting my way through the crowd just to get to her. She reached for my hand and pulled me through the would-be groupie bitches, male and female. I took one look at Niya and knew that she was overwhelmed. We made our way around campus as more and more people shouted to her and rushed in to get close to her. We found an empty lecture hall, went in, pulled the door closed, and she looked like she was finally able to breathe.

"Are you okay?" I asked as I watched her chest rise and fall with what I thought was relief.

"Yo, that shit was weird. What the fuck was that?"

I smiled a little bit. It was cute to see her scared. "That's going to be your life."

She looked at me with horror in her eyes. I walked over to her and let my hand rest on her shoulder. I looked at her, and as I played with her ponytail, I tried to get her to understand.

"Niya, this is only community college. If you want this, to be a star, to be a rapper, this will be your life, times one hundred. You are going to have to learn to deal with this."

"I know. I know that, Jamilla, I just wasn't ready. I just needed to wrap my head around it all. That video just went up today and look," Niya said, then pointed at the door. It was as if she knew, because just as she pointed, Marlo walked in.

"Hey, boo. People told me where I could find you. They are loving the video. Damn. I feel like a star," Marlo said. Then she threw her arms around Niya's neck and kissed her.

I didn't know what was more shocking: the fact that Marlo had just barged into the lecture hall, the fact that she had walked up to Niya, thrown her arms around Niya's neck, and kissed her, or the fact that she had just said that she felt like a star and Niya had smiled when she said it.

"You already have twelve thousand views," Marlo announced.

"*What*? It was only ten thousand when we left home this morning," Niya said as she pulled out her phone.

I was kind of stuck. I really didn't know what to say.

"Hey, Jamilla, girl. You see me in that video? That shit look sexy, huh?" Marlo winked at me as if we were on the same page. She was smiling and acting self-centered, while I was mean mugging and feeling confused. Hell no, we were not on the same page.

"Look, boo, you need to stop hiding in this room and go out and talk to people. They are showing mad love," Marlo told Niya.

As I stood there, for some shameful reason, I asked God not to let Niya find the strength to walk out of that lecture hall. I was the one who was supposed to help her overcome her fear, not a half-dressed skank who had just stepped into her life . . . for the moment.

Niya turned to me, and with a smile, she stated, "You know what, Milla boo? I think she's right."

With those words, a knife went into my heart and turned a bit. What in the hell did Niya mean when she said *she* was right? I was the one who d just told her to face her fears head-on.

I watched Marlo take her hand and pulled her toward the door. As I stood there looking at her back as Niya, my Niya, walked hand in hand with Marlo, something hit me. It crashed into me, like a wall devouring a car going at a speed of over 150 miles per hour. The truth in that moment acted like a three-hundred-pound bitch in heels, and she just sat her big ass right on top of my heart. The truth was . . . the truth was . . . Shit, I couldn't even say it to myself. I waited for Niya and Marlo to exit the room, just so I could have a seat and wallow in my undeniable truth. I wanted to cry, I wanted to run after Niya, and I wanted to stand there and tell her the truth, the truth I just couldn't face. Just as I gave up hope on being remembered, Niya turned around and held out her hand to me.

"Come on, Milla boo. You know I can't do this without you."

Hearing those words sent me into a fit of tears. I cried so hard, my chest hurt. I tried so hard to hold it back, but I just couldn't. To this day, I was not sure why I broke down, although I had a few ideas. I thought that maybe just when I figured she'd forgotten me, just when I thought that the only person who saw me couldn't see me anymore, she turned around and did just that. Not only did she see me, but she needed me too, and that feeling, to be needed by the person you felt the most for . . . there was nothing like it in this whole wide world.

She came over to me as my knees buckled. She got on her knees as well, dropping to my level, the level of desperation and emptiness, and she filled me back up.

"Jamilla, babe, what's wrong?"

I tried to tell her, but my sobbing came from so deep within me that my language of anguish was incomprehensible. She held me as I let all the doubt about myself, about her, and about us escape my body. I tried so hard to leave it on that floor where we stood. One thing I could say about Marlo was that she came over and looked just as concerned as Niya did. They both asked me what was wrong, but with Marlo so close now, I no longer wanted to answer. I did manage to get myself together, though. Marlo let me borrow her sunglasses, and with me right by Niya's side, we left the lecture hall to greet her new fans.

Chapter 42

Niya

Three weeks into this music shit and I was killing it. Well, I was starting a little buzz for myself. The video was doing great and had over seventy-five thousand views so far. The next song that I was going to drop was going to be "The Problems," the song that June had liked but hadn't thought was right for a first single.

It was a Friday night, and I was in Rodney's basement. This time, Jamilla was with me. She had never really spoken about what the breakdown she had had was about. I had tried to speak to her about it, but she would just say that for a brief moment, she had cracked, and that I had come in and saved her . . . as I always did. No matter what it was, I knew that I had to try to keep her close. I had never told her, but she'd scared me that day. Her cries had been so deep, so full. It had seemed as if she was crying out for help, but the truth was, I didn't know how to help her. All I could do was offer her my love and be there for her in any way I could.

"So, are you going to be the lead in this video?"

I had been wanting to ask Jamilla that all day and hadn't known how. I thought that she was perfect for it, because the song was about her. I had a gay girl problem, while she was dealing with her "straight" girl problem. I watched as her eyes bulged; she looked petrified.

"I am not a video ho," she joked, but I knew that there was way more to it.

"Come on, Milla boo. I really want you to be the lead in this one. I wrote it with you in mind."

She sat there for a minute before asking to see the paper I had written the lyrics on. Once she'd read them over, she shook her head violently.

"Oh, hell no. What will I look like being in a video with you talking about her need for pussy is starting to blossom?"

I had to laugh at that one. First, because the line was funny, and secondly, because the shit was true.

"When are you going to let this shit go, Jamilla? No one fucking cares what you are . . . well . . . besides you."

Chapter 43

Jamilla

I wanted to be in her video—hell, I would have been in the first one—but reading the line "as her need for pussy is starting to blossom" kind of had me rethinking even wanting to be in any of the videos. I was fine with everything else, but that one line . . . it got to me. So, I just sat there, smoking and drinking one cup full of Cîroc after the other, and just thought about things as Niya put the finishing touches on her song. I was in the land of the lost when I heard Niya talking to June.

"Nah, she said she doesn't want to do it. Just call one of them bad bitches from the other video and have them come through."

As I watched June turn to leave, it was as if my mouth spoke from the heart and not from my brain.

"I will do it," I declared.

They all stopped, looked at each other, and then to me.

"What did you just say?" Niya asked as she stared at me.

"I said . . . I'll do it. Are we filming today?"

Niya turned to June as we all waited for the answer. June asked to see the lyrics to the song, and then he read them over and took a second to think about things.

"Can we film this one in your room? Rodney was telling me that your joint is kinda hot, with all the posters and shit. That would be hot," June said as he played with his phone.

After Niya gave the okay, they all turned to me. I had only one thing to say.

"Let's go."

As we headed out the door, Rodney put his arm around my neck and said, "Now that you said yes, there's no backing out. I will tie you to her bed if I have to. You are way hotter than that other chick, so I am not letting you go."

I smiled and stepped out of his house. I waited for him to lock the door as Niya and June walked ahead.

June and Rodney had taken a good forty-five minutes to set everything up. As Niya and I waited on the couch for them to call us in, more smoke and liquor flowed through my body.

"You sure you want to do this? You seem kind of nervous," Niya said.

I laughed and leaned into her. She was right beside me, with her skin against mine. Her cologne was intoxicating, and I wanted to get closer to her.

"You can tell, huh? Well, as I thought about it, I thought about all the actors who have played gay characters. Some were straight and had no problem playing a gay role, so fuck it."

"So you're gonna get your *Brokeback Mountain* on, huh?"

We both laughed.

"You know what, Niya? I want you to know that I love you more than I could ever need you."

We locked eyes for a second, and the tension was thick. With me so close to her, her arm around my neck, and her lips so close, she broke the tension and started to laugh.

"You, you're fucked up," she told me.

I stared at her smiling lips and could think of doing only one thing.

"Yeah, I am. So what?"

She laid her head back and let it rest against the couch. *Damn.* I couldn't take being so close to her and not doing the one thing I wanted to do so badly.

"Niya?"

"Yes, Jamilla boo?"

Oh my God, she was so close. She was the only thing in view. She and her little peach-colored lips, her long, curly hair pulled back in a ponytail, her fitted hat. Even her damn jeans and T-shirt turned me on. She was so fucking perfect, from her head to her Jordans.

"I love you."

She smiled again, and that shit sent shock waves through my body.

"I love you too. I love you more than life itself."

That did it. I leaned into her, and at first, I kissed her lips softly. She pulled away—I guessed from amazement—but with one look into my eyes, she seemed to know what I wanted. When our mouths met again, a small moan escaped mine. It was as if I had been destitute, without a home, without a hope in the world, deprived of love. But when I felt her lips again, my luck had changed. I was now rich, not with money, but with love. I was rich with everything that I had been missing. It was as if, because of her, I was alive. Because of that kiss, I lived.

Our tender kiss became more aggressive as the need for more of her, the need for more of Niya, drove the reality of my sexuality home. My need for pussy was blossoming right before my eyes, and in that moment, I didn't give a shit. I wanted her, yes, and I needed her, and I loved her so damn much. The whole "I'm straight" thing seemed to fly out the window, and I kissed her as if I was really ready to let go of all the denial.

"Niya, Jamilla, we're ready," June called from the bedroom.

While I was in her embrace, it was as if the world slowed down to the pace of our beating hearts. I pulled away from Niya's lips reluctantly, and this time, it was my turn to ask.

"Are you ready?"

She stood up, took my hand, and said, "Hell, fucking yes."

The lights were low at first. Throughout the video, they would go from using a red light to a black light to a flashing strobe. The whole point of the video was that I was fighting what I was feeling. So we started out shooting the strained scenes, the scenes where I was fighting the fact that I loved this woman, and that came easy to me. She would pull me close; I would pull away. She would try to kiss me, and I would stand up and go sit in the chair, but soon the fight in me would lessen. My need for Niya was overpowering, and not just in the video.

The second half was what I enjoyed filming the most. Everything just came together so easily. Kissing her, being on top of her, letting her pull off my clothes, rubbing my body against hers, it all was just so easy. We were so free, so wild. The funny thing was that as Niya stayed in character and made sure to mouth her lyrics, I was totally gone. I had forgotten why I was there, and to me, this was real.

As Niya slipped on top of me, I opened my legs and enjoyed her. I pulled her into me, and the place between my legs throbbed. I kissed her and let her tongue leave my mouth and make its way to my neck. I moaned, and I took her hand from my breast and pushed it down. I pushed it past my belly button and let it rest between my legs. I wanted to scream when I felt the pressure of her thumb through my pants.

"Fuck that. Take them off," I demanded.

"Whoa, whoa. Do you want us to leave?"

Oh shit. I had been flung back into reality by Rodney's voice.

"No, no. Are we done?" I asked as I sat up and pushed Niya off of me.

The room was quiet, and no one answered.

"Hello. Are we done?" I asked again.

"Um, we just need some shots of you alone and a few of Niya," Rodney replied.

"Well, hurry up. I have to go home," I mumbled.

Just like that, my mood had changed. Hearing Rodney's voice had brought me back from what had felt like a dream world. I was a little embarrassed at how loose I had probably seemed to the two men. Niya must have sensed my shift in mood, because she didn't say much as they filmed my solo shots. She just sat there and smoked.

Chapter 44

Niya

There really wasn't much to say. I knew what had happened, and after our beautiful day, I just didn't feel like addressing that shit. Instead, I just sat and watched her. She was so damn beautiful, and just the thought of having her for that very brief moment was enough. After she finished her solo shoot, I walked her to the door and took the time to let her know that things were okay.

"Thank you for doing this, Jamilla."

She gave me a weak smile and said, "You're welcome. I can't wait to see it. Call me later?"

I didn't answer her. I just leaned out the door, and with my right hand, I pulled her into me from her waist.

"I meant what I said. I love you, boo," I told her.

She got close, with no rejection of my affection. I felt her take in a deep breath and heard her say that she loved me too.

That was when we heard it, loud screaming, the kind that either brought you out of your apartment or kept you in it out of fear.

"Yo, you hear that?"

Rodney had come out of my bedroom, and after he uttered this question, we all headed out the door. I was leading the pack and was the first one to lay eyes on the action. Once on-site, I stopped everyone behind me and motioned for them to stay quiet. When I looked around and saw that we were the only ones watching, I motioned for Jamilla to step up and peep around the stairway. I watched her, because I didn't want to miss her reaction. As we stood there, I tried my hardest to understand her facial expressions, but I couldn't. As she watched the three girls kick, punch, and slap Marie, it was as if she was just staring into air. She didn't come out of her trance until the three girls held Marie down, pulled down her pants, and one of the girls asked for the bat.

"Niya, we have to stop them," she said, with her eyes still on the action.

"Are you sure? Marie deserves this, all of it," I said, a little disappointed. I wanted them to take that bat and shove it right up her cunt. I wanted them to ruin her insides to the point where she wouldn't be able to have children. I wanted her to go through life knowing that her own actions had caused her inability to procreate.

"Yes, stop them now."

I stepped out from behind the wall slowly, with Rodney, June, and Jamilla behind me.

"Ladies, ladies, let me," I said as I walked up to the girls and held my hand out for the bat. "Jamilla, come stand by me."

I waited for Jamilla to join me. Then I asked the three girls to sit Marie up so that she was facing her stepsister. She was bloody, with damn near everything on her face bleeding.

"I know about that nasty-ass shit you helped Jamilla's mother do to her. Now I'm about to take this bat and shove it up your ass," I growled.

Like clockwork, Marie started to beg.

"Don't beg me. Beg her. My mind's made up. I'm about to fuck you nice and deep with this bitch." I looked over to my right. "Go watch the door and make sure that no one comes in the building," I said to Rodney.

He looked shocked as hell, but he still followed my directions. Once he was in place, I pressed the bat against her opening.

"Jamilla, please don't let her do this. Please!" Marie pleaded.

"Shut up, bitch. Who was there to stop you when you and Jamilla's mom held her down?" I asked as I added pressure to her slit.

"I will never do that again. Please, no, Jamilla! Please."

I looked over at Jamilla and held the bat up to her. "Take it and do what you want with it, but hurry."

Jamilla took the bat from me and walked up to her stepsister and just stared at her.

"Come on, Milla boo. We gotta wrap this up," I urged.

Finally, she spoke. "Get up," she demanded.

Once Marie was on her feet, Jamilla spoke again. "Let this be a warning and a thought that you must never forget. Always remember that it was me that saved you from a bat being shoved up your ass. When you think of what could've happened today, just remember that it was me, the girl you held down. The girl whom you smiled at as her own mother violated her. Remember that it was the girl whom your father has been molesting who saved you on this day. Now go."

I watched as Marie started to walk away, and felt that she was getting off too easy. "Ay, you, bitch. When you get home, make sure to wash your ass. You fucking smell like rotting fish. Nasty-ass bitch," I yelled.

Everyone fell into laughter except for Jamilla and me. I just continued to mean mug Marie, but inside, I was beaming. I had added insult to injury on purpose. The feeling of being laughed at would last longer than her black eye.

"As a matter of fact, Jamilla is coming with you," I told Marie. "When you get upstairs, you are going to say that you were jumped and you don't know by who. You are going to say that they would have killed you if Jamilla hadn't run up and fought them off."

I walked over to Jamilla, ripped her shirt, and pushed Marie toward her side of the building. I told everyone else they could go home.

Chapter 45

Jamilla

I felt like I was in the twilight zone. My mother and stepdad thanked Niya and me for saving Marie's life and treated us like royalty. I couldn't help but stand there and wonder if they would have reacted the same way if the shoe were on the other foot. If it were me who had come in all battered, would they have cared as much?

"We have to call police! Look at her. They almost kill her!" my mother said as she reached for her phone.

Niya shook her head. "No, I wouldn't do that. As they ran off, they said that if she called the cops, they would come back for her. Just take care of her, and we will keep an eye on her when she leaves the house."

Niya was quick on her feet when it came to responding to my mother. After talking it over with my stepdad, they decided not to call the cops, but something told me by the way he was looking at Niya, my stepdad wasn't buying our story 100 percent. So as my mother took care of Marie, I eased out of the apartment with Niya. We headed to her place. I needed to cloud my brain with smoke and drown my thoughts in liquor.

I hadn't said much to Niya as we sat in her room. I had mixed emotions about what had gone down, like I always did. Again, she was super "save a ho," and that meant the world to me, but on the other hand, the degree to which she did things was extreme.

"What are you thinking about?" she asked as she looked dead at me. I was on the desk chair, and she was on her bed. She had on jeans and had taken off her shirt. Her sports bra showed off her abs, and it was distracting.

"I'm thinking about you," I said as the alcohol and weed acted as a truth serum.

"Oh yeah?" she asked as she got up and sat on the edge of her bed. She reached out and pulled the desk chair over to her, sitting me front and center before her and between her legs. My body instantly tensed up as thoughts of her video shoot just that afternoon ran through my mind. I took the blunt from her fingers and inhaled.

"Just thinking about you and how much I love you. I also thought of how much the dark side of you scares me," I revealed.

At first she was smiling, but by the end of my last sentence, her smile had gone stale.

"I don't ever want you to be afraid of me. I would never hurt you. Understand?" As she asked this, she leaned into me and kissed my lips. The kiss was fast and could have been mistaken for a friendly peck, but deep down inside, I hoped not.

She went on. "I won't lie to you, but I will not think twice about killing anyone who hurt you. But me hurt you? Never." Again, another small, fast kiss. Her lamp was on low, and the music in the background wasn't rap, for a change. Alice Smith's voice hung in the air like the thick smoke that filled our lungs as she sang "Fool for You."

So there we were, me feeling like a fool in many ways. A fool because she was right in front of me, the woman that I loved, yet I still wouldn't allow her to be mine. A fool because I was fighting what I really was. A fool because although I should have known the truth, I was still very confused about who I was and what I wanted.

"Niya . . ."

"Jamilla?" she answered.

I couldn't let go of what was obstructing the truth. So I sipped and I smoked.

"Jamilla, tell me." Niya was right in front of me and made me feel as if she was reading my thoughts. "Jamilla, say it," she said as she pulled me even closer to her.

Still, I said nothing.

"You are going to tell me what you were about to say." She removed the cup from my hand and took the blunt away from me. She smoked as I sat there uncomfortably. "Why are you so afraid?"

"What am I afraid of?" I asked, hoping that she could let me in on my own fears.

"Why are you so afraid to love me . . . the way you *really* love me, huh?"

Inside I was screaming, *Oh shit. Oh shit. Oh shit.* But I answered, "I just don't know."

She looked at me for a brief moment, and when I felt her hand in my hair, I wanted to find out where this was about to go.

"Oh, you don't know?" Niya asked as I felt her finger roaming through the back of my hair. "Is this going to help you?" she asked, and then she pulled me in close to her and kissed my lips. "Tell me, Jamilla, do you know now?"

Another wet and delicious kiss. My body was begging my mind, asking it to throw caution to the wind. Her lips left mine and traveled down my neck. She was rough, she was intense, and she acted as if she would do whatever it took to get an answer out of me.

"Tell me what the fuck you were about to say, Jamilla."

I tried to speak the truth, but it just wouldn't come out.

"So . . ." A kiss. "You want to play this game with me?" Another kiss. "Jamilla, I am going to get this shit out of you even if that means fucking it out of you."

Now her kiss was long, wet, and forceful. She stood me up while our mouths wrestled to the sounds of Melanie Fiona's "Bones."

I needed to feel her. I needed to have her. I needed to have her love me. So after we landed on the bed, I let things go further than I should have. As she kissed me, she flipped me on my back, slipped her hands down my pants, and demanded an answer.

"What were you going to say?" she asked as her fingers met my clit, and even if I had wanted to, I wouldn't have been able to answer. "Look at you, eyes all rolling to the back of your fucking head. Tell me. Tell me what you were about to say."

The funny thing was, she was asking me to answer, yet her mouth constantly covered mine. The faster she moved her hand, the more open I became about telling her the words that were stuck on my tongue just a few minutes before.

"Go on. That's right, Milla boo. Tell me, baby. Just go on and tell me."

As my body was pulled to the edge with her skillful handiwork, I let it out. "Niya, baby, Niya."

"Say that shit."

I wasn't ready, but I had to . . . *Oh shit.* I was about to cum, and so were my words. I was about to ejaculate verbally the one thing that I just didn't want to release.

"Niya, oh fuck. Yes, Niya . . ."

"Fuck, Jamilla. Just say that shit."

I looked into her eyes, and I just couldn't hold back anymore. My body, my mind, my spirit were being taunted by her carnal powers. Sexually, she had defeated me, but mentally, I would still be the winner in the game of denial.

I reached up and pulled her lips to mine. Between kisses I said, “Niya, baby, I’m about to cum, baby.”

“Yes, Jamilla. Say it, baby.”

“Oh, *fuck*. I’m cumming. Shit. Fuck.”

“And?”

The answer never came, although I was sure we both knew what it was.

Chapter 46

Niya

It was crazy. She lay on my bed, sweaty, satisfied, and looked as if she has just seen a damn ghost. The air was filled with relief on my end, but I wasn't so sure about hers. My body had relaxed after hearing the truth after all this damn time. Sadly, though, as I looked at her, I saw that all pleasure had left her body after she came. She just lay there, staring at the ceiling, and said nothing. I was afraid to speak, afraid that I would say the wrong thing. So I waited for her to declare her stance on her revelations.

"I'm thirsty," were her first words. I got off the bed, went into the bathroom, washed my hands, and came back with a bottle of water. She took it from me and sat up as I got back on the bed. Her back was to me as she sipped her drink. I sat with my back against the wall and watched her from behind. I watched her back rise and fall as she took in and exhaled deep, long breaths.

"Jamilla, are you okay?"

"Yeah . . . I'm fine." She took another deep breath and still just sat there.

"Jamilla, look at me." I touched her back, but she pulled away, as if my touch was no longer needed.

"Niya, listen, what I just said—"

"Aw, hell no. We are not about to do this shit. It doesn't matter what you said or didn't say. We know the fucking truth." I could feel my face turning red. She was starting to piss me off.

"I wasn't going to say . . . I just, I just—"

"You just what, Jamilla?" I asked as I rolled my eyes. I was getting tired of her shit. Just when I thought that we had finally had a breakthrough, she wanted to take ten fucking steps back.

"I don't want you to think that what happened changed anything. I . . . I still don't think that I could really be with a woman."

I jumped off that bed and within seconds was on my feet. "What the fuck do you mean? Man, you know what? Forget it. Honestly, I'm sick of this shit. Do what you want, say what you want, and feel how you want. This game you're playing is called solitaire, 'cause I'm not joining in."

"That's a real fucked-up thing to say. Why the fuck can't you understand what I am going through? Look how long it took you to face the truth about who you really are."

"Really? You are trying to compare me to you? I have known that I liked girls for some time now. I didn't go around hiding it. I just didn't speak on it."

Jamilla started to laugh, and that shit boiled my blood. "So when Rodney called you out on the street, you didn't say that you weren't gay?" she said.

The stare off began. I was trying to think back to that night, but anger wouldn't let me take a trip back down memory lane.

"Look, you are going to have to face the fact that you like girls sooner or later. Whatever you do, stop using me as a crutch to lean on. 'Finger fuck me, Niya, but I'm not gay.' 'I love you, Niya, but I'm not gay.' Bitch, you *are* gay."

I didn't mean to call her a bitch, but fuck it. I was mad.

"*Bitch*? You are going to call me a bitch 'cause I won't admit to something I am not even sure of? Fuck you, bitch. Fucking dyke-ass bitch. How fucking dare you?"

I had to look away from her to stop myself from slapping her clear across the face. I was at my breaking point, and for some reason, I knew that it would take a while for things to get back to normal between us.

"Now ain't that the dyke calling the dyke . . . a dyke. Yeah, I'm a lesbian, but I can face my truth," I snapped. "How about you? You sure it's not getting too tight in that 'straight' box you're trying to fit into? You sure that the 'straight' air ain't suffocating you? Yeah, I'm gay, but at the end of my day . . . I know just who the fuck I am. I'm not a wannabe straight girl who likes to get finger popped by a full-fledged pussy-eating lesbian."

I got real close to her face and held her chin so that she would look directly into my eyes. "You are a fucking dyke, a lesbian, and no matter how you word it . . . that's what the fuck you are. Now, deal with that shit all on your own. I'm done. You say you love me. Well, now you are going to have to prove that shit. I think that I have done my part. Now it's time to show and prove on your end."

"Fuck you, Niya. Get the hell off of me," was all she said.

I looked around the room, grabbed my phone, and left her ass sitting right there on my damn bed. That shit was for the birds. I loved the girl with every fucking thing I had in me, but goddamn!

Chapter 47

Jamilla

She walked out, and to me, that was the ultimate disrespect. I wasn't sure if what I had just said was the truth or was built on emotions or not. Truth was, I had found myself looking at Rodney harder than I should have. He was cute, and for a few seconds while at his house, I had noticed him in a way I had never done before. It was quick, and I don't think anyone caught it, but he had made a joke, and when he'd smiled, it just made me stop for a minute. So with that feeling, how could I be a lesbian? I had never felt that way about women, just Niya. However, the feeling Rodney had given me with just a quick smile, I felt all the time for men.

The messed-up part about it was that Niya just wasn't giving me enough time to deal with my feelings. Why was it that not only Niya but the whole fucking world always wanted to put labels on people? Why couldn't we just live and love without having to be called gay, straight, or bi? That was so ridiculous to me. She had gone through that same damn thing in front of everyone, so you would think that she would understand. Everyone needed to do things at their own pace, in their own time, but no. She wanted to know things right away. Plus, she'd called me a bitch. That was the worst part of it all. Niya was an emotional creature, but above everything, she should know that I loved her. I tried my best always to tell her and always to show her, but still, she wanted me to pick a side, and I just wasn't ready for that.

At first, as I sat in her room, almost afraid to move, I felt as if she could still see me, see all my insecurities. I swore I wasn't trying to hurt her. I just needed time. I knew that in some ways I was wrong for letting her touch me, but I needed her touch. Being around her always did that to me: it made me want her in ways that I knew might not be right. Soon I decided to pour myself a cup of Cîroc. Under the bottle was one of her notebooks. I picked it up and found a blank page. I sat in her room, and everything I saw reminded me of the woman that I loved. I could smell her cologne in the air, her clothes that hung in her closet reminded me of her style, and her bed reminded me of what had just gone down. I picked up the pen that was on her night table and tried to write down my feelings.

Close to you . . .

Close to you, I feel safe. You feel like home; you feel like this is right where I should be. Tonight I watched you, and you were on top of me. I watched you breathe and thanked God for giving you life. Niya, my love, you are my world. You are the reason I love. Yes, Niya, I love you. Yes, Niya, I need you. And yes, one day I will have you. Just wait. Just wait for me to figure all of this out. I know what I feel, and I also know what I am fighting, but all I ask is that you wait for me. Trust in me, trust in our love, and just know that you will not wait for too long.

Damn. You're so fucking beautiful. Did you feel it? Did you feel when I leaned in and kissed your lips as you slept the other night? Today what you did for me, it gave me chills. Chills because I see what you are capable of, and chills because what you are capable of doing . . . was all done for me. The way you fight for me, even when I can't fight for myself, the way that you love me, even when I fight to push you away, this doesn't go unnoticed. See, when you sleep with me right next to you, I get wet. Wet because just the sight of you turns me on, wet because as you sleep, I want to wake you up so you can make love to me.

But . . . but . . . but . . . there are too many buts. There are too many reasons—reasons for us not to be, reasons that we can't be—but the reason we shouldn't be just makes me want to be with you . . . but just not right now. One day, Niya, one day I pray I figure it all out. See, Niya, I love you. I love you way more than I need you.

When I was done, I left the notebook open on her bed so that she could see what I had written, and then I went home. That night I stayed up, finished my book, and thought about Niya.

Chapter 48

Niya

I didn't do much that night I left. I called Marlo to see if she could come out, but she said she was out in Jersey, visiting her father. Since she wasn't available, I hit up Rodney, and he told me to come over to his place. I just needed someone to talk to, and he was a friend. When I got to his spot, he told me that he had been working on some new beats and needed to finish one up before he could take a break. So I sat on his couch in the basement, watched him work, and thought about Jamilla.

Touching her had been paradise. Being so close to her and feeling her as she let go of all her inhibitions was . . . it was . . . Damn, that shit was love. I had paid attention to everything about her as she opened up and let me inside. Yes, her body had felt good under me. Her wetness on my fingers had sent chills through my body, and her moaning had elevated it all, but it meant so much more than the physical. For the first time, I felt like she had let down her guard when it came to her sexuality.

Sure she had freaked off with Smiley, but this time around, she'd been so open to it all. Honestly, as I thought about her emotionally, physically, and mentally, I started to get turned on. I sat there thinking about fucking her, really fucking her. I had yet to taste her, and the truth was, I always held back from that. It was as if by touching her only with my fingers, I wasn't going all the way. I knew that if I tasted her, tasted her flavor, there would be no going back for me. I was already in love with her, so to me, going all the way could possibly turn her out, but . . . what if it didn't? Would I be stuck loving a straight girl for the rest of my life and never be able to have her?

"So, what's wrong Niya?"

I looked at Rodney as he came over to the couch. I twisted the top off of my bottle and smiled.

"Who said that there was something wrong. I just can't chill with my nigga?"

The smirk on Rodney's face let me know that he wasn't buying my shit. "Niya, come on now. Spill it."

I sat back and just let it all out. Afterward, Rodney asked, "So, is she gay?"

I sucked my teeth and threw my hands up. "Nigga, you tell me. Your guess is as good as mine."

"So wait. She does like dudes?" Rodney was asking questions I just couldn't answer.

"Man, I'm telling you, I really don't know. She says she straight but lets me finger fuck her until she cums."

"Yo, I was watching you two during the shoot, and I thought for sure she was gay, but the way she acted after . . . Man, I just don't know."

"That bullshit blows the hell out of me, man. I wish she would just pick a side and just stay there. Gay, straight, or bi."

"So what are you going to do, Niya? Are you going to try to hold on, or are you just done?"

I sat there thinking. If I could have Jamilla the way I wanted her, I would hold on for dear life, but this shit, this shit was killing me.

"I want to say that I am done, but I don't know, man."

"So . . . what if she started fucking with someone else, like a guy? Would that change how you feel?"

Rodney's last question made me look at him sideways. "Look, man, if she's straight, it's gonna suck, but I will have to respect that." I watched Rodney to see if what I was picking up was right, but I saw nothing there.

"So . . . I just want to tell you—"

My phone started to ring, cutting Rodney off.

"Oh shit. It's White Boy. I don't even feel like dealing with this dude right now."

"Go ahead and pick it up. Let's make this money, instead of sitting here thinking about Jamilla."

I picked up my phone, got an address, and found out how much drugs to bring. White Boy's flunky spoke fast and got straight to the point.

Rodney and I got to the meeting place with White Boy, and once we greeted him, I realized that he wasn't feeling too friendly.

"Where the fuck you two been? Y'all ain't up to making this money?" White Boy groused.

I could see that my being MIA for the past few weeks wasn't to his liking. I had made Jamilla a promise and was working on keeping it. Plus, I was feeling the music thing more than I thought I would.

"Nah, we just been busy. You can always get shit off of another nigga, that is, if you don't like the wait," I replied.

Having to make these runs was becoming a nuisance. Dealing with White Boy at times drained me. I had never really trusted him, and the info he had on me was unsettling. He laughed at my last statement as he smoked his Black & Mild.

"Oh, so that's how it is, huh, nigga? I can go elsewhere?"

I didn't answer him verbally, but the smirk on my face and the rise of my eyebrow let him know that my answer was yes.

"See how people get?" he asked one of his men. "They get a little shine, and all of a sudden 'You can go elsewhere.'" White Boy pulled out his phone and started playing "Team Take Yo' Bitch." "Yeah, you sounding real good. You about to blow up, huh?"

I didn't answer his question. Instead, I asked my own. "Man, can we get this over with or what?"

"Aw, what's the matter, Niya? You don't want to talk about your new venture?"

My quick temper was about to show itself. "Not when it don't have shit to do with you."

I was looking right at him, and my stance told him that I wasn't backing down. He started to laugh, and his goons joined him.

"You are a silly little girl. What makes you think that your music career won't have anything to do with me? Bitch, I own you."

It took me a minute to realize that White Boy was talking to me.

"What in the fuck did you just say?"

I reached for the gun on my waist while his men reached for theirs. Rodney jumped in front of me, with his hands in the air, and tried to calm the situation down.

"Whoa, okay? Everybody should just calm the fuck down."

My heart was racing, as if it would beat out of my chest. I was so enraged that I was ready just to let the bullets fly. I might not make it out alive, but it would feel great to put a bullet in his ghost-white ass.

"She better hand over that fucking gun before I get upset," White Boy said to Rodney. At first, I wasn't going to budge, but common sense kicked in when I looked around the room and saw that I was outnumbered. Rodney took the gun from me and stepped back. White Boy put out his cigar and walked over to me slowly.

"After what I did for you, you will always be in debt, understood?" he said.

I didn't answer. I just scrunched up my face and let the anger I felt on the inside rest on my lip as it curled up.

"Bitch, you think I'm playing with you?" he snarled. White Boy's hand was around my neck, and as Rodney tried to come to my aid, one of White Boy's men grabbed him. "Now listen to me and listen to me good. Outside of this drug shit, I want twenty-five percent of whatever you make on this music shit. You will pay me until the day you die. Now, I can make that sooner if you would like."

As I struggled for air, I managed to give him a response Niya style. "Fu-fuck you."

He laughed and squeezed tighter. Looking at Rodney, he said, "You better talk to your friend. As soon as she signs that first contract and starts doing shows, I want my money." With that, he let me go. "Now, get your fucking money, leave my drugs, and get the fuck out of here."

It took everything that I had in me not to go balls out and kill him right then and there. He was a brave man, and as Rodney and I headed out the door, his voice stopped us.

"See, I'm a fair guy. I pay for my drugs."

With my back turned to him, the roar of laughter from him and his two men came crashing down on me. I knew right away that White Boy was a dead man.

"Are you okay?" Rodney asked as I sped to his house.

"Yeah, I'm cool. It's just that White Boy got a lot of fucking nerve. I can't believe that he put his hands on me."

"Don't worry. We will find a way to take care of that nigga," Rodney answered as he lit a cigarette.

"Nah, don't even worry about it. I'm sure he'll get what's coming to him."

After that, I drove in silence. After the stunt White Boy had pulled, I didn't need anyone else to have any information on what I was doing. Rodney was cool, but after that night, whatever dirt I would do, I was going to take that shit to the grave with me.

Chapter 49

Jamilla

It was Saturday, around eight in the morning. The house was quiet as I thumbed through my book. It was all done. I had titled it *Rainbow Hearts*. It was based on facts, with a whole lot of fiction between the lines. I was going to give it to my English professor that Monday. Mrs. Turner had said that she would type it all up and edit it as she went along and would have the file to me within a week. Niya and I were both Libras, and I had to have the book in hand by September 26, which was her birthday. We hadn't made definite plans yet, but I knew that we would spend the day together. I was so nervous as I thought of her reading it. I had put so much of us into the book that I hoped that she didn't end up hating it. As I sat there thinking about her, I decided to text her since I hadn't heard from her since the night before.

Hey. I just want you to know that I am thinking about you. I love you.

I pressed SEND, and my heart raced a little. I didn't know if she was still angry about the night before. So I sat there and stared at my phone until it lit up with a text.

Hey. I was thinking about you too. Tell me, what were you thinking about?

Oh shit. Okay. I had to calm down. She always did that to me, always made me sweat a little. I thought about my answer for a minute, then texted her back.

Just thinking about you and how much I love you. Are you still mad at me?

Again, I sat there, anxiously awaiting her text.

Honestly, yeah. A little, but not much, though. I can't stay mad at you, Milla boo.

I smiled while texting, I miss you, Niya. After just one night without hearing from you, I miss you as if it has been years!

She texted back, I am not too far away, you know. Come see me! Come get in bed with me!

Damn. I had to cross my legs to stop what was happening between them. Thoughts of her pleasuring me intoxicated my mind, and for a brief moment, I was drunk from thoughts of her roaming hands. I got up to brush my teeth and wash up. As I walked to the bathroom, I texted, Be there in twenty minutes.

I texted her before I left my apartment and told her that I was on my way to hers. When I got there, she was standing at her door, leaning against the wall, smoking. Whenever a day or two passed without my seeing her—or in this case, fourteen hours—I felt all giddy inside. She was so beautiful. It was rare to see her with her locks out. Her hair was usually in braids or pulled back in a ponytail, but that morning, it was out, and her wild curls only added to her magnificence. I could tell that under her white wife beater, she had on no bra, and for some reason, I wondered if she didn't have on any panties under her boxers.

"So, you missed me?" Niya asked as she blew smoke out of her mouth. Her eyes were low, and so was her head. She lifted it and looked at me as her sentence seemed to dance in the air.

"Ye-ye-yeah, I did," I answered nervously. Her stance and her presence were causing me to stutter.

"You okay?" Niya asked with a slick smile on her face. She knew what she was doing to me.

"Yeah," was all that I could get out.

She moved to the side but didn't leave me much room to get by. My eyes were on her the whole time, and as my body brushed against hers, she didn't smile and her vibe was dominating. As I walked ahead of her, my skin was on fire. It was as if I could feel her eyes dancing against my back.

Once I got to her room, I sat in her desk chair while she closed her bedroom door and stood against it. She stood there, smoking, not saying a word. I sat in the chair, nervous as hell, excited by the sight of her, and wanting to know what was on her mind.

"What are you doing here?" she asked, still not moving, still with her back against the damn door.

"You told me to come and get in bed with you," I answered, now a little confused.

"Oh yeah? That's the only reason?"

Her eyes were small slits, and her head was cocked to the side. She wasn't looking at me, but down at the blunt in her hand.

"I mean, yeah. No. Well—"

She started to giggle, so I stopped talking. She walked over to me slowly, and once in front of me, she removed the rubber band that was holding my hair in a ponytail.

"You know I like to see that hair out. Now, tell me, you came over here only because I said so?"

Shit, shit, shit. My heartbeat was out of whack. She was too close, her voice was too soft, and her fingers were running through my hair. I couldn't answer. Hell, my eyes were damn near rolling to the back of my head.

She sat her blunt down in the ashtray, stood me up, and wrapped her arms around my waist. She hugged me tightly, and it felt good.

"Damn, Milla boo. I missed you, baby."

She had her nose and lips buried against my neck, and I could feel her words against it as she spoke. I hugged her back, and in that moment, my knees went weak.

"Really, Jamilla. I miss you whenever I am not with you. Thank you for your friendship."

That word—it was such a beautiful word, and being called her friend meant the world to me. But . . . but standing there in her arms, I didn't want to hear that word.

She picked me up, and with my legs wrapped around her waist, she put me on her bed. She was between my legs as my thoughts ran wild. As I waited for her to make her move, she just gawked at me. She stared, and then she kissed my neck. She whispered something that I couldn't hear, and afterward, she got off of me. She found her spot beside me, pulled me close, and just lay there. Now, what in the hell was I supposed to do with that? I thought that she would at least try to pull off my clothes, maybe kiss me, maybe touch me, but she did none of that. And there I was, thinking that it all was easier in bed.

Niya soon fell asleep, but I couldn't relax to save my life. She had fucked my head up by just really going to sleep. Had things changed? Had I pushed her away one time too many? Was I losing her, what we had, and what I loved so much? Well, lying there, so close to her, I felt uncomfortable. With no answers, lying in her arms only made me think even more. I got off the bed without waking her up and sat in the chair. I watched her sleep as I smoked the blunt she had left behind in the ashtray.

While I was deep in thought, I caught sight of her notebook, and I became curious about whether she'd read what I wrote the other day. I got butterflies in my stomach as I thought of the notes she used to leave for me in my notebooks. I got up, grabbed the notebook, and searched through the pages, hoping to find a note that would let me know that everything was okay, that everything was still the same. When I found the page with her writing on it, I sat back and read her thoughts.

To be madly in love, do you even know how that feels? It is as if I exist only in the land of insanity that my love for you has built. It is as if my thirst for you consumes me and dehydrates every ounce of stability in me. It is as if my hunger for you, which is growing with each passing day, ravishes my heart, allowing it to beat only when you are near me. Yes, I am madly in love with you . . . yet knowing that those feelings are not returned pains me most of all. To be madly in love, do you even know how that feels? No, No, sadly, you don't.

I couldn't believe my eyes, and instantly, they started to leak. My heart felt as if it had exploded in my chest and was leaking into my central nervous system. At first I couldn't move, but when my feelings started to erupt and caused me to cry out loud and shake uncontrollably, I had to get up. I went into Niya's hallway bathroom, grabbed a clean bath towel, covered my face, and just let it all out. I wept into that towel like I had never done before. I felt as if everything in me had shattered. I had ruined it all. I just knew it. Things would never be the same. Niya had realized that I didn't love her the way she loved me . . . yet! She had realized it and couldn't deal with it, or maybe she didn't want to deal with it anymore.

I didn't know what to do. So I sat in her bathroom and cried for a while. It was a deep, sorrowful show of what I thought was a loss of love. What was I going to do? When I was able to get myself together enough, I left her bathroom and went home. It would be three days before I saw or spoke to Niya again.

Chapter 50

Niya

When I woke up, she was gone, and instantly, I thought about her. There she was again, ruling my whole damn world, but I just couldn't help it. She was my drug of choice, and I the willing drug fiend. When I got my first hit of her, it was like nothing I had ever felt. She surged through my brain and became the dopamine that sent me into a state of euphoria. Unfortunately, just like the drugs that held my mother prisoner, Jamilla was somehow starting to feel as if she wasn't good for me, and that thought slaughtered my heart.

To be on top of her that morning, to hold back and not do the things I wanted to do to her, that shit was like executing everything alive in me. I had to force sleep just so I wouldn't think about it with her right next to me. My mind was becoming too clouded with the thought of not having her, and insanity wasn't too far behind my pursuit of her. How hard did I have to work? What else did I have to do to prove to her that I loved her like I had never loved before? My God, I would forsake life for her, I would reject the air that filled my lungs for her, yet she was still confused. She was still searching for the answers that I felt I had already given her.

Was I wrong for needing her the way that she had shown me that she needed me? Was my way of thinking off? Should I have been more understanding of her feelings? Sadly, I was starting to enter my selfish mode. I wanted to be happy. I had been through so much with my parents, with myself, and now I had to deal with White Boy. I wanted just to be fucking happy. I wanted to wake up and smile because all the bullshit in life that I had been dealing with had turned into Houdini and, *poof*, had disappeared.

So that morning, when I texted her to come over, I'd known what I was going to do before she even walked over to my side of the building. I'd known that I wanted to show her what it felt like to get a drop of what she wanted, to quench her thirst only for a moment and, *boom*, have it taken away. It was mean, cruel even, but I'd just needed her to feel it. This was her game, and I had played with the fucked-up cards she dealt from the minute I sat down at her table, without complaint. I had become monomaniacal, obsessed with every little aspect of her, almost possessed by just the thought of her and only her. But now things had to change.

What happened with White Boy had kept me up for a long while after I got home. I needed to adjust some things in my life; I needed to put *me* first. I'd stayed up thinking about how I would do that, because putting myself last had always been second nature to me. The thought of others had always preceded the needs of self, and because I had put others first for so long, I was starting to want more for myself. I loved Jamilla with all of me, and I would continue to love her. I just needed to change when it came to how I reacted to her. I had no idea how I would do this, for she was everything to me. She was everything. Even as I lay in that bed now and tried to will these things I was seeking into my mind, I couldn't help but reach out to her, just to see how she was. I picked up my phone and texted her.

Jamilla, I woke up and you were gone, and as I was lying here thinking about you, I just wanted to text and tell you to have a good day.

I waited for a good twenty minutes before I realized that she wasn't going to answer. Maybe that was best for now. As I got up and went into the shower, I tried to make sense of it all by telling myself that we both needed space, that maybe we needed to detox and remove all the toxins from our relationship.

It was around ten at night, and I found myself at Marlo's place. Her room was very feminine, with photos of herself all over the place. I had managed to hold myself back from going over to Jamilla's place or texting her again. Truth be told, I had called Marlo in hopes that her presence would act as a distraction. I had made a few deals, had a pocketful of money, so it hadn't been such a bad day. I had stopped off and picked up something cute for her, and that shit must have made her juicy. She squealed like a pig and jumped in my arms, and it kind of reminded me of Roxie. Now, that was a name I hadn't thought of in a while. At times, I missed her, but those moments were far and few between. But on days like the one I was having, she would have just added so much flavor.

I sat on Marlo's bed and waited for her to try on the tight number I had picked up for her. I knew that with her fit frame, she would do the dress justice.

"Yeah, I knew that shit would fit you well. Come here," I said after she'd put the dress on. I waited for her to walk over to the bed. Once she was within arms' reach, I stood up and pulled her close.

I grabbed a handful of her ass and tried to push Jamilla out of my brain. I kissed her, and it was as if she melted in my arms. Her kiss tasted good, just not as sweet as Jamilla's. Her body felt good, just not as good as Jamilla's. Man, what was I going to do? I knew I would do the same to her as I did to Jamilla, but this time, I'd teach Marlo a lesson. I would teach these straight girls that the best thing they could do was know what they really wanted and know who they really were. It had almost worked on Jamilla, and that night, I wouldn't leave Marlo's house without succeeding.

"You think it looks good on me?" Marlo asked as she pulled away from my kiss and turned around. We stood in front of her full-length mirror, and we admired the dress and her beauty.

"You are a sexy-ass chocolate thing. Yeah, you sexy as fuck, Marlo." My hands were rubbing her thigh. Her back was against me as I rested my chin on her shoulder.

"Am I the prettiest girl you have ever been with?" she asked as my hands slid behind her and squeezed her ass again.

"Hell yeah," I lied.

And with that lie, she was all mine. Marlo wasn't hard to read, so it was as if I had already finished her novel.

"Really? Please don't lie to me."

"Yes, Marlo, you are the hottest girl I have ever touched. Damn, girl. I can feel you trembling."

That part wasn't a lie. My hands had moved back to her thighs and were moving higher and higher. With one hand, I pulled up her dress, and with the other, I rubbed her inner thigh. She moaned as we watched everything that was going down in the mirror. The higher my hand moved, the more I could feel her feet move.

"Yeah, you're such a pretty bitch. Look at you. Are you looking?" I said.

I wanted her to watch everything that was about to go down. She was another straight girl walking on the "wild side," and I didn't want her to forget this.

The red little dress was now around her waist. Her panties were pink, lacy, and looked like something she would have on. My tongue played with her neck as my right hand rubbed the ridge of her panties on the side. I could almost feel her body begging for me to touch it. Her hips were moving to the waves of my fingertips, and her low, sensual moans played as the music to our sexual exchange. She was a sexy girl, beautiful even. Her model looks made me feel like a turnout queen. I was about to be the first girl ever to make her cum, and she would never forget me because of it.

"You like what I'm doing to you?"

I was teasing her, almost touching her wet spot, but not quite. I ran my fingers across the top of her panties, around the sides of them, but just not on what I would bet was her dripping wet pussy.

"Yeah, baby, it feels so good."

"How does it feel to have a girl make you wet?"

I was looking right at her, and she stared back. I watched as she licked her lips and smiled.

"It feels so fucking good, Niya. It feels so good."

"You want me to touch it? You want me to make you cum?" I asked before biting into her neck and licking my way up to her earlobe.

"Yeah, I do."

"Tell me again. Tell me that you want me to touch it. Tell me that you want a girl to touch that pussy."

I was looking at her as I ran my hand quickly across her clit. It was fast, over her undies, but she reacted nonetheless. She threw her head back and rested it against the front of my shoulder, but that was not what I wanted from her.

"Don't fucking look away, Marlo. Look at yourself, look at me, and look at what I am doing to you. Don't take your eyes off of that fucking mirror, you hear me?"

She picked her head back up, and as soon as our eyes met, I did it again, but this time as I quickly gave her clit a rub, my left hand met her left breast.

"Now, tell me what I want to hear," I demanded as her nipple hardened under my touch.

"It . . . it feels good."

So, she thought I was playing with her? I wasn't going to touch that kitty until she said what I wanted her to say. This wasn't just an ego boost. I needed her to say those words because every time she thought of this night, she would also remember saying that she wanted a girl to make her cum. That would either make her realize that she was a lesbian or help her to realize that playing these games just wasn't worth it. See, a lot of straight girls loved to play the "I kissed a girl and liked it" game. They knew damn well that they weren't even bi, let alone gay, yet they liked to play with gay girls' feelings.

"And?" I asked.

"And I want you to . . . to . . . to make me cum."

She needed a little more help than I had thought. I started to rub her clit. I rubbed it for a whole minute or two, still through her panties, just giving her a few moments of pleasure.

"And?"

My hands stopped moving, and I waited to hear her say the magic words. She was panting, and I could feel her heart racing as my left hand still played with her nipple.

"And . . . I want you, a girl, to make me cum." She put her hands over mine as she stared at me. "Come on, Niya. Make me cum. Please, Niya, I need you to make me cum."

Damn. Her begging was turning me on. She looked so helpless, as if me making her cum was her only wish in the world.

"Come on, baby. Don't stop now. You gotta make me cum, boo."

As we stood there, in front of that mirror, with her dress pulled up around her waist, I proceeded to turn Marlo out. At first I was going to use only my fingers, but then I decided that giving her the best head she would ever get in her life was the only way to go.

I pulled down her panties and let them fall around her ankles. Her bare pussy was soaking wet and was ready for my touch. As my fingers played tricks against her clit, the sound of her moistness filled the air. Soon her moans and groans followed. Her head rocked back, only for me to demand that she keep her eyes on the mirror. She threatened to let her knees buckle; I threatened to stop if she couldn't handle my finger play. My fingers against her wetness sounded like smacking lips.

"Niya, wait. I can't . . . I can't stand up anymore. Please, baby. Oh shit. Fuck. I can't."

I looked around the room, and with my right foot, I pulled over the chair that sat close to us. I sat her down roughly on it because she had pissed me off. I sat her ass right in front of that mirror and stood in front of her.

"Throw them fuckin' legs up."

I didn't have to ask twice. There she was, with that pussy in the air. We both could see it all. I fell to my knees and stuck out my tongue. I licked from her hole to her clit and stayed on it for a little bit. I sucked, licked, and pulled on that pretty little clit of hers, and soon my two fingers slid inside of her. I moved both of them with skill and watched as she fucked both my face and my middle and index fingers. She called my name, she grabbed my head, and then she tried to push it away and close her legs.

"Bitch, take that shit. You wanted to play lezzy games, huh? Sit still and take that shit, understand?"

"Yes, yes, okay. Oh God."

I toyed with her that night, drawing her closer and closer to the edge before I would back away and make her beg for more. Soon, her hips would be gyrating, and I would have to hold on to her to make sure that she didn't fall out of the chair.

To watch her cum, it was a beautiful thing. Her legs looked like they were fighting the air; her skin was damp from the heat we created; and her face, her beautiful face, was twisted and unfamiliar. She was in paradise, but I, despite the triumph of making her cum, felt little to nothing. If that had been Jamilla, tasting her would have been the epitome of satisfaction. With Marlo, it just gave me a short rush, and afterward, I came crashing down.

As she sat and caught her breath on the chair, I went into her bathroom to wash and sanitize my hands, mouth, and face. As I looked in the mirror that hung above her sink, I saw myself, and there was nothing there. Marlo was cool, but she was just a filler chapter. I'd used her to get myself from what was to what would be. She was a transitional passage, and her purpose had been served. After washing up, I told her that I had to go. When she asked for an explanation, I offered her none. Just told her that it had been fun and that she should never forget what we had, no matter how brief it was.

I would have thought that Jamilla would be on my mind at that point, but surprisingly, she wasn't. Instead, another girl who I missed just as much came to mind, and I needed to see her right then and there. I looked at my phone and saw that it was going on midnight. I went through my contacts, found the one I wanted, and dialed.

"Ay, yo, Rodney, what are you doing?" I said into my phone when Rodney answered. "So, can you meet me at

Smiley's place? Yeah, yeah, I know, but I have to see her. . . . Nah, I just don't want her to act all crazy and have her brothers fuck me up or something, so I'm not even going to call first. . . . Right. Shit wasn't right last time I saw her. . . . Okay. See you there."

Rodney was a bit shocked but said he would meet me there.

I sat in my car in front of Smiley's house and ducked down as Rodney went to her front door and waited for her to come out. She soon appeared, and I watched as she smiled and gave Rodney a hug. They stood talking for a few as I listened to their conversation through my phone. He had called my phone and then put his phone in his pocket so I could hear everything.

"Have you seen Niya?" Rodney asked.

She took a minute to answer, and with as much attitude as she could muster, she replied, "Hell, nah. The last time I saw her, she was throwing me out of her house. Can you believe that shit? And here I was thinking that we were friends."

"Come on, Smiley. You two *are* friends, but friends fight, and they also make up. So, would you want to see her now?"

Smiley didn't answer. She stood there thinking, I guessed.

"Look, Smiley. I know for a fact that Niya still cares about you."

"Oh yeah? How do you know that?"

Damn. Her question made me a little sad. No matter what, I would always care about her, and I wished she knew that.

"Maybe I'm not the right person to answer that question. Maybe you should ask her."

"I'm not fucking calling her. You will never understand, but that shit hurt, Rodney."

"You don't have to call her. She's here, in her car."

With that, I got out of my car, walked around it, stepped up on the curb, and leaned against the hood. She just stood there looking at me. She was maybe ten feet away and could see me clearly. I could also see her. The pain, the shock, and the anger that were on her face said it all.

Rodney took her hand, and at first, she put up a fight. I felt so damn bad as I watched her. She looked like she wanted to come over to me, but her pride was a roadblock. I had hung up my phone and listened as Rodney convinced her to come my way. She walked slowly, her thick body sweeping through the air gracefully, as a battle was still being waged within her. She would later tell me that she had been pissed but loved me, that she had never wanted to see me again but had missed me, and that she had wanted to punch me in the face but would never hurt me.

Once she was in front of me, for some reason, I felt like I wanted to cry. Didn't know why, but maybe it was 'cause I knew that I had hurt her . . . because of Jamilla.

"Hey, Smiley," was all I offered.

"Hey."

I was kind of stuck and didn't have the heart to say much more. I knew what I wanted to say, but I just didn't know where to start.

As we stood there, Rodney leaned on my car and started to split a blunt. I asked him to get us a bottle and handed him the money, which he refused to take. He walked away, and we were finally alone.

"I miss you, Smiley."

She rolled her eyes, and my hands started to sweat. I was acting cool, but inside, my mind and my heart were all over the place.

"Look, I guess I should start by saying I'm sorry. I should have never put you out of my house, let alone put my hands on you," I said.

"Whatever. You good."

Okay, so she was going to make this hard for me.

"Come on, Smiley. You know that you're my fave. Always have been and always will be my favorite."

I pulled her toward me. She fought, but it was really no fight at all. I pulled her between my legs and took in her scent. She always smelled so damn sweet, as if she bathed in Victoria's Secret Pure Seduction body spray. I had always liked that body spray the most out of all of them.

"Niya, come on. Let go of me."

Again, she tried to put up a weak fight, but I wasn't letting go.

"Niya, let me go!"

She pulled out of my arms for real that time, but as I tried to pull her back to me, her truth came out.

"No. Don't touch me. This is not a game to me. You hurt me so damn bad, Niya. You know what the fucked-up part about this is?"

I didn't answer her, because as she spoke, she'd started to cry. I could tell that she was trying to hold back her tears, but it wasn't working.

"You did that shit to me for another bitch. Yeah, that hurt, but your words . . . calling me a fat bitch . . . You knew that it would hurt me the most."

"I know. I know. I'm so sorry." Again, I tried to pull her to me, but she pulled away.

"Yeah, you knew, yet you still did that shit. Being with you, I was free. You never seemed to see the extra pounds. You always treated me as if I was the baddest bitch. You made me feel, as if for the first time, that I could be open,

I could be free, and I could be me without the insecurities. Without even knowing it, you helped me love myself, and with just a few simple words, you made me feel as if you took off your blinders and you saw me as the rest of the world does."

Goddamn. She was fucking killing me. I couldn't hold back anymore. Tears started to fall, even though I was trying to hold on to my gangster.

"I'm so sorry, Smiley. I swear to God I am."

"We had always been friends first, Niya, always friends first, and for you to do that to me, because of Jamilla . . . Well, I was fucked up for a little bit. I had fallen in love with my friend, and she didn't even give a damn."

I started to pace around her. I felt so damn low at that point. She was still crying, and so was I. I grabbed on to her from the back and kissed her neck.

"Smiley, baby, please, you have to forgive me. That shit was fucked up, I know, but please. I love you, and it will never happen again."

She turned around and hugged me tight. She didn't have to say a word, 'cause I knew that she had forgiven me.

After Rodney came back, we chilled outside and spoke about us, about me, and about life. She told me that she had seen the video and that she was so happy for me. When she asked about Jamilla, I told her that I was taking a break from her.

"Damn, Niya. I ain't know that things were that bad," Rodney said, all wide eyes.

"Man, I just got to wean myself off of that. I love her, she's my friend, but that's it, and I have to accept that shit," I revealed.

Both he and Smiley looked surprised, but it was all true. I would always be there for Jamilla, but like an alcoholic, I had to stay away until I could be around her without wanting a sip of her.

I knew that things might not ever be the same, but at least I had some part of Smiley again. I had a part of Smiley back, a part of a true friend. I drove home drunk, thanked God that I made it, and slept well. A day without Jamilla wasn't as bad as I had thought it would be.

Chapter 51

Jamilla

I had seen Niya's text when she sent it, but I just didn't know how to answer it. What I had read in her notebook, man, it was hard to swallow. I was going on thirty-six hours without speaking to her or seeing her, and it just didn't feel right. The funny thing was, after that one text, she hadn't hit me back up. That was not like her, and the truth was, I was hurting inside. As Mary's voice singing "Sweet Thing" came out of my radio, I tried to concentrate on finding the right person to do the cover for my book.

"I wish you were my lover, but you act so undercover," Mary sang.

Damn. There was no way that I would be able to think of anything else until I spoke to her. I hadn't seen her before, during, or after classes. I hadn't even bothered to wait for her to give me a ride and had opted for the city bus instead. I picked up my phone to text Niya but was stopped by a knock on my bedroom door.

"Jamilla, someone is here to see you. They are waiting at the door."

I jumped out of my desk chair and ran to the mirror. Why would she just show up without texting me first? I combed through my hair, checked for eye and nose boogers, and put on a little lip gloss. I pulled off the sweatpants I had on and threw on one of the pairs of extra-tight jeans she had bought me. If she was going to see me while still being pissed at me, I thought that I should at least look good.

I walked to the door and wondered why she just didn't come in and at least stand inside it. I took a few seconds to catch my breath and calm my nerves. When I felt steady enough emotionally, I pulled open the door and was shocked that it wasn't Niya.

"Rodney, what are you doing here?"

He smiled and asked, "What? Not happy to see me?"

There he went, showing off that sexy smile of his.

"No, no, it's not that. I just wasn't expecting to see you on the other side of my door."

"Can I come in?" he asked as he leaned against the wall. I took a second and looked him over. He was fresh to def. He and Niya always dressed well, with everything almost perfect and in its place.

"Sure. Come in. We can hang out in my room."

He walked in but didn't follow me to my room. I turned around and looked at him, as if to say, "You coming?"

"How about we go to my place?"

I stood there wondering what was wrong with my place.

"I need to talk to you, and I don't need anyone listening in," he said as he flashed another smile that was sure to get any straight female with a vagina wet.

I told Marie to lock up as I grabbed my keys and phone, and then I headed out with him.

"Niya won't be there, will she?" I asked as we got into his car.

"Nah. She's out working."

I rolled my eyes and sat back and enjoyed the ride.

We had been in Rodney's basement for about an hour, just chilling, listening to music, drinking, and drugging. Weed smoke filled the air, and its clouds danced in the air as it made us mentally fuzzy. He was cool and made me laugh. He was a great distraction. He came over to the couch and sat next to me. I looked at him, still laughing from his last joke, as curiosity crept in.

"You said you wanted to talk to me. What about?" I asked as I laid my head in his lap. I looked up at him, and for the first time, he seemed a little uncomfortable. "Aw, come on, Rodney. Don't get shy on me now," I said as I reached up and touched his hair. I had been wanting to do that for the longest, and the berry Cîroc had given me the courage to do so.

"I'm not shy. I just don't really know how to ask you this."

"Just spit it out, *Rodneyyy*," I said, elongating his name, as I tickled his neck.

"Okay, okay. Wait, I won't be able to talk with you playing with my neck."

I stopped messing with his neck and waited.

"Okay, so, what I wanted to know was . . . are you gay?"

My body went stiff, and I could no longer look at him. "Why would you ask me that?" I asked as I stared at the wall in front of me.

"It seems like you and Niya have things going on, and I wanted to ask and make sure before I told you something."

I didn't say anything for a while. I just sat there—we just sat there—smoking and breathing.

"What did you want to tell me?" I finally asked him. I wanted to know what his question was before I answered him.

I watched him breathe, smoke, and drink. I could tell he was nervous, because his hands shook as he held his cup. The shaking was slight but noticeable.

"So, um, well, I thought . . . I mean, I think that you're real pretty, and well . . ."

Oh my God. My heart was racing, and I couldn't believe my ears.

"What I am trying to say is that I like you, Jamilla. I know it's fucked up, but I just can't help it. That's why I wanted to know if you are gay and if you and Niya got something going on."

I couldn't speak right away. I needed to take everything in. *Wow*. He had blown my mind.

"Rodney, I'm not a lesbian. Niya and I are close, and I think that our close relationship blurs the lines for me at times. I love her, but I still like men."

What I should have said was that I still liked men *too*.

He flashed that beautiful smile of his again and said, "So, can we talk? I mean really talk?"

A part of me wanted to ask, "But what about Niya?" but I had to remind myself that I wasn't her girl and, well, I wasn't a lesbian.

"Yeah, we can talk. Go ahead. I'm listening," I joked.

"Nah, really. As long as you're free and unattached, I really wanna get to know you. And well, if you're bi, just tell me now. I just don't want any surprises."

I reached up, ran my hand through his hair, and let it rest on the back of his head. I leaned up, pulled him to me, and kissed him. When I did it, I wasn't sure of why, but later it hit me that I was trying to convince him that I was into men. I was also trying to convince myself.

"Ay, yo, Rodney. I just spoke—" June had come running down the stairs and stopped mid-sentence as Rodney and I jumped up and tried to get ourselves together. He just stood there, looking from me to his brother.

"What's up, June?" Rodney said.

The air was so fucking thick with guilt that it could almost be seen.

"I got a call about Niya doing a show and called her over. She's on her way here *now*. Yo, let me speak to you for a minute."

Damn. We'd been caught. I sat on the couch, on the verge of tears, as Rodney went upstairs with his brother. I was not sure if they thought that I wouldn't be able to hear their conversation, but every word was heard.

"What in the fuck are you doing, messing with Jamilla? You know that's Niya's girl."

"No she's not. She ain't even gay," Rodney answered.

"Man, this shit you're doing is going to be bad for business. How do you think Niya is going to feel when she finds out about this?"

"Man, she won't have to find out, 'cause I am going to tell her. Jamilla ain't her girl, so she should be cool about it."

Fuck. I wasn't ready for Niya to know about this.

"You're fucking crazy, dude. They may not be together, but you know Niya loves that girl, man. That shit ain't hard to tell."

There was silence before Rodney said, "Look, I like her, and I got a shot at actually getting with her. Niya is gay, and Jamilla ain't, so . . ."

With that, Rodney came back downstairs. I wanted to go home right away. He came back over to the couch and sat beside me. He threw his arm around my neck and pulled me close.

"You okay?" he asked.

The answer was, "Hell no!" but I nodded my head yes.

"Relax. I can tell that you aren't okay. It will be fine. I am going to be straight up with Niya—"

"No, not yet. Please, don't tell her. Let me be the one to let her in on things. Plus, we don't know where this is headed. Let's just chill and see."

I could tell by the look on his face that he didn't like that I didn't want to tell Niya that we had decided to talk and get to know each other, but I just wasn't ready.

He tried to respond, but June came down the stairs just then, followed by Niya. When she saw me, I could tell that she was shocked. I had slid to the other side of the couch before she made it down the stairs, but still, she was surprised.

"What's up, Rodney? Hey, Jamilla. What are you doing here?"

The room fell silent as everyone waited for my answer, which never came.

"Me and Rodney saw her while we were out, so we told her to come with us so she could hear the good news."

Thank God for June, 'cause I had gone blank. Niya still looked like she had questions, but June had news to give.

"Yo, man, I got some fucking great news. I uploaded the new video this morning, and that shit took off faster than the first one. Yo, Rodney. Pull that shit up on the computer. So, anyway, you know I used to do security for that A and R director guy from Gifted Records. Well, I hit him up and told him to check out the two videos. He hit me back and was really feeling your songs. He also said that he liked the amount of views the videos had even more."

She stood there as if she was in shock, as if she was trying to split her brain between what June was saying and the video Rodney had pulled up.

"So, what does this all mean?" Niya asked.

"You ready for this? He is having an artist showcase tomorrow, and he asked if you would want to join in. He said your set wouldn't be that long, 'cause you had only two songs out, but he would be willing to give you a twenty-minute set."

Everyone was jumping, screaming, and talking, but Niya just went over to the now abandoned computer and played her latest video. She sat there watching it and didn't say too much. I joined her on the couch, watched the video with her, and started to cry.

"Niya, this is it. This is the door you have been waiting for. It's open, boo."

She looked flushed with emotion. I was trying to read her, but it was hard. I was behind her, with my chin on her shoulder, as I looked over at the screen. I tried to reach around and take her hand, just to let her know that I had her back, but she quickly jumped up and completely disregarded what I had just said to her.

"So, how long do I have to prepare?" she asked June.

"That's the catch. The showcase is tomorrow night."

By that point, we were all shocked.

"There is no fucking way I am going to be ready for that shit. Are you crazy?"

June stepped in front of Niya and looked her straight in the eyes and spoke the truth. "You know, I was you not too long ago. I had the world in the palm of my hand, and I thought that I had more time. I wasn't ready. I had to get shit right first, thought I needed to perfect shit first, but look at me now. I could have been directing videos with the best of them, but I'm slanging shit with the rest of the 'normal-ass' niggas. Fuck being ready, 'cause if you wait for ready, ready will always pass you by. Take life as it comes to you, my nigga, 'cause right now, it's coming at you lovely, and believe me, shit can turn real ugly real fast."

Damn. June had us all thinking.

June went on. "Fuck being ready, Niya. No matter what you think, just *know* that you are ready. Plus, you ain't got no fuckin' choice. I already told him that you would be there."

After going over all the details, we were all ready to head out. I knew that I would leave with Niya. I wanted to talk to her and see where her head was at. I wanted to congratulate her and let her know that I was there for her and would help her in any way I could.

"Where are you going?" she asked as I got up to leave with her.

"I thought that I would ride home with you. I thought that we should talk."

She wasn't even looking at me. I was taken aback and was slowly getting angry.

"Nah. I ain't headed home. I gotta go back to work. Have whoever brought you here take you home."

With that, she slipped on her sunglasses and took the steps two at a time. I was pissed 'cause she was so fucking cool with that shit, as if I had never even mattered at all. June followed her up and left me in the basement with Rodney.

"You okay, Jamilla?" Rodney asked. His voice came crashing down on me, and in that moment, I was so embarrassed.

"Yeah, I'm fine. I just want to go home. And please, don't tell Niya anything about us."

Chapter 52

Niya

I couldn't deal with Jamilla. Honestly, I wasn't ready even to see her, and I couldn't understand why she was at Rodney's house. I made a mental note to let June know that if he saw Jamilla—I didn't care what news he had—I didn't want her over there without me. But that was the least of my worries. I spent the rest of that day shopping and making sure my clothes, shoes, and jewels were all on point. I knew that some people felt as if they should be accepted as is, but to me, people always wanted to be around a great persona. People loved beautiful, well-dressed people, and if you added swag to that, you were golden.

After shopping, I spent the rest of my night at home, getting my mind, body, and soul together. I practiced both of my songs over and over again in my full-length mirror. Hell, I even wrote a few new ones. I was going to throw a new one, just half of one, in for the showcase. I went over the new songs that I had written and settled on "Show Me Your Ugly, Show Me Your Pain, Boo."

Show me your ugly. Show me your pain, boo,
'Cause I came only to save you,
Heal the things from your past that haunt you.
Be a fool for you. Take a bullet for you.
Never let another mistreat you. I'll put a nigga six feet deep for you, so . . .

Show me your ugly. Show me your pain, boo, 'cause I will never hurt you. I came only to save you. I'll kiss it and make it all better, boo . . . but you gotta let me in.

When I first saw you,
I never thought that you would ever love me too.
See, I had walls up too,
But just like I fight for you, you fought for me too.
So let me love you. Trust me, my love remains true.

Show me your ugly. Show me your pain, boo, 'cause I will never hurt you. I came only to save you. I'll kiss it and make it all better, boo . . . but you gotta let me in.

In time, Jamilla boo, with me beside you
All that sadness will no longer reside in you.
You are strong enough to fix it, boo.
I am here for you only to lean on and strengthen you.
Together, we will conquer the world, boo.
All I ever wanted was for it to just be me and you.

I will fight for you. I will smile for you. I will love you and make it all better for you.

The broken heart you harbor, boo, will be the death of you. I am waiting to put it back together boo . . . but you gotta let me in.

Just let me love you, and that broken heart that we both know is the most hurtful pain in you . . . it will heal . . . and will barely leave a scar, boo, so . . .

Just show me your ugly. Show me your pain, boo, 'cause I will never hurt you. I came only to save you. I'll kiss it and make it all better, boo . . . but you gotta let me in.

I spent the next day with my granny. When I told her about the showcase, she cried. She knew how much music meant to me, and she had always felt that it was the only thing that linked me to my father. He was a music lover too, and when he used to come around, he always made her play music, and we all would dance.

"Niya, mi amor, I must bless you."

Oh God, here she went with her blessings. My granny was a Catholic, but with Dominican roots. She still lit her candles, prayed to her saints, and from time to time went and saw the "healer." He would give her oils and candles for her to light for herself and her family. I had always thought all that stuff was bullshit.

"The *curandero* say to me . . . he say something big will happen, and my Niya will need blessing. He say you will have problem. He say it will stop you from big things, so he give me to bless you. See, this save you, mi amor."

I looked at that shit in her hand and took it from her. I opened the bottle, and damn, that shit was strong.

"Granny, I can't put this on. People are going to smell it on me."

She twisted up her face, and I knew that she wasn't going to take no for an answer. "You wash already?"

"Yes, Granny."

"Okay, come. I put on you. No wash off. You keep on for whole day and night. You no wash until morning, okay? Now, me put on you, and I do prayer."

My grandmother wrapped her head in the scarf that the man had blessed for her. She lit her candles, lit her cigar, and shook her maraca to awaken the spirits that were believed to protect not only me but my family for generations. After that, she went to work. She prayed in Spanish as she rubbed the concoction all over me. When she was done, she made me blow the candle out as she dipped her finger in the liquid and made a cross on my forehead.

"You now blessed, mi amor. No one will stop you dream. You leave this house with protection."

***

It was going on seven o'clock as I finished getting dressed. The showcase was starting at ten, but I'd been told that I wouldn't go on until close to midnight, and that was cool with me. The closer it got to showtime, the more nervous I became. I had been to only one showcase, and that was because of June. If they weren't feeling you, you would know it. We were in the toughest city when it came to rap, so if you didn't come right, your career would be ruined. I texted Smiley and asked her for the millionth time if she was sure that she was going to be there, and again she said yes.

So I was pacing my room, going over my raps and how I would deliver them, when my phone started to go off. I picked it up, and the name that flashed across my screen turned my stomach. I took the call but wasn't too happy about doing so.

"Yeah?" was all that I said.

"Why so cold, nigga? You ain't a fan of White Boy no more?"

I didn't answer him and waited for him to say what he needed to say.

"All right, straight to the business, I see. Well, I was thinking about going to see Maggie, you know, the bitch that got three kids? She's a fine white bitch, but them kids drive me crazy. What you think?"

"I say go see the bitch. Where she live?"

He told me where she lived, and I mentally took down the address. Then I was ready to end the call.

"All right. We'll go see the bitch tomorrow. Have fun," I told him.

"Nah, nigga. I'm going to go see that bitch tonight. Around nine sounds right to me. Also, I know you be rollin' with that bitch nigga Rodney sometimes, but I wanted to let you know that if you go see a bitch of your own tonight . . . leave that nigga at home."

With that, he hung up. I sat on my bed and rolled a blunt that was so fat that it almost wouldn't seal. *Fuck*. The last thing I needed was to deal with White Boy . . . and by myself. What was he up to? His coded conversation was easy to decipher, but something just didn't feel right.

I had kissed my granny good night as she prayed me out the door. I was going to pick up what I needed and bring a couple of guns for insurance. I knew that White Boy would check for one gun, but on that night, I would rock with two. As I made it to my car, I heard her voice.

"Niya, Niya, you were just going to leave without me?"

I turned around and was floored by her beauty. Jamilla was dressed in all black, with tight pants and a sexy top to match. She was coming out of her shell as far as fashion was concerned, and I would have been proud to have her with me that night.

She went on. "I mean, damn, what in the hell is going on with you? I been texting you all day, and you don't answer. I called, and you still don't answer. Is this where we are right now?"

Half of me felt bad, but the other half of me didn't need this shit.

"Look, I am going to hit up Rodney and have him pick you up. I have something I need to do before I go there."

She twisted her nose up and threw her hands on her hips. "You have something to do? Like what?"

I rolled my eyes and attempted to turn my back on her, but she turned me back around.

"Answer me. What in the hell would you have to do that's so important that it can't wait?"

"Look, I don't need this shit right now. Just go back inside and wait for Rodney."

"Who in the hell are you yelling at? I don't understand you at all, Niya."

I heard my name being called, but it wasn't by Jamilla. When I looked up, my granny was hanging out the window, yelling my name.

"You no do this, Niya. So be nice. You no do this now."

With that, I unlocked the car doors. Jamilla jumped into the passenger seat as I got behind the wheel.

"Get out of the car, Jamilla."

"Where are you going?" That was all she kept saying for a few minutes. She just wouldn't let up and kept asking me about where I was heading.

"I got to make a fucking drop, okay? White boy on some new shit, and I have to see him tonight."

I waited for the long, drawn-out lecture that was about to come my way, but instead, all I got was a stern answer.

"I'm coming with you."

"What? Hell no. I am not taking you with me as I go and sell drugs. White Boy has been acting crazy, and there's no telling what may happen."

Jamilla didn't answer. She just sat back, put on her seat belt, and stared ahead.

"Jamilla, come on. I don't have time for this."

"Well, I guess that means that you should start driving, then."

I got to my stash house, got everything that I needed, and as soon as I stepped back in the car, Jamilla started in with her questions.

"Can you at least tell me why you are treating me like this?"

I had reached my breaking point. That night was supposed to be *my* night, but no one around me understood that.

"Look, how about you use your fucking brain." I tried to keep calm, but she was bugging the shit out of me.

"Use my fucking brain? Use my fucking brain? How about you use your fucking heart?"

I took in a deep breath and realized that my yelling would never penetrate that thick skull of hers, so I said what I had to say calmly as I sped through the streets of the city I held close to my heart.

"Jamilla, honestly, I just needed a damn break from you. Our relationship . . . that shit was becoming—is becoming—unhealthy for me. I live, sleep, and dream of you. My whole life is wrapped around you, and you being unsure of who you are, that shit drives me crazy."

"But, Niya, is it fair? Is it fair that what took you almost seventeen years to do, you want me to do in just a few short months? How long did it take you to come out? How did you feel when you were forced out of that closet, and even still, you were fighting not to come out?"

Sure, she had a point, but it still didn't change how I felt.

"I understand, but look how I treated Smiley. That was for you. Everything is always for you, and for a change, I want it to be all about me. When will I come first? When will people think of making me happy? When will anyone ever run to save Niya? My parents ain't do that shit, only my granny."

"Niya, that's not true. I love you, I am here for you, and it hurts that you don't know that."

I looked over at her, and I could see the pain on her face. My heart was begging me to stop the car and do what I had always done and cater to her, but my mind was in overdrive.

"I know you love me, Jamilla, but you come first when it comes to *you*. It's not a bad thing, but I would have loved for you to put me first a few times. We will always be us. What we have, that will always be. But . . . but . . . I just need more. In the time that we didn't speak, it was hard, but not as hard as I thought it would be. You know why?"

I waited for her to answer me. What I was saying wasn't easy at all. I felt a little messed up about it, but it needed to be said.

"Why is that, Niya?"

Her question was low and full of pain, but still, I told the truth.

"It's because even after playing all that we have been through in my mind, even after thinking about how much we love each other, I still was left with nothing. I was so busy being the savior that I didn't notice that I needed saving too. When I fall, I know that you will be there to catch me. You proved that to me when that shit went down with my mom. You proved yourself to me that morning. You proved your love. But even with all that, I still go to bed thinking about possibly never having you, while constantly, you play on my emotions."

"No, no, I don't. That's not—" I cut her off as fast as she started to speak.

"Yeah, you do, hon. You do. I don't stay mad at you, because I know that you do it without even knowing, but you do, and that shit has got to stop. Fuck this 'I love you, I need you, but I'm not gay' shit." Sorry, but this is just how I feel. I love you, and you are my best friend, but my obsession with you is unhealthy, and, baby, I am tryin'a find a cure so I can get right. You feel me?"

She didn't answer. I saw a few tears fall, and she tried her best to catch them. My insides felt like they were ripping apart, but she needed to feel this, the same shit that I felt every time she rejected me. I parked the car once I reached my destination, rolled up a joint, and smoked, while she declined the feel-good weed and turned up J.

Cole's new CD. "Sparks Will Fly" came on, and damn, that shit added insult to injury.

Jamilla and I sat in the alleyway without uttering too many words between us. I was on time, and yes, White Boy was late as hell. I looked down at my phone and texted him, asking him where in the hell he was. I had only a few hours to get shit done, but I hadn't planned on giving him that much time. Just when I was about to text again, I saw them. The red and blue lights right behind me made my stomach drop. I looked back, looked at Jamilla, and took a quick glance around me. *Fuck.* I was blocked in.

"Oh my God, Niya! What are you going to do?"

I looked at Jamilla with fear in my eyes. "I fucking told you to get out of the car. I fucking told you to get out."

The funny thing was, in that moment, my thoughts were once again all about her. The thought of my life being over, the thought of me losing the first opportunity that had come my way as far as music was concerned were secondary to Jamilla and what could happen to her.

"Roll down the window," demanded the cop who was standing by my window.

There were two of them, one on Jamilla's side and one on mine. I couldn't believe that this shit was happening.

I followed the cop's orders. "Yes, Officer?" I asked, trying to play it cool.

"What are you doing here?" he barked.

"My friend and I were just having a conversation. I stopped so—"

"Bitch, step out of the fucking car."

I was shocked, and when I didn't move fast enough, the officer on my side of the car opened my car door and yanked me out. Jamilla screamed my name, only to have the white officer on her side tell her to shut the hell up. I was pushed against the car as the officer felt me up. I would have said *searched*, but he went far beyond that.

He squeezed my breasts, pinched my nipples, and made sure to grab a handful of my ass.

"What the fuck are you doing?" I asked, trying to pull away from him. He grabbed my braids and slammed my head against the hood of my car.

"I'm doing what I got paid to do. Your ass is going to jail, bitch."

"What? Who paid you?" I asked as the shock of the situation kicked in.

"Oh my God! White Boy set you up," Jamilla said as the cop on her side searched her.

I was not sure what happened in the next few seconds, because I went dead inside. I couldn't hear, I couldn't see, and I couldn't move. White Boy set me up?

"So what? What are you? Her girlfriend? You two are lesbians, huh?" The white cop was talking to Jamilla, but with both of us pushed against my car, we just stared at each other. "Lookie here. We done caught us two dykes on the loose. Tell me something. Do you all eat pussy because you have to, or do you really enjoy it? I mean, it's not like you have a dick to really fuck each other, so is it done out of necessity?"

I could see in Jamilla's eyes that his words cut deep, but for me, they floated on the surface and angered me even more. The sad part was, I'd become used to hearing people talk shit about lesbians way before I even came out, so what he was saying and asking were nothing new to me. I just hated the fact that people always had to resort to using someone's sexuality as a source for insults.

"No, really, look at you, all dressed up like a real lady. You look like you got all dressed up for your boyfriend, but no . . . you got dressed up for another bitch. What is this world coming to?" Jamilla's cop asked her.

Jamilla started to cry, and if I could have, I would have killed both cops in the second.

"So, where's the shit?" asked the officer who held me down. He stood me up straight and was now looking into my eyes. I didn't answer him, so he slapped me across the face. "I'm not going to ask you twice, little girl. Where is the shit?"

I thought about punching him, but I doubted that it would do much, so instead, I head butted him. Years ago, my father had taught me how to execute the perfect head butt. He had always said that people might see a fist coming, but they would leave themselves wide open for a head butt. As our heads met, I was off a bit, and the collision caused a small gash on my forehead, but an even bigger one on his lip.

"Ah, shit. You fucking bitch." His insult came with another slap across my face.

"Let's throw these bitches in the back of the squad car and get this shit over with," the white officer said.

As Jamilla and I were thrown into the old police car, my world came crashing down, and I was sure hers did too. She was still crying, and it was all because of me.

"Listen to me. You won't go down for this. I am going to let them know that you didn't even know that shit was in the car. Don't cry, Jamilla. Don't cry."

She looked at me, and with everything in her, she asked, "But what about you, Niya? What about you?"

There we were. Thrusted in the middle of a shit storm, and finally, I heard what I had always wanted to hear. If only I could put into words what I felt in that moment, if only I could put that emotion into words, I would have used our time alone in the cop car to tell her exactly what her question meant to me. Instead, I leaned into her and forced a smile to appear on my face.

"Don't worry about me, Jamilla. This shit was bound to happen. Just look at my bloodline."

The expression on her face turned to disgust, and she let me have it. “What? Are you crazy? No, this will not happen like this. You have too many big things to look forward to. You are bound to lose everything.”

I didn’t answer her. She was right but . . . what could I do?

Chapter 53

Jamilla

I had to find a way to get us out of this. I was scared as hell, but I just couldn't let Niya's story end this way. I could tell by its looks that the cop car was old and probably didn't have any cameras. I also knew that we were dealing with two perverts by the way they had touched Niya and me. I couldn't believe what I was about to do, but it was worth a try. Since Niya was cuffed and I wasn't, I started to bang on the windows.

"Ay, Officer. Come here. No, please. Come here."

"Jamilla, just chill the fuck out."

I didn't give Niya's request a second thought. I continued to bang until the cop who had slapped Niya came my way. He opened the car door and asked me what I wanted.

"Look, you don't have to do this. I'm sure we can work something out," I said.

"You don't have enough money to work this out," he answered, and then he tried to close the door, but I stopped him.

"Please, sir. I'll do anything you want. Just let us go."

He stood there thinking. I prayed that he took me up on my offer.

"I got paid to do a job. What am I going to tell that man? If he would be dealt with, then maybe we could talk, but I won't be doing that dirty work."

I wanted to spit in his face. He couldn't kill anyone, but he could ruin the lives of two teenage girls. His partner joined us, and that was when I asked how much he was getting paid. He and his partner answered at the same time. He said he made thirty thousand, and his partner, the white cop, said fifty thousand. I looked at Niya and asked if she could top that.

With small droplets of blood running down her face, she answered, "Hell yes."

"Look, she will pay you sixty thousand dollars tonight just to let us go."

The cops stood there talking, and finally, the black officer, the one who had slapped Niya, said that we had a deal.

"Wait. Hold on now. What are we going to do with White Boy? He already paid us," his partner said.

"Who gives a shit? Look at your mouth. We'll just say they got away," the black officer replied.

My whole body was shaking. We were so close to having our freedom back that I almost couldn't breathe.

"Nah, man. He is going to have to get dealt with for me to feel comfortable," said the white officer.

"Don't worry," I told the white cop. "She will take care of it, trust me."

I looked over at Niya, and she nodded her head yes.

"Come on, man, make the fucking deal and let's take them to get the money," said the black officer. He seemed just as eager to get out of that alley as we did, but his partner wanted us to sweeten the deal.

"Nah, that still isn't enough," the white cop insisted.

I looked into his eyes and instantly knew what he wanted.

"What else do you fucking want?" Niya asked out of frustration.

"Her. I want a piece of her. I want some of that sweet lesbian pussy," he replied.

"Come on, Moore. Are you fucking crazy?" the black officer asked.

"Hell no! Take my ass to jail," Niya said without a second thought.

"Well, we have no deal, then. Excuse me, young lady," said the officer named Moore.

As Officer Moore went to close the car door, I stuck my left foot out and stopped him. "I'll do it."

"Jamilla, what the fuck? No, hell no!" Niya yelled. "Officer, close the door."

I turned to Niya and leaned into her. I wrapped my arms around her neck and hugged her tight.

"Jamilla, please, don't do this. Don't fucking do this. I'd rather go down for this shit. Please, Jamilla . . . don't," Niya pleaded.

I pulled away from her and could see the tears that were starting to form in the corners of her eyes, and that brought on mine. I hugged her again and whispered in her ear. "Niya, I would die for you. I would kill for you, and tonight I am going to give up my body for you. I need you to know that I love you. I need—"

"I already know, Jamilla. I swear I do. Please, Jamilla, Don't do this."

I could tell from her voice that the tears in her eyes were now flowing like a waterfall.

"Don't worry, Niya. I am used to this. I can handle this. I love you, okay? I need you to know that."

"I know, Jamilla. I fucking know. Man, please don't do this. You have been through enough of this shit."

"I don't have all goddamn night," the white officer said as I pulled away from Niya.

"Jamilla, no. Please, no. Oh, my God. Please, Jamilla, don't do this," Niya begged.

I got out of the car while Niya's screams decorated the night air. I didn't look back at her. I couldn't. Even with the car door closed, I could still hear her cries as she begged me not to save her. But she needed saving, and it was my turn to save her. It was *my* turn to save her.

Stepping out of the car, I knew that I was taking a big chance. The officers might go back on their deal, but it was worth a try. Officer Moore asked his partner to watch the alley, and then he pushed me on the hood of the car and slipped his fingers between my legs.

"I don't want a dead fuck. You better act as if you are enjoying this," he growled.

I looked him dead in the eyes and answered, "Don't worry. Been here, done this."

When he took my hand and tried to get me back in the car, I pulled away. "No. Not in there. Let's just do it right here on the hood."

"What? You don't want your little girlfriend to see and hear what's about to go down? I want you in that fucking car, or you can forget our deal."

I looked at Niya, and she looked like she was still screaming.

"Please, let's just—"

"Get your ass in that fucking car, or I walk."

I didn't have a choice. I waited for him to open the passenger-side door.

"Jamilla, listen to me. You don't have to do this. Let him take me to jail," Niya pleaded.

"I ain't taking you to jail. We made a deal. Now, shut the fuck up and watch me fuck your girl how you only wish you could," the officer told her.

Niya continued to scream and cry, but I just threw my hands over my ears and lay down across the front seats. My legs hung out of the car as Officer Moore spread them apart.

"You watching lesbo? You watching?"

With that, he pulled down my panties, pulled down his pants, and slid inside of me. I didn't feel anything. I didn't see anything, and I didn't care to. My hands over my ears shielded me from most of Niya's screaming, but . . . she could still be heard. I let the tears roll down the sides of my face and wet my ears, hoping that they would drown her out completely. I cried for her only. My poor Niya, I cried for her only. My body was there, but I let my mind disappear, as I had done on so many nights with my stepdad.

Chapter 54

Niya

"Jamilla, Jamilla, no. Don't fucking do it. Please, I beg you. Don't fucking do this."

I kept on screaming, but to no avail. I threw my body against the door. I did everything that I could to stop her with my hands cuffed behind my back, but the horror went on. I rested my head against the grill that separated me from the front seat and just closed my eyes and cried. I tried my hardest to drown out the sounds that escaped from that front seat, but they echoed, as if we were on a mountaintop. I shook my head from side to side while over and over again I said, "No, Jamilla, no."

Why did it have to be her? How many times did she have to get violated? How many times would her body be used and disregarded, as if it wasn't even hers? My God, what had I done? If only I had walked away when she asked me to. If only she had never stepped into that car.

My God, what had I done?

The cops made me leave my car, and they drove me to my stash house. I thought for sure that they would still arrest me once they got their money, but I guessed they were good for one thing that night . . . keeping their word. I didn't look at Jamilla once during that ride to pick up the money. I couldn't look at her without breaking down again. I held the weight of that night on my shoulders, and looking at her would just make it heavier.

"Is this all of it?" Officer Moore asked as I handed him the money.

"Yeah. I only got about two thousand dollars left. You want that too?" I asked after I lied.

"Nah, we aren't that damn greedy. Plus, we got your drugs. That will bring in some extra cash. Look, you better deal with White Boy, or we are going to be looking for you, understand?" I answered with a yes as the cops got back in their cop car.

"You just gonna leave us out here?" I asked while standing on the sidewalk with Jamilla. My question was directed to the black cop and not his partner.

"You got some cash on you. Catch a damn cab," he answered through the open window.

I sucked my teeth and spit toward the cop car. I was beyond disgusted with the cops.

"I don't know why I'm surprised," I yelled. "You just stood there as that cracker raped my young black friend. Thanks a lot, 'brotha.'"

The black officer reached for his door handle and was about to get out of the car, but his partner stopped him. He told him that they had my money and that my words didn't matter.

They drove off without ever looking back.

It took us thirty minutes to flag down a cab. I looked at my watch, and I had only forty-five minutes before I was due onstage, so I wouldn't have time to go back to my car. I had bagged everything that I had left in that stash house, and I took it with us. I still hadn't said much to Jamilla, and from the looks of things, she was also in her own world. I sat in the cab and thought about the money

I was able to save while slanging drugs on the cold, hard streets of Brooklyn. I had managed to save two hundred thousand dollars, and even with the money that went to the cops, I still had enough to leave New York comfortably. I also made up my mind about the drug game and knew that after that night I would be out of it for good. That was it. I was out.

We got to the venue where the showcase was being held with about twenty minutes to spare.

"Yo, where in the hell have you been? And what happened to your face?" June said when he saw me.

I was rushed by June to one of the dressing rooms, where Rodney and Smiley were already waiting.

"I just need to get cleaned up. I really don't have time to explain. Just show me where the bathroom is," I said.

I left the money with Jamilla and tried my best to get myself together in the bathroom. I had two braids in my hair, which I quickly took out, letting my hair fall freely. I returned to the dressing room and asked June for his sunglasses and switched shirts with Rodney since mine had dried blood on it. When I was all done, I didn't look too bad. I was able to hide the horror of my night behind the passion I felt for what I was about to do.

We all headed to the side of the stage, and I tried my best not to look as nervous as I felt.

"Niya, this is it. Just go out there and give it your all. Fuck being shy. Fuck worrying about what they think. Just go out there and give them the best of you."

I needed to hear that from June. I still couldn't really look at Jamilla.

"You are going to be great, boo, I believe in you," Smiley said as she patted me on the back.

"Yeah, you got this," Rodney added.

And as my name was announced, Jamilla leaned into my ear and said, "This is fate. This is destiny. Just step into it, and the world will be all yours."

I pulled her close, gave her a quick kiss on the forehead, and stepped into the light that had always been waiting for me.

Chapter 55

Jamilla

The police, the sexual exchange, the ride to her showcase—they had all seemed surreal. I'd been there, but I really hadn't been there at all. I wouldn't take it back. I would do it all over again just for her, just to make sure she didn't miss that night. So as I took a seat in the audience with her bag of money between my legs, I said a silent prayer. I asked God to help her forget what had happened just an hour before. Sitting there, I looked around the room and waited to see everyone's reaction to her. Most just seemed a bit shocked and perked up with interest. Her look was different from the norm. A pretty stud who came out with so much swag that no one would think that she had just been through hell.

Niya rocked the crowd as I smiled for her. If she didn't have their attention when she first came out, by the end of her set, all eyes were on her and heads bobbed to her sound.

"You know, I had a little, short joint I wanted to kick a capella, but as I stood up here and looked out there and saw her, saw how happy she is for me, and knowing how much she means to me, something different came to me. I just gave you my fly shit. Now I hope you feel this real shit," Niya announced.

And with that, she filled the room with everything that was authentic. She filled it with our truth. Her song went like this.

Baby, we young and reckless, young and reckless.
Bonnie and Bonnie, baby, we young and reckless.
I let the things I did forever affect us,
Pushing her away, too scared I'll never have her,
Tryin'a gain her trust, hoping one day it will just be us.
But I got her, just not the way I want her.
Heart so filled with her, feel like I'm about to burst.
Love and friendship merge, making us come first.
Fuck with what we got, and you'll need a hearse.
I was going to do this rhyme without even having to curse,
But fuck *and* shit *just seems like the only words that would fit*
'Cause the shit we just went through got a nigga feeling sick.
Something out of a flick,
Something I hope we'll be able to kick.
Bad decisions lead to improper procedure.
Seen her do things I wish I could erase,
But no matter what she been through, none of it will ever defeat her.
Thinking they can break her, but that just isn't the case.
Don't ever worry, baby. You'll always come in first place,
Baby, we young and reckless, young and reckless.
Bonnie and Bonnie, baby, we young and reckless.
I let the things I did forever affect us.
Just know that the shit you tryin'a prove, baby, I already know.
Living life fast got niggas screaming YOLO.
But no matter how many times we live through the rain, wind, or snow,

I want you right beside me, from the apartment in Brooklyn to the motherfucking chateau.

Baby, we young and reckless, young and reckless.
Bonnie and Bonnie, baby, we young and reckless.
We always love 'cause that shit so precious.
When we not together, nights always restless.
The way we love is always selfless.
When she's with me, she's my antidepressant,
And what we got forever effervescent.
Yeah, we young and reckless. Yeah, we take love and don't stress shit,
Shit you can't afford, 'cause our love . . . priceless
And with time and love, this shit . . . endless
Baby, we young and reckless, young and reckless.
Bonnie and Bonnie, baby, we young and reckless.

I had tried my best to bury what had happened that night, but I'd been numb until that very moment. While I listened to her words, the tears started to fall, and there was no stopping them. Everything flashed through my mind, and what had been suppressed emerged and landed on my chest. I got up, went to the back of the room, and just stood there crying. I would take none of it back, but I wished that it had never happened at all. I felt dirty, thinking of that man inside of me. The things that he had said and the way he had touched me left me feeling filthy.

As Niya's rap came to an end, the crowd went crazy. I watched her search the audience for me. I could tell she was about to panic, until her eyes landed on me. She lifted the mic to her lips, and it was as if she saw no one else in that room but me. While looking dead at me, she said, "I love you."

I was making my way backstage to tell Niya how well she did when I was stopped by a man with a suit on.

"I saw you, you know, standing in the back, crying. Did her lyrics touch you that deeply?" he said.

I looked at the man and was about to keep on walking, but for some reason, I told him the truth. "Yeah, they did, and they always do. She's special that way. She touches your heart when she's not even trying."

We stood there, and from the look on his face, I could tell he got it.

"Yeah, she's a star," he observed. "You can just tell. But let me ask you this. What about how she looks? She seems to roll harder than most of the niggas I know, and that's just her stage presence."

I smiled, because Niya's presence could never be missed. "Yeah, but that's what makes a star. She's different, she's real, and she's just her. No gimmick. She always gives just Niya."

He stood there thinking before he asked, "And her being gay . . . Do you think that she will femme it up a bit?"

I laughed. "Hell no. She's a 'take me or leave me' type of chick."

I left him standing there and headed backstage. Her dressing room was packed, and everyone seemed to crowd around her. It seemed like everyone wanted to know who this Niya chick was. She was just starting to make a name for herself, yet she had reporters, music executives, and new fans all around her.

I stood in the doorway, watching her. She smiled for pictures and answered questions, but I could tell that she just wasn't there 100 percent.

"She did great, huh?" Rodney asked when he came over and stood beside me. I couldn't even look at him. I felt as if he could see the night's events on me.

"Niya, this is the dude I was telling you about," I heard June say to Niya.

In walked the guy I was just talking to, and June introduced him to Niya.

"That shit rocked," Suit and Tie said to Niya.

She thanked him before she let him continue. I wasn't really listening to everything the man was saying, because he was talking so fast and seemed to have so much to say. But when I heard the words *L.A.* and *Atlanta*, my ears perked up.

"Yeah, I have shit poppin' in Atlanta too. One of our artists just worked with the Brazilian Barbies. Are you thinking about relocating?" he said.

Niya looked my way as she said, "Yes."

"Well, take my card. Call me Monday morning, and let's talk business."

Suit and Tie was gone as fast as he came in, and it seemed like the groupie train rolled in.

"Ay, we about to head to Rainbow Dreams. Who rollin?" June asked with a full bottle of Cîroc in hand.

My prayers were answered when Niya said she wasn't going. I just wanted to go home and take a shower, and I wanted her to take me. I needed to talk to her before this night ended.

"Come on, Niya. Do you know how many business cards I got for you? You are about to blow up, baby. This is your night."

June was on a hundred, and I couldn't blame him, but he also had no idea what we had been through.

"Nah, me and Jamilla ain't going. Just drop me off at my car before you turn up," Niya told him.

"Niya, are you sure that you don't want to come with us and celebrate? You turned this night into your night. You deserve to party," Smiley said as she ran her hand up and down Niya's back.

"Nah, Smiley. It's cool. I just really don't feel well."

***

We had been driving in silence, as if we were in our own worlds. I was so tired that I couldn't find the energy to speak. We pulled up to our building, Niya got her things out of the trunk, and together, we entered the building. It was an eerie feeling, us standing there in the middle of the lobby, with our flights of stairs waiting to separate us. It was as if we should not have been there, as if our presence surprised the air, which just wasn't meant for us. But by the grace of God, neither Niya nor I would sleep in a jail cell that night. Only by the grace of God had we cheated the cruel hand fate had dealt us.

"Niya?" Her name was all that I could say. We had been standing there, not looking at each other, not speaking. Words had gathered in my throat, but they were wedged between my heart and my teeth.

"Jamilla, baby, we don't have to talk about it. We never have to talk about it."

She wouldn't look at me. I just needed her to look at me.

"Niya, look, we, I . . . you know that—"

"No need to talk, Jamilla boo. I already know what it is. I have always known."

Still, her eyes graced the floor.

"But we need to talk. We need to make sure that things are okay."

"They are. Just go home, take a shower, and try to sleep. We don't have to talk about it, Jamilla. We don't ever have to talk about it. Just go."

"But, Niya—"

"Just go, okay? Please, just go. I know everything that you want to tell me. I just want you to know that I'm sorry and that I love you, but right now . . . just go."

She was trembling, and her face was turning red. I was afraid that she was breaking, that she was breaking right before my eyes. I got close to her and just hugged her. I hugged her until she said it again.

"Jamilla, just go."

Chapter 56

Niya

I just couldn't be that close to her, knowing what I had caused. I watched her walk away only because I was dying to look at her, but I just couldn't look into her eyes. What she did for me that night would haunt me for the rest of my life, and in that moment, I was just trying to deal. When I got inside my apartment, to my surprise, my granny was still up. I stood with my back against the door, but I could see her on the couch.

"Niya, mi amor, I so happy you come home so soon. I stay . . . I stay up until my Niya come and tell me everything. Come to de living room."

I couldn't move. Facing my grandmother with so much on my heart was another conquest that I just wasn't ready for.

"Niya, honey, you hear me?"

I couldn't even answer. Flashes of that cop and Jamilla filled my brain. I just couldn't move. I could hear her getting up, and I swear to God I tried to will my feet to move. I just wanted to run into my bedroom, but I just couldn't move.

"Niya, qué pasa?"

My granny stood in front of me, and I wanted to answer her, but I couldn't. I started to bang the back of my head against the door, and I didn't know why.

"Niya, what is wrong? *Cuál es el problema*?" My granny pulled me away from the door and into her arms. There, for the first time that night, I felt safe.

"Granny, it was all my fault. It was all my fault."

"Mi amor, tell me. Tell me what happen. *Tienes que decirme qué pasó para yo poder ayudarte.*"

We were now on the floor, with me in my grandmother's arms. She rocked me back and forth as I screamed and cried.

"Tell me, Niya. You have to tell your granny what happen."

"That spell that you did before I left? You were right, Granny. It saved me, Granny, but . . . but it used Jamilla to save me. It killed her and saved me, Granny. Oh my God. What did I do, Granny? I'm so sorry. I'm so sorry."

"Niya, you have to say what you problem. I will help, but you tell me first."

At that point, there was no holding back. I had had enough. All my life I had fought to be strong, all my life I had *had* to be strong, and I was tired. I lay in her arms and told her everything. I didn't just start with what had happened that night. I told her about me dealing drugs, about what really went down with Rodney, and about the happenings with White Boy. I even tried my best to get her to understand my love for Jamilla. The love I felt for her before that night and the love I felt after what she did for me seemed like two different things now.

When I told her about Jamilla sleeping with the cop, she said to me that Jamilla was my living angel. She said that the liquid she got from the voodoo man did just what he said it would. It protected me from deviated dreams, and Jamilla in a sense stopped the bullet. She said that no matter what I did or said that night, Jamilla would never have gotten out of my car when I stood screaming at her in front of my building. She said it was all fate, from our first real meeting on that stoop to her being my angel that night.

"So now, in the morning, we go see *tu padre.* He know how to fix that *puta* White Boy."

I had fought everything when it came to my father, as if I was holding a grudge against him. He had never really been there, giving me only pieces of himself from time to time. But that night, when my granny said that she would call on my dad for help, I knew that adding him to the mix was my only way out. I knew that this was going to be his chance to save me, and after years of fighting every battle by myself, I welcomed him with open arms. I was tired and in need of rest.

Chapter 57

Jamilla

I stood in the shower, trying to wash away the dirtiness I felt scorching my skin. Niya, without trying to, had made me feel as if she couldn't stand being close to me, as if I disgusted her. With thoughts of her repulsion for me burning our night's events into my brain, I tried to scrub my skin off. Part of me was happy that I was standing in my tub, because my night could have turned out differently, but it also bothered me that it had been so easy for me to give up my body. It made me question my self-worth. Did I really have so little consideration for my body that I was willing to give it up just to save us? Whatever the case might have been, it just left me feeling ill.

Once out of the shower, I turned on my computer and let it boot up. I looked at my phone the whole time I dried off and got dressed. I wanted her to call or text, and I wanted to do the same, but . . . what would I say? I even picked up the phone and held it in my hand, but still, I drew a blank. So instead, I went to my computer and checked my e-mail. I was so thankful to find my teacher's e-mail waiting for me. She was done with the edits on *Rainbow Hearts*. I looked at my calendar. I had only about a week to get the cover in and the formatting done. I e-mailed both parties, paid them, and had their word that they would put a rush on both things. I went to bed with Sade playing in the background and hoped to dream of happier times with Niya.

I stayed in bed most of the next day. On Sundays my house was always filled with delicious aromas, as my mother cooked a big Haitian feast. I looked over at the clock that was beside my bed, and it read three in the afternoon. I lay there for a little longer and decided to jump in the shower and at least comb my hair. Before going in, I looked at my phone and saw I still had no call or text from Niya. I broke down and reached out to her, hoping that she was okay.

Hey, big head. I just wanted you to know that I was thinking about you. I love you, Niya.

I jumped in the shower and let the hot water soothe me. After getting out, I still didn't have a text back from Niya. My stomach was growling, so I headed to the kitchen to see what my mother had cooked.

"Jamilla, go to the store and get some Malta."

I looked at my mother sideways, because my stepdad was the only one who drank that shit. Why would she send me to the store for the man she thought I was trying to steal from her?

"Send his daughter," I answered without a second thought.

"You know we don't like her going out by herself after the girls fought her. Ale pou mwen."

I rolled my eyes and took the money from her. I turned the music on my phone on high, put in my earbuds, and headed out. It was a little cold out, but I had forgotten my jacket. I hurried to the store and got what my mother wanted. I was halfway home when I again checked my phone for Niya's message, but I still had nothing from her. When I felt someone grab me from behind, I screamed and dropped the bag in my hand.

"What are you fucking doing? You scared the hell out of me." I was clutching my chest and breathing heavily. Rodney was smiling, as if he thought it was funny.

"My bad, baby. I was just happy to see you. Plus, I called you, but you didn't turn around."

"You made me break my stepdad's Malta. What is wrong with you?" I asked, a little annoyed.

"My bad, Jamilla. I will buy you some more. Don't be mad. You looked so cute while screaming."

He made me crack a smile.

"Come on, Jamilla. Let's go back to the store. Have you heard from Niya? June and I just left her apartment, but no one answered the door."

"No, I texted her, but she didn't hit me back. Why are you looking for her?"

"People have been getting at June all day about this girl Niya. She's blowing up, and everyone wants to know who she is."

As we walked to the store, I thought about life and how messed up it could all be. Whenever I looked at celebrities, I always saw the glitz and the glamour. I would dream about being them. To have people scream your name, show you love no matter where you went, and to have people look up to you . . . I had always thought that life was easy for them. It wasn't until that moment that it hit me that they were human too. Sure, we saw them shine, but now I wondered what was behind the bright lights and smiles. Were they dealing with things like family, depression, anger, hurt, and pain? Niya just had what should have been the best night of her life. Her dreams were unfolding and coming true right before her eyes, yet misery had preceded her happiness.

After getting my stepdad's drink, we headed back to my building, and Rodney walked me to my door.

"I've been thinking about you ever since I saw you last night. You looked so beautiful, but I really didn't get a chance to tell you," he said.

"Thank you. That means a lot."

"Were you and Niya okay? You two seemed weird."

I was about to answer him and tell him everything. It was as if I needed to talk to someone, anyone, about it, but my mother opened the door, interrupting us.

"Oh. Who is this boy?"

"Hi. I am Rodney."

My mother smiled and shook his hand, which shocked me. "Why you stand in the hallway? Come in and eat the food with us."

My mouth hung open as I watched her move to the side to let Rodney in.

"What are you doing?" I asked my mother as I entered the apartment.

"I like you talking to him. He boy. You need to talk to boy only."

I rolled my eyes at her. She was so stuck on Niya being a girl, and it disgusted me, although I was doing the same thing.

By the time Rodney left that night, my mother was acting like she was in love with him. She made him promise to come over the following Sunday. As we stood outside my front door, he joked about how much my mother liked him.

"Please. She's just happy that you're a boy."

He stopped smiling, and it hit me that maybe I shouldn't have said that.

"Plus, it doesn't matter what she thinks. It's all about what I think of you, and I think you're pretty freaking great," I added quickly.

There. He was smiling again.

"Can I pick you up and give you a ride to Kingsborough tomorrow?" he asked.

I thought about it. I still hadn't heard from Niya.

"Yeah. That would be cool."

He smiled and leaned in and kissed me softly, lovingly. I liked it, but still, my mind was on her. As I locked the door after saying good-bye to Rodney, my phone vibrated. I looked at it and saw I had a text from Niya, finally.

Waiting at Rikers to see my dad. This shit feels weird. And I love you too.

I took a seat and instantly wished I was with her, but all I could do was text back.

Damn. I'm shocked. Just breathe and say all that you need to say. I'm proud of you. Good luck. And hit me up once you leave.

Chapter 58

Niya

I sat in that waiting room, with my heart pumping blood, anger, hurt, and excitement. No matter how mad I was at my parents, I still loved them, and we had still shared some good times. My granny sat with me, holding my hand. She always knew when I needed her, even when I didn't say it, and her offering something as small as just holding my hand gave me strength.

"Karee?" the guard called out. My grandmother and I stood up and waited for my father to enter. It had been a few years since I had seen him, so I was nervous.

When he walked into the waiting room, I looked at my granny, and she was smiling. He was big, and you could tell he was lifting weights. He looked healthy, and that made her happy.

"How you holding up, baby girl?" he asked me after approaching us.

I didn't know why, but I teared up as I leaned in to kiss him. When things were good with him, they were good, and I had missed that. He kissed my grandma, and she told him about the package she had brought for him. He thanked her, and after that, he turned to me.

"So, baby girl, I saw you on the Internet. That shit was dope. I am really proud of you."

I smiled. "Thanks, Dad. This is just the start of it all, and truth be told, this is all 'cause of you. I got my love of music from you, and I thank you for that. You didn't have a problem with any of it?"

I could tell that my words had touched him, but I wasn't sure how me being so open about being gay sat with him.

"Why would I have a problem with any of it? All I have ever wanted for you was happiness and for you to follow your dreams. If you can do all of that while being *you*, that's all that I can ask for. Plus, these niggas out here ain't shit these days. Better you fuck with bitches. Oh, my bad, Mommy."

My grandma gave him the stink eye for using the word *bitch*, but they made me laugh.

"So, we got about an hour. Tell me what's up," he said.

I told him about everything that had gone down with White Boy, from selling to him, to Roxie and her man, to him rolling up on me, demanding money off of my shows and earnings from my music in any form, even CD sales. I made sure to speak low and tried my best to keep shit coded.

"See, that's where you fucked up right there. How many times did I tell you that if you're going to do some dirt, make sure to get dirty by yourself? I don't give a shit if it's a friend or a foe. Do shit on your own, 'cause all friends can turn into damn foes in the blink of an eye."

I didn't answer, 'cause he was right. When he did come around, he always made sure to drop his street knowledge on me.

"I am going to need you to stay off the streets while I handle this. No school. No work," he said.

"I'm off that," I answered. I wanted him to know that selling drugs would forever be in my past.

"Good, 'cause you're too talented to ruin your chances. So there's this guy I know, Marcelo. They call him the Get-It-Done man."

"Yeah, I know him."

"Good. I want you to go and see him. I want you to say these words. Jack said he has a pain in his ass that makes his head hurt, and he needs you to take care of that before it reaches his heart too. He also asked if you've seen that nigga White Boy."

"That's it?" I asked with a scrunched-up face.

"No. And tell him that I will be calling him at Willie's spot tonight, around nine."

"But I thought you just said that you should always do your dirt yourself?"

"Yeah, well, in this case, Marcelo owes me one. I am sitting in here, and he's free, so I am as dirty as I can get. It's his turn."

There was no need really to talk about it anymore. The rest of our visit was spent talking about old times, and before we left, my father asked only one thing of me.

"How is your mother?"

My face turned sour. I quickly told him about the last time I saw her, and he looked saddened by my reality.

"Niya, go check on her. Do it for me. Do it for your granny."

I looked at him, I looked at my grandmother, and I really thought about my mother.

"All right, Dad. I got you."

He kissed my granny, and afterward, he kissed me. I wanted to hold on to him, but as always, I had to let him go and watch him walk away. We had to sit down until all the prisoners left the room. Before he exited through the door, he turned to us and said, "Just two more years, just two more years."

As I drove home with my grandmother, the car was silent, as it appeared that we both were lost in the land of our own thoughts. When we hit the Brooklyn borough, she spoke up while taking my hand.

"Mi amor, you know you papi love you, just like you mommy. I love you too, Niya, but I hope you change now. Seeing you papi in jail and you mommy on the street, it kill me. I want good for you only. You become a star and show them the best thing they did was make you. You are special. You are a gift, mi amor. I know it soon as you mommy push you out. I pray, and that night I have dream you someone big in this world. I know you will be big, Niya. I see it in my dreams. Now, you take my dream, you step out of my dream, and you make it true. Learn your lesson, mi amor. Leave the street behind."

When we got home, my granny made a quick dinner, because she knew I had a message to pass on. It wouldn't be hard to find the man my father called Marcelo. He was always in the same spot.

"Gran, do you know why that man owes my dad a favor?"

She took in a deep breath and said yes, with no other explanation.

"Well, tell me what you know."

She got up, went into her tin jar, and pulled out a neatly rolled joint and lit it. "When your papi do the robbery, that man go with him. Your papi tell him no violence, but that man no listen. He go in, beat the Chinaman up, and when police catch your papi, the other man get away. Your papi never tell on him. The police say they know he no rob the bank alone, but your papi . . . he never say nothing."

I thought about things, and after I ate, I threw on my jacket. As I headed for the door, my grandma came over and put her hand on my forehead and prayed for me.

***

As I walked the streets, I looked down at my phone and saw that I had a few missed calls and text messages. When I called June back, he told me the good news about the people who were calling him for me, but I told him that I wouldn't be able to handle shit due to being really sick. I told him that the doctor said that I couldn't even go to school, and that the only reason I was out was that I was filling my prescription. He agreed to let me get back with him in a couple of days, and that ended our conversation.

Next on my list was Marlo. She had been blowing up my phone nonstop since I turned her out, but I just really wasn't feeling her anymore. The last thing on my mind was pussy. I saw the text from Jamilla and really wished that she'd been with me when I went to see my dad. I missed her more than I led on, but she would only cloud my mind with more of her "I'm straight" bullshit. So, I told myself that I would text her back some other time and went on to find the Get-It-Done dude.

When I walked up to him, he was alone. Just sitting on an old shopping cart that was lying on its side.

"Hey. Went to see my dad, Jack, today, and he had a message for you. Do you know who I am talking about?"

I waited for him to speak, but all he did was nod his head yes.

"Jack said he has a pain in his ass that makes his head hurt, and he needs you to take care of that before it reaches his heart too. He also asked if you seen that nigga White Boy. He said to go down to Willie's spot around nine tonight, 'cause he would be calling you."

"That's it?" he asked as he picked up his newspaper and started to read the sports section.

I started to say yes, but I had a request of my own. "From what my pops says, you owe him one. Is that true?"

My question seemed to freeze him in space. After a few seconds, he looked up at me and answered, "Yeah, that's true, but after this, all dues will be paid."

I reached down beside him. Picked up his pack of Newports and took one out. I pulled out my lighter, lit a cigarette, and told him how I felt about things.

"See, this is how I see it. You not only owe my father, but you owe me too."

"Oh yeah, and why is that?" Marcelo asked as he lit his own cancer stick.

"'Cause you were with him that day, and he never told on your ass. And because you two were into robbing places, I grew up without him. You're out here on these streets. You see how hard life is. You also know my pops, and you know that even with all his bullshit, he's a great guy. Yeah, *he* robbed that store, but you were with him, so . . . that makes you an accomplice to my stolen childhood." I was laying it on thick, but it was worth a try.

"So, what in the fuck do you want from me, little girl?"

Yeah, I could hear the anger in his voice, but him asking me what I wanted showed that he was at least willing to listen.

"I want to be there when you handle this for my dad."

"Is that it?"

"No. I want you to handle this one yourself. Can you do that?"

He stood up and looked me dead in the eyes. "Now, why would you want that?" he asked. Looking into his eyes was like looking into a black hole. He seemed empty inside, and it gave me chills.

"'Cause the less people who know about this shit, the better. Plus, I need some information from him, and after I get that info, I am going to hire you to do a job."

I watched as his lips slowly curled into a smile. "A paid job? Now, that's what I like to hear. I will make sure that you are there."

I put out my cigarette and asked him to take down my number.

"No, no need for that. I only take calls from the pen. When I need you, I know where to find you."

I walked away with a chilly feeling creeping up my spine. It was a scary thought that a man like that would know where to find me.

I went home and stayed there for the next week. I didn't speak to or hear from anyone until my fourth day of solitude.

Chapter 59

Jamilla

This was the third morning Rodney was picking me up for school, and Niya was yet again a no-show. I called her, I texted, and I even knocked on her door, but nothing. When her grandmother opened the door, she told me that Niya wasn't home, but I could tell that she was lying. There was no way that she wasn't there. Her birthday was only a day away, and I needed to see her. I needed to speak to her, and I really just wanted to spend time with her. I missed her so much. Hanging with Rodney was cool. He gave me all his attention, and I loved that. When we weren't together, he texted me until he went to sleep, and in the morning, he texted me while he was still in bed.

"Hey, beautiful. So happy to see you, boo."

I was standing in front of my building, waiting for him. I guessed I was deep in thought, because I didn't even see him walk up. He was behind me, with his arms around my waist, and he planted a small kiss on my neck.

"What in the fuck are you doing? What did I tell you about that? What if Niya was walking down?"

I pushed him off of me roughly and looked up at the window to Niya's kitchen. The blinds looked like they might have moved a little, but I wasn't sure. I knew that her grandmother always left the fan on in there, so that could have been the cause.

"Yo, when are you going to tell her? I'm tryin'a make you my girl, and I don't want to have to hide the fact that I'm falling in love with you."

I was stunned. Stunned, but still pissed.

"*Love*? What do you mean, you're falling in love with me? We have been hanging out for only a couple of days."

I started to walk away from him, but he just followed me.

"Yeah, that's what I said. Is there a problem with falling in love with you within a couple of days? I mean, I have known you for some time now."

I didn't answer. Hell, I couldn't.

"Stop walking, Jamilla. Look, that's the facts, so tell me how you feel."

I stopped walking and looked into his eyes. "I don't know what to say to tell you the truth. I guess I wasn't expecting to hear that."

He shoved his hands in his pockets and looked down at his shoes, then back at me. "It's cool, I guess. I just can't help it. You make me feel different, so . . . I'll wait."

"Wait for what?" I asked, although I already knew the answer.

"Guess I'll wait for you to fall in love with me too. Hey, I know you like me, so being the smooth nigga that I am . . . it won't take long."

Seeing him smile made me smile too.

"Look, Rodney, I am going to catch the bus instead of riding with you. I just need to think about things. Is that okay?"

He nodded his head yes and came in for a hug. I held him at arm's length and tilted my head to my building.

"So, when are you going to tell Niya?"

His question hung in the air as if it were thick smoke, which caused me to have trouble breathing. I started to back away from him before answering.

"I don't know, Rodney. I really don't know."

That was all the truth.

Between classes, I texted Rodney and told him that I would also take the bus home. Things were moving too fast with him, and I needed space. I wasn't ready to tell Niya anything, so he needed to pump his brakes on that issue. My life had changed because of Niya. It seemed like everyone on campus wanted to be my friend ever since they'd found out that Niya and I were close. People were always asking me about her when I wasn't with her, asking about her music, when her next video would be out, and that day was no different. As I walked out of my English class, I heard my name being called and turned around to see Marlo.

"Hey, girl. What you been up to?" she said.

I stood there and gave her a tight-lipped smile. "Hey."

"Them shoes are real cute, girl. Niya get them for you?"

I didn't answer her. I just waited for her to get to her real question.

"So, girl . . . you seen Niya? I see she hasn't been on campus, and I'm getting a little worried."

I rolled my eyes and just offered her a simple no.

"Come on, girl. Don't lie. I know that you are real close to her. I know you've seen her."

I started to walk away while answering over my shoulder, "No, sorry. I haven't seen her."

"Well, tell her to call me. I need to see her."

"I'm sure you have her number, Marlo. Just go ahead and hit her up." She wasn't about to use me to run her whore errands.

I walked into my house and fell on my bed. I lay across it the long way while going through old texts from Niya in my phone. I wished she would talk to me and see me. I missed her and needed to make sure that we were okay after that crazy night with the cops.

Niya, I miss you. I need to see you. Answer me please. I need to know that you are okay.

I sent my text and waited and waited and waited. My heart hurt, and I just didn't know what else to do.

"Hey, Jamilla. This came for you."

I sat up and looked down at the package that Marie had laid on my bed before retreating. I had uploaded my manuscript on CreateSpace and had put in my order for the proof as soon as it was available. I wanted to open the box and hold my first book in my hand, but it didn't feel right not sharing this moment with Niya. I had ordered two copies, and she was supposed to be here with me.

Niya, I really need you. Please, answer me.

I waited and waited and waited, but still nothing. I slid the box under my bed and promised myself that if she didn't answer my happy birthday call or text, I was going to her house and pushing past her granny. I needed to see her; I needed her to share this with me. I spent the night texting her and ignoring the text from Rodney. He wasn't who I wanted in that moment.

Happy birthday, Niya. I miss you, baby. I will see you today. I am on my way to Kingsborough, and I hope you have a great day. I love you.

I texted Niya her happy birthday text after calling her three times with no answer. I was starting to get pissed.

That day, while in school, all I did was think of her. What we had couldn't be over already. We had to get past whatever this was. Our love was too strong for whatever this roadblock was. So after my last class, I went home, did my chores, showered, did my hair and makeup as best as I could, and put on a dress that Niya had bought for me but that I had never worn. I waited for my family to fall asleep before I headed out.

Chapter 60

Niya

I was already up when Jamilla's text came through. If it weren't for her text, I would have forgotten my own birthday. I stood at the kitchen window and waited for her to appear. I watched her every morning, just needing to get a simple glance at her. She was still the most beautiful thing that I had ever seen, not that things would change in just a couple of days. But our couple of days apart felt like centuries crushing me. I missed her to the point that my head and heart would hurt at just the mere thought of her.

So I stood there at the window every morning, and that morning, nothing had changed. I had been up for almost twenty-four hours with no sleep, I was drunk as hell, and I was in a terrible mood. So many things were running through my mind, but none more dominant than that night with Jamilla and the cops. I hated myself more and more with each passing day. All the blame was on me, and I just couldn't face her—not yet. At times, I felt as if she deserved someone better than me in her life.

Who was I? A fucking drunk, a drug dealer, a lesbian who was dealing with Mommy and Daddy issues, who at times counted on her love a little too much? See, all this time I was thinking that she treated me as if she needed me more than she loved me, but . . . I did the same damn thing. I used her, used everything that was good in her.

Her pureness somehow healed the broken and painful parts in me. Her love and her need for me made me feel wanted, as if I had a purpose in this world. She made me feel like a redeemer, a liberator, a protector. She made me feel whole. She completed me; she rescued me from a lonely existence that was sure to eat me up alive. See, I needed her too. I. Needed. Her. Too!

Once Jamilla was out of sight, I tumbled over to the bathroom, undressed, and got into the shower. Afterward, I didn't even dry off. I just stepped out, sat on my bed, and conked out. I didn't wake up until Marlo and what seemed like all of Facebook started blowing up my phone.

I rubbed my eyes when my Facebook notifications said I had over two thousand birthday wishes. What was even crazier was the fact that I didn't know a good 90 percent of the people who had taken the time to wish me a happy birthday. When I looked on Instagram, there weren't as many, but there had to be a few hundred. That made me smile. My head was a lot clearer, and I wasn't so drunk, but the first thing I did was pick up the bottle of Patrón that was next to my bed and take a big swig.

After checking social media, the next thing I did was check my text messages. A few friends who weren't my friends on Facebook had texted, but most were from Marlo. I must have had about fifteen from her. The very first one was her sending me her birthday wishes, but the others were her saying that she needed to see me, she missed me, and she loved me, and the last one was a picture. I sat up once I made the photo bigger. She was naked and looked so damn good. She was on her back, with her legs spread, and my God, I was turned on from the minute my eyes landed on the picture. I texted her back.

My bad. Was sleeping. Thanks for the b-day wishes. What are you doing? I hope you didn't slip on any clothes. ☺

It seemed like as soon as I pushed SEND, she messaged me right back.

You tell me what's up. I am tryin'a see you. I miss you and want to try my hand at fucking the shit out of you. ;) Maybe a birthday fuck?

With this message, she sent another picture. This time, she was playing with herself.

I can't drive. Been drinking. Why don't you come through?

Again, her response was lightning fast.

Just give me the address, and I'll be on my way.

I thought about it and had only one demand.

Okay, cool. But I want you to come over here with nothing on. Just you and that wet pussy of yours.

I waited to see if she would still come.

That's fine. I'll borrow one of my mom's long coats. Send me the addy.

I got out of bed, got myself together, and threw out the empty bottles that littered my room. Other than that, it was still pretty neat in there.

"Niya, mi amor, come. Come see."

I walked out of my room to see what Granny wanted to show me. When I got to the kitchen, she was holding a cake in her hands that had nineteen candles on it.

"Happy birthday, mi amor. You make wish now."

Damn, I loved that lady. She always made everything better. Looking into her eyes, I could tell that she was both happy and thankful that I had made it to see my nineteenth birthday. For a while, we ate cake, listened to Héctor Lavoe, a Puerto Rican singer whose salsa music always got her to dance. For the first time in days, I was smiling and enjoying myself. I rolled a few fat blunts, and Granny and I got drunk and high as hell. Soon she would have to sit down, because she danced too much and because the liquor and weed would get to her. And of course, she would never admit that she just couldn't hang.

"Niya, put down the music. I need to sit. *Uno momento*, I will get up again."

I smiled and turned the music down.

"Oh, Niya, you see, I old now. I used to be the best salsa dancer in Santo Domingo."

"It's cool, Granny. I've been told that you can't hang."

We laughed, and I kissed her forehead. As I poured her another drink, there was a knock at the door.

"Maybe it's you friend Jamilla. She look for you, Niya. Why you so mean to her? She so nice girl."

I told her that it wasn't Jamilla as I headed for the door.

"Hey, you. I missed you," Marlo said as she walked into the apartment. She opened her coat and showed me all that she was working with. I pulled her inside, pushed her against the wall, and closed her coat.

"Slow down, girl. My granny's up."

She looked embarrassed, and it was cute.

"Calm down. She didn't see you." I pressed my body against hers and kissed her lips.

"Niya, who is this girl?"

I turned around to find my grandmother behind us. She gave Marlo the stink eye off the bat.

"Hey, Granny. This is Marlo, a friend from school."

She stood there, looking at Marlo, then turned back to me. "*A mi no me gusta ella*, Niya. Jamilla, call Jamilla."

I was shocked but had to laugh. I thanked God that my granny had said that she didn't like Marlo in Spanish. I took Marlo's hand and started to walk to my bedroom. I turned around and let my granny know that she had nothing to worry about, that I really didn't like Marlo and that we shared nothing too serious.

"A mi tampoco me gusta. No te preocupes. No es nada serio."

Marlo and I had been in my room for a good twenty minutes before she started talking shit.

"Oh yeah? You think it's that simple, huh?" I said.

"How hard can it be to be good at eating pussy? I have one. You got one. It shouldn't be hard. If I know what I like, that means I can please you."

I wanted to see what she was working with. After all, it was my birthday. A good nut would add the icing to my birthday cake.

We were on my bed, so I pulled her on top of me. I kissed her and waited for her to make her move, but she just stayed on my lips.

"See?" I said between kisses. "You're fuckin' up already. You are taking too long on this boring-ass kiss. Make your move, ho."

As Marlo smiled, I realized that she was one of those types who liked to be mistreated in bed. Fuck her right and call her all kinds of names—that was what would make her cum. I had picked up on it the last time I was with her. Every time I'd called her a bitch, she'd moaned a little louder, and she'd fucked my face a little harder.

She did the "licking and kissing my breasts, tummy, and inner thighs" thing, but I was ready for more. I let her slip off my shorts and watched her face as her eyes landed between my legs. I was clean shaven, and from what I had been told, I was pretty down there. So she should have been happy. Even I had run into a few that scared the hell out of me. Some of them had looked like an ugly-ass catfish, and if that was the case, I would just play with it a little and send them home.

"Go ahead. What in the fuck are you waiting for?"

I took her by the back of her head and pulled her face toward me. Her mouth was warm and wet, just how I liked it.

"Yeah, lick that shit. Yeah, now suck on that clit."

She was a great student, a fast learner. She was so nasty that she let her tongue slip to places I didn't even tell her to lick. She did what I told her to do. When I said, "Suck," she latched on to my clit and nursed it. Yeah, she was a great student.

"Oh shit. Yeah, bitch. Just like that, right there. I'm about to cum. Fuck . . . I'm about to cum."

I pushed her off of me with my foot. She fell onto her back, and before she knew what hit her, I was on her face. I pinned her arms down with my knees and rubbed my wet slit against her lips.

"Come on, ho. Lick that pussy. Look, Ma. No hands. Look, Ma. No hands." I was teasing her by quoting lyrics the old "No Hands" song by Waka.

I rode her lips and tongue until the tingling feeling came back to my stomach. I pulled off my shirt and let my naked body kiss the Libra-scented night air.

When I looked down, I could see in her eyes how turned on she was, and that pushed me over the edge.

I tried to push myself deeper into her mouth as I came and told her how good a ho she was. It took me a minute for me to get myself together, but soon I was between her legs and making her cum with just my hands. Again, when we were done, I didn't see the need for her to be there anymore. I felt bad about it, but that was just how it was. I lay there with her and made small talk, but once she looked like she was getting tired and ready for a nap, it was really time for her to go.

"So, I hope to see you again," I said as I sat up in the bed.

"You can see me all night long if you want, baby."

I lit the half of a blunt that was sitting in the ashtray by my bed and gave her the okeydoke. "I would love to, but . . ." I picked up my cell phone and read the time. "It's after ten, and my grandma is going to be coming in here soon. I'm not supposed to have anyone here after ten."

She looked disappointed, but at the end of the day . . . she wasn't my girl.

I stood up and waited for her to join me. I walked her to the bathroom, and we both cleaned up. I really did feel bad as I watched her mope around the bathroom. She was a cool girl, but I could see right through her. She hadn't been checking for me before I started hanging out with Jamilla or before my videos. And who in the hell needed another Roxie? When she was done, I walked her to my front door and showed her a little kindness.

"You made my day. You know that?"

She smiled, and I could tell that it was real. "Niya, I want you to know that I really like you. I have never met anyone like you."

Damn. I kind of felt bad now.

"You're real cool too, Marlo. You're real cool." That was all that I could give her.

"I know that we haven't spent a lot of time together, but I just like you. At first, I just thought that I was going to run game on you." I started to laugh as she continued. "That's the truth. But as I got to know you, I realized that you have more to offer than money. I really do like you, and after you left the other night, I felt like I had fallen in love with you."

I was speechless. I had wanted to turn her out, but having her fall in love wasn't in the cards for us. So I pulled her to me and just kissed her. I knew that I wouldn't speak to her or see her after that night, so I gave her a kiss to remember.

"Niya?"

As soon as I heard the voice, I knew who it was. I pulled away from Marlo, as if I was a kid who had just got caught by her parents. My heart raced, and my head felt light, as if my hand had got caught in the kitty jar.

"Jamilla, what are you doing here?" I asked.

I kept my eyes on her face, but it was void of any emotion.

"It's your birthday, and I couldn't let this day go by without seeing you."

I glanced over at Marlo, as if I had forgotten that she was even there, and looked at her as if I was asking her why she was still there. "So, you should be getting home," I said.

If looks could kill, Jamilla would have been dead the minute those words left my mouth. Marlo looked at her and then back at me, and I could tell that she was not happy.

"Why don't you walk me out?" Marlo said.

I wanted to tell Marlo that she was not more important than Jamilla, but I was not cruel. "Nah, I have to talk to her. Be safe."

I hugged her and kind of pushed her out the door toward the steps. Once I had done that, my eyes went to Jamilla and stayed on her, and damn, she was beautiful.

"Hey, you look nice," I said as she walked over to me. I walked her into my house and closed the door. We stood behind it in the dimly lit hallway, she against one wall, I across from her and against the other.

"Happy birthday," she said with a smile.

"Thank you. I'm happy you stopped by." I was nervous. I had so much that I wanted to say to her, and I held back so much.

"I have a gift for you."

She held her hand out and waited for me to take the neatly wrapped gift from her hand. I took it and unwrapped it slowly. It was a box that had not been opened yet, and I asked her what it was.

"Just open it. I have not seen it, either. I wanted to wait for you, for us to see it together."

I ripped the box open, and once I pulled out the two books, it hit me. I took in a deep breath as my eyes registered what I was holding in my hand.

"Oh my God, Jamilla. This is your book. Wow. I am so proud of you."

I looked up at her and could see the tears in her eyes. I was so damn happy for her. I looked back down at the books and handed her one. I watched as she held it and turned the book from front to back and side to side. She looked like she was in paradise. Her dreams were in her hand, and for a brief moment, I stayed quiet just to let her take that trip to dreamer's paradise.

"It's so beautiful, Niya, and to be standing here with you, I . . . I am just so happy."

I left my wall and hugged her tight. I smiled as she cried tears of happiness.

"You did it, baby. You did it."

I let her go and stood beside her. Her cover was beautiful. Two girls from the back. One looked like a stud; one like a femme. They were holding hands, and although most of the cover was black and white, there were small things in color, and each was a color from the rainbow. I read the title, *Rainbow Hearts*, over and over, and the subtitle, *A Funny Little Thing Called Fate*.

"Don't just hold it and look at it. Open it and read the acknowledgment page," she ordered.

I opened the book and took my time reading all the pages before her dedication, even the copyright page. Once I got to the page she wanted me to read, I took my time with the words and took it all in.

To Niya. Because of you, I am alive. You came into my world and changed not only the things in it, but me and my heart too. I love you, and I am no longer afraid to say it out loud, and most importantly, I am unafraid to say it to you and believe it myself. You are the rainbow that drowned out the darkness, and you made my heart beat.

I was so touched that my eyes started to get cloudy with tears.

"Jamilla, I don't know what to say. Wow, Jamilla. Just wow."

"So you like it?" Her question shocked me.

"Jamilla, I love it. I love everything about it. This is the best gift I have ever gotten in my life."

She smiled, and that, unlike the lie I had told Marlo, made my birthday.

"So, the show the other night . . . Niya, you killed it."

It was sad. That should have been the most memorable night of my life, and it would be, except for all the wrong reasons.

"Yeah, I wish that I was really present for it."

"I love the freestyle you did at the end. Really touching. That guy who came in and spoke to you thought so too. What did you think about him?" she asked, but I really didn't understand why.

"I mean, he was cool. There were so many people coming at me after the show that I really didn't give him much thought."

"No, I mean about him saying that he works out of Atlanta and L.A. Have you thought about us leaving after we finish our freshman year of college?"

Damn. My mind had been so cluttered with the shit going on in my life that I hadn't really given it much thought.

"To tell you the truth, Jamilla, I really haven't even thought about it."

"You still want to leave, right?" she asked, as if she was holding her breath.

At that moment, I really wasn't even sure about moving anymore. Things between us were off and on, my granny would be alone, and I, well, I just felt like I . . . Hell, I didn't know. Maybe I was scared, maybe I was just in a messed-up state, or maybe I thought that I would fail. I just didn't know why I was having a change of heart.

"Niya, we have to go. There is nothing for us here but crime and too many bad memories. Granny could come with us, but you and I, we have to leave."

I looked at her and knew that she was right, but I just wasn't sure. I told her that I would give it more thought, and once I had an answer, I would give her one. I knew that I should go, but whether I would go was the question.

Chapter 61

Jamilla

Leaving her was torture. The space between us was too damn wide, my need for her was even bigger, and I wanted to tell her so. It just didn't seem like the right time, so I just spoke about the book and about her show and how well she'd done. When she asked me what else I had been up to, I couldn't really answer, because most of my free time had been spent with Rodney. So as I turned to walk out her door, my heart was heavy. I felt as if I was hiding so much from her, and it hurt.

"Happy birthday, Niya. I really hope that you enjoyed it."

"I did because of you. I have missed you, and getting this book as a gift that has made my night."

I turned back around and stood there, wanting to run into her arms and have her kiss me and hug me.

"You want me to walk you to your side of the building?" she asked as I stared at her.

"No, I can make it. You should get some rest."

I turned to walk out, but she took my hand and pulled me to her. When her arms reached around my waist, I melted inside.

"I'm proud of you, Jamilla boo. I really am."

***

The walk to my apartment was harder than I thought it would be. Thinking of her, for some reason, made me emotional. Seeing Marlo leaving her place and then being able to see my book for the first time with her right next to me made me feel an array of emotions. I stood in front of my front door and tried to get myself together, but it just wasn't working.

"Where'd you go this time of night?" said a male voice.

My front door had flung open, and my stepdad was standing there. I rolled my eyes and tried to get past him, but he was blocking me.

"I went to take someone their birthday gift."

"Oh, you go see your girlfriend or you go see the boy? You have so many people, I cannot count."

Once he said that, I used all my strength and pushed him out of the way. This time it worked, as I knocked both him and the beer that was in his hand down.

"You don't hear me?"

Once I was in front of my bedroom door, I turned to him and told him how I really felt.

"Why don't you go and question your fucking wife, you sick fuck?"

"Ay, you don't talk to me like that. They called your mother to go work. So now I question you."

My face twisted with disgust as I answered him. "Go fuck yourself. You don't get to question me. You have a wife and a daughter. Do this stupid shit with them."

With that, I went into my bedroom and locked my door. I didn't even bother to take off my clothes. I just lay across my bed, went through old text messages from Niya, and cried. I missed her with all of me, and I needed to have her the way I used to have her. I needed her love.

When I opened my eyes, I just lay there for a minute. I almost didn't believe what had happened. It had been so long that I was shocked. I sat up and looked down. *Shit.* I really was wet. The cold had woken me up, and the disbelief brought me to reality. *Damn.* I had wet the bed. Instantly, I felt embarrassed. I slid off the bed, with my head hanging low, and wondered how this could have happened. I had been doing so well, and *boom*, look at me. Was it the stress of the situation with Niya? Was it my stepfather? Or maybe the secret I was hiding with Rodney was eating away at me. I just couldn't put my finger on it, but one thing was for sure. I felt so low and dirty.

I got out of my clothes, threw on my robe, and took all the sheets off of my bed and threw them in the corner with my wet clothes. Thankfully, I had never taken the plastic cover off my mattress, so I just had to wipe it off with a mixture of bleach and water and put on new sheets. I picked up the pile of sheets and clothes and headed for the washing machine in the kitchen. Once in there, I could see the light from the television, which meant that my stepdad was in the living room. I hurried and started the washer and headed to the bathroom. I made my mixture to sanitize the plastic that covered my bed and headed back into my room. I closed my door, and with tears in my eyes, I wiped the urine off my bed, dried the plastic cover, and started to put on new sheets.

"You pee in the bed again?"

My stepfather's voice scared me and caused me to jump up and let out a low scream.

"Get the hell out of my room."

He was clearly drunk. I could tell by the way he slowly blinked and leaned against the wall.

"Oh, so, you take it away from me, like you a big girl, you give it to him, her, and you still pee pee in the bed. Oh no, you not grown up. You still my little girl."

My heart started to race. I hadn't felt this way since before Niya held the gun up to his head.

"Get out of my room, or I will scream," I said as I looked around the room for something that could be used as a weapon.

"Go. Okay, scream. You think I don't know you make my Marie scream? Yes, I know it's you."

Once he said that, the fight to leave my bedroom was on. I clawed and slapped him as he tried to hold me in the room. I made it all the way to the front door, opened it halfway, only to have him slam it shut.

"Get away from me!" I screamed as I ran back to my room and pushed the door closed. I tried to lock it, but he was against it, pushing to open it, as I stood behind it, trying to keep it shut.

"I am going to hurt you, you hear me?"

I was so terrified because he was winning the door battle. Finally, he pushed so hard that I went flying back and fell, hitting the back of my head on the corner of my dresser. I tried to shake it off, but my head was spinning and hurting. When I reached back to rub it, my hand felt wet and came back in front of me decorated with the color scarlet. I struggled to get up and couldn't. I held on to my nightstand for support, but it leaned forward, making everything that was on it fall. I thanked God for that, because my phone fell within arm's reach.

"Yes, show me my stuff. Yes, that is mine, and tonight I am going to feel it with this."

The room was still spinning, but I could see what "this" was. It was his penis, and it was hard and ready to enter my body. As the blood from my head warmed my back, I pushed CALL next to Niya's name and prayed that she picked up. As soon as I heard her voice, my stepdad knocked the phone out of my hand. He grabbed a handful of my hair and stood me up and threw me on my bed.

"Niya, Niya, help me. My stepdad, Niya. Please, *Niyaaa.*"

I kicked, punched, and did all that I could to keep him from entering my body. I just couldn't let that happen.

Chapter 62

Niya

I was in a deep drunken sleep. I could still remember the dream that I was having when my phone woke me up. I was in a big house, a big, beautiful home that was empty. I kept looking for my granny, but I couldn't find her. I kept yelling for her, asking her if she liked the house that I had just bought her, but I just could not find her. So when my phone rang, it made me jump out of my sleep and sit up. I looked at the name that flashed across my screen and wondered why Jamilla was calling me at six in the morning.

"Hello?"

All I heard was her voice screaming my name and asking for help. At first, I just sat there, wondering if I was still in a dream, but when she shouted my name again, followed by the words *help* and *stepdad*, I hopped out of bed and took off running. I didn't stop for my shoes or shirt. I ran out with just some red-and-white boy-cut undies and a wife beater on. I took the steps two at a time and made it to Jamilla's side of the building in record time. The front door was unlocked, so I burst in. As I stood in her entryway, I listened for her cries. Once I realized they were coming from her room, I ran in and saw red. He, her stepfather, was on top of her as she fought to push him off. I didn't really know what happened next, and I wouldn't know until the day Jamilla told me.

Chapter 63

Jamilla

When I saw Niya behind him, I was able to breathe. She yanked him off of me and slammed him to the floor. I wasn't sure where she found the strength, but I was grateful that she had it in her. She jumped on top of him and delivered a barrage of punches into my stepdad's face. I sat there, trying to catch my breath, and watched the beating he was enduring and wished he was dead.

"Jamilla. Oh my God! She is going to kill my dad."

I turned and saw Marie, and then I looked back at Niya. I couldn't tell if the blood on her fists was hers or his.

"Niya, that's enough," I said between deep breaths."Niya. No, Niya. *Don't.*"

Niya had moved on from her fists to the buckle of a belt that she had picked up off my floor. She had wrapped the belt around one of her fists and had made sure the buckle stuck out. Over and over again her fist met my stepdad's face. He was screaming, and in his drunken state, he was no match for her. I screamed her name over and over again, but nothing would stop her. I even tried to pull her off of him, but she pushed me away with her left hand as her right one continued to do damage. There was only one person who I knew could stop her, so I ran to Niya's apartment and woke her grandmother up.

"You have to come to my house. Niya is going to kill my stepdad."

She was out of bed and standing in my apartment within a minute.

"Niya, Niya, mi amor. Ay, Dios mio. Niya, stop."

I thought that hearing her grandmother's voice would bring her back to us, like it had with her mother, but it didn't. It took me, her granny, and Marie to pull her off of him. Her white wife beater was covered with blood, and sweat made it cling to her body.

"Ay, what is this? Oh no! Call the police now," cried my mother, who had just walked into my room, holding her chest.

Marie walked over to the house phone, but Niya's granny backhanded her so hard that she flew into the wall.

"You think you call the nine-one-one on my Niya? No. I know everything you and your crazy husband do to Jamilla. You call them, I tell them everything. We all go to jail. Now, tell that little *puta* to lock your door and come back. We all sit and talk, and we fix this. You tell me your choice."

Time seemed to stand still. All this time, I had looked at Granny as if she was just that—Niya's elderly grandmother, who stayed quiet and smoked her weed. But the lady before me . . . There was nothing elderly about her. She stood with power and made the air in my room so thick that I had to take deep breaths to feel as if I was getting air in my lungs.

"Oh my God! Your lesbian come here and kill my husband, and I will call the police. She kill him!"

With just two steps, Granny was in my mother's face, and my mother was dealt the same fate Marie had been handed just a few seconds ago. My mother flew into the wall and held her face. Granny was right back in her face as soon as she hit the wall.

"*Estás loca*? I say no police. He no dead. *Comprende*? You let him touch Jamilla. You touch Jamilla, I make cops take you to jail. Okay?"

My mother sat there and had the nerve to turn to me and ask why I was telling people outside the house about what happened inside the house. Thank God Granny was there to yank her up.

"You have one minute, *uno minuto*, understand? Tell her lock the door and come back," Granny growled.

My mother had no choice. Marie did as she was told and, afterward, she came back to the bedroom.

"How you let this man touch you daughter? You so sick. I know my Niya is wrong, but this is what we do. I take Jamilla to my house. She no stay here no more," Granny said.

"You crazy. You no take my child," my mother said, as if she had ever really cared for me.

"You child, you child? What you do for her, huh? She tell you what he do, you do nothing," Granny said in her thick Dominican accent.

"He not do that to her. She go with her boyfriend. She go with your lesbian and do sex."

I watched as Granny took a deep breath and tried to hold her composure. "Okay, you no call Niya lesbian again, okay? And yes, I take her. She no safe. Make him tell you what he do to her."

We all seemed to look at my stepfather, who was still on the floor, moaning and groaning. No, he wasn't dead, but he was about to answer for all his wrongdoings when it came to me.

"Yes, ask him what he do to you daughter. Ask him," Granny insisted.

We waited for my mother finally to pop the question. She walked over to her husband, kneeled down, and picked his head up and placed it in her lap. Never mind her daughter, who had a gash on the back of her head and still had blood running down her back.

"Jackson, you not do nothing to Jamilla. I know, yes?"

I held my breath and took Niya's hand, her left hand. I squeezed it until my fingers started to go numb. I waited and waited and waited.

"You better speak up, motherfucker, or I am going to finish your ass off." Niya's voice was steady and straight to the point. There was no wavering. When her words graced the air, she meant every part of what she said.

"Yes, Nicole, I touch her."

Again, my mother grabbed her chest, but his head was still in her lap.

"Poukisa ou fè sa?" My mother, Nicole Jean, had the nerve to act shocked and ask why he would do that. She had known the truth for so damn long, because I had told her, but she was in denial.

"*Mwen pa konnen*, Nicole. Okay? I don't know the answer. This is what I know. They touch me when I go to school, the teacher. . . . She make me touch another girl that go to that school. I don't know, okay? I don't know."

The room was silent.

"So you do that to my Jamilla? You tell me she lie, and you in this house . . . you sex her?"

"No, no sex. I touch. No sex."

"Until tonight. You said that you were going to rape me with your dick tonight, remember that?" Jamilla interjected.

Niya took her foot and kicked him in the thigh. She would have done it again if her Granny didn't tell her to stop.

"*Mwen pa ka kwè bagay sa.* You, Jackson, you?"

"Oh yes. You better believe that now," Granny answered, to my mother's surprise. "Oh, I am Dominican, but I learn to speak it there, because there so lot of you there, and Niya's papi come from Haiti. So yes, he do that. You have to believe it now. He tell you."

"Nicole, it's not my fault. I grow up that way. That's what I know."

"Oh no. He no do that to his daughter. He know he wrong. He no touch his daughter," Granny observed.

"Has he?" I asked Marie, and she shook her head no.

Again, Niya was on the attack.

"Jamilla, take her home. I finish with you mommy," Granny said.

I am not sure what happened in that apartment after I left. All I knew was that my mother and Marie started to bring my things over to Niya's house. Within two hours, the only thing that once belonged to me that was in that apartment was my furniture.

Once they were done bringing my things over, Niya's granny sat in the kitchen, smoking, as Niya showered in her bathroom. Before I went in and took my own hot bath, I had only one question.

"Did my mother kick him out?"

Granny took one long pull of her blunt and looked out the window. "No. She say she keep him. She can't pay bills if he leave."

I thanked her for everything she had done that day, turned around, walked into the hallway bathroom, jumped in the tub, turned on the water, and cried under the running faucet. They were a mixed basket of tears. Some from joy, some from pain, and some from that deep down feeling I got when I thought about being out of that house. I was free. I, Jamilla Jean, was free.

Chapter 64

Niya

When I got out of the shower, Jamilla was still taking her bath. I joined my granny in the kitchen and pulled the joint from her fingers. I took a few pulls, scrunched up my face, and headed to my room for my blunts.

"You have got to stop smoking that paper, Granny. Blunts, that's where it's at," I said as I kissed her forehead and sat back down beside her. As I split the blunt, my grandmother asked me a question that I was not expecting.

"So, now you and Jamilla move to Atlanta?"

My hands stopped moving, and I just stared at her. "How did you know that?"

She didn't answer my question. Instead, she nodded her head at the blunt and asked me to finish rolling.

"You know what, Niya? You will go with her. You no good here. You go."

I sealed the blunt, lit it, took a few long pulls, and handed it to her. "Did Jamilla tell you about Atlanta?"

"No, she no tell me nothing. I hear the night she come when Marlo here," she answered through the smoke. "You go, you hear me? You no stay in Brooklyn. You will die here, mi amor, and I no live if you die."

"Come on, Granny. No one said that I would be dying anytime soon." I tried to hold her hand, but she pulled it away.

"Yes, Niya, you will die, or you turn out like you mommy or papi. You sell the drugs. I watch you beat a man today like you will kill him, and yes, you kill before. Niya, your road no good, and now you get off. You leave with Jamilla soon, okay?"

"I am not leaving you, Granny. I just can't."

She started to laugh, and finally, she held my hand. "You no worry about me, Niya. I am gangster like you and like you parents. You see me slap Jamilla's mommy?"

We both started to laugh, but to me, leaving her just wasn't an option.

As I sat there, I took the time to really look at her. The fine lines on her face showed the years that had been good and bad to her. The calluses on her hands proved that her life might not have been easy, but knowing her showed that it all had been worth it. I marveled at her salt-and-pepper hair and remembered when there was more pepper than salt. I looked at the heavy folds around her beautiful eyes and knew that I had to be near her until the very end.

I loved the woman who sat before me, even more than my very own mother. She was the one who had bathed me, who had fed me, who had kissed my boo-boos. She was the one who had made me love me, and that was priceless. When a teacher gave me shit at school, she was the one who would go there and set them straight. And when the world became too heavy, her arms lifted the weight. Her arms sheltered me from the pain and the ugliness the world housed. Her arms were the only place I had to go to so I could experience everlasting love. No, I could never leave her. I just couldn't.

Like the mind reader she always seemed to be, she spoke up and left me without a choice.

"Mi amor, you must go. No questions. *Entendido*?"

We sat and smoked in silence. From time to time, I would reach over to her, kiss her face, and she would smile. I moved closer to her, ran my hands through her long, thick hair and kissed her. I loved her, and as I sat there, I tried to picture a day without hearing her call me mi amor. . . . And I couldn't.

Granny and I smoked heavily, and by the end of our sack of weed, she went in to take a nap. I planned on going into my room to join Jamilla, but first, I just needed a few minutes to gather my thoughts. So as I stood on the other side of my bedroom door, I thought of her. There she was, in my bed, in my home, and in my heart. I had dreamed of the day that she would go to bed with me and wake up right next to me. I had longed for the day when I could just hold her close for hours on end and not have to worry about her having to go home. But with her so damn close came so damn much. We were in a weird place, and we both knew it. We loved one another, yet we both pushed and pulled. I loved her, she loved me, she needed me, and I needed her more. *Damn.* Shit was so funny.

There she was, in my bed, the same bed that I would lie in some nights and wonder if I crossed her mind. I always tried to will her into thinking of me in the very same moment that I was thinking of her. I would say to myself, *God, please, just help her feel my thoughts. Just help her feel my love.* I needed her to know that what I felt was the realest shit the world had to offer. Damn. I just needed her to know that I would give her the world, but not only that. I would also give it up just for her. She was just so damn . . . At times, it was hard for me to find the right words.

Just the sight of that smile crushed me. Crushed me because it would cause me to stop breathing. It would almost cause my heart to stop beating, or so it seemed.

And the more I fought to rid myself of this unhealthy infatuation, of this lovesick illness that would be cured only by her love, the more I fell. I would fall deeper into the vast abyss known to me as Jamilla's heart, and it was impossible for me to find my way out. And it wasn't that her heart was evil, but her inability to give herself to me fully was cruel. Even with the facts that should have stopped me in my tracks, I let my heart lead me to her waiting warmth.

I turned the doorknob to my bedroom door, fully knowing that I would have to settle for only half of her, but to me, just having half of her was worth it for the moment. I slid into bed next to her and pulled her close. I breathed her in, experiencing a cloud nine overload that came only with her being so close. Everything about her awoke all my senses. She smelled like ripe peaches, and I wanted to bite into her. As I looked down at her, she truly was the most beautiful girl that I had ever laid eyes on. Her breathing was soft but seemed to pound a romantic rhythm into my soul, and her lips . . . her lips were sweet enough to send a diabetic into a coma. My kiss didn't linger long; I just wanted to taste her lips. She was still half asleep when she turned and faced me. She smiled with her eyes closed, leaned into my lips for another short kiss, and wrapped her arms around me. We fell asleep holding onto each other, as if we never wanted to let go.

"Niya, wake up. It's time." My granny woke me up without waking Jamilla and asked me to follow her out to the hallway.

"What is it, Granny? I'm tired." I stood there rubbing my eyes like the little girl I really was as I whined about not wanting to get up.

"Your papi is on the phone. He send his friend for you."

The childish shit was over. I walked into the kitchen and took the phone from my granny, who had walked ahead of me.

"Dad?"

"Don't talk. Just listen. I don't have much time."

I stood there for ten minutes and listened to my father's instructions. By the end of the conversation, he had only one warning for me.

"There's no going back after this."

I took in a deep breath before I replied, "I am my parents' child, so I have been on this road before."

I hung up, threw on some clothes, and told my grandmother that I was leaving. She came over to me, prayed for me, and told me to make sure that I tied up all my loose ends.

I walked out of my building with Get-It-Done man and jumped into a car that appeared to be stolen, with its popped locks and busted steering wheel. I stayed quiet until he spoke about my granny.

"After you came to me and before I called your dad, I wondered if you would have the heart for this shit. But then I took a look at your bloodline, starting from your grandparents."

I sat up a bit when I heard the word *grandparents*. I knew a lot about my mother's parents, but I really knew nothing about the people who had birthed my pops.

"Your dad was always a crazy nigga, but that's who he was destined to be."

"What do you mean by that?" I asked as I stared him down.

"What? Don't tell me that you don't know about your father's parents." Get-It-Done man looked at me as if I was crazy. "Man, they were running a kidnapping ring that branded them two of the most ruthless criminals New York had ever seen."

I didn't answer, mostly because I was shocked.

"And that lady you live with, your mother's mom, shit, that lady never took no shit."

"Yeah, Granny thinks she's hard," I said while laughing.

"Nay, she don't just think she is. She's proved that shit time and time again. She used to hold your dad's money for him. Well, one day, some little nigga thought that he could run up in her spot for that shit."

My heart was racing. Just the thought of Granny in danger raised my blood pressure.

"So, what happened?"

"That little nigga went in breathing but came out dead."

For the rest of the ride, I thought of the origins of the blood that ran through my veins, and it scared me.

"Well, there they are. Two dead and one still breathing just for you," Get-It-Done man announced.

I stood in the basement of a seedy bar, face-to-face with the man who had taken so much from me without even knowing. Flashes of Jamilla's face snapped in front of me, as if I was watching a slide show from that night with the cops. White Boy sat between his two henchmen, with his hands tied behind him. He didn't look like he had a scratch on him.

"How did you get them here?" I said.

Get-It-Done man nodded to a needle that sat on a side table. I walked over to it, made sure it was empty, and walked back over to White Boy.

"This is some crazy shit, huh? Not too long ago, you were on the other side of them ropes," I told him.

"Fuck you, bitch."

I smiled. "This shit ain't gonna take too long. I just want their names."

White Boy spit at my feet before asking, "What names?"

I took the needle and stabbed him a few times through the cheek. "You know what the fuck I'm talking about. The cops. I want their names and their precincts."

White Boy was soft at the core. A few more jabs to the face with the needle, and he gave up all the information that I needed to know.

"So . . . what now?" he muttered.

I stood there and thought about what my father had said. He had made it clear that I was not to kill White Boy. He had told me that killing one person and allowing the other to die was enough blood on my hands. I thought about the family members who had most likely stood in my shoes years before, and about how I was sure that I was cut from the same cloth as them. Lastly, I thought of that night. The cops, Jamilla, him, her, him on top of her . . . Man, fuck that!

I didn't thug out and pump bullets into him. I didn't go crazy and stab him forty, fifty times. No, this was more personal. I wanted to feel death take over his body; I wanted to feel life leave his body. I kept eye contact with him as my hand wrapped around his neck. I smiled as his eyes seemed to pop out of his head. I breathed easy as his body went limp, and I continued to squeeze the life out of him. Choking him just seemed so damn right, and it allowed me to feel as if his soul now belonged to me.

"Damn, girl. That was some cold-ass shit you just did. Looks like that killer instinct didn't skip a generation, huh?" Get-It-Done man said.

I didn't answer him. I just repeated the names of the officers to him and where they worked and asked for the price.

"What kind of shit you talking about?"

It didn't take me long to spit out what I wanted. "Cut off their dicks. If they live, they live. If not, I won't lose sleep over it."

"Fifty Gs. Twenty-five for each," he shot back.

I asked him to drop me off back at home so that I could get in my own car and get his money. Two hours later, I was meeting back up with him and making the exchange.

"You want me to come and get you for this one too?" he asked as he counted his money. As I sat in the very same basement of the bar in which I had killed White Boy, I thought about his question.

"Nah, I don't need to be there. Just cut their dicks off and send them to a news channel, any station, with a note that says, *Even cops have to pay for their sins. Raping young girls never goes unpunished.* And with that note, send in their badges. That way when I see it all over the news, I'll know that the job is done. I am giving you three days."

With that, I walked out of the bar and never looked back.

Chapter 65

Jamilla

Darkness filled the room, and I wondered if it all was just a dream. I sat up quickly and searched for the light. I had to fill the room with clarity, and the light was the only way that I would get any. My heart raced as the thought of still being in my mother's house filled my mind. If I was still there and the thought of being free was just a dream, at that point, I would have jumped out the window. I stumbled around the room and finally flicked the light on. As I looked around the room, it hit me that I was in dire need of a bathroom. I opened Niya's bedroom door and almost made it. Tears filled my eyes as the warm urine leaked out of me and flowed down my legs.

By the time I made it to the bathroom, my bladder was half empty. I sat on the toilet and emptied my bladder of the other half. I couldn't stop the tears as I thought of the embarrassment I would face if either Niya or her grandmother found out. Once I was done, I wiped myself and instantly started looking for the cleaning supplies. I had left behind a trail of pee and wanted to get it cleaned up right away. As I headed out of the bathroom with the supplies, Granny's door opened, and as her foot stepped on the urine, she looked at me as I stood at the end of the hallway and then back down at her foot.

"I'm so sorry, Granny. I will clean it all up. I'm so sorry."

Before she could even answer, I was on my knees, spraying and cleaning every drop of pee that I saw. My tears merged with the pain that inhabited my soul and showed itself on my face. My soft whimpers were transformed and became loud sobs, and all I could do was repeat how sorry I was.

"Okay, okay. Jamilla, stop. You no need to say sorry."

Granny had come over to me and was trying to help me, but my hands were moving too fast. As my bare knees dug into the wood floor, my hands moved the rag and the spray vigorously. I needed to clean it all up as fast as I could, as if I was wiping away the memory of it ever happening.

"Stop, Jamilla. Please, baby, you no need to do this. *Cálmate*, Jamilla. *Cálmate*."

I was not sure when it had happened, but I found myself in her arms, being rocked back and forth.

"You know, Niya tell me you problem. I want to tell you, if you no let go of all the pain and because you mad, you no heal, baby. Please, go in shower. I clean."

"No, please. I have to clean it up," I said as I tried to pull away from her. Instead, she held me tighter.

"You know, you clean for me that morning with me baby. She poop. You clean it without make one face. That day, I know you are the one for me, Niya. That day, I know, in your heart, you are pure, Jamilla. You not only clean the bathroom that day, no. You show me you . . . You show me you heart. So listen to me. You clean for me, so I clean for you. No questions. Just you go shower, and I clean, okay?"

I looked into her eyes, and I knew that I was safe.

"No worry. You shower. I clean before Niya get here. Hurry up. I need to talk to you, and I need you help."

She didn't leave me much of a choice. I got up from her loving arms, showered, dressed, and when I came out, I sat with her for our talk.

"Jamilla, you and Niya leaving today."

I sat across from her, with confusion written all over my face. "What do you mean? Where are we going?"

"I hear you talk to her. You say you want to go to Atlanta, no? So, we pack all the stuff, and you go."

I didn't know what to say. How could we just get up and go like that? "But what about school? What about our things? Are you coming with us?" I had so many questions, but it was hard to get all of them out while my head was spinning.

"My cousin who there will get you enrolled in classes. She work for college there. I want Niya to leave tonight. If she stay, the streets will kill her like they did her mama and papi. I cannot live to see that. I will die if she stay and no leave."

I watched as she smoked and let her mind drift to a place that I knew I would never understand. I wanted to ask her what she was thinking about, but I left it alone.

"Okay, you help me. We pack clothes now." She got up, but I stayed sitting. "Let's go, Jamilla. We pack clothes, and I send rest of stuff when you get to Atlanta."

"But Niya won't want to go," I said as I stood up slowly.

"Niya will have no choice. I tell her when she get home. Now, no talking. Come."

I was so scared of what Niya was going to do once she came home, but this was between her and her grandmother. I was ready to leave but was also a little fearful of what this move would bring. Sure, I would finish school, but what would come next? As I packed, I made my mind up. I would work on my second book while really pushing *Rainbow Hearts*. Niya's dream was about to come at her full force, and I didn't want just to sit back and get lost in her world. Yes, I planned on being right by her side, but I didn't want to forget about the one thing that would make me happy . . . my writing.

Granny and I packed for a good two hours before I heard the front door open and close. I held my breath as Niya's footsteps got closer and closer. When she walked into her bedroom, her eyes said it all.

Chapter 66

Niya

"What's going on here?" I looked from Jamilla to my grandmother, and neither of them said anything. "*Hello*? Why are you packing up my room?"

After the night I had had, I just wanted to go home and bask in the killing of White Boy, but no. I had to come home to some bullshit that no one could explain.

"Mi amor, sit down, honey. Let me talk."

Oh shit. If Granny was at a loss for words, it had to be something bad.

"I'm going to step out and let you two talk," Jamilla said as she damn near ran out of the room.

"What's going on, Granny? And no, I don't want to sit down."

My granny looked dead into my eyes and said the words I feared the most. "Today you leave to go to Atlanta. You call the man who say you can come, and you tell him you coming now."

I cocked my head, with discontent. "I'm doing what? Nah, I ain't going no damn where."

My room seemed to be closing in on me, and I took a seat on my bed.

"Niya, you go, and you go *today*."

My head started to spin, and air wasn't filling my lungs as it should.

"Granny, I'm not leaving. I am not going to leave you here just so I can go to Atlanta. I need more time to plan. I need to find an apartment on my own, so you can come too—"

"Niya, I come later. For now, you and Jamilla, you two go."

I stood up and started to pace the room.

"Man, fuck that. I'm not leaving, and I need you to understand that. I'm not fucking leaving you."

I wasn't trying to disrespect her, and I was sure she knew that, but I just couldn't leave. She was my life. Most of the time, she was the first person I saw when I woke up and also the last person I saw before I went to sleep. What would I do without her? No, there had to be a way for her to go too.

"Niya, *escúchame*! You need to calm down, okay? I am doing this for your good. You need to leave this place. Look what I had to wake you up for tonight. To watch a man get kill. That is a crazy life. Tell me, what did you do when you get there?"

I looked at her and told her the truth. I told her how I smiled as White Boy's soul left his body. I told her what I wanted done to the cops, and I told her that I had to wait to see if things got taken care of.

"Oh my God, Niya. This no good. I understand you get even, but where your soul go to now? You are my angel, Niya. Now you so dark inside. You too beautiful person to be dark."

I started to laugh and cocked an attitude. "You don't think I know my bloodline? This shit was bred in me, Granny. A dark heart is part of who I am."

She walked over to me, slapped the dog shit out of me, and afterward pulled me close and hugged me tight.

"Niya, mi amor, my angel, my heart, you are you, not the people before you. Oh, Niya, your granny loves you so. I don't see how my life will be when you go, but you must go. You have to, mi amor. If you stay, I will lose you like you mami, like you papi, like so many before you."

As she spoke, I started to cry. I begged her to let me stay. I told her that I wouldn't be able to live without her. I told her that she was me, and I was her, but still . . . she said I must go.

"Granny, please, not yet. Just give me time so that I can bring you with me. Please, Granny, please."

She tried to push me away from her chest, but I held on even tighter. In her arms, I felt safe.

"Mi amor, I always with you, no matter what. I need you to go and live the dream you dream. I will come soon, Niya. It no take too long. Come on, Niya. You break your granny heart crying like this."

I didn't care what she said. I wasn't letting go.

"Granny, you just don't understand. Please, Gran, I need you. Who am I without you? If it wasn't for you, I would still be hiding. Please, Granny, I will die without you. Do you hear me? I just won't make it."

That was when her own tears started to fall. I could feel the tremble radiate from deep within her, and I knew that this was just as hard for her as it was for me. So, for a short while, we just sat there, with me in her arms. Me, unable to let go of my backbone, the woman who was my mother, my father, my God, in a way. And she . . . Well, I never asked her what went through her mind, but her arms told me the untold story. To me, the way she held me told me that I was her second chance at motherhood. Maybe in some way she felt as if she had failed my mother, failed herself, but with me came redemption. That was what really gave me the strength to let go of her eventually. It was the thought of her wanting better for me. It was the thought of the love I knew she had for me that made me realize that what she wanted for me . . . was the best thing for me.

"Okay, mi amor. Now you call the man and tell him you come to Atlanta now. After, we finish packing."

When I called the guy who had spoken to me at the show, the only thing he asked was how soon I could get there. He spoke about jumping right into the studio and how he was going to make me a star. When I told him that I would be driving out to Atlanta that night, he assured me that he would have a place for me to live as soon as I got there. I let my granny speak to him, and he answered all her questions adequately, so there was no turning back.

We got up and packed the important stuff. By four in the morning, my car was packed and I was standing in the living room, waiting for my dad to call. When the phone rang, my granny told him that she was in fact able to get me to understand why I had to leave and that everything was packed. When she handed me the phone, I was the first to ask a question.

"So you were in on this too?"

My dad started to laugh, but I didn't find things funny.

"Listen, when she first told me that she was going to make you go, I told her, 'Good luck.' I know that I haven't been around much, but from what I do know, you seem as hardheaded as me."

"I really don't want to just go and leave her, but—"

"Don't you worry about her. She will be just fine. Just go out there, do your thing, and move her there when you can. I saw your videos online and, baby girl, you have a great shot at making it. Don't let this street shit kill your dreams. There's a whole bunch of talented niggas who are six feet deep or in a damn cell. I don't want that for you."

I didn't say much, mostly just listened.

"You go out there and do your thing, baby girl. I'll be out soon, and I promise to make up the years I have lost with you. Your granny been laying some real shit on me lately, and she opened my eyes. Did you see your mama yet?"

I took in a deep breath and rubbed my temples. I knew that I had to stop and see her before I left, and I was hoping that at the very least, it went better than the last time I saw her.

Chapter 67

Jamilla

I made it seem as if the only reason that I left the room was to give Niya and her grandmother room to talk, but that was only half the true. When it hit me that I was really going to be leaving, I knew that I had to call Rodney.

His voice came on the line, deep and sweet. "Hey, baby. What's up?"

"Hey, I really don't have much time to talk, but I need to let you know that Niya and I are leaving for Atlanta . . . tonight."

I heard what sounded like shifting on the other end, and I knew that Rodney must have sat up in his bed.

"What do you mean, tonight?"

I took in a deep breath and tried to speak fast. "Niya's grandmother wants her gone tonight. I guess shit is getting too hot for Niya, and Granny wants her out of New York. Niya called the guy from her show, and he said that he will have a place for her when she gets there. Plus, Granny has family there who will get us in school."

"Yo, what the fuck is going on? You can't just fucking leave."

I waited a few seconds before answering. "I'm leaving Rodney . . . with her. I have no choice."

I waited for him to speak, wondering what he was thinking. "Where are you?" he finally asked.

"I am in front of the building. I came out so Niya could talk to her granny."

"Okay, stay there. I'm coming to see you," Rodney said, and I heard keys jiggling in the background.

"I don't have time for—"

"Jamilla, I *am* coming to see you. Be there in ten minutes."

I guessed I had no choice.

I could hear the tires on the car as Rodney turned the corner. He stopped in front of the building and waited for me. I hurried to his car, praying that Niya didn't see me, and jumped in. At first, he just sat there looking at me. Damn. He was so damn cute. His skin was so smooth, and it looked as if it had melted into a fresh haircut.

"So, you are really gonna leave me?"

I took a deep breath and asked him to drive. A few traffic lights down, I answered him.

"Yes, I am really leaving. Some crazy shit went down at my house, and I don't live there anymore, so I have to go. Plus, I want to go. Not that I want to leave you, but I just want out of New York. I am so ready for a fresh start."

"What in the hell went down at your place?" Rodney's face was twisted with confusion.

"Nothing I want to talk about right now. Look, I just wanted to let you know that I was leaving. I can't be gone for too long right now."

"Damn. That was cold as shit," Rodney said as he pulled the car over at a random spot.

"No, I didn't mean it like that. I really am going to miss you, but I just don't have much time to sit and talk. Niya will be wondering where I am soon."

We sat there, with him saying nothing, not even looking at me.

"Rodney, come on. Speak to me."

He turned to me and leaned toward my side of the car. He gave me a quick kiss and answered, "I'm just going to miss you . . . that's all. We were really just starting to get to know each other on a personal level, and now you're leaving. This is so fucked up."

I didn't say anything, because what I really wanted to say was that what we were doing, and not me leaving, was wrong. Instead, I just pulled his lips to mine again and kissed him. I savored the flavor of his lips and wondered if I would ever get to taste them again.

When Rodney dropped me off a block away from my building, I looked at him before getting out of the car and couldn't think of what to say, so he spoke.

"Don't worry, Jamilla boo. I am going to make sure that I see you soon. As soon as you get to Atlanta and you know the address, text me the info."

As he kissed me good-bye, I couldn't help but think about how weird it was to hear him call me Jamilla boo. That was Niya's thing, and it just didn't sound right coming out of his mouth.

While walking back to Niya's place, I took in all that Brooklyn had to offer. Although I was ready to leave the place I called home, I knew that I would miss it.

Chapter 68

Niya

The car was packed, and I couldn't believe that I was about to leave New York. Those streets were all I knew. They had raised me, they at times had made me cave, and they had made me who I was. I leaned against the car and waited for my grandmother to come down. I told myself that I would not break down again. I didn't know how long it would be until I saw her again, and I didn't want her last image of me to be my tearstained face.

"Are you ready for this?" Jamilla asked.

"No," I answered as I lit a blunt. "Are you?" I asked in return.

"No, but I'm hopeful that this is the right thing to do."

I thought about it and silently prayed that it was. As I prayed, Granny appeared at my side.

"Okay, mi amor. You pack, and now you can go. First, you and Jamilla stand here. I bless you."

I couldn't help but smile. I should have known that she wouldn't let us leave without blessing us with her potions and prayer. I took Jamilla's hand, and we stood right there on the street as my granny prayed and sprayed us with her concoction. Afterward, she did the same to the car before coming back over to us.

My heart skipped a few beats as I peered into her eyes. My mind, body, and soul said, "Stay," but I knew that I couldn't. She pulled Jamilla to her and hugged and kissed her.

"You save my Niya, and with you, I know she safe. God send you to my Niya. I know this. You are the angel she need. Make sure you watch her for me. You know she crazy, just like her family. Thank you, Jamilla. *Te amo*."

I watched the two women I loved embrace each other and show genuine love toward one another. When she let Jamilla go, she turned to me.

"Oh God. Now it hard to let you go, mi amor. Come. Hug you granny."

I was keeping it together while she was falling apart. My heart broke in a thousand little pieces as I fell into her arms.

"I love you, Granny. I love you more than anything in the world."

"I love you, mi amor. I always with you here," she said, pointing to my heart. "Okay, you go. You go see you mommy before you leave New York, yes?"

I smiled. Granny was going to be Granny till the end.

"Yes, I am going to see her before I leave."

"Okay, now you go. Call on the phone when you get there. I love you, and you my Niya for always, okay?"

I hugged and kissed the woman who had raised me, and I prayed that everything she was, everything she had given me, and everything she had taught me left New York with me.

Jamilla and I got in the car, and before we left, Granny made me make one more promise. I rolled my window down.

"Niya, you leave here, you leave all the dark here. You no look back. I know you a star. I know Jamilla know, you family know, you friends know. Now you need to know. You leave everything bad here. You will be new, so you act new. You are good only . . . no bad. You new, okay?"

I reached through the window, took her hand, kissed it, and said, "I promise, Granny. I promise."

***

Later that day I picked up my money from the stash house and went on to search for my mother. I drove the streets, looking for my mom. I knew where she liked to hang out, but for some reason, that night I wasn't having much luck.

"Man, fuck this. I tried."

I started to leave the block I was searching when Jamilla stopped me.

"No, Niya. You told your granny you would see her before we leave. Just park the car, and maybe she'll show."

"I don't have time for this shit. I just wanna get out of here."

"Just park the car. If she doesn't show in the next thirty minutes, we can go."

Just as I thought that thirty minutes would be too long of a wait, I heard her voice.

"Fuck you. My pussy is worth way more than twenty bucks."

My mother had jumped out of the car that had stopped right beside us. She looked a mess, and the tantrum she was throwing in the middle of the street with a trick was worse. I jumped out of the car as my mother argued with the older black man who was sitting in the neighboring car, and grabbed her arm. I walked her to the curb, with her cursing all the way.

"Nah, fuck that. Weak-ass mothafucka thinks he can just fuck for a dub? I don't fucking think so."

I could tell that she was high out of her mind.

"Mom, it's me, Niya."

I waited until the memory of me splattered across her face.

"Hey, cutie. You got some money Mommy can hold? I'll pay you back."

I clenched my jaw in an effort to hold back my pain and anger. "Look, Ma, I just came to say good-bye. I'm leaving New York."

For the first time in years, my mother looked as if my presence had an impact on her.

"But what about my mother? Who will be with her? And what about me? Won't you miss me?"

"Granny is the one who is making me leave. I would tell you to check in on her, but you would only cause more problems."

She looked as if my statement had hurt her, but I meant every word.

"You know, Niya, I don't want to be like this. I know that this shit is slowly killing her. I know—"

"So *stop*. Get your shit together. I have been hearing the same story from you since I was a kid. Don't you think it's time to finally make good on all your promises? Do you want Granny to die with this shit . . . with you on her heart?"

She said nothing. She just looked down at the ground, and slowly, pity crept in and I started to feel bad for my mother.

"Look, I just want to make sure that you don't go over there fuckin' with her while I'm gone. When you think about going over there and stealing from her, just think of me. She did the job you and my pops didn't do. She loves me the same way she loves you, and that should be enough to stop you."

"I know Niya. I know."

I stood there and watched her light a cigarette before reaching for the piece of paper I had written my number on.

"I gotta go, Ma, but really think about what I said. Here's my number. Call me if you or Granny needs anything. And, Ma, if you are ever really ready to change your life, I'll be waiting for you."

I pulled her close and wrapped my arms around her waist.

"I love you, Ma. Always know that."

For the first time in a long time, she hugged me back, and I could feel the love. I took out some cash and handed her five hundred dollars, hoping that it might keep her off the streets for a few nights.

"I know that I don't show it much, but I do love you," she said.

I told her that I knew that she loved me . . . the only way she knew how.

"And one day, I'll get clean, I promise."

As those words left her mouth, a car slowed down beside us, and she called out to the driver.

"Okay, baby. I gotta go," she told me.

I shook my head as I watched her walk toward the car. She looked back at me, smiled, and seeing the light in her eyes gave me a little hope.

"Don't worry, baby. I'm gonna call you when I'm ready."

And just like that, she was gone.

As I headed back to the car, flashing lights stopped me in my tracks. I stood there for a minute and called Rodney.

"Hey, Rodney. Just wanted to let you know that I am leaving for Atlanta tonight."

"What? Why are you leaving so soon?"

"Shit got hot, and Granny wants me gone. I'm not sure how this shit is gonna go, but once shit pops off, I want you and June to come through. I'm taking you niggas to the top with me."

"Damn, Niya. That's crazy, but I'll make sure to pass on the message. As soon as you're settled, just hit me up and we'll be out there. I'm ready!"

"I got you. Don't worry. If it wasn't for you and your brother, none of this shit would be poppin' right now. But

I was also calling to ask you about the tattoo shop you go to. Is the name the Tatt Shop?"

"Yeah, that's it. You about to get tatted?"

I stood there, looking at the flashing sign. "I'm thinking about it. You know, something to remind me of home while I'm gone."

"Well that's the best place to go. Ask for Big Mike, a big white dude. He'll rock your shit out."

We said our good-byes as I headed to the car.

"Jamilla, come with me for a minute," I called as I got close to the car.

She looked as if she didn't want to get out of the car. "Where we goin'?"

I pointed at the tattoo shop and watched as her eyes got big.

"No," she said as she stepped out of the car.

"Yes," was all that I answered.

Chapter 69

Jamilla

My stomach turned as I watched the needle dig into Niya's neck. I thought she was crazy when she told the artist that she wanted to have *Brooklyn* tattooed on her neck with musical notes, but when he was done, it was dope as hell.

"I'm not done yet. I want this on my lower neck, centered."

I tried to read the paper that she was showing to Big Mike, but she wouldn't let me.

"Damn, Jamilla. You all up. Just wait and see," she scolded.

I sat there, racking my brain, trying to think of what crazy shit she was about to get tattooed on her neck. I watched the man change gloves and ink, and as his hand pressed the needle against her neck again, I watched each letter. *J . . . A . . . M . . . I . . . L . . . L . . . A.* I was in shock. She had had my name inked on her neck for all the world to see.

"What do you think?" she asked as I just sat there, staring. I wanted to run my fingers over it but knew that I couldn't.

"It's beautiful . . . just as beautiful as you," I answered as my heart raced.

I didn't say much more for a short while. I just held her hand as the man added a few more musical notes and moved on to the piece on her back, which she said was for her granny. She read it out to Big Mike, and he worked his magic on the words and the portrait of Granny in her younger days.

I got a family tree
That don't got enough leaves.
A bunch of dark souls birthed from rotten seeds.
Thank God for my granny, a woman at war,
Fighting to win these battles galore.
I got a family tree that may not be like yours,
But I could never hate them, so for them I will soar.
See, my family is much different than yours.
If it wasn't for my granny, I would be rotten to the core.
Thank you, Lucinda, for all that you've done.
Even as I leave you, our hearts beat as one.
No matter how near or how far you'll be to me,
Your love has set the bar so tall, from the ceiling to the floor.
Because of you,
I'll always live free and be a star.
For Granny Lucinda Ramirez

As the car surged toward the New York state line, I looked over at Niya and wanted to ask her the same question that I had asked just a few hours before.

"You know what? With you by my side, I know that I'm ready. How about you?"

She took my hand and simply answered back, "As long as I got you, I'm ready for anything."

We took our time to take it all in before it all became just a memory.

Chapter 70

Niya

Three months later . . .

I was sitting in the Santino Hill recording studio and couldn't believe the shit that was coming out of the speakers.

"Man, I ain't rapping over this bubble gum shit. I have told you time and time again that I need some dope beats," I groused.

Santino Hill was the boss at Hill Top Records and also the man that I liked to call Suit and Tie. I had been in Atlanta for three months already, yet nothing had progressed. The only thing that was poppin' off was one fight after the other. He was always trying to get me to go mainstream, while I wanted just to be me.

"Look, Niya, I let you have this whole thugged-out stud shit that you're on, but you need to go a little softer with the songs. We need balance just until the public gets to know you."

"Thugged-out stud shit? This is who I am, and I'm not changing for anyone."

Santino took in a deep breath and tried to intimidate me with his stare. It was not working.

"I am not trying to change you. That whole 'you need to put on a dress' shit is played out. This ain't the year nineteen ninety-nine, so I'm not asking you to change that. After I asked you once, I never brought that back up again. I ain't on that wack shit. What I do need you to understand is that because your look is so hard, we have to find a way to slide you in without them thinking of how you look. I ain't asking you to put on a damn dress. I just want you to lighten up on the songs."

I looked at him and gave him an honest answer. "Hell no. I'm not rappin' over this wack shit."

"What in the hell you mean, no?"

I could tell that I had just pissed him off, and I didn't give a damn.

"When I first came here, you said that I had free range to do me. Now you tryin'a pull this 'You need to soften up' bullshit on me. My look, my sound, that's all me. So either you take it or leave it."

Santino started to laugh. "I want you how I want you. I pay *you*. I got a contract with your name on it. If you don't like how I want to run *my* shit, I'll just sit your ass on the shelf until your contract is up. How about that?"

By then, I was standing up, with my backpack in my hand. I looked at him up and down, sucked my teeth, grabbed my crotch, and said, "Shelf me, then, 'cause I ain't with that 'New Age, naked female rapper out here tryin'a push sex' bullshit. I'm street, I'm a lesbian, and I can only be me."

I headed for the door, his words following me.

"I'll give you a few days to think about this. I know you got a hot head, so I'll wait for you to come crawling back."

I was heated, and the first person I called was Jamilla. She was the only person I had to vent to. I told her to meet me at the café on Peachtree Street, and within twenty minutes, we were in the restaurant and seated. As I went over what had happened at the studio, she seemed distracted by the loud group of girls who sat at the table behind me.

"Hello? Are you listening to me?" I asked as my temper grew even hotter. Moving to Atlanta wasn't all that it was cracked up to be, or maybe it was just my mood. I did love the city and the beautiful Georgia peaches with phat asses, but I had thought I would be on the fast track out here. The only time I really smiled and was truly happy was when I saw headlines on the news about two cops being killed in New York and having their dicks mailed to their precinct.

"I'm so sorry, Niya, but I am freaking out right now. The Brazilian Barbies are right behind you."

I gave a quick glance at the annoying girls behind me and rolled my eyes. "Well, how about you go and sit at their damn table, then?" I knew that I was being a brat, but I needed her ear.

"Okay. I'm sorry, boo. I was listening. So what are you going to do? This has been going on since we got here. I know he's paying our rent and giving you seven hundred dollars a week, but you don't really need his money. What are you waiting around for?"

"The contract, Jamilla. I signed the contract."

As she opened her mouth to reply, the DJ turned up the music in the ultrahip café, and it took me a second to realize that my voice was coming out of the speakers.

"Oh my God, Niya. That's 'Team Take Yo' Bitch.'"

I was in shock. I didn't think that anyone knew about my music in the A.

As Jamilla and I sat there in shock, one of the girls who was sitting behind me got out of her seat and started to dance to the music.

"Girl, that's my shit, and I ain't even gay," another girl said.

A third girl asked, "Who in the hell is it?"

Jamilla leaned over the table and told me to tell them that it was me, but I couldn't move. I just sat there listening to my song and watching the girl dance.

"Fuck it. If you won't say nothing, I will."

Before I could stop her, Jamilla was on her feet and heading to the DJ booth. The music was loud, but it really wasn't loud enough to require Jamilla to yell at the DJ. It was obvious— well, at least to me—that she wanted the girls to hear her yelling, "That's Niya over there. The song you're playing, that's her."

It was as if I was standing outside of myself, watching everything go down. I was able to catch the reaction of everyone who was within earshot. The first to turn to me was the DJ. He smiled and nodded for me to come over to him. Second to turn to me was the girl who was dancing to the song. Her mouth was open, and I could tell that she was surprised. Last to look my way were the girls who were with her. They didn't look too impressed, but I could tell they were curious nonetheless. When Jamilla started waving for me to come over to her, I got up and prayed that my legs wouldn't give out.

"Hey. Niya, right?" the DJ asked.

I nodded my head up and down, unable to say a word.

"Damn. It's really nice to meet you. As soon as you walked in, I thought that I had seen you somewhere, not even realizing that it was from your YouTube videos. I listen to your songs every chance I get."

I shook the hand he had extended and thanked him. He went on about the club he DJ'd for at night and mentioned how crazy the crowd got when he played my underground shit. I programmed his number in my phone and promised him that I would come through and check the club out.

"See, Niya? They like your shit," Jamilla said as we headed back to our table.

"You are something else. You know that?" I replied.

She was beaming from ear to ear, and I had to give it to her. I would have still been sitting at that table if it weren't for her.

"Umm, excuse me. Did I hear her right?" said the girl who had been dancing before as she stepped right in front of me. I hadn't noticed before, but with her in my face, I was floored at how beautiful she was.

"What did you hear?" I asked with a smile. If only she knew that smile was hiding sweaty palms.

She swiped her hair off her shoulders, and with a curl of her lips, she asked, "Did I hear her say that you're Niya? I mean, you do look just like the girl from the video."

"You're Brazil, from the Brazilian Barbies, right?" Jamilla asked. She was smiling from ear to ear. She had been listening to their latest CD day and night and was a big fan.

Shit. That was when it hit me.

"Yeah, that's me. I mean, yeah, we *are* the Brazilian Barbies." Her answer was quick, as if she was in a rush to get back to me. "You know, I'm a big fan. I love your songs and videos. You're dope as fuck."

I did a quick overview of the chick standing in front of me, and as much as I hated to say it, she took the place of the most beautiful girl I had ever seen. Plus, her telling me that she was a fan only made me smile a little harder.

"Picture that. The lead singer in the biggest girl group is a fan of mine? Damn. This must be my lucky day," I replied.

"Nah, I'm the lucky one. Who are you signed to?" she said as she looked me over. I could almost feel her eyes burning through my body.

"Well, I'm signed with Hill Top Records . . . I think."

She smiled and asked what I meant by "I think." I asked her if she had time, and she said yes and invited

Jamilla and me back to her table. Thirty minutes later, I had poured my guts out and laid it all on the table. To this day I still didn't know why, but fate was at work.

"Man, fuck that dude. That label is wack as fuck, anyway. We worked with him as a favor to my stepdad, and it was hell," Brazil revealed.

"Yeah, well, as I said, I'm not even sure if I still have a deal after walking out, so I guess he really doesn't even matter."

Brazil barked for her phone, and an assistant came running over with it in hand.

"You damn right he doesn't matter. Are you looking for another deal? I mean, it doesn't sound like you're doing much over there, and that's crazy. You are wasting your time, and in this music game . . . that's like death."

"I know, but I signed a contract with him, and he said that he would shelve my ass until the five years on it was up."

Miss Brazilian Barbie jumped up and threw her hands on her curvy hips. "He said what? Man, fuck that lame. You tryin'a do some business or what? I know a star when I see one, and, baby, you're it. Just let me know, and shit could change for you overnight."

Goddamn. My head was spinning, but I was smart enough to say, "Hell yes."

We exchanged numbers, and she told me that she would be calling me later on that day.

Jamilla and I went back to our table. We watched them leave as we sat there in a euphoric trance. I went through my phone, searching for her number, as if seeing it would prove that all that had just happened was real. When I came to it, I read her name over and over to myself. *Brazil Noelle, Brazil Noelle, Brazil Noelle.*

"Oh my God, we just had a conversation with Brazil Noelle. Do you think she's really going to put you on? Did you see her outfit? She was hot, right? They were right to make her the lead. She outshines the other two girls. I think one of them is her sister or half sister. Wow. She was everything you think a star will be when you meet them."

I had to cut Jamilla off, or she would have gone on and on. "Damn, Milla boo. Calm down, baby," I said with a laugh. Truth was, I was just as excited inside too.

"Man, this is it, Niya, I just know it. Fuck Santino. She is the real deal."

I looked at Jamilla and told her that I really hoped so.

By the time midnight rolled around, I had lost all hope. My phone hadn't left my hand since I left the restaurant, but Brazil hadn't called. I thought about calling her but didn't want to turn her off and seem too pressed. I was about to lose my mind, so I got out of the chair I was sitting in, peeked into Jamilla's room, and asked if I could come in. She was on her laptop but put it down and to the side.

"Did she call yet?"

I guessed my frustration was written all over my face. I didn't answer her. I just slid in her bed, lay down beside her, and pulled her close. I took in a deep breath and smiled when her sweet scent filled my nostrils.

"You always smell so good, Milla boo. I miss this. I miss you."

The three months had slipped by, and we were seeing less and less of each other. I was always in the studio, listening to those wack-ass beats. She would come with me sometimes, but not enough times to keep me from missing her.

"I miss you too, Niya. I really do," she said as she melted into my arms.

"So what's keeping us from each other? Even when we're home, we are in two different worlds half the time. I just miss what we had. I miss the closeness. So tell me, how is the book thing going?"

She perked up and smiled when I asked about her book. She always did.

"Things are going well. I have joined a whole bunch of Facebook groups, and two want to discuss the book."

"Facebook has reading groups?"

She laughed at my ignorance. "Yes, Niya boo. The two that want to read my book are called My Urban Books Club and Don't Read Me, Read A Book. I cannot wait to have these discussions, but I am also so nervous."

I smiled and hugged her even tighter. "Don't worry, boo. You're gonna rock that shit."

As she went on about her book and all the new authors she'd been talking to, my phone started to vibrate. At first, I just looked down at my pocket. I would have missed the call if Jamilla hadn't yelled for me to answer the phone.

"Hello?"

"Hey, Niya. This is Brazil Noelle."

"What's up?" I asked, sounding a little down. I also wondered if it was a Hollywood thing she was doing when she used her whole name.

"Don't tell me you're in bed already. It's not even one yet."

I sat up and tried to sound more alive. "Oh, nah, not at all. I was just chillin' with Jamilla."

"Good. Give me your address. I'll be there to pick you up in about an hour or so."

Damn. Just like that, I guessed. I laughed and loved how bold she was. She didn't ask. . . . She *told* me she was coming to get me.

"I'll be ready."

I gave her the address, and before she hung up, she added one more thing.

"Just you. This is a private meeting."

After hanging up the phone, I sat on Jamilla's bed while my head spun.

"So . . . what did she say?"

I stood up and headed for Jamilla's bedroom door. "She said she wants to meet up with me in an hour. Guess that means I have to jump in the shower and get dressed." I stopped once I reached the door and turned to her. "This is all because of you, boo. All you."

Chapter 71

Jamilla

Yeah, it was all me, and I was happy for her. I really was. I had a feeling that this was the right move for her and that it was all happening for a reason, but . . . I couldn't shake the feeling of jealousy. I saw it in Niya's eyes as we spoke to Brazil, and there was something in Brazil's eyes too. Niya looked at her like she looked at me. I told myself that Niya was starstruck, just as I was, but . . . I was just hoping that this was the case.

I waited for Niya to come out of the shower and went to her room to "help" her get ready, but the truth was, I just wanted to ask more questions. As I sat on her bed and watched her dress, I probed a little more.

"Why would she want to meet up with you so late? Do you think that she really wants to talk business at this time?"

Niya was so wrapped up in picking out what to wear that I hoped she didn't pick up on my attitude.

"I mean, that's what she said. What do you think of these shoes with these jeans? Too loud?"

I glanced at the Lanvin sneakers she held in her hand but didn't even bother looking at the jeans. "Yeah, they look cool. So, do you think she will get you a deal? I'm sure what she's offering will be much better than the deal you have now."

Niya glanced at me with a big grin on her face. "She sure does look like she has a lot to offer, huh? Did you see that ass?"

I knew she was playing, but I was in no mood to hear about Brazil's ass. I sucked my teeth and stood up to leave.

"Aww, come on, Milla boo. You know that body was out of fuckin' control. Yes, Lawd!"

She was laughing as she searched through her closet and couldn't see my face, thank God.

"All right. Well, I hope everything goes okay. Can't wait to hear about it."

I left her room and stayed in my room until she came in to say that Brazil was outside. I walked her to the door and couldn't believe that this girl had come to pick Niya up in a Rolls-Royce. She didn't even bother to get out and greet Niya. The chauffeur opened the car door for Niya, and all I could see were those long honey-colored legs that belonged to Brazil Noelle.

I didn't have much to do after she left. I ate ice cream, commented on a few posts on Facebook, and listened to a blog show. After that, I was left twiddling my thumbs. I looked at my phone and thought about calling Niya and asking her how things were going, but I went against that thought. I didn't want to seem like the nagging friend who wasn't invited. So I went through the contacts in my phone. His name came up, and it made me miss him. I pushed CALL next to Rodney's name and waited for him to pick up.

"Hey, baby. What's up?"

I smiled at the sound of his voice. "Nothing. Wishing you were here. What are you doing?" I got in bed, turned down the lights, and got comfortable.

"Working on some beats. I—"

"Oh, sorry. I can call you some other time." I was disappointed that he was busy and was about to be a total bitch.

"Come on now. You know I wanna talk to you. I can work on that shit later. So tell me, what do you have on?"

The smile that was creeping across my face turned into a low laugh. He was so naughty.

"I miss you. You know that?" I said.

I could almost hear him smiling as he said, "Send me the address to your place again. I have something I want to send you."

"What is it?" I asked excitedly.

"Just wait and see. So, tell me, what do you have on?"

I looked down at myself and told him the truth. "A T-shirt and panties . . . pink panties."

I was so thankful that I had him to keep me company. I knew that he wouldn't hang up until I told him that I was tired.

Chapter 72

Niya

I was nervous as hell, but I tried to play it cool. My breathing was damn near snatched from me as soon as I stepped into the car. Brazil, who had to be at least five feet nine inches tall, had on a little black dress that seemed even shorter because of her extremely long legs. Her hair was pulled up into a high bun, which allowed me to see the depths of her beauty without her curly hair getting in the way. Her features were so damn exotic that one wrong move by the hand of God and everything would have been all wrong, but damn, were they *right*. Looking into her eyes was like looking into the eyes of a rare species. They were brown. They were green. Hell, I think that they were even gray. Whatever the case might have been, they were so beautiful that it was almost painful to look into them. Her stare didn't make it any better. It was as if she was looking into me, and she wasn't shy about staring.

Her body was lean and thick at the same time. Her skin, the color of warm honey, looked sweet, and I wanted to lick her and see if I was right. I didn't know if I wanted to keep my eyes on her face and admire her bone-straight nose, her semi-full lips, with a deep dip in the middle of her top lip, or if I wanted to slip down to her body. As I sat there, nothing but sinful thoughts crossed through my mind, but I didn't even know if she was gay . . . or at least bi . . . curious.

"Are you okay? You're so quiet," she said.

I smiled. I knew that she had to have seen me looking over at her every two minutes, but I just couldn't help it. I watched her uncross her legs, and it was as if I could hear a loud bang when she crossed them again.

"Yeah. It's just a little hot in here."

If I wasn't sweating, I was sure that I would start any minute. It was as if I could feel the power she held just by sitting beside her. Maybe it was her being a celebrity and the fact that she was one of the more famous people in the world at that moment, but goddamn. The car was closing in on me. Her presence was overbearing, and that shit turned me on. She didn't even have to say much. It was all just her.

She didn't tell me where we were going, but by the time the car stopped, we were sitting in front of a palatial estate.

"I am about to give you the break of a lifetime. Make sure you don't fuck it up," she said.

"Where are we? Who lives here?"

She smiled and leaned over to my left ear. Her lips were close to my ear, and her voice was low, deep, and sweet. "I live here with my parents and brother. Ever hear of Green Note Records? Well, that's us."

I sat there, realizing that I needed to do more homework on this chick. Had I heard of Green Note Records? Hell, yeah, I had heard of them. I just didn't know that they were the label behind the Brazilian Barbies. I guessed I needed to start paying more attention not only to rap but to music overall.

Brazil and I entered her home, and it was everything that I thought it would be. I had only had dreams of homes like this, and here I was, standing in one.

"Did you pick her up?" a female voice asked. It reminded me of Brazil's voice, but it was more mature, almost even sexier. When I was able to put a face to the voice, I knew instantly where Brazil got her beauty.

"Hey, Mom. This is—"

"Niya, I know. I checked out your stuff since my daughter couldn't stop talking about you. You're hot." Her mother shook my hand, and if you asked me, something was deeper in that wink she just gave me. Could have been wishful thinking.

"Thank you. I know it's nothing major, but it will be."

"You're fucking right it will be. I heard you were stuck in a shitty deal with Santino's wannabe ass." Her mother was even more intense than Brazil was. She was standing close to me, looking dead into my eyes and sizing me up.

"It is what it is, but I'm hoping to move on to bigger and better things," I told her.

She smiled and finally let go of my sweaty hand. I thought that she would also step back, but instead, she got even closer. So close that I could smell the scent of her sweet breath.

"Get your head out of them clouds and watch over your shit. Sit back, think about it, and then make a decision. You're either going to make the wrong one and fuck your life up, or you make the right one and move on to bigger and better things," her mother said.

"Boom, and there it is," Brazil said.

Her mother stepped back as Brazil cosigned her last statement. What she said opened up my eyes and made me realize how loose I had been with my business. Between school and the studio, I had left everything else in someone else's hands.

"Is Daddy home?" Brazil asked.

"He's been waiting for you to bring him the next big superstar. He's waiting in his office."

Brazil took my hand and started to lead me toward her father's office, but I kept my eye on the mysterious creature she called Mom.

"Bye-bye, Niya. I hope the next time I see you, you'll be on your way to becoming the star that I know you are . . . with *our* company."

Damn. I guessed I was about to have the world offered to me, but at what cost?

The office was dark and looked rich. Everything seemed to be made of thick black glass. I sat in front of a man who seemed to hold all the power in the world in the palm of his hand. Carmello Green of Green Note Records was *the* man, and everything about him said so. As I sat there and listened to him tell me about how big a star he would make me, I thought about the three people I had met so far who lived in this house. They all had one thing in common. They thrived on the supremacy they commanded when they walked into a room. It was as if they lived without fear, as if being afraid was never an option. It went far beyond being conceited. Nor did they hide behind their wealth. No, this was something that was bred from within. Brazil had it and was clearly born with it due to her bloodline, but that just made me wonder about her parents.

Carmello Green was a big man, tall and built like he had been lifting weights his whole damn life. As he spoke, I couldn't help but picture The Rock, Dwayne Johnson. It was as if they had covered him in chocolate and sat him in front of me. But it wasn't just his size. The way he spoke, how sure he was of himself, and honestly, the fear I felt—that shit was real. And her mother . . . Shit. There were almost no words for her. She was beautiful, intense, and scary all at the same time. The whole mood of the house felt that way, powerful but deadly. It gave me chills, but in some crazy way, I wanted to be a part of it. I knew that I wouldn't sign anything that night. I was done with just jumping into things without reading the fine print. I also knew that I was almost sure that I would sign with them, if I could.

"So what are your thoughts so far? Are you ready to step into the real world of rap? Not that backroom bullshit that Santino got you on," Carmello said.

"Yeah, I'm ready for it all. I want to become a legend, someone who shows the world that no matter what you have on, as long as you're you, no one can stop you."

Carmello slammed his hand against the table and smiled. "That's what the fuck I'm talking about. You're different, and I knew that as soon as Brazil showed us your YouTube videos."

"Yeah, well, although Santino isn't trying to change my look, he sure as hell is trying to change my sound . . . trying to get me to go all pop and shit."

"Aww, fuck Santino. He doesn't know what he's doing. See, with us, you are going to get to be yourself. You can be who you are and do what you want . . . as long as your records sell. We don't censor shit around here."

"That's some bullshit. You may not censor the rappers, but you're on my ass like white on rice," Brazil interjected with a roll of her eyes.

"Come on now, Brazil baby. You are the number one–selling girl group in the world right now. That's a whole different arena than rap, but let's talk about that later." He looked at me. "So, Niya, what do you think?"

"I'm signed to Hill Top Records. I can't just—"

"If that's your only worry, well, then . . . you have nothing to worry about. You let me deal with Santino."

I sat there and thought about things. I was not sure how much time passed with me just sitting there and not saying a word, but neither of them rushed me.

"Give me the contract, give me three days, and you'll have an answer. As long as I don't have a problem with Hill Top Records, I'm pretty sure we have a deal," I finally said.

My heart was pumping so fast that I thought I was going to pass out. Now it was Carmello's turn just to sit and stare at me. I wanted to know what he was thinking, what he saw when he looked at me, and if I had just blown the biggest chance at stardom I had been given thus far.

"Three days, and I want an answer. Don't worry about Santino. I know how to deal with niggas like him. I do want you to keep in mind that I want Brazil to jump on a remix for "Team Take Yo' Bitch." She wants to step out and swim on the wild side for a while. Even if you don't sign a full contract with us, I would like you to at least consider doing that with us."

Brazil jumped out of her chair and ran over to him. She got in his lap and kissed his face. "Really, Daddy? Please say you're not playing with me."

Carmello smiled as he looked into his daughter's eyes. "No, honey, I am serious. I will take baby steps with you as far as you wanting to do more things outside of the Brazilian Barbies, but you have to promise that if I give you an arm, you won't take it, cut the motherfucker off, and run with it."

"No, Daddy. I promise I won't. Oh my God, Niya. You have to do it."

Brazil stood up, allowing her father to do the same as I followed suit. He extended his hand, and I took it, and he held on to mine as he spoke.

"While you're at home, thinking, make sure to look us up. We have an all-star lineup, and so far, no one has failed. Don't let your destiny pass you by. You fucked up one time with that Hill Top bullshit. Don't do it again. Now, Brazil will show you out, and I'll have the contract hand delivered to you tomorrow morning."

***

"Thanks for coming over, Niya," Brazil said. "I am so excited for you. I really do hope that you sign with us. We are the majors, baby."

Brazil seemed to be more excited than I was, but I knew that wasn't possible. She walked me to the waiting car and took my hand once we got to it.

"Let's step into the car so I can take a picture with you," she said.

"Shouldn't I be asking *you* to take one with me?" I asked as we got into the car.

She turned on the light and pressed the side of her face against mine. She snapped a few shots with her cell phone and answered my question afterward.

"Nah. I am about to post this all over Twitter, Facebook, and Instagram. I am going to tell my fans that I will be doing a song with none other than the hottest lesbian rapper on the scene. Wait. Is it okay if I put *lesbian*?"

I couldn't help but laugh right in her face. "It's not hard to tell. Know what I mean? It's cool, I guess. It's just that I don't want to be known as the greatest lesbian rapper, just the greatest rapper, period. But it's cool for now."

At first, she just sat there with her head cocked to the side, but slowly, a smile crept across her face. "Damn. That was some deep shit, and I totally get it. That's why I want to branch out and just do me. The girl group thing is fine, but I'm so limited. I just want to be free. Fuck always having to be the good girl, 'cause, baby, I'm as bad as they come."

Something in her eyes told me that there was nothing but truth behind her words.

"That you are, Brazil. That you are," I answered as I openly admired her body with my eyes.

I watched as the confident fame monster became shy and girly all of a sudden.

"Good night, Niya. I'll be praying that things go my way and you sign to Green Note Records."

"But don't they always go your way?"

I couldn't lie. When she smiled, it did something to me.

"Yeah . . . they kinda always do."

A weird silence fell upon us, and I had to intervene.

"Thank you so much for bringing me here tonight. This is a once-in-a-lifetime occurrence."

"Well, you heard what my mother said. Don't fuck it up. Good night, Niya. Hope to see you soon."

I didn't want her to go. I could have just sat there with her all night long.

"Yeah, I hope I see you really soon too."

She smiled at me and jumped out of the car. I watched her walk into the house and close the door before I told the driver where to go.

I had a million thoughts swimming through my head that night. The deal that I had, the deal that was just offered to me, and Brazil Noelle played a major part and acted as the water that filled the pool of confusion my brain was swimming in. Something deep down inside said that this was it, that my life was really about to change, and not on some bullshit level.

Chapter 73

The Green estate, the house that was built from deceit . . .

Brazil walked back into her home, feeling very different. Her encounter with Niya had left her excited yet confused. She couldn't understand what was happening, and it gave her a disturbing feeling. She stood behind the heavy doors that she had just locked, and tried to put her thoughts in order.

"So, what do you think? Will she sign with Green Note?" her mother asked. She was sitting on the left side of the imperial staircase, awaiting her return.

"I don't know, Ma. I really hope she does."

"You better make sure she does. Come with me. Let's take a ride."

Brazil followed her mother to one of her cars and knew that her mother was about to lay something serious on her. She always did when they took a ride that late at night.

So as the Atlanta moon missed their skin while they rode in the Bentley convertible, plans were put in motion.

"That girl reminds me of someone, and trust me when I tell you this. She will blow up with or without Green Note."

"I know, Ma—"

"You don't know shit. Shut your damn mouth when I'm talking, and maybe you'll learn something."

As always, Brazil wilted and waited for her mother to finish. There were times when she would feel brave enough to talk back to her mother, but that night, something told her just to sit back and listen.

"You keep saying you want to go solo and be the bad bitch of the music world. Well, that girl is your ticket."

Brazil wanted to ask her mother how so, but she knew that she would tell her, anyway.

"No matter how much people want to deny it, the younger generation isn't taking any shit when it comes to being who they are. I see it out here every day. Young girls proud of being studs who stand out from the rest. Lesbians, bisexuals, and the boys are in on the fun too. It's as if being a part of that world while still holding on to the straight world really works for you celebs. So here's what you're going to do. You are going to make sure she signs with us, and after that, you're going to do a song and video with her. Soon you'll start to have lunch with her, go to parties with her and even award shows. You'll walk the red carpet. You'll text her and get really close to her."

"Okay, but why?"

Her mother shook her head and decided against calling her a dumb little girl like she really wanted to. "Because, Brazil, that will get people talking. Soon you'll be all over the blog sites and magazines. You'll take her on the yacht and make sure the paparazzi snap shots of you lying on her, kissing her even."

"Kissing her?" Brazil asked with wide eyes.

"Don't worry. You won't be swimming in the lady pond for long. Just long enough to create some buzz. That way, when you do step out on your own, the world will be ready for you."

The rest of the ride was filled with minor details. What Brazil's mother didn't know was that deep down inside, this mission wouldn't be so hard to complete. Brazil's little crush on Niya would soon grow. What was meant to be a publicity stunt could very well become bigger than anyone could conceive and could spiral out of control.

Chapter 74

Jamilla

It was Sunday evening, and when I came out of my room for breakfast, Niya was at the damn table, staring at the contract again.

"Would you sign the damn thing already? You had a lawyer look at it, and he told you that everything looked right. What are you so nervous about? You know you got this."

She was such a damn Libra. Couldn't make up her mind to save her life.

"I know, Jamilla boo. I just like looking at it. When I called Granny and told her that I was asked to join the same label as the Brazilian Barbies, she said she liked their songs. I thought she was bullshittin', but she started to sing one of them. That was some funny shit."

We shared a laugh, but inside, I couldn't help but wonder if the new journey she would soon be on would push us further apart.

"Just sign the fucking thing. Oh, guess what I did today? I started sending the book out to some publishing companies."

She got up and came over to me. She wrapped her arms around my waist and hugged me tightly, and it felt so good.

"Here you are, telling me that I got this, and you are already on it. It's going to happen, Jamilla boo, trust me."

"It's been so long since we have really spent time together. How about we watch the award show and just chill? We can smoke and laugh at all the wack-ass performances. Wait, isn't Brazil's group one of the performers?"

I watched as Niya's smile broadened to lengths I hadn't seen in a while. I rolled my eyes, hoping that she wouldn't catch it.

"Oh yeah. That's right. Turn to that channel that does the red carpet. Maybe we'll see her on there. Bring the smoke and blunts. I'll roll the first one."

I didn't say a word. I just did as she asked and sat beside her with an attitude. The whole first forty-five minutes was spent with me listening to Niya go on and on about what she thought Brazil would have on, if she would show up with that dude from the boy band whom she was dating, and even what song she thought the group would perform. Seemed like she'd done some research. Niya had never really been into the Brazilian Barbies like that, so I just sat and listened.

"Okay, the show is about to start. I'm gonna run and make us some drinks," she announced.

I sat on the couch, pouting like a three-year-old. I didn't like the feeling that was brewing deep inside. Maybe I just wasn't used to her showing so much interest in someone else. As I waited for her to come back into the living room, I read the little bottom ticker on the screen that kept viewers up to date on the news. As my mind drifted back to the issue at hand, I thought I saw Brazil's name. I sat up and waited for the news ticker to come back around again. As I sat there and read the news, my eyes felt as if they would pop out of my head.

"Oh shit!" I yelled without even trying.

"Are you okay?" Niya asked from the kitchen.

"Yo, get in here. Brazil got beat up."

"What did you just say?" Niya asked as she walked out of the kitchen and set the drinks down on the coffee table.

I reached for my laptop and went to the most accurate celebrity blog I could think of. As soon as the page loaded, I saw that Brazil's battered face was the first and only post on the front page. I walked over to Niya and sat the laptop on her lap. I was scared to see her reaction, but I couldn't keep this information to myself.

"What the fuck? This nigga put his hands on her?" Niya bellowed.

I grabbed my computer before she threw it. Niya's face was bloodred as she jumped off the couch. I watched her as she picked up her phone and, I was sure, tried to call Brazil.

"Fuck!" she shouted.

I watched as she hung up the phone and tried calling again. When no one picked up, she walked over to her contract and dialed the number that was at the top of it. Again, she got no answer. She went back over to the television and turned up the volume.

"How could he do this to her?" she murmured.

We sat and listened to the blow-by-blow as the reporter received the news in her earpiece. It seemed as if a fight had broken out between Brazil and her boyfriend when the couple was on their way to the award show. When the picture of Brazil's face appeared on the screen again, the swelling, cuts, and bruises left her almost unrecognizable. I sat beside Niya and could feel her body trembling.

"Calm down, Niya. You'll talk to her soon."

I took her hand and just sat with her. For the next few hours, we flipped through the news channels, hoping to get more of the story. At the rate we were drinking and smoking, I knew that Niya would be in a dark place come morning. She just kept asking how a man could do that to a girl, to his girlfriend at that.

That was when it hit me. You really never knew what these celebrities were going through. I remembered sitting at the computer and admiring the relationship Brazil had with her boy band boyfriend. At times, I would ask God why I couldn't be her. She was beautiful, talented, rich, and famous. She seemed to have what every girl in the world wanted. *Now look at her and how things are unfolding for her*, I thought. All I could do was shake my head at my private thoughts. I guessed that should show me that I should be happy with who I was, what I had, and who I had in my life.

Chapter 75

Niya

I didn't sleep that night. I stayed up all night and blew Brazil's phone up. I wasn't sure if I was out of order or not, being that we had just met, but I just couldn't help it. I stayed up, hoping that the news or the blogs would have more information about what had happened or how bad off she was, but they just kept repeating the same things over and over.

I didn't even leave my room. I had a bottle of Cîroc and all the weed I needed in my room. Jamilla tried to get me to open the door a few times, but I just stayed silent and pretended to be asleep. *Fuck.* I needed to talk to Brazil. By the time eight in the evening rolled around, I was going out of my mind. I staggered to the shower and tried to clear my mind in there, but that didn't work, so I thought that maybe I needed some food. I left my room and tried to move in silence, but that didn't work.

"Why didn't you open your door? I know you heard me knocking," Jamilla said as I stood at the kitchen sink, eating a cold slice of pizza.

"I was sleeping." That was all I offered her, and that was all she was going to get.

"Why are you so fucking cold with me? I wasn't the one who beat her ass."

I stopped eating, took a real hard look at Jamilla, and threw the pizza down in the sink. I wanted to really let her have it for even going there, but I changed my mind and just walked away. I thought that Jamilla knew me well, but her choice to follow me showed me that she didn't know enough about me to know just to leave me alone. I wasn't in the mood for her shit.

"So that's what we're doing now? You're just going to walk away from me?" she snapped.

"Jamilla, just leave me alone," I answered with my back to her.

"Nah, fuck that. How long have you known her, and you're already acting like this? I'm your friend and I care about you, but look how you're treating me."

I was in my room by that point and tried to close my door, but she walked in and closed it herself.

"Yo, Jamilla. I asked you to leave me alone. What's your fucking problem?" I sat on my bed and watched as she rolled her eyes.

"You! You're my fucking problem. You don't even know that girl like that, yet you're locked up in your room, acting like a little bitch over her."

I just kept telling myself to ignore her. I knew that I wasn't in the right frame of mind, so I was trying my best to keep it cool.

"Look at you. All drunk and shit. You over here worried about her, yet you don't give a second thought about not spending time with me, not seeing me, not—"

"This shit ain't about you."

She was really starting to piss me off. I had never seen such a selfish side to Jamilla, and I didn't fucking like it.

"Oh really? It ain't about me? Well . . . isn't that some new shit? I see. What now? She's your new Roxie, your new Marlo?"

I could feel the heat in my face and knew that if she didn't leave my room, it would only be a matter of time before I blew up.

"Jamilla, you better leave me the fuck alone. I'm not for this shit tonight."

She tipped her head back and let out a hearty fake laugh. "Oh, so, you not for *this* shit tonight?" she asked, pointing to herself. It was then that I realized that her speech was a little slurred and that she must have had a few drinks herself.

She went on. "I remember when you were always for this shit. I remember when you used to *love* this shit. I remember when you wanted *all* this shit. Guess your love ain't worth shit."

I wasn't too sure what was happening, but her questioning my love made my whole face feel like it was on fire. I jumped off the bed and almost felt as if I was out of my body and watching myself. *Do not put your hands on her*, my brain yelled to my heart. So instead, I grabbed her arms under her shoulders on each side and held on tight as I shouted in her face.

"How fucking dare you say my love wasn't real? I fucking ripped out my heart and handed that shit to you on a diamond fucking platter, and what did you do? You threw that shit back at me, as if it wasn't worth shit."

"You didn't give me *shit*. You can't share that side with everyone else, Niya. If it were mine, it would be mine alone."

"You are such a selfish bitch. You know that? I was ready to ram a bat up Marie's ass for you. I was ready to kill. I breathed for you, bitch, for you and you only, and you didn't give a fuck, because you are not gay. Remember that shit? Remember shoving that shit in my face in front of everyone at Kingsborough? Remember saying it time and time again as my hands were in your wet-ass pussy, yet you still denied it. What the fuck do you want me to do? Sit around and play sike-dyke games with you? *Fuck that*. You want me to finger fuck you, but you don't want *me*? Fuck you, bitch! Motherfuck you!"

I let her go and went back and sat on my bed. She stood there, and I waited for the tears that I was so sure would come. I waited and waited and waited, but nothing. Instead, she walked over to me and tried to slap me. I grabbed her hands and pushed her away from me, which caused her to fall back on her behind. I stood up and knew that I was about to lay hands on her ass. I grabbed her shirt, stood her up, and pushed her against the wall and held her by the shoulders.

"Look at you! You in here worried about Brazil, yet you are the same motherfucker her boyfriend is. Go ahead. Hit me," she yelled.

I stood still and tried to control my breathing. As hard as it was to hear, I knew she was right.

"Hitting you would only make you feel like you have the right to treat me the way you did. Nah, I ain't gonna hit you, 'cause, see, my love for you won't let me. That's right. That shit was real. Yeah . . . *was*. I would have given you the world, Jamilla. I would have given you the world. I even offered you all of me, without leaving none of me out, not even a drop, but you didn't want it. You toyed with all that I had to offer, and today I see why. You are selfish, and that's why Brazil bothers you. It's because you're a taker. You take and take and take, until there is nothing left. You filled up on the love that was left in me and did nothing with it. Do you know how hurtful that is? Do you know what it's like to look at you every day and know that the person I love the most only used my love to make herself feel better and didn't give it back?"

She was trying her hardest to hold back the tears now, but soon they would wet her face. I could feel her stance softening under my hands as she tried to tell me that I was wrong.

"I do love you, Niya. Think of what I did for you that night. I did that because I love you."

I couldn't let her throw that night in my face, not right now, not when I was forcing her to face the truth of our relationship.

"When in the fuck are you going to prove it past that? I know what you did for me, and I will never forget it. The truth is, Jamilla, I know you love me, but while I was *in love* with you, you were just loving me. I mean, come on. We've been arguing about the same shit since we met. I can't do this shit anymore, and I certainly can't keep having the same conversation over and over again. I'm just tired, Jamilla. I just wish you could have fallen in love with me too . . . instead of playing your fucking games."

"And you call me selfish? How could you say that I'm not in . . . ?" She stopped mid-sentence and couldn't even finish saying what I'd been dying for her to say with so much on the line.

"You can't even fucking say it, and that's why I'll fuck Brazil or whoever else I want. Man, get the fuck out of my room."

I let her go but stayed there. We stood there, eye to eye, truth to truth, and she just couldn't face hers. I would have stood there all night, peering into her eyes, if my phone didn't ring. I reached in my pocket, pulled out my phone, and looked at the number. I didn't recognize it but picked up the call, anyway.

"Hello?"

"Niya, this is Carmello. Made your mind up about that contract yet?"

I moved away from Jamilla but kept my eyes on her as I spoke into the phone. "I have been trying to call but couldn't get anyone. Is Brazil okay?"

"Niya, this call is about the contract. How are you feeling about it?"

He was making me angry all over again.

"I have a few things that I want to request. If these demands can be met, I'm all yours."

I waited while silence filled the air.

"Are you busy right now?" he finally asked.

"No. Why?" I asked, hoping that he would ask me to meet him somewhere. I needed to get out of this house.

"I'm sending a car for you."

I hung up the phone and turned to Jamilla. "Get the fuck up out of my room. I need to get dressed."

She tried to approach me, but I wasn't having it. "Niya, I—"

"Get the fuck out."

I waited for her to leave my room before I locked my door and got dressed.

Chapter 76

Jamilla & Niya – Paradise Lost

Jamilla

Niya had been gone for only a few minutes before I started to panic. What had just happened, and why did I feel as if it was death? When I'd gone into the kitchen to talk to her, I'd sworn that I didn't want things to end up this way. I just couldn't understand why she was so worried about Brazil when she had just met her. I was used to being the only one she cared about like that. I didn't know. . . . Maybe I had overreacted. Maybe I should have just been there for her, but what about me? I still needed her to be there for me. I still wanted to be the only one she cared about. A little selfish, maybe, but that was the truth. We were moving apart, and instead of going to her and telling her that it was bothering me, I'd fucked things up.

Niya

I enjoyed the ride to Brazil's house. It gave me time to cool down and think. Honestly, I was shocked at how it had all gone down. Those feelings had seemed to spring up out of thin air. Feelings that lurked deep down inside and that were fighting their way through the pain and disappointment of our love had seemed to decorate the air in my room, and it had been intense.

As angry as I was, I had wanted to tell her that the words I spoke were birthed from her unreturned love, the love that I would still, to this day, give up the world for. I had wanted her to look at me and tell me that I was wrong, and I had wanted to believe her. I had wanted her to say, "Yes, Niya. I am in love with you too," and I would have been ready to give her my all again, but she just couldn't. How long could I try to force her hand at love? How long could I leave my needs unfulfilled for her?

As the driver pulled up to the house, I received my first text from Jamilla but left it unanswered.

Jamilla

Niya, if you're not there yet, please call me, I texted.

I looked down at the glass in my hand and knew that I had to stop drinking. I was pacing the floor in the living room while I thought about losing Niya for good. I was going crazy as I envisioned my life without her. No, that could never happen. I sent her another text since she didn't answer my first one.

Come on, Niya. Please. I'm sorry. I don't want you to be mad.

I waited another five minutes before texting her to call me again. That night made me realize that I needed more friends. I really needed to speak to someone, but I had no one but Niya. I also realized that I feared being alone. I wanted someone there for me. . . . I *needed* someone to be there. I didn't want to throw myself a pity party, but I felt as if I was heading in that direction. Why in the fuck wasn't she texting me back? I would rather have fought with her than for her to ignore me.

I went into the kitchen and thought about pouring another drink but went against it. I rolled up and waited for the weed to calm my nerves. I sat there smoking, thinking about the things Niya had said to me. Was I really being that damn selfish? How could I be when all I was telling her was that she didn't really know Brazil? She knew *me*, not her. I sent her another text, and my words were starting to show a bit of anger.

Niya, stop acting like a fucking child and hit me back. Grow up and talk to me.

Niya

I sat in front of Carmello for the second time that week and wanted to ask him about Brazil again, but he was strictly business. He had his lawyer there who would adjust the contract after the negotiations, and I wished I had mine with me. Although my lawyer had told me what to ask for and what to look for when I was looking over the revised contract, I still wanted him there. I was a bit drunk still and didn't want to fuck myself again with another bad record deal.

"So, your terms. What are they?"

I got nervous but said, *Fuck it*. All he could do was say no.

"First, I want to talk about the up-front money and the back end. I want more of both."

I went on and told him that I wanted a quarter million, and not the 150 that he had offered. I also negotiated the points I would have on the records and future royalties.

He was quick to agree to a higher signing bonus, but it took some work for us to meet in the middle as far as the back end was concerned. Soon, we came to an agreement that would leave me rich if everything went well and him wealthier.

"What else?" Carmello asked as his lawyer took notes.

As I had walked into his office and had waited for him to come in, I had thought more about Jamilla and me. I had thought that maybe we just needed some space. Maybe we needed to be away from each other to know if this thing we had really was real. Plus, I just wanted to help put her writing career on the fast track. I knew that doing so would make her truly happy.

"Do you have any connections with the book world?"

I could tell that my question puzzled him, so I waited for him to throw some questions my way.

"What do you mean, the book world?"

"Well, I have a friend who just self-published a book and sent it out to a few publishers. I want to know if you can call someone to help get her a deal."

Carmello smiled as I waited to hear what he was thinking.

"I don't specialize in books, but I'm sure that if I make a few calls, I can deliver that deal for her. I know that the owner of Cash Flow Records just launched a publishing company, so that will be an easy deal. Anything else?"

Damn. Carmello made all of this seem so easy.

"So can we add that as a clause to the contract? If Jamilla doesn't have a book deal within, let's say, a month—"

"She'll get an e-mail from them as soon as I make that call, trust me. Just leave her contact info, and they will get at her."

I breathed easy as I ran through a few other things that I wanted. As my pocket vibrated with more of Jamilla's texts, I was signing my first big contract.

Jamilla

As I wrote Niya another text, Rodney's incoming calls just pissed me off. He wasn't who I wanted to speak to. I needed to hear from Niya. I needed her to know that I loved her. I needed her to know that my anger about Brazil was jealousy, but she wouldn't pick up.

> What the fuck is wrong with you? What? Should I kiss your ass for you to text me back? I am trying to tell you that I do love you. Text me back.

I pressed SEND and waited. Still nothing. "Fuck her," I yelled as I mashed the blunt into the ashtray. Why was she doing this to me? Didn't she know that I loved her? Didn't I prove that already? As I continued to talk to myself, I heard a knock on the door. I ignored it until the person started to knock even louder.

"Who the fuck is—" I couldn't continue to speak when I opened the door. At first, I thought that I was too damn drunk or high, because my mind had to be playing tricks on me.

"Hey, baby. Surprise."

I was not too sure of the look that sat on my face, but I was sure shock was mixed in there somewhere.

"Rodney, what are you doing here?"

Niya

The house was dim, and the darkness was created by something far deeper than the lack of lighting. I got chills as I headed for the front door. There was a sadness, an evil, a gloom that radiated through the house, and I couldn't help but wonder about Brazil. It killed me that

I was about to leave the house without even getting an update on how she was doing.

"Niya?"

I looked around and tried to find the voice. Like one might with a cat, all I saw were her eyes before she appeared.

"Hey, Mrs. Green."

She had on a long, black, sheer robe, with just her bra and panties underneath. Even amid all that darkness, I could still see her fit body. Again, she got real close to me as she spoke, a little too close for comfort.

"You remind me of someone from my past," she said as ice clanged in the glass she held.

I could smell the liquor on her breath, and it made me want some. I reached for the heavy crystal that was in her hand, took it from her, took a big swig, and asked her who.

"No need to name drop. It's just . . . every time I look at you, I see her. From your hair to your skin to your eyes, you make me miss her even more."

I stood there as her hand swept over my hair. Her fingers slid down a handful of strands until she reached the tips.

"Why don't you call her or go see her? I can tell by the look in your eyes that you really do miss her," I replied.

She didn't answer right away. I stared at her to see if the tears that were forming in her eyes would eventually drop. They didn't.

"It's too late for that. . . . I chose all of this," she said as she waved her hands in the air, pointing out the house, before she continued. "I wanted all of this instead of her. Biggest mistake of my life."

"It's never too late to change your mind," I answered before finishing off the strong liquor that was in her glass.

"For me, for us, it is."

Her voice was so filled with agony that her anguish seemed to leave her body, float to me, and cause me pain somewhere deep down within me. I put the glass down on the piano that stood beside us, making sure to put it on the cloth, and moved closer to her. I was not sure why, but I put my hands around her waist and pulled her to me. I hugged her long and hard, and she let me. We stood there, with her seemingly mourning the loss of a beautiful friendship, and with me in fear that I would end up right where she was.

"I knew the minute I saw you that you were special, just as special as her," she murmured.

"Yeah, well, I'm sure you were very special to her too."

When I said that, she melted in my arms, and I . . . did the same. We hugged as if that was all either of us had ever needed. It wasn't sexual; it was just one person being there for the other. When she let me go, she picked up the glass and took my hand.

"Come with me. My daughter wants to see you."

Jamilla

Rodney and I were sitting on the couch, and I just could not believe that he was sitting right next to me.

"So, wait, you're here to stay?" I asked.

Why in the hell did he think that he could just show up and move in?

"Yeah. My mom bitched a little bit, but I told her that I would enroll in college out here. June will be coming next week. Didn't Niya tell you?"

My anger rose through the roof. "You mean she knew?"

Rodney started to laugh, as if all this was funny. "Yeah she knew. I just didn't give her a date, 'cause I didn't want her to tell you. I just told her that I would be here this month. You're not mad that I'm here, are you?"

I tried to fix my face and smile. “No. I mean, I’m surprised, but no.”

Rodney leaned into me and hugged me, but I felt nothing. After a few seconds, I pulled away from him and reached for my phone. I texted Niya.

Call me ASAP.

And then I waited.

Niya

I followed Mrs. Green up the stairs and couldn’t wait to get to Brazil. The house seemed even bigger than I had initially thought, and it seemed to take forever to get to Brazil’s room.

“Hey, Mom? Delilah is coming over. Is that cool?”

I turned and saw who I had learned was Brazil’s brother during my research. He was a star basketball player in his high school and seemed to have a lot of buzz around him.

“Yeah, that’s cool. Niya, this is Rio. Rio, Niya.”

I shook his hand before he turned and went back to his bedroom. Finally, we made it to Brazil’s bedroom, but before I went in, her mother had a few last words for me.

“You know, you are the only person she wants to see. If you can, try to act like you don’t notice the damage done to her face. I keep trying to tell her that the swelling will go down and the scars can be fixed, but . . . Anyway, I just want you to know that you must have had an impact on her in the short time that you have known her, ’cause she just kept asking for you.”

She knocked on the door, and when we heard Brazil say, “Come in,” she walked away. I entered the room and found Brazil staring out her bedroom window. Her back was to me, and I was almost scared for her to turn around.

"Hey, Brazil. It's me, Niya."

She didn't turn to face me but answered, "How are you?"

Was she crazy? Fuck how I was doing. I was here for her.

"Honestly, I have been worried about you. I couldn't stop thinking about you."

"Yeah, you and the whole world. I can't even leave this fucking house, because everyone is worried about me."

"Well, I thought about you for more reasons than one. I may be out of line, but ever since I met you, I haven't been able to stop thinking about you."

She was silent for a while, still not facing me.

Finally, she spoke. "Why is that? Have you been thinking about my beauty? Have you been thinking of the girl you saw before yesterday? Because if that's who you are thinking about, she may be gone for good."

When she turned and faced me, I took in a deep breath. Her face was so swollen and bruised. Her lower lip was split, and it looked as if it must be painful for her even to speak. I moved toward her and pushed her hair out of her face.

"Nah, she's still here. All this shit will go away, and because of it, you will be even more beautiful, because you will be stronger."

"But, Niya, I am in the business of beauty. Yes, people like our music, but my looks are what get me the endorsements. They are why I am Brazil Noelle."

It was so fucked up how this industry shit could really mess up people's outlook on themselves. I wanted to ask her where *her* self-confidence was, without the business bullshit, but I didn't. I just gave her the love that she needed.

"You are Brazil Noelle because of who *you* are. You are beautiful because of who *you* are, and that outer shit . . . it will heal. As I stand here looking at you, I don't see the swelling and all that other shit. I mean, I see it, but I still see the bad bitch who was shaking her ass in the restaurant to my shit. You're still that bad bitch, and from the looks of it, you will be bad no matter what. You could still kill most of the bitches in the game right now, looking like Martin did on that one episode when he went up against the boxer Tommy Hearns."

That made her laugh, so I smiled.

"Shut up. I don't look that bad," she said as she hit me on the shoulder.

"Nah. I'm just fuckin' with you. But what are you going to do about the press? You can't just stay locked up in your room until you heal."

She thought about it for a second and asked me something that I was not expecting. "What if I wanted to get away? Would you come with me? Maybe we can work on the remix to 'Team Take Yo' Bitch.'"

I was stunned. Go away with *the* Brazil Noelle? "Really? I mean, yeah, I would come. Where are you trying to go?"

She didn't answer me. She opened her bedroom door and yelled for her mom and waited for her to come in.

Her mom walked in with a fresh drink and a long white cigarette in her hand. "What do you need, Brazil?"

"I was just talking to Niya about getting away for a little bit. I feel trapped here. I just want to leave the country."

Leave the country? Damn. I was really happy that Santino had insisted that I get a passport.

"Where do you want to go?" her mother asked.

I guessed that was how the rich did it. They just got up and went, and that was including their kids.

"Didn't you and Dad renovate that house in Brazil? Are they done working on it, and did they finish the studio?"

"Yeah, it's all done. When do you want to leave?"

"If we leave tonight, do you think that Dad will get things together so we can record the remix to Niya's song and work on my solo stuff? Hell, we can even shoot the video out there once my face gets better."

"Wow, Niya. Looks like you did what we couldn't do. She's smiling. Let me call a few people to make sure the staff is there when you two get there. Don't worry about Daddy. I know how to work him," her mother said as she dialed a number on her cell phone.

She spoke to a few people, and within ten minutes, she told us to pack our bags, because the plane would be ready in two hours.

Jamilla

Rodney was so hyped about being in Atlanta, but my mind wasn't on him. I had yet to receive a text from Niya, although I had sent her one after the other.

"Yo, let's go out. Let's celebrate. When is Niya coming home? I want to surprise her too."

"I'm not sure when she's coming back. She went to go meet with Carmello from Green Note Records."

His eyes got big as I ran down the story of everything that had gone down, but I left out the part about me and Niya's fight.

"So you mean to tell me that I will have a chance to make beats for her while she's under his label?"

For the first time that night, I really smiled. Rodney was so excited and looked like a big kid.

"If she signs with him, you will."

"Oh my God. Look how great things are unfolding. You got your book thing. How is that going, by the way?"

"So good I even sent it out to some publishers."

Rodney jumped to his feet and pulled me up with him. He picked me up and hugged me as my feet left the floor.

"Damn, baby, we are going to be the motherfucking dream team. You will blow up as a writer, and I will be killin' these niggas with my beats. We can't lose. Fuck that. We going out. I saw Niya's car outside. Where are the keys?"

I really didn't want to go out with him without speaking to Niya first, but what more could I do? Maybe this was all meant to happen this way. Maybe Rodney and I were meant to be. I didn't know, and some parts of me didn't want to know. Hell, what I did know seemed to be getting away from me; what I really wanted alluded me.

"Just let me get dressed," I said as I headed to my bedroom.

Once there, I told myself that while I was out, I would text Niya a few more times. I wouldn't tell her that Rodney was here in a text, but I really hoped she called me. *Damn.* Life was a funny motherfucker. Leave it to the gods to have Rodney show up on the night Niya and I seemed to be falling apart. I shook my head at that funny little thing called fate and hoped that it knew what it was doing. I loved Niya with all of me and prayed that one day soon she would believe that.

Once dressed, I looked for Niya's extra set of car keys, found them, and handed them to Rodney. I wrote a note telling Niya that I had gone out in her car and that I would be back. I also wrote that she should call me, because I had something to tell her.

"Yo, where should I leave my bag?" Rodney asked as he pointed to his duffel bag, which sat by the front door.

"Just leave it there. You can put it away when we get back."

As we headed out to the car, I texted Niya again and wondered where Rodney would be sleeping until he got his own place.

Niya

Brazil had four trunks full of clothes and everything else she thought she would need for our trip to Brazil. They were all put into the truck that would follow us to my house, then to the airport. The only people who would join us there were her assistant and her hair and makeup people, being that the house in Brazil was fully staffed. That was shocking because she was the same age as me, only seventeen. I had always heard about the freedom these child stars had, but I was now experiencing it firsthand.

When we got to my apartment, I dreaded going in and facing Jamilla, but at least I wouldn't be staying long. I went in and headed straight for my bedroom closet. On my way there, I read the note Jamilla had left behind but didn't give it a second thought. I pulled out two suitcases, then packed one with shoes and the other with clothes. I packed all my toiletries in a carry-on and made sure that I had plenty of cash, my bank card, my passport, and a blunt and weed to smoke on the way to the airport.

After I made sure that I had everything that I needed for the trip, I picked up the notepad that I always left beside my bed. On it I wrote, *Going to Brazil with Brazil. Not sure when I'll be back. You know where some money is if you need anything*. I dragged my bags to the kitchen and was about to tape my note to the fridge, but something stopped me. I looked at the duffel bag by the front door and wondered how I had missed it on my way in.

So she was going to leave for a while? Really? The duffel bag couldn't hold that much, so I knew that she wouldn't be gone for too long, but she was just going to leave? To me, that just proved my point. If she was so ready to leave without even fixing the situation and facing the truth, what the fuck was I even wasting my time for? I loved her, but maybe we were just meant to be friends. Maybe that was what fate had in the cards for us.

In that moment—I couldn't even lie—that shit hurt like hell. Jamilla had my heart, even though I didn't want her to, and I knew that it would take time to heal. I was lovesick and needed to rebuild the empty space she was going to leave in my heart. So, I taped the note to the fridge and left . . . hoping that she would at least be there when I came back.

The car ride to the airport was smooth. I was happy to know that Brazil smoked from time to time, and she helped me smoke the fat blunt I had rolled. She sat close to me and seemed relieved to be leaving America. She talked about how much she loved the country she was named after. She told me that her mom was half Brazilian and that every year, they made sure to visit Brazil. She said that her mother had told her that she was conceived there and that she knew from the minute she found out that she was having twins that she would name them Brazil and Rio. I liked hearing her talk about herself, the person, and not the star. While in that car, just being close to her and listening to the "real" her, I knew that something was brewing inside of me for her.

Soon, we were standing on the tarmac at the airport, in front of her family's private jet, waiting for the suitcases to load.

"Let's take a selfie. You have to take one with your phone so we can tag each other," Brazil told me.

Man, life was changing, and it made my head spin. We took our pictures and tagged each other with hashtags that read #Her, #JetSet, #GetAway, #Niya, #Brazil, #Us, #NeverYou, #TeamTakeYoBitch, #SheTookYo-Bitch, #Recovery, #LeaveUsAlone, #RockStarShit, and #PeaceAtLast.@NiyaSoDope@BrazilianBarbieBaby.

Within ten minutes, her pictures had over twenty-five thousand likes, and the requests from people to follow me was out of control.

"Don't worry about the requests. I'll have my assistant, Kelbe, take care of them for you," Brazil promised.

We started to climb the stairs to the plane, with her in front of me, but before I could step on the plane, my phone vibrated with a text. When I looked down, I read the text, and it was Jamilla asking me to call her. I went to my contacts and was about to push CALL when Brazil's voice stopped me.

"Come on, Niya. I can't wait forever."

Something about her words struck a chord with me. I had to just let shit ride when it came to Jamilla. I just had to force myself to let go. I turned off my phone and entered the plane as I thought about her last text to me.

"Yeah, well, neither can I, baby. I just can't wait forever."

Chapter 77

Paradise Found . . . For Now

São Paulo was a welcome getaway for both Niya and Brazil Noelle. Both girls had time to, in a sense, lick their wounds. Brazil's face was healing nicely, and with the best plastic surgeons at her beck and call, she knew that things would be okay. The girls spent every waking moment together. The bond that was forming would last as long as either of them wanted it.

That day, as they recorded the remix to Niya's song, something magical happened in that studio. Neither of them knew why or how these feelings had come to be, but neither of them fought them. It was something about working together, feeling the creative juices run through their veins. They got each other; they were wrapped in each other's vibes. It was as if their souls spoke the same language without even having to utter a word.

After the song wrapped and Niya asked for everyone to clear out of the studio, she knew she had to speak about what she was feeling.

"I am really happy we took this trip together. I'm also happy that I am getting a chance to really get to know you," she told Brazil.

The truth was infused with the liquor both girls had consumed, and their actions would reek of the potent Brazilian weed that swam in their systems.

"Niya?"

"Yes, Brazil?" Niya moved closer to her, almost needing to feel her skin.

"I like you," Brazil said as Niya pressed her body against her.

"Man, I feel like I fucking more than like you at this point," Niya answered as her arms wrapped around Brazil's waist.

Brazil standing there in her skimpy bikini didn't help dilute the sexual thoughts that danced around in Niya's head.

"You know, I don't know you well yet, but . . . I feel as if I need you," Brazil said.

Niya's heart raced as she remembered feeling that way and writing it to Jamilla. She had crossed Niya's mind often during the past few weeks, but each time Niya would quickly push thoughts of Jamilla out of her mind, as she did on this day.

"Don't worry. I know that feeling well," Niya answered.

"So, if I feel as if I need you, and you feel the same way too, why don't we just say fuck it and have each other?"

Brazil's words were like sweet samba music to Niya's ears. Niya held Brazil tightly, and both women fell deeper into each other as they shared their very first kiss to the sounds of Brazil's verse on the "Team Take Yo' Bitch" remix.

Seeing her makes me sweat.
Bet you would have never bet
She's my little secret, well kept.
With just one look she makes me wet.
They asking what's a Barbie without her Ken babyyy?
I say, "Fuck a Ken. She's the perfect blend, babyyy."
My heart is torn. She's here to mend it, babyyy.
Thought I was straight, but she makes me want to bend, babyyy.

Nothing better than a studdd, baby.
Nothing hotter than a studdd, baby.
Nothing sweeter than a studdd, baby.
She got me needing her, wanting her, feeling her, babyyy.
The shit she do to this body, babyyy.
I'm up to bat and I'm playing for her teammm, babyyy.
She said she want it, I said, "You can have it, babyyy."
Fuck a nigga. I want a studdd, baby.
Team take your bitch. Got your bitchhhh, babyyy.

Things would forever be different now. Although Brazil's mother wanted her to use Niya as a ploy to gain more gay fans, Brazil threw all of that out the window. She was really falling for this girl who had seemed to win her heart out of nowhere, and she knew that truly loving her wasn't far behind.

As for Niya, she just kept telling herself that this was where her heart should be. It should belong to a girl who was willing to love her back. It should be where the two people involved were able to love freely.

For Niya
The space between us is killing me.
The words that were spoken no longer exist, and you can't hear me.
The love we have seems fleeting, and that is like death to me.
This shit between us, this unspoken hurt haunts me.
We look at each other, yet we can't see.
I want what was, but that just can't be.
I am losing you, and, Niya, that thought is drowning me.
Sleepless nights with thoughts of her loving you murder me.

Murder the hope of us and what we were always meant to be.

Niya, I scream your name, hoping that you'll hear me.

Niya, my love, be there for me.

Love me.

Care for me.

Rescue me.

Can't you see life is meaningless if you are not there with me?

But wait . . . there it is.

I have made this all about me.

Niya, my love, I do love you.

I do want you.

I do need you.

Niya, my love, let's start with a clean slate.

Niya, my love, our love, it was all fate.

Niya, my love, I hope it's not too late.

Jamilla

A Note from the Author

Like love, a beautiful, heartfelt book that is birthed from the purest place may prove elusive. For me, capturing something as rare as the Niya series was pure bliss.

When I think back to the start of it all, I know that I just wanted to write a book for me. I wanted to enter Niya and Jamilla's world because they invited me in. So, while basking in the purity of it all, I knew that I didn't want to dilute it with what I thought it should be. Nor did I want to portray it as something it wasn't. No, I just wanted to write freely, as freely as these characters came to me.

The more I wrote, the more I fell in love, but that did not stop me from asking myself if this book would mean something to anyone but me. I knew that each word that left my fingertips had torn its way through my heart, but still I wanted to know, would the rest of the world understand it? Would they feel it as I did? Would they be able to feel each word?

Even with all these questions floating around in my head, I pushed on and stayed true to the story that was meant to be, and for me, when it was all done, I knew that it was fate. I did not choose these characters. They chose me. And, my God, was I grateful. I got the chance to experience pure love, true friendship, devastation, and perseverance. The words that decorate the pages of *Niya* for me are life changing. Just like the lives of my two main characters, Niya and Jamilla, this book made me, and at times, it caused me to cave. It took me to the hollowest and darkest places inside of me, and with the love between these two ladies, it brought me back to the light.

The characters' light, their radiating wholesomeness, even when they are at fault, salvaged the damaged parts in me. Niya and Jamilla gave me hope. They taught me that to dream is to have a belief in yourself. They showed me that a dreamer's heart will forever beat, and within their world, I learned to believe in my dreams once again.

So, readers, I thank you. You all got a glimpse of the deepest parts of me, and you understood. You even understood the things I could not comprehend until now. So many of you opened your hearts to the story, which I wrote only because I had no choice. You openly received the love of Niya within the pages, and for that, I thank all of you.

Continue to open your mind and your hearts, and enjoy. Always remember that love is blind. It does not see race, religion, or gender.

We are love!

Sincerely,

Fabiola

Contact Fabiola Joseph

Twitter – @Soulofawriter
E-mail – Soulofawriter3@aol.com
Facebook.com/Fabiola.Joseph3
Instagram – TheArtOf BeingFabie

12-16

Books by the Author

The Art of Deceit

Porn Stars 1. More Than Just Moans
(coauthored with Matthew Ramsey)

Porn Stars 2. The Beginning of the End
(coauthored with Matthew Ramsey)

Rebel's Domain

Pricey: Playing in Traffic

"The Bully Bangers"
(short story)

"Truth or Death"
(short story)